# Praise for *The Wives of Halcyon*

'Eirinie Lapidaki's storytelling prowess shines through this masterfully crafted narrative about strength, solidarity and faith. It's in the quiet whispers of strength that we find our loudest roars, reminding us of our shared human resilience.'

RUBY SLOANE, @xrubyreadsx

'An enthralling tale of female strength, vulnerability, and solidarity in a dangerous and unpredictable universe. The author has created such beautifully complex and flawed characters. It's definitely one of the best books I've read this year.'

MATINA TZOUMERKA, @breathing_pages

'A uniquely compelling and profound book with real and raw characters, I felt totally transported into the setting and emotionally absorbed by the story. It is an insightful tale of female fortitude in the face of manipulation and coercion.'

POPPY SMITH, @poppysreads

'An extraordinary debut novel... This is an astute and gripping tale of coercive control, about power and about misplaced trust. The isolated Scottish setting adds such depth to the narrative and the bonds of motherhood are beautifully portrayed. A novel that raises questions about power that can be gained by one man's charisma and words. Female characters who are precisely drawn, exposing their flaws and vulnerability, but most especially, their strength.'

ANNE CATER, Random Things Through My Letterbox

'A fascinating story.'

ILONA BANNISTER, author of *When I Ran Away*

'A brilliant and completely addictive read.'
RUTH HOGAN, author of *The Keeper of Lost Things*

'An astonishing and extraordinary debut.'
CHARLIE CARROLL, author of *The Lip*

'What a gripping journey this was! Hats off to Eirnie for this fabulous book. A stunningly written, powerful tale of power and control, and what happens when people lose themselves in the face of coercion.'
JESSICA RYN, author of *The Extraordinary Hope of Dawn Brightside*

'*The Wives of Halcyon* is a worthy addition to the 'cult' novel genre – a gripping page-turner which celebrates the strength and resilience of women, in even the most desperate of circumstances.'
CAROLE HAILEY, author of *The Silence Project*

'I loved this fierce and perceptive book. It questions female solidarity, faith and redemption and answers with skill, wit and not a little provocation. Clever and satisfying!'
JANET ELLIS, author of *The Butcher's Hook*

# The Wives of Halcyon

Eirinie Lapidaki

Legend Press Ltd, 51 Gower Street, London, WC1E 6HJ
info@legendtimesgroup.co.uk | www.legendpress.co.uk

Contents © Eirinie Lapidaki 2024
The right of the above author to be identified as the author of this work has been
asserted in accordance with the Copyright, Designs and Patents Act 1988. British
Library Cataloguing in Publication Data available.

Print ISBN 9781915643193
Ebook ISBN 9781915643209
Set in Times.
Cover design by Rose Cooper | www.rosecooper.com

Born in the north-east of England, Eirinie Lapidaki studied English Literature at St Andrews and completed her MLitt at Newcastle University.

She began writing her debut novel, *The Wives of Halcyon*, while working as a bookseller at Waterstones, and early chapters won a Northern Writers Award from New Writing North. Eirinie is currently working on her next novel, about the wellness industry and its impact on women's bodies, inspired by her battle with the chronic condition adenomyosis.

She lives in Gateshead with her husband, her daughter and her dog.

Follow Eirinie on Instagram
@eirinie.writes

*For my Nell*

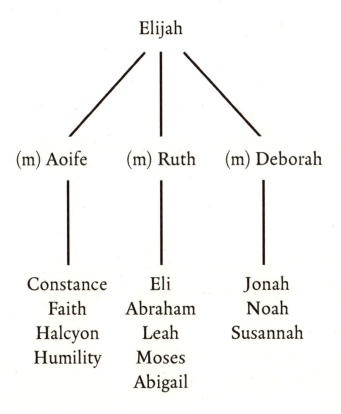

Elijah

(m) Aoife        (m) Ruth        (m) Deborah

Constance         Eli            Jonah
Faith          Abraham          Noah
Halcyon          Leah         Susannah
Humility         Moses
                Abigail

Can man make for himself gods? Such are not gods!

Jeremiah 16:20

# Prologue

## Revelation

Halcyon is gone now. The farmhouse where three of my children were born has been demolished; cold stones once covered in flaking whitewash turned to rubble, floorboards taken up, grey roof slates reclaimed. And our meagre belongings – worn-out boots, mugs and plates, bed linens – taken away to some evidence room. They could still be there, those relics of our old way of life, gathering dust. Most likely they have been thrown out, to lie in a skip or a landfill site awaiting the End of Days. The barns and outbuildings have also been dismantled, taken for scrap, the poured concrete floors where worshipful knees once knelt jackhammered into oblivion so no trace is left behind. Caravans towed. Charred remnants of the fire vanished, like we were never there at all.

Halcyon was erased to deter the gawkers, the obsessives, the surviving believers. But the one-track road from Abercraig is still there, narrowing as it winds away from the village towards the old settlement. You could follow it still, admiring the undulating hills broken through with patches of heather and harsh grey rock, stopping to photograph the snow-capped mountains which rise in the distance. Two streams break the road, narrow and pretty and cold. They are two distributaries from the larger stream which formed one of the borders of our land, so although you can't stand in the same river twice you could get out of your car and walk the length of either of them and know that you were close to the spot where we lived. The surviving livestock were sold, so you won't see any of the sheep which once grazed the hardy grasses, but maybe you will spot a stag or an eagle in the distance. If you decide to drive on and take your chances on the road, which is paved with small stones that dislodge and catch in the wheels of your car, you will end up driving through the spot where our gate was and into the old heart of Halcyon. If you are very prepared, really invested in your trip, you might have a copy of those grainy aerial shots which got published during the trial. There are no landmarks any more, but you could pace it out roughly – this is the farmhouse where the wives lived, this is where their church was, here's where all of the children slept. Such people do exist, I've learned. People who will take that road and record themselves tramping over the land, looking for ghosts or souvenirs. Telling a story which isn't theirs to tell.

I tell my story as infrequently as I can. I'm still ashamed by the part I played in it all, embarrassed by my stupidity, frightened by how far astray I was led. I have spent enough time in therapy to see myself as a survivor, and enough time in the tangled web of my mind to see myself as a perpetrator. When I've spoken to other people about it, people who weren't there, it's obvious that they see me as a fool. They nod sympathetically and say all the right things, but behind their careful words and kind eyes I can sense the question they most want to ask – how did you not see it coming? They are desperate to know how so many people could walk headlong into such an obvious disaster waiting to happen. To follow a man with such unquestioning obedience, oblivious to the writing which must surely have been on the wall from the beginning, like the signs in *The Wizard of Oz*: *I'd turn back now if I were you.*

Most people, the ones who have spoken to me and the ones who have spoken about me, come to the conclusion that we were all brainwashed. He had brainwashed us. A pied piper, marching us away from our homes and jobs and along the craggy road to Halcyon. Personally, I don't hold with the brainwashing idea, but I do like to think about the word. Brainwashed. If I didn't know what it meant, if I'd just heard it for the first time with no context, I would think it sounded like a good thing. I imagine a brain, as grimy as a city dweller's lung, being submerged in a glittering Highland spring. The fresh water runs over the brain, washing away the dirt, smoothing it like a stone until it emerges unburdened, unworried and clean.

# Part One

# Chapter One

## Aoife

Mostly, I forgot about the life I had lived before we moved to Halcyon, in the same way that you forget what winter feels like on a balmy summer day. It wasn't so much that I couldn't remember the world outside our compound, or the things I had done there; I just had no reason to. Occasionally, a memory would pop up in my mind – the sound of my boots against the paving slabs as I walked to work; the particular smell of chip fat and coffee and smoke which clung to my hair and clothes after a shift. Collapsing onto the sofa at the end of the day, too tired to do anything except turn on the TV and lie there, half watching, half dozing, until it was time for bed. What struck me when those memories surfaced was just how small my life had been, how empty, how *boring*. Halcyon had given me a purpose. It had made my life fuller. It had made it interesting.

For as long as I had known Elijah, he had dreamed of building a community, somewhere far away from the evils of the modern world, where like-minded people could live and work and worship together in peace. Halcyon was the realisation of his vision, but it was our shared achievement – our baby. He was the ideas man, but the details, the logistics, were all me. It was his job to say something like 'we need to be fully off grid, I want us running on wind power', and it was my job to make it work. And I did. Every time.

Our hard work had paid off, and we were thriving. Our farmhouse, squat and sturdy, was the centre of Halcyon, and at the centre of the farmhouse was the temple.

I was the last one to arrive at temple that morning, and when

I opened the door everyone was already seated for prayer. The temple was a small room, with damp emanating from the dark stone walls. Elijah wanted the space to be sacrosanct, free from any markers of the twenty-first century, so unlike the other rooms in our farmhouse, this one had not been wired with electricity. The only source of light came from a small window above his pulpit, the Scottish morning sun travelling weakly through it down into the space, illuminating the motes of dust which floated and eddied in its path. Elijah's pulpit faced the room's entrance, but he acted as though he hadn't noticed me and continued to stare up to the heavens, his arms remaining outstretched as the door creaked closed behind me.

I took my place next to Ruth, at the end of the row, and settled onto my knees. Even then, over ten years after our first meeting, I could not get my fill of Elijah. He was older of course, but still the same striking figure he had always been. When we'd first met, I had been taken by his shock of black hair, his broad, strong shoulders, his calm, assured stance. This was a man, I had thought, built to bear the weight of God's instructions. From my kneeling position he looked more imposing than he did in the old days, readier to face his challenges. He was the only man I could imagine who could wear ancient jeans and an argyle jumper and still look as though he had stepped straight out of the Old Testament.

'Lord!' he began, his voice reverberating against the unadorned walls, 'We thank you for granting us another day in our Heaven on Earth, and pray that we might do you service today. We thank you for granting us your bounty here at Halcyon, and for protecting us from the sins of the world outside its safe walls.'

Elijah expressed the same sentiments every morning at temple, and then again later on at church, and at evening worship. It was our mantra, our Lord's Prayer. We responded:

'Thanks be to God and our Holy Prophet.'

Other than the opening prayer, things were very different at temple to how they were at church and evening worship. At temple, it was just the four of us, the innermost family: Elijah at the helm, then me, then Ruth, then Deborah. We were his disciples, and because of our privileged position within Heaven on Earth his decisions and his prophecies were shared with us first. At the start, these prophecies had filled me with joy, but

God's latest revelations had been more difficult for me to accept, and slowly there had been less dialogue. I prayed a great deal.

'Some troubling news.'

I looked up in alarm, and for the briefest moment my eyes met Ruth's. Elijah continued, his low voice rumbling.

'The Devil has brought doubt and fear into the minds of our sinful neighbours. Since our mission reached out to Abercraig several weeks ago, our success there has raised concerns with some of the villagers. I have prayed, and decided to stop all of our local missionary work. God has told me not to waste any more time on these sinners; they have lost their chance at salvation. We need to remain vigilant, as some threats have been made to our property. Let me know the instant you see anything or *anyone* amiss.' He paused and gave us a knowing smile which did not quite reach his eyes.

Elijah bowed his head to indicate the start of silent prayer. I looked down at my knees. At almost ten miles away, the people of Abercraig were our closest neighbours, and we had had run-ins with them before. When we first bought the farm there were some rumours spread which caused a bit of a stir, but Elijah went over and charmed the village council and everything was sorted. If it came to it, I was sure he would go out and speak to them again.

Out of the corner of my eye I could see Deborah, her hands clasped virtuously in her lap, as unfazed by the revelation as she had been by Elijah's bombshell the previous week. Ruth was now breathing steadily, apparently focused on her prayers, but I had seen her flash of concern. The three of us were still, glassy pools of water, the gentle ripples left by the glance Ruth and I had shared had already faded into our depths. Deborah remained as shallow and unmoved as a puddle. I closed my eyes and prayed that the villagers would leave us alone, and not get anyone else involved. I also prayed about his bombshell, and wondered if Ruth was praying for the same thing.

Once temple was over and Elijah had gone, Ruth and Deborah and I rose to leave. Deborah clutched her swelling stomach with one hand and supported herself against the wall with the other. Although she was only around five or six months along, she already seemed fit to burst and the buttons of her dress strained against the force of her belly. Whenever I picture Deborah, she is always pregnant, like the Virgin in a nativity scene, only I'm sure Christ's mother was never so smug. She even looked like the Virgin, or at least the Virgin as she had appeared in every nativity play I'd seen – long fair hair, wide-eyed, angelic. Although her pointy little nose reminded me of a pig's snout.

'How are you feeling, Deborah?' asked Ruth, extending a hand to pull her upright. 'How's your back?'

'Much better thanks,' she said, 'the willow was a massive help. Like really, really helpful. I slept better last night than I've slept in a long time.'

Once upon a time, when pregnancy was something that happened to me, Ruth had offered me willow and pressed my stomach to feel the position of the baby. She had been a midwife before she'd married Elijah. All of the babies born in Halcyon were delivered by her steady hands and had their first cries lulled by her low, lilting voice.

It had been my idea to bring Ruth into our family. Elijah and I were four years, two children, and one church deep into our relationship. Faith, our youngest, was almost two years old and there was no sign of a little sibling making their way to join her. Elijah was stuck in a spiritual cul-de-sac; unsure of the direction we needed to take the church, and concerned that God's reluctance to bless us with another child was an indication of some misstep he had made or a sign he had unintentionally ignored. Grey clouds had gathered above our once happy little unit, and every day I would wake with a knot in my stomach, terrified of the impending flood. At home in the flat, we barely spoke. We went on as normal in the church, but even there the undercurrent of love which I had relied on seemed to be fading and I was becoming a colleague, not a wife. I had reached breaking point, but the failure of my marriage was not an option. It was Helen, the wife of John, Elijah's right-hand man, who had pointed me in the direction which had saved us. I had been unsure of Helen at first; John had developed something of a reputation in the café where I had worked, and surely any woman who would marry a man like him must be a little off-kilter herself? But she was kind and wise, and by that point, my closest friend.

'I know this might sound obvious, sweetheart,' she had said as we worked alone in the church hall kitchen, preparing snacks for the playgroup children, 'but have you turned to your Bible?

God wants you to be happy in your marriage. I know he'll point you to your answer if you look.'

So I looked. And I found. Elijah had started preaching more and more about the old patriarchs, and their many children from many wives, but even he seemed surprised when I broached the subject with him over dinner when Constance and Faith were in bed. Surprised, but intrigued. Surprised, but happy. Surprised, but satisfied. We spoke about the potential for jealousy, and although it was something I prepared for, I never felt it. Or at least, not at first; watching Ruth then, though, with her tender hand on Deborah, I couldn't help but feel a little pang of envy. I missed our gentle, easy camaraderie. I missed being the one that people cared about the most.

We walked out of the temple and into the kitchen together, removing our headscarves as we went. I knew I should go to the office for an hour before church and run through the finances, but instead I sat down and let out my relief with a slow exhale. The log book could wait a moment.

'Oh Aoife,' Deborah said as she sat next to me, 'that's exactly how I feel. Still, are you looking forward to the Feast of the Prophet tomorrow?'

I closed my eyes. Deborah would be the wrong person to talk to about my worries, with her exhausting optimism and holier-than-thou attitude. She had been a member of the church since she was a teenager, her and her mother, before the mother had died of liver failure or some such thing. At twenty-six she was almost ten years my junior, but she seemed far younger. So much of the work had already been done by the time Deborah was able to understand the church, and even more had been done before she joined our family. The foundations of Halcyon had been laid, and she seemed to think that meant there was no longer any urgency in our mission. She seemed to forget, as she mixed her home-made soaps and oversaw the children's lessons and crafts, that we were living in the End of Days.

Before she could speak again, I raised myself up out of the sagging folds of the sofa and walked out of the room without turning to say goodbye. Sequestered in the dim hallway, I allowed myself a moment of quiet contemplation before beginning my working day. The devil, after all, makes work for idle thumbs. My own thumbs had been far from idle for many years, and in the early days of our community I had spent my days side by side with the rest of them, renovating the crumbling barns, fixing up rusty caravans, and building our kennels and coops.

More recently, I had kept myself occupied with less strenuous, but equally vital, matters in the farmhouse office. The office sat at the back of the house, and if there had been a window it would have overlooked the deep, velveteen mountains and dancing streams which guarded our horizon. But there was no window; the sash had been rotted through so thoroughly when we moved in that we'd had to take it out and board up the gap with a sheet of ply. Instead, the whitewashed stone walls were adorned with glossy prints depicting Bible scenes. There were twelve, one for each month of the year. This was because each image had been carefully cut out of an old calendar and pasted up with water and flour. The picture of Christ in His manger, surrounded by the Virgin Mary – this one dark-haired – Saint Joseph, and an array of livestock, was my favourite. I liked the awed way that Joseph looked at Mary. In the bottom-right corner, cursive print read: 'December'. They were my only decorations.

In the place of ornaments and knick-knacks, there were stacks of heavy ledgers in which I kept track of our finances, noting every expenditure, every donation, every tithe from the early days of Heaven on Earth up to the present. Before we moved north, when I had use of a computer, I could manage all of my week's work on a Thursday afternoon and be finished in time for evening service. Of course, we were a smaller group then, and our members lived in their own homes and held down jobs with regular incomes coming into our account. Even so, the past few months had been harder work than they should have been. The little rows of numbers which once came together so easily had become reluctant to add up, and I spent many fruitless hours staring at the page, willing myself to spot the simple mistake which, when remedied, would solve all of my problems.

# Chapter Two

## Ruth

Stepping out of the farmhouse and into the yard was a religious experience. The cobbled stones under my feet had been there for over one hundred years, but the craggy green mountains which surrounded our settlement had been there even longer, since God Himself shaped them for us with His loving hands. They were darker in places now, rust red, burgundy, plum, where the patches of fern and heather grew, reminding us all of the turn in the year; an endless cycle of death and resurrection which played out around us in technicolour glory. I loved to look at those mountains in the mornings, especially in Fall, when the mist still lingered around their ragged peaks – God's curling, frosted breath. Occasionally, I would spy a stag a little way in the distance, and we would watch each other with interest until one of us moved away. Almost as magnificent to my eyes were the barns and outbuildings we had breathed life into when we'd arrived five years ago; the church, the schoolhouse and the community barn stood around the yard like three stone hives. They were not as beautiful as the land they were built on, not by a long way, but they were a reminder of our own little miracle of Creation.

Pulling the hem of my skirt out of my boots, I walked away from the centre of the settlement to the barn where I spent most of my days. In theory, I was the colony's resident medic, but we were mainly a healthy group. Aside from attending to the odd birth or injury, I found myself spending most of my time turning my nurses' training to our livestock. I grew up surrounded by farms, and although I couldn't get away fast enough at the time,

I'd begun to take great pleasure in dealing with the animals once we'd moved to Halcyon.

There was something serene about the huge beasts which walked slowly and gracefully towards me each morning; sometimes I even allowed myself to fuss them, running my hand over the pelt of one of our cows before settling down with my stool and bucket, or brushing out the donkey's coarse grey fur. Of course, the animals weren't there to be fussed. I did not name the chickens before we slaughtered them, just like I didn't name the cows or sheep. 'Adam already named the animals on the sixth day,' Elijah reminded us when we first moved to the farm, 'you do not need to name them again.' He was looking at the children when he said that. City-stifled, until that moment they had only seen animals in picture books, and they had barely been able to contain their excitement.

I milked the cows first thing, losing myself in the gentle and familiar rhythm of their breathing, the steady movement of my hands. It was a good time to pray, sitting there on my low wooden stool, listening to the spurts of milk hit the metal bucket by my feet. Once my work there was done and the milk had been poured into our little silo, I took the three halters from their hooks on the wall and one by one attached them to the cows' heads. They were padded, but still heavy and old-fashioned, and I worried that they must be uncomfortable. I wanted to talk to the cows as I fastened the buckles, to apologise for the inconvenience, to reassure them that we were headed right out to pasture, but I didn't. 'You can be so sentimental, Ruth.' I could hear Elijah's voice in my head as I knotted their lead lines. 'Everyone says so. No wonder Aoife doesn't take you seriously.' He said it so often that I could imagine the exact tone of his voice – gently reproachful. I would always nod. 'I'll work on that.' And then I tried my best, but whatever I did I could never manage to be as efficient as Aoife.

The three lead lines gathered into my right hand, I pulled open the gate which kept the cows in their pen and walked them out of the barn. I took another breath of the cold morning air and set off up the gentle slope to their pasture. I had made this journey so many times that my boots had begun to wear away a little trail in the hill's mossy earth, revealing patches of the stone beneath, and I could walk it without thinking even once about where to put my feet. The cows followed behind, their own hooves sure against the uneven ground. Once we reached the top of the hill, I lingered for a while before unfastening the cows. All of Halcyon lay before me like a picture postcard; our stone buildings and shiny white caravans, and then further out the fields where we grew our crops. Already people were hard at work – I could see them going about their business, hear as they sang hymns and chatted as they checked the hives and reinforced the bunker.

I was watching the cows drink from the stream when I was startled by a series of loud bangs and yells coming from down the other side of the hill, which made me drop the lead lines to the ground. It was only when the sound continued, this time louder and more intense, that I realised what was happening. Behind me, a little way down the slope, was an old coal bunker that the children had dragged out there to use for their games. It had become a kind of training ground for Halcyon's younger inhabitants to prepare for the End. The possibility of seeing my children was too much to resist, so selfishly I gathered the cows' lines and picked my way down to the source of the noise.

As I'd expected, the miniature bunker was surrounded by a group of children. A quick scan of their faces told me that none of my biological kids were amongst them, but I could see Constance and Faith – Aoife's oldest girls – and a cluster of others. I tried not to let myself be disappointed, but the feeling sat in my stomach like a stone. They were hitting the sides of the box with long pieces of firewood, making the corrugated steel thunder and shake. Constance was taking running leaps to kick at it with her boots. Some of the smaller children were smacking it with the palms of their hands and screeching through the cracks in the metal. I hugged myself against the chill as I continued towards them.

Ryan, the oldest in their crowd, was the first one to see me. He handed a small silver stopwatch to another boy, Ollie, and bounded over to where I was standing.

'Sorry, Sister Ruth,' he panted, 'I hope we didn't give you a fright. We were just practicing.'

I smiled. I remembered Ryan from when I had joined the church, and whenever I looked at him I could still see the chubby four-year-old he'd been then – all big eyes and dark curls. His voice broke a little when he spoke, and I wanted to reach out and ruffle his hair.

'No need to apologise, honey, I was just coming down to see

how you all were doing. Whose turn is it now?' I asked, pointing to the coal bunker which the other children were still battering.

'Oh, it's Humility, Sister.'

Humility, another of Aoife's; her youngest. Halcyon, her third daughter who was the same age as my Abraham, was nowhere to be seen.

'And? How's she doing in there?'

Ryan turned to Ollie, who was still clutching the stopwatch in his bony white hands.

'How's Humility getting on, Ollie?' he called.

Ollie glanced down at the watch, and then back up at me and Ryan. I had to strain to hear him over the ruckus as he spoke.

'She's only been in a couple of minutes,' he said, 'but she's already crying.'

Ryan shook his head. 'Females.'

The way he said it made him sound like Elijah, and I shivered. The game was something that had made me uncomfortable when it had been first introduced, but it was the invention of one of the more senior church members – not Elijah himself, but John, his assistant – and there wasn't much I could do. I'd been convinced, eventually, that it was good for them to practice for the End. That it would make the real thing less scary for them.

A second later, the lid of the coal bunker creaked open and Humility emerged, wet and dirty, her small face red and blotchy and streaked with tears. She struggled to climb out, her feet catching at the bottom of her dress, which reached down to the tops of her boots. My instinct was to comfort her, but I managed to fight it. Word would certainly get back to Elijah if I did. The children stopped their attack on the little tin hut, but as she rejoined their group they started up with a chorus of boos and jeers. Somebody threw a small stone, which bounced off her shoulder and made her cry even harder, and I watched with a lump in my throat as she gulped and wiped the tears from her eyes.

'Honestly, Humility, that was pathetic,' said Constance, rolling her eyes, 'you're four now. You're getting too big to be acting like such a baby. What are you going to do when the End comes? God isn't going to stop sending his wrath down to Earth because you're *crying*. Isn't that right, Ryan?'

She turned to where Ryan and I were standing and gave us both a smile.

'Yeah,' said Ryan, 'the hordes of sinners won't just turn away if they hear a cry-baby. It'll probably make them even more angry.'

Humility sniffed again and rubbed her shoulder. 'Will not.'

'It will, too,' said Constance. 'Anyway, it's my turn next. I'll show you how to be brave.'

With that, she closed herself into the coal bunker and the banging started again. Ryan handed Humility a stick of her own, which she took with a gleeful smile, tears forgotten. Content that all was well, I took my cue to leave.

'You all watch out with those sticks now,' I said as I waved, 'I don't want to have to give anyone here any stitches.'

The threat of stitches sent a thrilled shriek through the little gathering, and I could still hear them long after I started my descent down the other side of the hill. Even though my own children hadn't been there, it had been good to see the rest of them up close and at play. Adults made me nervous, unsure of myself – how to act, what to say – but babies and kids were different. They were easier to understand, more like animals in that sense, and I could always find my voice around them.

The children had been my first responsibility. With God's guidance, I had brought the smaller ones into the world, frightened only by the secrecy which shrouded the whole practice within Heaven on Earth. In the hospital, or even in my routine home births, a doctor was never far away. One could be called in to assist if something were to go wrong. Even before we came to Halcyon, when I delivered the Heaven on Earth babies who were born in the city, I did not have that luxury.

Midwifery was never my calling, but I was desperate to leave home and my father was a pastor, so he had firm views as to what was appropriate for a young woman to do with her time. My godmother, who lived in London, suggested I come stay with her and study midwifery. This was deemed a suitable career for me, better even than just plain old nursing because I would not have to deal with any men 'up close', as my father would say. It was either that or stay in the Midwest, plus I liked babies, so I got my visa and I went. I visited home just once after that, for Christmas during my second year of training. My godmother made me stay in London for my first Christmas; she was anxious that I would be overcome with homesickness and never come back. When

I finally returned to the States, I watched my father preach his Christmas sermon, and ate the food my mother cooked alongside my grandparents and my siblings and counted the days until I could be back in London, where interesting things happened to interesting people.

Back home, my mother braided my hair into cornrows in silence while we listened to the radio or watched some soap opera on TV, but in London I went to a real hairdresser who created intricate coiled designs against my scalp with her long, manicured fingers. She would gossip to me about the other customers and about her life, complaining about her boyfriend and her boyfriend's mother, who liked to interfere with her business and tell her how to raise her kids and what she should wear. Michelle, my hair lady, and the other girls at the hospital opened up a whole new world to me. I liked to listen to their stories about wild nights out, although when they invited me along I turned them down. It was one thing to hear about their adventures, and something very different to participate in them myself. I loved those girls when we worked side by side, but the thought of them after work, when their uniforms were swapped for high-heeled shoes and short leather skirts, frightened me. Their lives out of the hospital seemed messy and exhausting. The only other black trainee midwives both went to extra efforts to include me, but after a while their invitations dried up before stopping altogether, leaving me equal parts lonely and relieved. It wasn't too long before I started going back to church, where people were always on their best behaviour and I knew exactly what to expect from them.

# Chapter Three

## Aoife

As I sat in the front row of our church at Halcyon, I resisted the urge to turn my head and watch the other congregants as they made their way in to worship. When I first joined Heaven on Earth, church services had taken place in the living room of Elijah's first-floor flat, which stood unexceptionally within a terrace of identical Victorian homes in the leafy outskirts of the city. There were only around fifteen of us at that time, including myself, but even so there was hardly enough room for us all. Elijah would stand and preach in the bay window, so that the comings and goings of students and harried families which played out on the street below formed a background to his sermons. Despite its inhospitable size, the flat had been furnished for this very purpose, and chairs and sofas of all descriptions had been laid out in the approximation of pews in an ordinary church, with a small aisle down the centre leading to Elijah's window pulpit. A collection of mugs, just as cosily mismatched as the living room furniture, were laid out in the kitchen along with bags of herbal tea for after. Our refreshments were often supplemented with the home baking of various congregants, namely Helen, Lois, and Pauline, all of whom came with us to Halcyon. The effect of the homely setting and informal furnishings, combined with the provision of food and drink, was that I felt instantly welcome when I first joined the church. Before I'd found them, I had been homesick and desperately lonely. After, they became a second family, and then, my only family.

Helen took me under her wing from the first, and every service in the flat was subsequently spent by her side. In the weeks between my engagement and my wedding, I'd stayed with Helen and John at their house in the suburbs, and on my wedding day it was Helen who'd helped me to get ready. I even wore her wedding dress; a high-necked, long-sleeved gown, white of course – Elijah had absolved me of my one prior fumble with a boy from back home – in which I felt as beautiful and as grown up as I ever had. The ceremony took place in Elijah's flat. There was no paperwork, no documents to suggest that our union was sanctioned in the eyes of the law. It was witnessed, Elijah said, by God, not man, because the purpose of our marriage was to honour God, not man. It sounds like a cliche, but our wedding was truly the happiest day of my life. Standing there in the bay window of our church, surrounded by friends and pledging myself to a good and Godly man, all felt right with the world. I had been so happy that I hadn't even minded that John was the one officiating.

Many things had changed since the days of cramped church services in our living room; our congregation had grown, our family had grown, we had moved from the flat to the hall and then north from the city, and settled in the Highlands, where life was harsh and beautiful and closer to God. Our new church was a barn, larger and grander, certainly, although some things remained the same. The haphazard collections of furniture. The devotion of the people.

Deborah's long blonde plait swished from side to side as she turned her head towards one person and then another, and I did my best not to roll my eyes. She was just striking up a conversation with Helen, who sat behind her, when Elijah entered and a hush descended. My seat at the very front of the room meant that I could see his face clearly. The two wrinkles which had recently appeared on his broad forehead were deepened with concern, and his hands were balled into tight, tense fists. He barely relaxed for the opening prayer, which reverberated against the empty walls: 'God! We thank you for granting us another day in our Heaven on Earth, and pray that we might do you service today. We thank you for granting us your bounty here at Halcyon, and for protecting us from the sins of the world outside its safe walls.'

'Thanks be to God and our Holy Prophet.' The voices of our congregation rose together in response. Almost one hundred joined together as one.

Elijah began.

'We say this prayer every day. We know its words as well as we know ourselves. God gifted this prayer to us so that we could praise Him and thank Him. I thought to myself today that our prayer is like a diamond. Precious, valuable, and multi-faceted. Just like different colours and aspects of a diamond reveal themselves as the light moves, so it is with our prayer. It is a great sign of God's wisdom that the words which He revealed to me have many meanings, meanings which reveal themselves to us as our situations change, as we move through different seasons of our life's journey. He has recently drawn my focus to the final line of our beautiful prayer. The line with which we thank Him for protecting us from the sins of the world which lie outside Halcyon's safe walls.

'You are all aware of our recent outreach mission to Abercraig. Last night, this mission ended. Brother John had been in the village to collect two Godly young people who had wished to join our community here and in the next life. Unfortunately, the parents of these young people intercepted this mission, and we were forced to leave them behind. Brother John was waiting at the bottom of the driveway in the car, ready to bring these new recruits to Halcyon, when he was viciously attacked. Threats of violence were made to his person, our vehicle, and the community as a whole. We are taking this very seriously. I ask that you keep these two young people in your prayers, but also that you pray for the safety of our community. The threats made against us betray a gross ignorance about Heaven on Earth and our mission here at Halcyon, and I fear that we have not felt the last of their anger. I have prayed for guidance, and God showed me the answer in our own prayer. We will no longer be reaching out to Abercraig and the surrounding areas on missions, and I ask you all to be vigilant of outsiders or anything out of the ordinary. Remember, it's your sacred duty as citizens of this holy land to report anything, anything at all, that goes against our way of life.'

I knew that there was a man from Abercraig within the congregation, Aaron, who had joined us a year or so before. He had been saved during a mission trip there, and his own parents had also been angry about his decision to join us in Halcyon. He was one of the few colonists who had not come up with us from the city. He was a pleasant man, young and Godly and hardworking, and I hoped that Elijah would reach out to him and make sure he understood he was one of us, not an outsider, and still a welcome and loved member of our community. I was considering that this could be a pastoral duty which might feasibly fall to me, when Elijah took a breath and continued his sermon.

'Let this also be a lesson to us all,' he said, his eyes meeting mine for the briefest moment, 'of the dangers of the so-called *traditional* family. Parental bonds should never be stronger than the bonds between us and our Father God. These cruel parents may have denied their children the opportunity for eternal salvation, and for what reason? Because they value their earthly love over His heavenly love. They were frightened that their children loved God more than they loved them!'

Before, Elijah's delivery had been deliberate and sombre, but this new direction had filled his words with the passion and vigour which had first inspired me all those years ago. He had always had strong feelings about so-called 'nuclear families', and they were a subject which never failed to inspire him to righteous anger. Couples in Halcyon were married, but lived apart from one another in gender-segregated caravans, coming together only for pre-approved 'private' visits when Elijah decided that the schoolhouse was looking empty. I secretly wondered if his control over this most intimate aspect of his congregants' lives stemmed from his desire to have the most children of them all. Between us three wives, he'd fathered twelve children – my four, Ruth's five, and the three which Deborah had given him, not including the baby currently floating in her obnoxiously young and healthy womb. Unlike the others, our children knew who their father was – he was our Prophet after all, and what would be the point of so many heirs otherwise? But even for my oldest girls, the concept of 'mother' must have become a lost word in a dead language – as it had for me.

'How selfish can a person be,' he continued, 'that they value their meagre earthly happiness over the eternal happiness of others? Are they animals, that they don't understand anything other than what they see in front of them? Satan lives in these people and their shallow understanding of love. If they were not so very dangerous to us, we could almost pity them. Sadly, they are determined to push their warped beliefs onto us. They think *we* are the dangerous ones!'

A less dangerous group of people you could never hope to meet. We were a collective of all ages, all races, all backgrounds, all of us united by our faith in our Prophet and in God, and of course by our steadfast belief in the Halcyon project. We were parents, some of us grandparents. Of the eighty members of the community, almost thirty were children and babies. I wondered what the villagers thought we could possibly do to cause anyone any harm.

Once the sermon had finished, I shifted and stretched my neck as subtly as I could, all while trying to avoid John's gaze. John was the administrator, the lackey, the man on the ground, and he was stepping up to the rostrum to give the day's orders.

'Thank you, Elijah, for another powerful sermon,' he said, running a hand through his greying blond hair. 'I wanted to follow up on the point Elijah made there about reporting anything you see which goes against our way of life here – I hope you all remember that Elijah doesn't just mean any strangers you might spot around the compound. It's your duty to come to me if you see one of your fellow Brothers or Sisters in Christ straying from our path, if you hear someone say something which goes against our teachings. Let me know. We're in the final days here, people, and we can't be running the risk of inviting Satan into Halcyon when we're all so close to salvation.'

I felt a twinge of annoyance. He was right, of course, but the delight he seemed to take in rooting out sin was unbecoming. Many an evening we had been sitting in the farmhouse eating dinner when John had scuttled in, desperate to divulge to Elijah – and Elijah alone – the most recent infraction which he had uncovered. We wives would be forced to stand in the hallway, our dinners congealing on our plates, for the duration of the interruption which *just couldn't wait.*

Reading from a sheet of handmade paper – yet another ill-fated experiment of Deborah's, the clumpy fruits of which we were compelled to use up – he called out names and tasks. Mark and Niall to repair the roof of caravan M-3. Lisa, Annie, and Lois to the greenhouses and beehives. Alfie to lead the same group of men as yesterday to reinforce the roof of the bunker. And so on, everyone listening keenly for their name, careful not to drift off and miss their assignment. It was a crisp autumn day, cold but not freezing, clear and bright. Ideal weather for much of the outdoor work on the schedule, and people were keen to get outside and make the best of it. Two children whose faces I could not quite make out held the great barn doors wide open, and I turned to watch the exodus.

Elijah, too, stood by the exit, but instead of blessing the congregation as they left, he was focused on one person alone. They were shorter than Elijah, and although my position at the far end of the room obscured my view, I could guess who had captured his attention so entirely. We exited row by row, and following this convention I would be the last to leave. Elijah knew this too, and while it was possible that he was too engrossed in his conversation to pay attention to the other people passing him by, I knew him well enough to realise that this was a calculated move, and he would dismiss his mystery companion before Ruth, Deborah or I could get to the front of the church. With the entire congregation facing the other way, and Ruth and Deborah engrossed in their own private, whispered conversation, I took my chance and leaned out into the aisle, craning my neck to see around the bobbing heads of the people filing out ahead of me. A gap emerged for long enough for me to spy the person who was so captivating to my husband.

After we moved to Halcyon, I found myself predicting worst-case scenarios. Poor crop yields. Trouble with electricity. Arrest. I took a perverse pleasure in it, because if the worst were to happen, at least I would have the small satisfaction of having been right. I had guessed by the intent look on Elijah's face, the particular angle at which he tilted his head, a gesture visible even from across the barn, that he had been speaking to Jemima. Somehow my usual self-satisfaction at a correct guess was not enough to soften the blow of what I saw before me. It was as though the room went out of focus, like a scene in a film where a woman looks across a crowded bar and sees the love of her life, one clear figure in the centre. Except there were two figures, one tall, handsome man and one small, bird-like girl tucking her hair behind her ears in the absent way that teenagers have, and hanging on to every word the man was pouring into her head. She looked down shyly and laughed at something he had said, and he leaned even closer to her. My face already felt flushed, but when he reached out and touched her arm, it burned. I had had my suspicions before, but now I was certain. When Elijah had dropped his bombshell, when he had told us about God's desire for him to take another wife, he didn't tell us exactly who he had in mind. But I knew. It didn't take a genius to work it out. The only single women in Halcyon were either older – not Elijah's style – or they were teenagers. And there was only one of those who would fit the bill: petite, quiet Jemima.

The row of women ahead of me began to file out, and I turned to see if Ruth or Deborah had noticed that I had moved. Ruth was still turned towards Deborah – she hadn't even realised that it was almost time for us to leave – but Deborah was staring straight over her shoulder and directly at me. Her expression remained blank, but she maintained eye contact for just long enough that I knew she understood what I had been looking at. It was too late to deny it. All I could hope was that she wouldn't speak to Elijah about it. I returned her cold stare, hoping that my countenance was just as inscrutable as her own; perhaps I could convince her that she had been wrong, and that I had nothing to hide. In earlier days, I might have even taken the time to change the story completely, and have her feel as though she was the one who ought to feel guilty for staring at *me*. But I had grown too tired to play such games, as satisfying as they had been, and in all honesty I had also grown a little too worried that I would no longer come out on top.

Instead of challenging Deborah, I allowed myself to lead our row down the aisle and towards the door, my posture straight, my eyes looking fixedly ahead. I noted that I had been correct about Elijah; by the time I reached him, he had dismissed Jemima and had turned his attention fully onto John. As I drew closer to him, I prepared my face with a smile, waiting for him to wish me a blessed day, but he was too distracted to notice me and I passed by without acknowledgement. I turned my face away before anyone noticed that I had been ignored. Outside, I spotted Jemima standing by the schoolhouse. She was taking a headcount, watching carefully as each child returned indoors for their morning lessons. Occasionally, one would stop to talk or hug her, and she would lean in and smile. I spotted Humility, wrapped up in a trailing scarf and a little red hat that I'd not seen before, holding hands with a slightly older girl. When she reached Jemima, my youngest daughter let go of her friend's hand and flung her arms around Jemima's skinny legs.

# Chapter Four

## Ruth

We were all stifling yawns as we shuffled, one after the other, into the church barn after a long day of work. My eyes were bleary and stinging from tiredness, but I was glad to be there. My own, lonely bed promised nothing but hours of exhausted wakefulness. Elijah told me he had mentioned my insomnia to Deborah and Aoife, who had both agreed I couldn't sleep because I wasn't doing enough work during the day, and I agreed with them. My dread of the nights made evening worship even more appealing – there was plenty of opportunity to tire myself so much that by the time my head hit my pillow, I wouldn't be able to do anything *but* sleep. In theory, anyway. In practice, it never worked, no matter how much energy I put into worship. Still, just like Deborah likes to say: God loves a trier.

The chairs had been set out ready for the night in two concentric circles. I took my place next to Aoife and Deborah on the women's side of the inner circle, and waited for Elijah to arrive. All of the adults were there, shifting to get comfortable on their seats and talking quietly, when he made his entrance. John followed in after him, and the chatter subsided as Elijah took his place in the centre. He was the only one of us who didn't look tired; instead, he was almost vibrating with energy. I could sense it coming off him as he looked around the room, doing that thing he had always done where he seemed to meet everyone's eye at once, making sure that everyone felt included. I felt a giddy thrill as he looked my way. The room felt smaller with him in it, more compact. When he started to speak, his voice echoed.

'Before we start our worship tonight,' he said, pacing the

centre of the circle of chairs like a lion in a cage, 'we have some business to attend to.'

The congregation sat up a little straighter, and I felt Aoife turn to look at me. I wondered what she thought I had done.

'The world is full of sinners. We know that. The Bible tells us that.' He patted the heavy black book in his hand. 'But the reason that we, the Church of Heaven on Earth, came to Halcyon was so we could *escape* the sins of the world.'

I nodded, and a few people around me made some sounds of agreement.

'So I am sure you can all begin to imagine how very,' he paused, '*disappointed* I was to find that one of our number here, one of *you*, has brought sin into this most holy place.'

Again, he cast his eyes around the circles of chairs. This time they were searching, and when they lingered on me my stomach turned over. Had I committed a sin without realising? Had someone seen me talking to the children that morning, and told John that I'd been looking for my own kids? If that was true, there would be nothing I could even say to defend myself, because they would be right. I knew deep down that I had no reason to worry – even if someone had held me accountable to John, wives' sins never got aired out at evening worship. We'd be punished, sure, but in private. We were always careful to keep our dirty laundry safely inside the farmhouse. And yet my stomach still turned somersaults as the congregation squirmed and Elijah continued to pace. Last week, one of the women had been accused of stealing bread. Shanti. She and her husband had joined Heaven on Earth a year or so before we left for Halcyon, and her family had been angry about it. She was quiet and smiled a lot; I had always liked her. Elijah had drawn her into the centre of the circle to make her confession, and she had spent each mealtime since then with her hands tied behind her back.

'We know that the End times are coming, and they're coming quickly. Next year, next week, tomorrow – we can't be sure when, which means we can't afford for one of our number to tempt Satan into Halcyon. We need to be pure, and cleansed of sin, so that when God brings his wrath down on the world, we can be assured that *we* will be safe. When someone here sins, they threaten to bring the righteous vengeance of God down on *all of us*.'

His voice rose as he spoke those last three words, and I jumped a little in my seat. The words were still reverberating around the barn when he continued on.

'And so,' he said, 'this sinner amongst us must atone, before they seal our fate with their actions. Do you agree?'

The cheer started in the men's half of the room, and spread outwards until everyone was clapping and stamping. Some of the men whistled, but of course none of us women did.

'Good!' roared Elijah, picking up his pace around the circle. 'Now, whoever in this room has sinned, I need you to stand up and confess so we can absolve you!'

Across the room where the men were sitting, there was a murmur. Elijah changed the direction of his pacing, and strolled over to the source of the disruption.

'Stand up and speak up, please.'

I chewed my bottom lip.

It was Colin who stood up and walked into the centre, the men parting away from him like he was a leper. Colin was about ten years my senior, just over forty or so, and looked so much like my father that the first time I'd met him I'd been lost for words. He even wore the same type of glasses, the old-fashioned kind with those thick tortoiseshell rims, although Colin's were wrapped with Scotch tape around the sides where they'd broken while he'd been working on the bunker a few months ago. He'd been an optician, I remembered, when we'd still lived in town. He'd given us all free eye tests before we left for Halcyon, after his store had closed for the day.

'Brother Colin,' said Elijah, 'please can you speak out and tell the congregation what sin it is you have committed?'

Colin cleared his throat.

'I am sorry, Elijah. During our most recent visit together two nights ago, I expressed to my wife Lois that I missed being able to see our children whenever I liked. I said I wished that we could live together with them, like we'd done before we came here.'

Elijah gave a big, exaggerated nod. 'And how, Brother Colin, did you describe our arrangement of children living in the schoolhouse?'

Colin shuffled and looked down at his feet. He was a little taller even than Elijah was, but he looked so much smaller.

'I said it was ridiculous, Elijah. I'm sorry.'

The room was filled with the sound of fifty adults drawing a sharp, shocked breath all at once.

'You have four children, Colin, isn't that right?' Elijah gave no time for Colin to answer, but continued, pacing around him. 'And by all accounts, they're very good, Godly children. They do as they're told, they say their prayers, they work hard. Do you love your children, Colin?'

This time he did pause, and Colin nodded.

'Of course you do,' said Elijah. 'We are almost all of us parents here. We all love our children. We love every child of Halcyon, just as we all love one another. So, why, I wonder, Colin, do you want your children to burn in hell?'

Colin spoke, though his head was bent so low that it was impossible to hear him. I felt my muscles tense. Elijah bent so he was looking right up into Colin's downturned face.

'Say again, Colin? Do you want your children to burn in hell? To spend eternity in torment, away from God and the rest of the church?'

'No, Elijah.'

'Then why do you want them to love you more than they love God?'

I could hardly watch what was happening, but I couldn't bring myself to look away. Deep down in the very pit of my stomach, I knew that Colin's sin was not so far from my own, and my cheeks grew hot with shame as Elijah went on. I had never been dumb enough to say it out loud, to broadcast my sin like Colin had, but the deep, empty longing for my babies hollowed me out every night as I lay alone in my bed. On either side of me, Aoife and Deborah sat still. I could hear their easy, regular breaths. Their consciences must have been clear.

Elijah turned to the congregation as Colin stood, motionless, waiting to see what would happen. When Elijah pointed at Lois, I saw Colin wince. 'Lois,' he said, 'can you stand up for a moment, please?'

Behind me, Lois's chair scraped the floor as she stood. Everyone turned to look at her, but I kept my eyes on Colin. Beads of sweat were beginning to form on his temples.

'Sinners,' said Elijah, 'never just endanger themselves. Sin drags down everyone it touches. That's what makes it so dangerous.'

Around me, everyone nodded. I nodded too.

'When you exposed your wife to your sin, you put her in danger. Fortunately, Lois did the right thing, but women are more susceptible to sin than men, and we could easily be telling a different story tonight if your wife had less fortitude. I think it's important that you remember that.'

I could feel Lois shifting on her feet. She knew what was coming – we all did.

'Lois, in order for your husband to learn his lesson, he needs to see you punished. Please can you take your coat off and stand outside?'

Colin's shoulders sagged as he watched his wife pick her way through the circle of chairs to reach the door.

'Because of you, Lois will stay outside for the rest of worship. And for the next three days,' he held up three fingers to Colin, and then to the rest of us, 'I want none of you to speak to Lois. You may not look at her. You may not acknowledge that she exists. Colin needs to learn that his actions have consequences for others.'


Even though I knew Elijah was right, and it was important for Colin to learn his lesson, I still struggled to shake my guilt. Elijah once pretended that I didn't exist for a whole week, a punishment that still made me feel sick when I thought about it.

Later that night, just as I was beginning to spiral further away from any possibility of sleep, I was disturbed by a loud bang, followed by the sound of footsteps in the hallway outside. For one shameful moment, I let myself hope that Elijah had felt my sadness and was coming to check on me. I promised myself that if it was him, I would come right out and tell him about my sin and take whatever consequences came after. I pulled back my quilt and slid my feet into the thick pair of knitted socks which I used as slippers. I sent up a prayer – *please let it be him*. And then another, more cowardly part of my heart sent up another – *please don't let it be him*.

We all kept wind-up torches in our rooms in case of emergencies, and I fumbled under the bed for mine, knocking over an empty and rarely used chamber pot in the process. Conscious of the creaking floorboards beneath me, I picked my way across the room and opened the door onto the landing. There was no Elijah. Instead, I looked down to see the sharp little face of Russell the ratter blinking in the torchlight. Dazzled by the sudden light, it took the dog a moment to realise that the door was open, but once her eyes adjusted, she scampered straight past my legs. A couple of weeks before during a routine check-up, I had discovered Russell was carrying a litter, and by this time she was as round as a ball; so round, in fact, that I couldn't believe my eyes when she took a running leap and jumped straight onto my bed.

Elijah had very strong feelings about the difference between animals and humans; even Russell's name had been something of a compromise. Our two sheepdogs were both nameless, but she spent so much of her time with us, keeping our buildings and stores free from vermin, that we couldn't just keep calling her 'the dog'. At first, Elijah had been reluctant to name her, quoting the same Genesis passage which he had used with the children about the farm animals, but eventually he had relented just enough to name her Russell. He reasoned that by naming her after her breed, we weren't over-humanising her. She was allowed into the farmhouse only as a working dog. No petting her, no loving on her, no feeding her. There was no point in anyone making a rule about letting her on the furniture – we would have been no more likely to let Russell sit on the couch than to invite one of the sheep to stand on the kitchen table. But there she was, illuminated by the pale stream of torchlight, curling up on the pillow where my head had been resting just moments ago as though she had done it a thousand times before.

I closed the bedroom door and padded over to the bed. Russell raised her head slightly in acknowledgement before settling again as I slipped between the sheets and lay my head down on the pillow next to her. She smelled of fresh air and straw. I knew all of the animals in Halcyon: all of their individual quirks, what they liked to eat, which ones were jumpy, and which were calm. They were my daily companions as I went about my business on the farm, but I realised that I had never once reached out and touched that dog just for the sheer joy of it. Although the room was cold, I brought my hand out from beneath the quilt and placed it on her rough little back. She stretched a little and readjusted herself so that she was as close to me as possible. That night, with Russell's cold, wet nose against my ear, I slept better than I had in years.

# Chapter Five

## Aoife

After almost six years at Halcyon, the night-time routine was something the four of us had reduced to a fine art. Once evening worship was over, we would take it in turns to use the outhouse; Elijah first, followed by me, then Ruth, and finally Deborah. Returning to the house, we would make our individual cups of heather tea and take them to our rooms, where a filled basin lay in wait for washing faces and brushing teeth. It was rare to bump into another wife tramping along the garden path to the toilet, but I always made sure to time it so I would pass Elijah as he made his way back to the house. Sometimes he would brush his hand against mine, and I would relish the thrill of his touch on my skin. It was a stolen moment, and our carefully honed schedule meant that these fleeting extra-curricular meetings could only be afforded to me. On the nights Elijah and I shared, I would usually return to my bedroom to find him waiting for me on the bed, half-dressed and deeply engrossed in his Bible. I loved how easily and quickly he could focus his mind – he would have been alone in the room for no more than ten minutes, and already be oblivious to anything other than the words on the page in front of him. Eventually, he would look up at me and smile, as though my presence was the most delightful and unexpected surprise. *It's you*, his eyes would seem to say, *of all the people in Halcyon, how wonderful that it's you*. He'd always been very good at that. Then the Bible would be closed and laid to one side and one rough hand would move to unbuckle his heavy leather belt, his eyes staying on me, moving up and down my body.

That said, no such thing had happened now for three months.

I would open my bedroom door and he would barely glance up from his Bible. I would undress, slowly, my body aching in need of him, willing him to put the holy text to one side, to reach for me – even just to look at me. But when he finally laid his Bible down, it was just to turn off the light. Our last ten nights together had ended in quiet, heavy darkness, my hand desperate to reach out across the no man's land between us. *Still,* I thought, pulling on my boots – *there's always tonight.*

The anticipation was already building as I opened the door onto the crisp autumn night. I was almost certain that he hadn't returned to the house yet, as he'd still been speaking with John in church when I left, so the question was less *if* we would cross paths, but *when*. Feeling for the washing line we used to guide ourselves through the darkness, I made my way carefully along the cobbled path. As I walked, I listened, hoping to hear something that would indicate his approach; instead, all I could hear was the crunch of gravel beneath my feet, the shallow rhythm of my breath, and the familiar sounds of the farm settling itself down for the night. I had been so certain that I would meet Elijah along the path that I was surprised when my feet made the final step off the gravel and onto the hard slab of stone paving that indicated I was nearing the outhouse door. I knocked. Silence. I knocked again, pausing just a second before trying the handle – I did not want to stand there for too long, knowing that Ruth would not be far behind me.

It was quiet in the outhouse. The little stone room was empty of life, except for one large black spider clinging to the whitewashed wall like a full stop. I hoisted my skirt and pulled down my knickers. The sound of urine drumming against sawdust broke the silence of the night. There was a basket of newspaper next to the toilet, cut into neat little squares. I was never sure how old the newspapers were – the odd words which caught my eye could have been from any time – and I never had any interest in reading them. I didn't even know exactly where they came from, other than the obvious fact that they must have been imported into Halcyon from the outside world. With Elijah's recent decision to cease all missions to the neighbouring villages, I wondered where we would get our toilet paper from now on. Once I was finished, I took a handful of clean sawdust from the bucket and sprinkled it into the bowl, erasing the evidence of my visit.

My return journey to the farmhouse was much faster, the guiding line barely skimming my hand as I headed towards the gentle glow of the porch light. It was my night, so even if there was to be no sex, no intimacy of any kind, at least I didn't have to lie there, sleepless and angry, picturing him with Deborah. And still, some hope lingered until I arrived back in my room to find the bed empty, Elijah entirely absent. Somewhere along the garden path, my eagerness to see him had mingled with frustration. He had disregarded our nightly routine, a routine which was almost as sacred to me as the Halcyon earth beneath us. An image flashed before my eyes of a scene from earlier in the day – Elijah and Jemima standing together by the church door, looking intently at one another. I took off my clothes hurriedly and clumsily, tossing my skirt and blouse and jumper onto the floor by my side of the bed, trying not to wonder where he was. Standing naked in the middle of the rug, the rest of my many garments in a pile at my feet, my resentment grew further. I took such pleasure in undressing in front of him. We had no mirrors in Halcyon. Instead, I saw my reflection through his reaction to my body. His eyes were my mirror. If he wasn't there to see me, then where was I? I pulled on my nightgown, a flannel creation which was ugly but warm, and reluctantly got into bed alone. Despite our attempts to conserve electricity as much as possible, I left the lightbulb blinking dully above me, reluctant to fall asleep and miss his arrival.

It wasn't just the nights; we had been spending our days apart more than we ever used to. In the time before Halcyon, we shared a cluttered office space in the corner of our living room. We organised our soup kitchen there, our free community nursery, bingo for the old folk and Christmas collections for the food bank. It was there that we'd laid plans to rent out the old community centre to house our growing congregation, and there where we'd stayed up late into the night discussing the prospect of inviting Ruth into our inner circle of two. After that, Halcyon became the next project to consume our waking hours. Now, I saw him for worship, surrounded by other people, and at our silent mealtimes. One night in every three was all we had to be together, and now he'd thrown that away too. Maybe he'd decided to stay another night with Deborah instead.

I woke to the sound of my bedroom door bursting open. I

jumped, and it took a moment for my heart to slow down enough to realise where I was and what was happening. When I came to my senses, I saw him there in the doorway, a reverse silhouette against the darkness of the hallway behind him. It was truly night-time now, and the rest of Halcyon must have been fast asleep in their beds. His hair was wild and unbrushed, sticking up in the way it always did after he had run his hands through it, and he now wore an old nightshirt over his jeans, his heavy workman's boots caked in flaking mud. With one hand he held the heavy wooden door open, and in the other he clutched his heavy old Bible – dog-eared and bursting with fluorescent sticky notes and sheets of paper turned black and blue with his heavy hand writing. His eyes were dark and unfocused.

'What's the matter?' I asked, sitting up in bed.

Bleary-eyed as I was, I could tell from the flare of his nostrils and the narrowing of his eyes that I'd said the wrong thing. With a slam of the door he entered the room proper, and I flinched automatically at the sound. He turned off the light with the smack of his fist and we were plunged into darkness. I heard my own voice, a scolding stage whisper:

'What are you doing?' I hissed. 'You'll wake the whole house!'

I felt myself flush – I hadn't meant to speak, and I saw my words flutter in the space between us like a great red rag. Until then, there had still been a chance that the night could be salvaged, the anger channelled to lust, but of course I'd ruined it. *Silly bitch,* came the voice in my head, *silly nagging bitch. You just had to open your mouth.* He was silent, and for a moment I believed he had snapped out of the rage which had overtaken him. Instead, it morphed into a different mood, a mood which had once been rare, but which was now becoming increasingly more common. He went from explosive anger, the reverberations of which still buzzed in the air, to an electric form of fear which I was frightened to touch. He clambered onto the bed, still in his boots, like a terrified child. I no longer wanted to be close to him. Instinctively, I retreated as far as I could into my pillows.

'I'm the last thing this house has to worry about,' he whispered, his voice low and conspiratorial. 'This house is in about as much danger as it's possible to be in, but not from me. This whole *place,*' he gestured wildly around himself, 'is hanging by a fucking *thread* and I'm the only one who's trying to do something about it.'

My heart dipped in my chest, and visions of the End flashed through my mind. We knew it would be coming soon, some awful event which would force us down into the bunker to await The Rapture. What did he know? He was close enough to me now that I could see the whites of his eyes in the darkness, and feel his hot, heavy breath on my face. The sound of his teeth grinding anxiously gave me goosebumps, but as scared as I was there was an excitement there too. A little thrill of pleasure that he was talking to me again, trusting me, just like the old days. I tried not to let it carry through into my voice:

'What's going on?'

He grabbed me by the shoulders.

'What's going on, Aoife, is that the parents of those two brats from the village told John they were going to call the police. The government have had it in for me from the very start. They know who I am, and they know I'm here. They hate what I'm doing here. You know that; they'll take any sniff of a scandal and come bursting through the gates and take me away. This is my Gethsemane, Aoife.'

'Okay,' I said, almost disappointed. 'Well, you know, even if that's true about the parents of those kids from Abercraig calling the police, what can they do? This is our property. We're living peacefully on land that we own. They don't know what we're doing here, and they've no grounds to take you away or harm you, or any of us.'

The silence that followed was a heavy one, and I could almost hear Elijah's mind trying to reconcile my words with his paranoid fantasy. I knew that what I was saying was less than true – the police might not have any idea what was happening in Halcyon, but as Godly as our lives were, we were going against the law of the land. Ruth, Deborah and I shared a husband. With every unregistered child here, we had broken the law. And only God knew the whole raft of other minor infractions: taxes unpaid, the uninsured jeep. I prayed that he didn't think of those things, that what I had said would at least pull him out of the state he was in. Eventually, he spoke.

'They don't care about whether or not I've actually done anything wrong. What had Christ done wrong? They had to stop him because he was preaching the truth, and there's nothing they feared more. If everyone was like us, they would have no power. And it's the same people. They're terrified of me.'

'What?' I said, struggling to follow his jumbled line of argument, 'Who are the same people? The same as what?'

'The same people who killed Christ, you stupid woman. You don't understand anything important. The Order, they're in charge of everything and they'll kill me just like they killed him. They can't have another Prophet on their hands. If you don't understand that, I don't even know what you're doing here.'

His words were hard now, and venomous. I would have preferred a shout, a smack, to the seething disdain I heard when he spoke in that moment. Even the unfamiliar fear which had been there before would have been better. I took a sharp breath in, as though I'd been punched in the gut. In the darkness I watched his mouth, which had been contorted in rage and fear, twist into a cruel smile.

'Are you going to cry?' he asked, fake sympathy dripping from his lips. 'Go on then, cry. I don't know what you think you have to cry about.'

Elijah had been right. I had been about to cry. I couldn't remember the last time I had cried. I blinked the prickling tears back and swallowed the lump in my throat. *Pull it together, Aoife.* I focused back on my husband. His energy was shifting between terror and rage, as if he couldn't decide whether he wanted a fight or an embrace. I chose for him, reaching out and taking him in my arms. I expected him to resist at first, but instead he yielded immediately, and we lay down together, holding on to each other as if for dear life. I was still just about awake when his breathing began to slow, but not by much, and I'm not sure who fell asleep first.

# Chapter Six

## Ruth

When I came into the kitchen that morning the porridge was already beginning to congeal in its pot on the range stove, and the fire which warmed it was dwindling. I was downstairs later than usual; my deep, heavy sleep had carried me past the dawn, and I had slumbered through the cockerel's crow and the morning activities of the rest of the house. Elijah, Aoife and Deborah's bowls had already been washed and were drying on a threadbare tea towel by the sink. It would have been a quick meal, with everyone rushing to get their daily chores done before the Feast of the Prophet, but the thought of them all sitting together without me for any length of time made tears prick in the corners of my eyes.

I poked at the dying flames, hoping that I could revive them for long enough to warm my breakfast. The more I prodded, the more ash appeared and the fire started to smother itself, so I spooned out what was left in the pot into my bowl and sat down at the table. Our meals were now usually silent affairs, although we rarely took them alone. We tended to sit at the big kitchen table, one of us on each side, chewing in silence. The sound of knives and forks scraping plates was our only soundtrack. Dinner times in particular reminded me eerily of childhood meals at my grandparents' house. My grandfather was a disciplinarian, even more than my father was. There was no talking at dinner. My siblings and I would sit in silent terror, trying to remember all of the rules: elbows off the table, no yawning, no wriggling, never put your cutlery back on the table once you'd picked it up. Most importantly of all, and this was also a major rule for mealtimes in Halcyon, finish every scrap on your plate. Food production was too difficult, produce too scarce, to leave anything but the barest bone behind.

Once, early enough into one of my pregnancies that I didn't even know I was pregnant yet, I had been so sick that I had barely been able to eat a bite of food. We were having mashed potatoes, I can remember clearly, with boiled carrots and offal. The potatoes had been too thick, the carrots slimy and sweet and cold, the offal spongy and strong. My stomach had turned. Elijah and Aoife and Deborah were slowly clearing their plates while mine remained almost untouched. All eyes were on me and I forced myself to take one more mouthful of everything. I had barely swallowed when my mouth began to fill with saliva and I was hit with a wave of nausea so overpowering that I couldn't do anything to stop myself vomiting. Deborah gasped, and Aoife's eyes widened in shock or perhaps embarrassment. Elijah barely looked up from his meal. Weak as a kitten, I had cleaned up my mess as my sister wives looked on in stunned silence. Once I had finished, I took myself off to bed, thinking of nothing but my sudden overwhelming need to lie down and close my eyes against the whole day. I was woken several hours later by Elijah coming into my room; I remember being surprised to see him, because it wasn't our night together. He passed me my dressing gown and took me by the hand. Together we walked down the stairs and around to the back of the house where our compost bin sat waiting, barely visible in the twilight. He opened the lid and lying on top of a slurry of eggshells and bones and garden waste was my dinner. Even before Elijah took the knife and fork out of his pocket, I knew what he wanted me to do. He must have stood there for over an hour watching me eat. The sky darkened around us, and as it grew colder, he took off his own jacket and placed it gently over my shoulders. Once I had finished every last morsel, he walked me back into the house and tucked me gently into my bed. 'You're forgiven,' he had said. 'I love you.'

The memory was almost enough to put me off my breakfast, but I shut down the part of my mind that cared and ate the porridge as quickly and unthinkingly as possible. All I wanted at that moment was to get out of that cold, empty kitchen. It was time to be a good, productive member of the community.

There was no church or temple that morning, because of the

Feast, and everyone was working through their chores as quickly as they could. When I finished up with the animals, I came right back to the house to take my bath and get ready. One of the older children had already been in and filled up our tin tub with water boiled on the stove, and the kitchen door was closed. We usually just washed ourselves in basins, so the tub was a rare treat. I stood in the hallway clutching my towel and bar of soap, listening to the sounds of water as Aoife took her turn. Eventually, the door creaked open and Aoife peeked her head out of the crack. Her black hair was dripping wet, and she was wearing an old bathrobe which I recognised right away as Elijah's.

'I hope you weren't waiting there for too long, Ruth,' she said, pulling the robe tighter around her neck, 'it's all yours now. I'm heading back into my room to get ready. Just give a wee knock when you're done so I know when I'm all right to come out.'

She swung the door fully open and turned to walk back to her bedroom, which led off of the kitchen. Her feet left damp prints on the stone floor, and I tried not to look at her. It felt too intimate, seeing her bare legs sticking out from under the thick navy fabric. I waited until I could hear her opening her wardrobe before I undressed and lowered myself into the water. It was already cooling down, so I took a deep breath in before lying back fully until I was totally submerged. We had to be completely clean for the Feast. It was our biggest celebration, Easter and Christmas paling in comparison. October twenty-fifth: Elijah's birthday. He would be forty years old, not that we ever mentioned his age. I re-emerged from the water, rubbed the sliver of homemade soap across my body, moving as quickly as possible before the water had a chance to get any colder. I could hear Deborah shuffling around outside the door, waiting for her turn.


Dried and dressed, I pushed open the door to the community barn. The noise was nearly overwhelming after the quiet of our kitchen: people talking, dragging benches across the concrete floor, setting out platters of food. Four rectangular tables, each long enough to seat around twenty, had been laid with knives and forks. Each place setting was identical, and the wooden benches were bare, except for at the spaces where the inner circle would be sitting – Elijah, John, Aoife, Deborah, and I all got to sit on cushions.

Along one wall, women were busy arranging food on trestle tables ready to serve to the queue of diners. I could smell the savoury scent of chicken stew, the rich yeasty bread, steaming buttery vegetables, some kind of steaming dessert with preserved fruit. This was a special occasion. Soon, hungry colonists would be lining up, and an equal portion of everything would be set on their plates.

Helen banged the dinner gong and the few people who hadn't already been inside came chattering through the doors. Lois walked in alone and deflated, and sat at the edge of a bench as far away from Colin as she could get. Alfie and Adam, who were at the same end of the table, carried on their conversation as though she wasn't there at all. Other than the cushioned bench, there was no seating plan, although there was an unspoken rule that parents did not sit by their biological children. My five trooped in quietly with the others from the schoolhouse. Eli and Abraham had been born in the city, but the youngest were all Halcyon born. Moses, who was almost three, had one of his sweet hands clasped in Deborah's. I was stung by a pang of jealousy, which made me feel ashamed. Still, I desperately wanted to be the one to take his little hand in my own, to feel the grip of his small fingers. Constance, Aoife's eldest, was carrying Abigail. *My* Abigail. She was sucking on the end of one of Constance's long brown braids, and her own curly hair had been pulled away from her face into a topknot. I felt my eyes become hot with tears, and I blinked them away before anyone could notice.

'Busy morning, Ruth?' asked Aoife. Her hair was still damp from her bath, and she hardly looked at me when she spoke.

I wanted to tell her that I'd milked the cows, taken them to pasture, fed the chickens. Assure her that I was no sloth. But there was still a lump in my throat and the words got stuck behind it, so I just smiled again and nodded, hoping she wouldn't ask me anything else. By that time, Deborah was heaving her legs over the bench to sit down at her place across from us. She had barely got herself settled when the doors swung open again to reveal Elijah and John. The room rose to its feet.

# Chapter Seven

## Aoife

Despite everything which had happened the night before, my heart soared at the sight of Elijah. He had been gone by the time I'd woken up that morning, and I had worried that he would still be as distressed as he was when I last saw him. The Feast of the Prophet was too big an occasion in our church. It could not be spoiled.

I was pleased that my fears had been unfounded. I could tell as soon as he smiled his wide smile at the cheering congregation that everything would be all right, that he was back to his normal self. It was the fear of the End, I reassured myself; it was getting to him. He had such a burden to bear, and all things considered, he bore it beautifully. I had known him for years, and in that time those heavy moods had come and gone – it had always been me who had been able to save him from them. I watched with pride as he stopped and shook hands with various people on the way to his seat, the room ringing out with applause. I was clapping too, my palms buzzing. With all his stops, it took him a while to reach his spot to my left. I turned and looked up at him, still clapping, as he surveyed his kingdom. The whole barn was turned in our direction, and I smiled too, not just at Elijah but at the knowledge that as they looked at him they were also seeing me by his side. Seated at his right hand, just where I belonged.

Elijah liked it when we wives looked at him a certain way, eyes wide, interested, smiling. He said it showed respect. Recently, I'd had to make a concerted effort to get the look just right – the combination of our vanished sex life and the possibility of a new wife had made it difficult – but in that moment, it came as naturally as breathing. Jemima, I was aware, was standing at the far table by the door, surrounded by a gaggle of other children, out of sight, his sight, and I hoped, out of his mind. *I* had almost forgotten about her as I gazed up at his grinning face. Even his eyes were smiling, those beautiful delicate creases betraying true joy. He had the most wonderful eyes; brown and gleaming and wise, under thick brows and long lashes. His lashes, longer even than my own, were almost feminine. They didn't make him girlish, though – nothing could do that – just even more striking than he already was. His skin still carried a light tan, even though we were reaching the end of October, from all the time he spent outdoors. Mentally, I traced every line, every mark, every freckle. Just two more nights and he'd be mine again. And we'd be back to normal.

He raised his arms. The applause stopped, and the congregation sat down.

'My wonderful, loyal friends,' his voice boomed and bounced off the corrugated walls, 'we are here today to celebrate the Feast of the Prophet. I know for certain that this will be our final feast in this life – the End will be upon us soon, and by next October we will be feasting with our Lord in Heaven!'

The room burst out into applause once again, and some of the men stamped their feet and whooped. I had to resist the unladylike urge to whoop myself.

'Look at this bounty we have before us, friends, and look at what we've built here! They said it couldn't be done. They said we were fools when we made this journey, that we'd be back before the end of our first winter. Well, they were wrong!' With the word 'wrong', he leaned down and banged his fist on the table with such force that the crockery jumped into the air. 'We showed them! We showed them just what can be done when you have an Almighty God on your side!'

His eyes were wide with passion, and little beads of sweat had broken out on his forehead.

'Now,' he went on, 'I know we can all smell the delicious food which our women have so lovingly prepared for this Feast, and I'm sure we're excited to tuck in. But before we queue to be served, I would like us to offer up a prayer through song. God, we thank you for granting us another day in our Heaven on Earth, and pray that we might do you service today. We thank you for granting us your bounty here at Halcyon, and for protecting us from the sins of the world outside its safe walls.'

'Thanks be to God and our Holy Prophet.'

'Psalm twenty-three,' he said, and began to sing.

I had always associated that particular Psalm with funerals, *though I walk through the valley of the shadow of death, I will fear no evil*, but I sang along with the rest of the congregation, enjoying the sound of our voices all joined together.

When we finished, Elijah called for everyone to take their place in the queue for our meal. None of us in the inner circle had to queue, of course – this was the Feast of the Prophet and we were the wives of the Prophet. Annie took our plates for us and filled them, giving Elijah a little more than everyone else. The food was just a slightly better version of what we usually ate in the farmhouse, better probably just because Deborah had had nothing to do with the preparation of it, but I had a feeling it was significantly more than the general population of Halcyon was used to getting. As it was a special occasion, talking was very much allowed, but everyone was too distracted by the food on their plates so the main sound in the room was the scraping of cutlery against enamel.

I barely tasted my meal, so focused was I on my proximity to Elijah. I could feel the warmth coming off his body, our sides almost touching on the bench. I moved my foot so it rested against his. When he didn't react, I allowed myself to move my leg too, so it pressed into his own. That was when he turned to look at me. He gave a small smile, and gestured for me to lean in so he could whisper something in my ear. The feeling of his breath on my skin sent waves of heat through my body, and I had to inhale deeply through my nose to calm down.

'Aoife,' his lips were almost brushing my ears, 'I need you to do something for me.'

I nodded. I would have done anything.

'Go and fetch Jemima.'

My ears were ringing, suddenly, with the sound of my own blood, and I worried I might faint with the toxic combination of rage and grief which had engulfed me as soon as those three syllables came out of his mouth. Je-mi-ma. That was how he had said it, as though he was savouring the taste of her name on his tongue.

I rose, moving slowly to avoid tripping over my skirt or the bench. I was vaguely aware of Ruth and Deborah watching me go, but my full concentration was on staying upright, putting one foot in front of the other, and not screaming. Jemima was helping one of the smaller children cut up their food when I reached her. I couldn't bring myself to touch her bony little shoulder, so instead I coughed. She looked up, wide-eyed and frightened. *Good*, I thought, *you should be frightened, you little harlot*.

'Follow me,' I said, making my voice as terse and sharp as I could.

I didn't even wait for her to disentangle herself from the bench before I strode back towards Elijah. I liked the thought of her scampering along behind me, struggling to catch up.

Elijah barely looked at me when I got back. His eyes were focussed on her. When I went to retake my seat by his side, he shook his head.

'Let Mim sit there. You can go around the other side, next to Deborah.'

And then he was gone. Leaning in towards her, that whorish girl, that nasty child, whispering. What was he saying? And why was he calling her Mim? For the duration of our marriage he had never called me anything but my full Christian name. My stomach twisted into a knot of rage as I sat down next to Deborah, my buttocks feeling the hard wood of the bench for the first time.

I forced myself to take another deep breath. I wanted to be like a swan, serene and calm, no hint of the crazed paddling feet beneath the surface. Serene and calm and – but weren't swans vicious? I turned to Deborah, who was mopping up the last of her stew with a piece of bread. I waited until she was just about to pop it in her pretty pink mouth before I spoke.

'Well, you've certainly polished that off, haven't you, Deborah?' I heard my own voice, hard and cool, amid the low chatter and scraping of plates. My accent, usually subdued after years of living away from County Kildare, always pitched up when I was angry, and I could hear it rising then. Elijah and Jemima did not look up from their whispered discussion.

The bread was already in Deborah's mouth by that point, and I watched as she froze, holding it there.

'Although you know that eating for two is a myth, don't you?' I said. 'No need to turn into a greedy guts just because you're expecting.'

I let out a venomous laugh. Deborah's watery grey eyes had widened, but she didn't say anything. I leaned in and spoke in a stage whisper:

'If I were you, I'd watch your figure a bit more. You'll not be the youngest model for much longer, and when all you have to offer is your looks ... No offence meant of course, *Sister*.' I spat the word. 'Of course, I'm just looking out for you. But when all you have is a pretty face and a young body, it's awfully easy to be forgotten about when a prettier face and a younger body comes on the scene.'

I looked meaningfully over at Jemima. Elijah had his arm around her shoulders. The sight made me do a double-take, but no one else seemed to think anything of it; Ruth was staring at her plate, and John appeared to have vanished. I turned back to Deborah, watching her eyes for tears. *Come on you little cow, cry.*

I was just about to open my mouth again when Elijah stood and the room fell into silence.

'I hope we have all enjoyed our delicious meal?' He paused, allowing the congregation to answer him.

'Yes!'

'Good!' he said, 'I'm glad. I said before we ate that this will be our last Feast of the Prophet here on Earth, so I think we ought to make it a special one. Do you agree?'

'Yes!'

The answer was loud enough that I didn't have to respond myself. Instead, I opened and shut my mouth in time with everyone else, my silence lost in their voices.

'Excellent! I have a surprise for you all, one which I think you'll enjoy.' He smirked and I prayed that the surprise had nothing to do with Jemima, who was looking up at him wide-eyed, interested, smiling. 'But first, I think this is a good opportunity to share some testimony.'

Elijah pointed at one person after another, and they rose and spoke. I had heard everyone's stories so many times that they all blurred into one.

'I met Elijah just after I had got a new job, I was stressed, everything I did was about money. He showed me that there was more to life.'

'Thank you, Elijah. You brought God into my world just when I needed Him the most.'

'I was thinking about ending my life when Elijah invited me to a service in the community centre back in town.'

'I'd never felt so much love in a room before.'

'Elijah saved my mother's life. He turned her away from sin and he reunited us, and I'll always be so grateful.'

That was Deborah; Elijah loved getting her to trot out her sad little story on occasions like this. He stood and watched, beaming as the compliments rained down on him. When Deborah had finished speaking, he didn't point at anyone else. Instead, he spoke up again himself.

'Thank you to everyone who shared,' he said. 'I think it's so important to speak our testimonies. They remind us of the importance of faith, of placing our trust in God. Even when we ourselves can't see how something might end, we have to remember that God knows. That *I* know. And that we won't let you come to harm. With that in mind, I would like to share with you my surprise.'

*Please don't let it be about Jemima, please don't let it be about Jemima, please, please.*

'While we've been testifying, Brother John has been laying out glasses of water by your plates. I have noticed that some of you have taken sips already – don't worry if that's the case, but if you haven't, I would appreciate if you could wait until I've finished speaking before you do.'

John appeared at my left, a greasy waiter, and set a glass for me and a glass for Deborah down on the table.

'This isn't just ordinary water – well, most glasses glasses are full of ordinary water. But five,' he held up a hand, fingers splayed, 'contain something else too. You won't be able to taste or smell the difference, but after a few moments you'll notice… something. The glasses have been given out at random, although I've told John not to give any of the *special* glasses to the children. To make it fair, I've also asked John to make sure that one of the special glasses be served to one of the inner circle.' He gestured to Ruth, Deborah and me. 'I don't want to be accused of playing favourites.'

The room watched in silence. I couldn't believe what I was hearing. 'Special' glasses? What on Earth could be in them? I wracked my brains – LSD? Cyanide? Surely not. He had never spoken to me about anything like this. But then, he had not spoken to me properly for so long. My mind flashed back to the previous night. He had been out of his mind then. If he had been speaking with John just before…

'The End is coming so soon, friends. We need to be ready. I need to know that everyone in this room has faith, and so, when I give the command, I want you to pick up your glasses and drink. Show me your faith! Show everyone in this room that you deserve your place amongst us in these very final days!'

He raised his own glass to his lips, and drank. My heart was hammering so hard in my chest that I worried for a moment that I might have some kind of attack. Everyone around me was lifting their glasses and drinking. Next to me, Deborah had already downed her drink and was sitting serenely, hands patiently folded in her lap. With both hands I picked up my own glass. Elijah looked down at me, his brow raised expectantly, one hand clutching his empty glass, the other resting heavily on Jemima's shoulder.

I brought my glass to my lips and swallowed the cool, flavourless liquid. I held his gaze as behind me the coughing and spluttering began.

# Chapter Eight

## Ruth

Back in 2008, after I qualified as a midwife, I decided to move out of my godmother's place in London and try out somewhere new. I applied for about ten positions in hospitals and birthing centres around the country, but none in London; an omission that I didn't share with my godmother. I had been living with her for the whole duration of my studies, and was starting to get worn out. My father's rules had been too rigid, but Therese, my godmother, had no rules at all – a choice she worked hard to keep from my parents. Back home, I could leave the house for church and pre-approved church-related activities, school, and to help my mom run errands. I had to keep my hair just so, my nails filed way down, and the room I shared with my sister immaculate. Trying to please him had been difficult and exhausting, but it was possible. Therese wanted me to 'live my life' and 'have fun' and 'stop being so uptight', and pleasing her was difficult and exhausting in a whole different way. After four years of being dragged out to bars and parties where I was simultaneously the youngest and most boring person, having my orange juice and coffee spiked with liquor, and being set up on dates with men who painted murals, I had had enough. Moving to Newcastle was my chance to start again; I was twenty-two years old, and ready to begin life on my own terms.

It was my roommate Chrissy, another nurse, who told me about the Church of Heaven on Earth.

'You'd like them, I think. They seem like your kind of people.'

'My kind of people?' I wrinkled my nose, unsure what she was trying to say.

'Oh, you know I didn't mean…' Chrissy blushed. 'I just meant, they seem nice. Like, they do nice things. Lois from work, her and her husband go there. They run a free creche and do a soup kitchen, and I think some other stuff too? I'm like, not religious or anything, but they definitely seem like the kind of church I would join if I was, you know, going to join a church.'

I had been in the city for three weeks by then, and had tried three different churches, none of which had seemed right. On my fourth Sunday in Newcastle I took the bus from my apartment to the hall where Heaven on Earth held their services, and knew straight away that Chrissy had been right. These were my kind of people. First off, they welcomed me with open arms. Lois, one of the receptionists from work, recognised me right away and called me to sit with her and her husband and their little boy. Everyone there seemed so incredibly *nice*. Elijah was a draw, too. I liked the way he talked about faith, and what it meant to live like a Christian in the modern world. When the service was over, he filled my mug with tea from the urn and asked me about myself. When I talked, he seemed interested. He said he hoped he would see me again soon.


Eleven years later, I pulled myself out of bed, a dull throbbing pain pulsing behind my eyes. Elijah had not come to bed, and I'd been relieved. He'd scared me with his stunt with the water, in a way he hadn't ever scared me before.

He had waited until everyone had taken a drink before clapping his hands together. He kept them clasped as the room looked back up at him, waiting to be told what five of them had just drunk.

'I am so proud of you all,' he said, his knuckles turning white, 'so, so proud. You've shown your faith today, shown me that you all deserve to be here with us at the End. I'm pleased to say you have all passed the test.'

He smiled.

'Each and every one of your glasses contained nothing more than God's own Highland water.'

I hadn't realised that I had been holding my breath until I felt the air rush back into my lungs. Just water. Nothing more. Elijah would never harm us. Those terrifying coughs from the congregation, the urge I'd had to clutch at my throat, had been from fear, not poison.

On the other side of Elijah, John let out a loud and hearty laugh, as if Elijah had just pulled the funniest prank he'd ever seen. At first the sound echoed emptily around the room, until Elijah laughed too – then everyone joined in. Even little Jemima, next to me, put her hand to her mouth and giggled. My own laugh came out sounding like a rough honk, not a laugh at all really, just the strangled sound of relief. The only person who was silent was Aoife. She'd had her gaze fixed on Elijah since he had issued his instruction, and now she was staring up at him with thunder in her eyes. Had she been in on it, I wondered? Had Deborah? Was that why they had both finished their glasses so eagerly? My own glass was still almost full; I had barely swallowed any of it.

I took the opportunity while everyone was laughing to drink the rest, so if anyone checked afterward they would think I'd been just as obedient as my sister wives. The laughter went on for what felt like forever. Every time it slowed, someone would laugh louder and everybody would start up again. It was contagious, and by the end I let myself get swept up too, just glad that it was over, that no one had been hurt, that Elijah hadn't really wanted to harm us. Relieved too, I guess, that we had all done as we were told. I didn't like to think what punishment Elijah would have brought down on anyone who had stood up and refused.

The Feast went on for hours after that. We sang more hymns, Elijah preached, and when the autumn sun went down the women lifted the lid off the cabbage soup and brought out another platter of bread and we ate some more. By the time we were dismissed, everyone seemed to have forgotten about the test, as if it didn't bear thinking about. People laughed and talked all the way back to their caravans, their voices fading into the night as we wives walked back to the farmhouse in silence. I waited and waited for Elijah that night, keeping my door shut to Russell even though I could hear her padding around on the landing, running through what I would say to him when he arrived. Thinking about what he might say to me. Would he even want to talk? Would he just want to make love and then fall asleep, as he usually did? The cool grey light of dawn was coming through my window by the time I realised he wasn't coming.

The following morning, after work, I decided to visit the schoolhouse. It had been a long time since I had been inside. Like all of the farm buildings in Halcyon, the schoolhouse had been renovated lovingly but inexpertly by the many hands of our church. We had an architect and two engineers in our midst, but they had been too busy working on the bunker to spare much time for anything else. Inside, tarpaulin had been strung up to separate the sleeping quarters from the school. These hanging tarps had been used as canvases by Deborah, who at Elijah's request had spent painstaking days writing a selection of 'child-focussed' Bible verses on them in huge black letters. I always forgot just how imposing the great banners were, and how stern they made God's loving words.

**FROM THE LIPS OF CHILDREN YOU, <u>LORD</u>, HAVE CALLED FORTH YOUR PRAISE.**

**LIKE ARROWS IN THE HANDS OF A WARRIOR ARE CHILDREN.**

**FOLLY IS BOUND UP IN THE HEART OF A CHILD, BUT THE ROD OF DISCIPLINE WILL DRIVE IT FAR AWAY.**

**LET THE LITTLE CHILDREN COME TO ME FOR THE KINGDOM OF <u>GOD</u> BELONGS TO SUCH AS THESE.**

Even the last verse, which had been my favourite ever since I was a little girl, sounded harsh thanks to the heavy black text in which it was written. Elijah was proud of the banners, but although Deborah pretended to be pleased with how they had come out, I could tell she felt that they did not look exactly how she had intended. I wondered what the children made of them, or if they noticed them at all.

The porch opened up into the classroom side of the building, where rows of children sat cross-legged on the floor listening intently to Jemima, who at barely sixteen was one of the barn's older residents. Jemima. She had been there yesterday, had taken Aoife's seat at Elijah's side. I'd tried not to look as she'd leaned into Elijah, whose strong, familiar arm had encircled her shoulders. I did my best not to think about it as I watched her from across the room; she was demonstrating something, but I was too far away to see what. I was amazed by the children's undivided attention, especially as Helen and Danielle were busy laying out lunch on a trestle table nearby. Annie, who was tending to a little cluster of gurgling toddlers in another corner, looked up as I closed the door behind me and gave me a quizzical stare. Abigail was sitting on her lap, playing with the buttons on her cardigan. With a tentative wave in Annie's direction I ducked through an opening in the tarp into the dormitory, trying not to think about Abigail or Jemima or the Feast.

If it had been a long time since I had been in the school, I doubted if I had ever been into the children's sleeping quarters even once. The first thing that struck me was the smell, which transported me back into the changing rooms in my high school gym in Illinois. The second thing that stood out was the order in which the space was kept. Bunk beds and cots were lined up as neatly as soldiers, and bins of folded clothes labelled by contents did not look as though they had been rifled through by twenty-five children a few hours ago. Unable to resist, I came to the first bed and inspected the sheets – although the linens and blankets were mismatched, the little bed was made up as neatly as could be. I was so impressed by the hospital-like precision, which surely couldn't have been achieved by a child, that I didn't even notice Deborah until she spoke. She was sitting on the floor.

'Hey, Ruth! Is everything okay?' Her stage whisper, presumably to stop her voice carrying through the tarpaulin divider, sounded cheerful enough, but she looked concerned. It was only then that I realised she must have thought I was there for a particular reason, and I wished I'd never come at all. What if she thought I wanted to talk about the Feast of the Prophet? What if she brought it up herself?

'Oh,' I said, 'yeah of course, everything's fine.'

She looked at me expectantly until I spoke again.

'I got done a little earlier than usual this morning so I thought I would take a walk. Can I help with anything?'

Deborah gestured to the little piles of folded clothes around her with a gentle smile.

'You've timed that pretty well, Ruth. These have come back from being washed but I've just this minute finished folding them.'

'Oh, I'm sorry,' I said.

Deborah let out a sweet peal of laughter which echoed around the room, then put her hand to her mouth in mock embarrassment.

'Don't be daft! You're too sweet, Ruth, but you know I'm just teasing. Although...' she paused for a second, 'there is actually something I could use your help with.'

'Sure, anything!' I said quickly, stepping towards her.

'You can help me get up.' She reached up her arms to me like an overgrown toddler, and I heaved her onto her feet. Once upright, Deborah shook her head, 'I'm getting too pregnant for this.'

I wouldn't have dared agree with her out loud, but she was looking particularly large and I was keeping a close eye on her during her check-ups, doing my best to figure out if she was having twins again. I thought it was a miracle that she had managed to get down on the floor in the first place. Instead, I smiled and said, 'Well, looks like I came along at just the right time after all.'

My usefulness apparently exhausted, I was just about to make my excuses to leave when a burst of chatter from the classroom signalled the end of lessons and the beginning of lunch.

'That sounds like my cue to head next door,' said Deborah, 'I like to lead their mealtime prayers when I can.'

But instead of making a move in the direction of the schoolroom, she stayed where she was.

'Why don't you join me? It'll only take five minutes, and then we can head back to the farmhouse together for a bite to eat?'

Before I could answer, Jemima peeked her head through a gap in the tarp. She must have been completely engrossed in her lesson when I'd come in earlier, because she looked surprised to see me.

'Oh, err, hi,' she said, blushing slightly, 'am I all right to, I mean, please may I come in?'

Deborah nodded and beckoned her forward with a smile. 'You're very welcome to join us, Mim, but we were just about to head through ourselves.'

It took me a second to figure out that Mim must have been short for Jemima, and I wondered if any of my children had been granted schoolhouse nicknames of which I was unaware.

'I didn't know you were here, Sister Ruth. I'm sorry. I didn't mean to interrupt.'

She could barely look me in the eye, and I realised with wonder that she was waiting for me to grant her some kind of pardon. I supposed it made sense – in the hierarchy of Halcyon I was, somehow, the most senior person in the room.

'That's quite all right,' I said. I was so unused to any show of power that I had to borrow my words from Aoife, and they tasted foreign in my mouth.

Jemima – Mim – looked relieved, although she still kept her

gaze low. She had grown up in the church and I had seen her most days since she was five years old, but I suppose I hadn't really studied her for a long time. Even yesterday, when she had taken Aoife's place next to me, I had done my best not to look at her at all. Up close, I was surprised by how pretty she was, even with the peppering of acne across her chin.

'What can we do for you, Mim?' asked Deborah.

Was I imagining it, or did her pleasantness, usually so natural, seem slightly forced? Maybe she was just anxious to go say grace with the children, and was a little resentful of the hold-up. Nothing to do with Elijah's announcement last week, or Mim's seat on his right the day before. No. Nothing like that.

'I just wanted to catch you before you went for lunch,' said Mim, managing to lift her head high enough to look at Deborah while she spoke. 'I wanted to say thank you for letting me run the scripture lesson today. It was fun.'

'You're very welcome, sweetheart,' said Deborah, softening slightly, 'I'm sure you did a lovely job.'

Mim smiled, relieved.

'Off you go then, get yourself some soup before there's none left. I'm coming through just now to say a prayer with you all.'

With a nod at Deborah and a strange little half curtsy to me, Mim scurried back through to the classroom. We watched her go in silence.

'Sweet kid,' I said.

Deborah raised an eyebrow. 'She certainly is.'

# Chapter Nine

## Aoife

Schoolgirl stuff. That's what it was. Stupid, silly, petty schoolgirl stuff that should have been as far beneath me as it was possible for anything to be. But it still bothered me. The three of them standing there, chatting, pally as anything. I had been looking for Ruth, and when I was told that she'd last been seen going into the schoolhouse I had thought there must be some mistake. Only, there she was. And not just her, but Deborah too, and worst of all there *she* was. The girl. Jemima. Or what was it that he was calling her now, some sickly-sweet diminutive? Jem? Mim? Mim. When he said that at the breakfast table that morning I had almost choked on my porridge. It had been just the two of us there, and I had taken the opportunity to bring her up in conversation – conversation being allowed on occasion at breakfast, although never at dinner.

'Your idea with the water glasses at the Feast of the Prophet yesterday was really inspired, my love,' I said, choosing my words carefully. 'What a clever way to make sure everyone is faithful and ready for the End.' No hint of criticism. No shouting. Not a whisper of my real feelings about the whole thing, which were … what exactly?

He let out a pleased grunt of recognition.

'It was nice of you to let Jemima sit up with you, too. Did she have anything interesting to say?'

Elijah looked up and I thought I was in for it, but instead he tilted his head. 'Jemima? Oh, you mean Mim.'

Her name was like a spell – as soon as it escaped his lips he was transformed into a teenager with a crush. He flashed me a smile.

'Oh,' he said, 'Mim was just fine.'

I could have spat.

Seeing them all together had just been salt in the wound. Only the Lord himself knew what they were saying about me, huddled in their little coven. Deborah, especially, was very free with Elijah, telling him just what she thought of me at every opportunity she got – it made sense that she would be doing the same with Ruth and Jemima, trying to turn them against me. At least Elijah was honest, careful to relay her spiteful words with compassion and love. I could rely on him for that. For all his faults, at least he cared enough to tell me the truth. *Maybe they weren't talking about you at all*, came the voice in my head, venomous and wise, *maybe they were talking about his trick with the water. Maybe they were all in on it, and that's why they polished off their glasses so loyally. He probably ran it by them all first.*

I walked out again quickly, before any of them could spot me and accuse me of spying on them. To my shame, I felt tears prickling in my eyes and heat rising to my face. How could I let two women and a teenage girl make me feel this way? *Pathetic,* piped up the voice in my head, *you're absolutely pathetic, Aoife.* The voice was right. Why did I care if they hated me? Why should I mind if Deborah thought I was bossy and stuck-up and past my best? Who cared if Elijah had shared his plans with them and not me? It had felt like two against one for a while, so why was it important that I would soon have three sister wives against me?

Before I could come up with a concrete plan of what to do next, I found that I had passed out of the centre of Halcyon and was walking towards the perimeter fence. Instead of turning back, I decided to keep on walking, hoping that it would clear my head. I took a breath, inhaling the fresh Highland air. I tramped on by the caravans, which were mainly empty at that time of day, and the hives and the greenhouses, my eyes fixed purposefully ahead. I had learned a long time ago that a little confidence can take a person a long way – if I'd been shuffling, looking shifty or wary or lost, someone would have come up to me and asked where I was going, or they would have gone to tell Elijah or John that I was wandering. If I looked like I knew what I was doing, I could do anything that I wanted.

Without my noticing, Halcyon had burst into an autumnal flame. It happened every year – I would pay no attention at all to the land around me until it was almost too late to appreciate the changing colours. The deergrass and heather were a blazing russet red, and I let myself admire them as I picked my way towards the perimeter, carefully avoiding the stones and hard tufts of spiked grass which stuck out at random intervals. It wouldn't be long until winter came, and the golds and oranges and reds were replaced with dead browns and greys, covered with snow and treacherous with ice. I had wandered so far that the only sign that I was still in Halcyon at all was the chain-link fence (to keep the livestock *in* and the nosey neighbours *out*), and the wooden watchtower which stood, quaint and empty, waiting patiently for the End of Days. The sheep grazed, placid and uninterested in anything but the mossy grass at their feet, occasionally meandering over to one of Halcyon's winding streams for a drink. An eagle swooped high overhead in the wide grey Highland sky, circling gracefully through the air. I looked out ahead to see how far I was from the edge of our land, and that was when I noticed the car. It was a big four-by-four, fancier than ours, the sort that belonged to wealthy landowners and gentleman farmers across the British Isles. I was surprised that I hadn't noticed it before, even though it was parked at quite a distance from the perimeter and obscured slightly by a mound in the earth. Without thinking, I picked up my pace and strode towards it. I don't know what I expected to do when I reached the edge of Halcyon – dig out under the fence to investigate? Fortunately, the decision was made for me; as I continued my approach in the direction of the vehicle its door swung open and a figure leapt out. I stopped. This was the first person from outside of Heaven on Earth that I had encountered in a long time. Perhaps they sensed my unease from afar, because they bounded towards me with an exaggerated show of friendliness. It was a man, I realised, not quite as tall as Elijah but still broad and imposing in his own way. He gave a long, languid wave.

'Hullo!' he called.

I responded with a tentative wave and continued on my path towards him. We both reached the edge of the perimeter fence at the same moment and I was able to study him properly. My initial assumption that this person was some kind of wealthy landowner was reinforced when I saw him up close. He wore a waxed jacket, unbuttoned enough to reveal a woollen jumper and a red and white checked shirt underneath, and he had the floppy, public-schoolboy haircut and lazy grin of someone who lived a carefree and privileged life. I thought he might have been out on a fishing trip, but I couldn't see a rod anywhere on his person, and he wasn't wearing the sort of waders you'd need for the river which bordered us. Maybe he had left them in the car.

'Who are you?' I asked, surprised at the breathiness of my voice. 'What are you doing here?'

He let out a hearty laugh and shook his head.

'Malcolm,' he said, 'pleased to meet you.'

His voice was rich and warm, like a smoky Scotch whisky.

'Pleased to meet you,' I echoed.

'I would shake your hand, but…' he gestured to the fence between us.

'Oh, that's okay.' I looked down, embarrassed by my embarrassment, and noticed his wellington boots, expensive-looking and squeaky clean, through the gaps in the fence. I wondered what he was noticing about me.

I scolded myself internally. I had complained earlier about the rest of them acting like a bunch of schoolgirls, and there I was, unable to look a man in the eye. *Pathetic. Pull yourself together.*

'What did you say you were doing here, Malcolm?' I tried to convey breeziness and assertiveness all at once in my tone, but breezy was something I rarely tried to be, and I worried that the effect made me sound more demanding than I would have liked.

He laughed again, and I couldn't help but feel pleased. He lifted both hands up in a jovial surrender. 'You got me there. I didn't. I've recently inherited the land around here. Not your land, of course, but the rest of it.'

We looked at one another in silence for a short moment before he spoke again.

'I've heard a bit about the man who owns *your* land,' he nodded at the expanse of Halcyon behind me, 'and I thought he might be interested in some kind of offer.'

'I'm not so sure about that. I know him fairly well and I don't think he'd be interested in selling or buying. We've got just about the right amount of land for us. And you wouldn't want this land anyway, when the weather is bad the river floods and half of the pasture is under water.'

I could see him thinking, trying to figure me out. I'm ashamed to say that I enjoyed it.

'Do you think I might be able to chat with him anyway? I always thought that you should get to know your neighbours.'

I shook my head and turned to leave. 'He's not much of a people person, I'm afraid.'

'Wait!' he called.

I turned back around.

'I'm so sorry,' he said, 'that wasn't very neighbourly of me.'

'It was not.' Although I tried to sound hurt, I was secretly almost giddy with pleasure. I wasn't used to receiving apologies.

'I do think it's good to know your neighbours though, and if…'

'Elijah.'

'Elijah. If Elijah isn't much of a people person, then maybe I could get to know you? That way if I need to borrow a cupful of sugar or a bag of flour one day, I know who to go to.'

I smiled.

'That certainly sounds sensible to me,' I said. 'I shall keep an eye out for you coming along with your mug of tea.'

A dimple appeared in the left corner of his mouth when he grinned.

'Perhaps it would be a good start if you told me your name?'

'Aoife,' I said.

'Nice to meet you, Aoife.' He lifted his right arm as if he were about to shake my hand, and awkwardly stuck his forefinger through a hole in the chain link. He looked at me expectantly, and with a sheepish giggle I placed my own finger next to his. We linked them together and shook as best we could, separated as we were by the great metal fence. Other than my husband, he was the first man to touch me in almost twelve years.

I stayed out a little longer than I had planned to, and returned to the farmhouse with a sick, guilty knot in my stomach. I counted the things which I had done wrong. Number one, I had wandered off in the middle of a working day. Number two, I had stood and talked to a man, unchaperoned. Number three, that man was not a member of Heaven on Earth. Number four, I had let that man touch me, albeit with an entirely innocent part of his anatomy on an entirely innocent part of my anatomy. And worst of all, number five, I had enjoyed myself in his company. Not only was that sluttish and immodest, but with the End looming it was a potentially dangerous waste of time. The End. Somehow, speaking to someone new had made the End seem less – final.

Less urgent. Less *real.* Which was ridiculous. What had I been living in preparation for these past twelve years if that was the case? I shook my head, trying to dislodge the thoughts before I opened the front door.

When I walked into the kitchen where Deborah was preparing our evening meal, I expected her to notice some kind of difference in me, as though my transgressions would be branded onto my forehead. I had braced myself for an interrogation – *where have you been? With who? Why?* – and was relieved and disappointed in equal measure when she barely looked up from her chopping board.

'Hi, Aoife,' she said, returning almost instantly to her work, 'you all right?'

I made a small noise in response, although what it was supposed to mean I couldn't say, and busied myself by setting out four lots of cutlery. It was typical of her to be so oblivious. She was too simple to even still be annoyed with me about the way I'd spoken to her at the Feast. If she had talked to me that way, I certainly would not be looking at her now. Outside, I could hear the rest of the colony chatting as they traipsed to the community barn for their tea, tired but happy after a day of hard work. We were soon joined by Ruth, who filled a jug with water before taking her place at the table. Every sound was amplified by our silence as we waited for Elijah to arrive, each of us sitting patiently in our designated spot. Occasionally, Deborah rose to check the food, which smelled like it might be beginning to burn.

'Well, Deborah,' I said, leaning back in my chair to look at her as she stood by the stove, 'that certainly smells interesting. You really do just follow your own rules with cooking, don't you?'

I watched, stomach fluttering, as her shoulders froze. When she didn't say anything, I decided to keep going.

'I'd say it was admirable, if we weren't the ones who had to eat it every single day.'

Deborah's hand clenched around her wooden spoon as I let out a high-pitched laugh.

'You know, I remember reading something in a newspaper years ago about how burned food can give you cancer. Let's hope for our sakes that the corrupt media didn't get something right for once!'

I looked over at Ruth, but she didn't meet my eyes. My words kept ringing in my ears, and I had just opened my mouth to speak again when Deborah interrupted me.

'Wow, thanks, Aoife. I really value your opinion. Maybe, if you're so keen for a change from my cooking, you could give it a try once in a while. I'm sure Ruth and I would enjoy whatever five-star cuisine you'd manage to rustle up with our daily rations.'

'Well, I hardly think there's any need for that attitude, *Deborah*.' I stood up. 'I do plenty of work, not that you'd notice, actually keeping Halcyon running. It's not easy, you know, managing the accounts for a place like this.'

'Oh, I'm sure you're right,' she said, the corner of her mouth twitching, 'but we can't all be as clever as you. Saying that, I'm pretty certain you didn't bother yourself with cooking or housework before we came here, either. Didn't you just get Ruth to do it all for you?'

Before I could think of a retort, Ruth spoke up.

'Not that I minded a bit, Aoife. I was happy to do it.'

I forced a smile, trying not to wonder what else they said about me behind my back.

'That's nice of you to say,' said Deborah to Ruth, 'but you know, I wonder sometimes how happy Elijah could have been. Poor man, only the Lord knows how he coped before you and I came along.'

It wasn't like her to talk back, and my hand rose, reflexively, to slap her. It would have been worth whatever punishment Elijah dished out, and it would have been a big one I was certain, given Deborah's condition. The only thing that stopped me was the sound of the front door opening, followed by Elijah's familiar footsteps in the hallway. When he appeared in the doorway, he seemed surprised to see us there, waiting for him.

'Elijah!' Deborah chirped, turning to him with a smile as she took her seat. 'You must be famished. Why don't you sit down?'

He shook his head gruffly, as though he couldn't believe how stupid she was. As much as I was pleased to see it, his manner with her took me by surprise – he'd never acted so brusquely with Deborah before.

'I'm not staying,' he said.

'Oh?' I could hear a strain in Deborah's voice as she tried to remain cheerful. She was usually so effortless.

'I have to go and pray. About adding Mim to our family. I need to speak with God and I can't hear Him over your infernal *chat*.'

They were staring at each other so intently that I began to feel as though I was intruding on a private conversation.

'Do you know when we can expect you back?' she asked.

Once again, he fixed her with a look of pure distaste.

'No.'

The tension in the kitchen crackled, as though we were all waiting for lightning to strike.

'Oh, okay,' said Deborah, 'that's fine, but if you could just give a sort of rough ide—'

Elijah was not a violent man in the traditional sense. He dished out his punishments cold, when the heat of the moment had died away and you thought your indiscretion might have been quietly forgiven or forgotten. He had never smacked me in a temper, never bruised my face or blacked my eye. Which is why, I think, we were all so shocked when he interrupted Deborah's prattling request by picking up a heavy stoneware dinner plate from the kitchen worktop and throwing it so it soared inches above her head, before smashing against the kitchen wall. If she hadn't ducked, it would certainly have grazed the top of her scalp. Had he meant for it to get so close to her? Surely he hadn't intended to actually hit her? The electricity had gone from the air, and the three of us sat in stunned silence. Elijah was panting a little, and he hadn't taken his eyes off Deborah, who was white as a sheet and gripping the edge of the table with what I could only assume was fear.

'I will come back,' he said, 'when I decide that I want to come back. I am not beholden to you. Don't ever tell me what to do again.'

He spoke deliberately, almost calmly, waiting for Deborah to nod in agreement before leaving the kitchen. He closed the front door gently, but the sound of the latch clicking into place echoed down the corridor and made me wince. Nobody said a word as Deborah mechanically began to plate up our dinners, and we sat and ate in silence. One by one we finished our charred food, ignoring the ceramic shrapnel which had been scattered across every surface.

# Part Two

# Chapter Ten

## Deborah

I wanted to kill him. I imagined how it would feel to leap onto his back as he left the room – in my fantasy I was nimble and not almost six months pregnant – and tear his hair so his head snapped backwards. I could almost feel the soft flesh of his throat giving way under my nails, the warm spurt of blood. He would be too shocked to do anything but fall to the floor, clutching at his neck, writhing under my weight as I straddled him and pummelled his face with my balled-up fists until he lay still and lifeless on the kitchen floor. 'How dare you do this to me?!' I would scream, raising my voice louder than I'd dared to for years, as Aoife and Ruth looked on.

At the very least, I should have left when he did. Packed a bag, picked up Jonah and Noah and Susannah, and followed him straight out of the open gate, into the Highland night. What would they have done? What *could* they have done? Nothing. But it was like something turned off in my brain when it happened, and I couldn't do anything at all any more. How dare he, after everything? Especially after his disgusting stunt at the Feast of the Prophet – that evil bullshit with the drinks, making my babies watch on, thinking that people around them were going to die. I'd almost killed myself trying to be normal and pleasant after that, and for what? For years I had played along, keeping everything in, and when it finally clicked that I was playing a losing game and the time came to let it all out, I realised that I couldn't. It's like when people say to kids, 'stop pulling faces or the wind will change, and you'll be stuck like that'. I'd played the cowed wife for so long that the wind had changed without me even noticing, and I was suddenly unable to be anything else.

That was the danger of my survival technique. The chameleon, quick-change, be-who-they-want-you-to-be personality which I had had down from the day I realised, as a child, that not everyone's life looked like mine. That to stay safe, wherever I was put, I needed to mask up and play whatever part was needed. It had kept me going through the early years with my mother and a childhood in care, but then in Heaven on Earth it had got a bit stuck. There was no need to change it up, because everyone needed the same from me, so I just kept the 'Prophet's Wife' mask on all the time. It had actually started to get comfortable, and when I needed to take it off, I couldn't, because there wasn't really a normal Deborah face underneath any more.

The next few days passed in a hazy dream, which was almost lucky really, because it meant I couldn't beat myself up too much about what had happened, or what hadn't happened. My mam used to say I was a 'nervous sleeper', because any kind of emotional surplus always exhausted me, and that was how I passed the days after Elijah left. Sleeping on my feet, walking around Halcyon like a pregnant zombie. I hadn't even realised that I'd been doing it until I returned to my body one morning, all of a sudden. I was midway through scrubbing the kitchen floor, and I woke up so abruptly that I actually felt a bit frightened. I had no way of telling exactly how long it had been since Elijah had left, how many days and nights I'd managed to pass without being present in my body or my mind. I had a sense it had been a few – two, three, four? Time passed differently in Halcyon, anyway.

Crouched there on the floor I stared at my hands. The cold water had turned them as red as the kitchen tiles and they seemed to belong to someone much older. I was clutching a rag, and my knuckles looked chapped and sore. After not feeling anything for however long I had been out, all of my emotions flooded back at once with an intensity that I hadn't felt since I was a teenager. Since moving to Halcyon, I had been a lot of things: frightened, miserable, desperate, lonely. And I was still all of those things, but I was something else as well, something that I hadn't been for such a long time that I almost didn't recognise the feeling as it simmered and bubbled inside me – I was angry.

With great care, I manoeuvred myself up off the floor; my legs had gone numb, and I had to regain my balance by gripping the countertop. The windowpane was beaded with condensation and outside the morning sky was just beginning to lighten, a peaceful blanket of mist still hanging in the air. The rest of Halcyon would be waking up very soon, but for now the colony was still asleep. Suddenly, I couldn't bear to stand there in the stillness any longer. Abandoning my sodden rag in the sink, I crept out of the silent farmhouse and across the garden path towards the outhouse. It was the only place in all of Halcyon that I could be certain of some privacy. Within its whitewashed stone walls, I wasn't Deborah the Third Wife; I wasn't a wife at all. I could almost begin to imagine that I was somewhere else altogether. I sat on the cold floor with my back against the wooden door, oblivious to the spelks of wood which pierced through the loose knit of my cardigan. The outhouse was the place that I came to cling on to myself, although I would have to start trying harder. If the scene in the kitchen the other night had proved anything, it was that I was no better than the rest of them. Ruth was once brave enough to emigrate halfway across the world, and now look at her; it was as though she'd been lobotomised. Even Aoife. When I first joined Heaven on Earth, she had terrified me. She had reminded me of a pagan queen, or an ancient warrior saint, black hair streaming down her back and blue eyes like something from a fairy tale. I had thought Halcyon would have been the making of her – really it should have been, she wasn't made for domesticated city life. When we first moved here, she had come into her own, some dormant pioneer blood bubbling to the surface. The graft of building a settlement from almost nothing had made her even more beautiful and terrible than she had been before, but once it was done, once we fell back into a routine, it was like she withered before my eyes. Seeing Aoife disappear into herself like that was the real worry, the real shock. If it could happen to her, how could I be surprised that it was happening to me? I could furiously read as many squares of recycled newspaper as I liked and sing as many pop songs under my breath as I could possibly rescue from the fog of my lost teenage years, and it wouldn't be enough.

My anger rose again, and I was relieved. With anger, I thought, would come the will to do something, *anything*, that would improve my situation. I needed it, and to keep it up I would have to force the flames to burn bright and hard enough to swallow me up, so I could burst up from the ashes like a whole new woman, like a – I wracked my brains for the word for the magical fiery bird I'd seen on TV as a kid. But it had vanished, along with a million other little bits of pre-Halcyon knowledge. *Never mind.* I shook the disappointment out of my head and I slid the bolt back to open the door. If I wanted to fan the flames of my rage I knew exactly where I would have to go.

I managed to make it to the schoolhouse without seeing another soul, although I could hear Aoife and Ruth moving around in their bedrooms when I returned to the house to change into some clean clothes. Everyone else must have still been in their caravans because of the cold. I wondered if the kids would even be up yet – I was rarely over there at this time of day – and if they weren't, what I would do. The door to the barn opened with a creak. Inside, the weak morning light was beginning to come through the high windows, making the children look sickly and pale. They were lined up for their morning exercises, led by Mim and under the watchful eye of Helen, who was leaning against the wall with her arms crossed tightly around her chest. I spotted Jonah and Noah straight away; they were two of the smallest ones there, their dark shaggy heads bouncing up and down as they star jumped in time with the others. As soon as I saw them my heart swelled, and I remembered why I had gone along with the whole thing in the first place. I'd had to convince Elijah that I was the most loyal, the most trustworthy, or he would never have let me spend so much time in the schoolhouse. Except for Helen, all of the other women in Halycon had to take turns working their shifts there to avoid spending too much time around their own children, just in case. Aoife and Ruth were lucky to see their kids from across the room at church, but I got to see mine every day. Even if it did piss me off that they looked so much like their father. Even if they knew they were his, but didn't really, fully know that they were mine. When I found out that I was pregnant with Susannah, I hoped that she would inherit something of mine – blonde hair, grey eyes, the shape of my mouth, anything at all – but when she was born, she came out with the same shock of brown hair as the other two. And now, at a year and a half, it was obvious that she was the spit of him.

I was so distracted watching them that I didn't notice that Helen had moved from her spot until she put her hand on my arm.

'Deborah? What are you doing here? You're awfully early!'

'Oh,' I said, 'I had an early start today. Sorry to disturb you. I hope you don't mind?'

Helen stifled a yawn. 'Not at all. Elijah usually pops in around this time to check on the children, see how they're getting on. You know?'

I did not know.

'They love it,' she said, gesturing at the kids, 'especially Jonah and Noah. And Susannah too, actually. The way she clings on to him when he picks her up, we always have such a job tearing her away.'

My fists clenched. I thought back to all the mornings that I had turned up at the schoolhouse to find little Susannah tearful and distressed, only for her to twist herself out of my arms. As betrayed as I was, I felt vindicated by the rare acknowledgement that I would be more interested to hear about Jonah and Noah and Susannah than any of the other children. That they belonged to me. Oblivious, Helen carried on.

'The boys have been asking when he'll be calling in to see them since they woke up this morning. He hasn't been for a few days and they really miss him.' She stopped herself and gave my arm a gentle squeeze. For a second, I hoped she would say that they'd miss me too if ever I wasn't there, but why would they? 'Of course, they're too small to understand that he has more important things to be worried about at the moment. He's in my prayers, Deborah. You are too.'

Helen's revelation about Elijah's morning visits had left me reeling, so it took me a second to realise that she had finished speaking and was waiting for a response from me.

'Thanks, Helen.'

'Are you going to stay for breakfast?'

'No. I don't think so. I need to sort a few things out back at the house, but I'll be back before too long.'

The kids had stopped their star jumps and were jogging on the spot when I turned to go, still in their military straight lines. I tried as hard as I could not to look at the boys again before I left. For the first time in my life, I didn't want to see them. When I got outside, I put my hand on my stomach. I felt my anger growing. Something had to be done.

# Chapter Eleven

## Aoife

Things seemed strangely light after Elijah left, but as the days went on his reason for leaving started to weigh heavily on us all, and the scene in the kitchen kept playing over in my head when I least expected it. I barely saw Ruth, who spent every daylight hour with the animals, and for the first time ever, Deborah looked downright miserable. I kept seeing her wandering around Halcyon like a lost puppy, her face drawn, eyes completely blank. Elijah and I had had our disagreements before, particularly in recent years, but as far as I knew he and Deborah had never had so much as a cross word for as long as they had known each other. I almost felt sorry for her.

Almost, but not quite, because I had more pressing things on my mind than the state of Deborah and Elijah's relationship. Or maybe I should say that the cracks appearing in their foundations had inspired me to up my game slightly, and to use the time Elijah was away wisely enough so that when he returned, he would be reminded of my – for want of a better phrase – overall superiority to Deborah. I couldn't stand for any more surprises, and so I needed to work my way back into the little circle of trust which had closed me out without my noticing.

I began to spend most of my waking hours cloistered in my office at the back of the farmhouse, wrapped in a quilt to keep away the encroaching October chill, surrounded by all of our ledgers from the past twelve years. I stared at the neat lines of numbers, written by me, until they were all I could see even when my eyes were closed. I knew I must be missing something somewhere. When we had moved from Newcastle to Halcyon, I had transcribed all of our records from the old computer onto paper. Could I have made a mistake? I combed through every line, trying to see if I had written something glaringly incorrect, but there was nothing. I counted the money in the petty cash safe so many times that my hands became grubby, even though I knew too much was missing to be found there. Far too much, in fact. We seemed to be down almost one hundred thousand pounds, somehow. A figure which seemed to grow each time I recalculated it, as though week by week our savings were just leaking out of some invisible hole. Elijah had been away for four days, and I had nothing to show for my efforts at all. The missing money was nowhere to be found. On my excursions from the farmhouse I could hardly look anyone in the eye. I thought of everything these people had done for us, donating their wages, selling their furniture, their cars, their homes, all so we could build Halcyon from practically nothing. They had given so generously and trusted us so deeply, and I had repaid them by losing their hard-earned money. When I had spoken with Elijah about it in the past, he had simply shrugged. 'There's more to life than money,' he had said. But I knew him well enough to notice the darkening of his brow. He was, deep down, concerned.

When the office walls seemed to be closing in, and the air became too stuffy for me to concentrate any more, I would take walks. The best route, the one where I was less likely to be disturbed by other church members, was the one I had taken previously around the perimeter fence. I would be lying if I tried to claim that the hope of meeting Malcolm again hadn't crossed my mind as I set out one early afternoon following a lonely lunch at my desk, but it wasn't as though I was heading out with the single aim of crossing his path. Plus, it seemed absurd to think that he would be there a second time, especially when he hadn't appeared the day before or the day before that. He was a busy man, I reasoned, as I trudged beneath the big white sky. It must take a lot of work to manage such a huge amount of land.

The blazing beauty of autumn which I had only just been admiring was already fading to ash. It was practically November now, winter-time drawing in like a familiar beast to wipe away the colour from our small world. Soon the sun, already setting earlier and earlier each night, would barely show its weak pale face, and the colony would settle into a sad hibernation until the gold and purple and green of spring arrived in April. It would soon be too cold to justify a walk around the perimeter, and I would be stuck in the farmhouse.

I had just about talked myself out of the idea of ever bumping into Malcolm again when his car slowly rolled into view from behind the hillock where it had been parked last time. I wondered how long he'd been waiting there, and if he had come out just to talk to me. We both reached the fence at the same moment, and I did nothing to hide the smile which twitched at my lips.

'Well hello, Aoife,' he said, still zipping up his coat, 'fancy seeing you here.'

'I was just out for a stroll, you know. This is my route.'

'Oh?'

'Yes,' I said, 'I've been stuck in my office all morning and thought I might go mad if I didn't get out to stretch my legs.'

I looked right at him as I spoke this time, searching his face. He had very fine laughter lines around his eyes, and they creased when he smiled – the only thing about him that reminded me of Elijah.

'Well, I'm certainly glad to see you. I actually came out this afternoon with the express hope of bumping into you again.'

Then it was my turn to say, 'Oh.'

'I enjoyed our chat the other day. This part of the world is beautiful, but it can get rather lonely. And you're an interesting person to speak to.'

'Well, I'd hardly say interesting. We don't do much of anything here that would be interesting to the rest of the world.'

I could tell, from the way he spoke, that he was trying to flatter me; I had lived thirty years outside of Halcyon after all. Still, just because I knew what he was doing didn't mean that I couldn't enjoy it. So what if he was still only interested in our land? I twisted a loose strand of hair around my finger and tucked it behind my ear.

'You say that, but we've been talking here for hardly a minute and I'm already intrigued as to what you've been doing in an office all morning. I didn't realise you sold produce from here.'

'No, we don't, everything we grow or make stays here in Hal— on the farm. But I run the accounts for our church.'

'Really?' he said, 'and is it interesting work? I can't say I envy you, accounts are my worst nightmare.'

I let out a little laugh. 'Mine too. I'd always thought of myself as pretty good at numbers and things, I did half of a degree in business studies once upon a time, but I just can't seem to get the numbers to add up at the minute. It's as though the money has just... sorry, I'm being boring. Not even *I* like talking about the accounts, and they're my job.'

I realised, of course, that he might actually be very interested in our accounts. I didn't think it could do too much harm for him to get the hint of an idea that we were struggling to balance the books, if he was interested in buying the land. If he thought there might be a chance we'd sell, and that I was the woman holding the purse strings, he might keep stopping by.

'Not boring at all,' he scratched the back of his neck with his gloved hand, 'but I wonder how a woman like yourself, with no less than half of a business degree, found herself doing accounts for a church in the back end of nowhere?'

'Well, now that really is a boring story.'

I had only ever told Elijah about my half-degree. It was the biggest shame of my life that I'd given it up. Homesickness for Grainne and my mother had sent me into despair, and I had fallen so far behind on my work that I had failed every end-of-year exam. The thought of retaking had made me feel sick, and so I quit. The irony was that I was too embarrassed to tell my family what I'd done – they had been so proud of me for going – that I didn't ever go back home. I wrote letters talking about lectures I never attended and classmates I barely remembered, and sent through the dates and times of exams which I saw posted on the campus notice board. I kept meaning to tell them, promising myself that I would, but it felt easier not to. My mother, who came very late to parenthood and was well on in years, suffered from poor health and couldn't travel, and Grainne couldn't leave her, so they never visited. I think Grainne might have guessed, but she never said anything, and my mother died thinking that her younger daughter was going to be a graduate. I promised myself, after that, that I would never give up on anything else – a dramatic, teenage promise, but one I kept.

He laughed. 'I don't believe you for one minute, you know. But even if it is. Indulge me.'

'Oh, well, all right then,' I said, trying to make my voice nonchalant, 'I dropped out of university after my first year. It wasn't really for me, but I couldn't just go back home, so I hung on in Newcastle where I'd been studying and I was working as a waitress—'

'In a cocktail bar? Sorry, that was awful.'

'Oh, no, nothing like that. It was a horrible little café that was open all hours of the day and night, so we got all of the drunks and junkies. And that was where I met Elijah.'

'Your husband?'

I nodded, pleased that we had skipped forward to a subject I knew I could speak on without shame. Elijah. I'd never given up on *him*.

'And was he a drunk or a junkie?'

I blushed. 'Oh certainly not,' I said, 'he was ministering to them. He'd come in and buy them a meal and sit and talk with them. I would stand there behind our horrible Formica counter and just listen to him talk, it was incredible. Eventually, he started to talk to me too, and I remember being absolutely beside myself. The other girls who worked there were so jealous, they all had a thing for him. Back then, he was so, well, he was so good. Just in every way. He took me on a date once, when we were first courting, and he bought a *Big Issue* from every seller we passed on the way from my flat to the restaurant. He cared about people. He made me feel like I was a better person just for being around him. Have you ever met anyone like that?'

'I'm not sure,' he said, when he eventually spoke.

'You would know if you had,' I said. 'Back then it would just glow off him, the good. I felt, and you might think this is silly, but I felt like I was spending time with Christ himself. He just drew people, he always knew what to say or do or ask to make someone comfortable. I've never met anyone else quite like it.'

When I stopped talking, Malcolm's face was still and serious. I had said too much, scared him off. But I couldn't help myself. It was nice to remind myself of how Elijah had been in the old days, when the weight of the world wasn't laying quite so heavily on his shoulders. When he shared his plans with me.

'And now?' he asked.

'What do you mean?'

'Twice there you said "back then". I just wondered, and you can tell me to shove off if this is too personal, what's changed?'

'Well, we don't have any homeless people in Halcyon.'

The word 'Halcyon' tasted different on my tongue when speaking it to a stranger – something I had never done before, and I must have sounded stern because Malcolm took a step backwards and shook his head. The sky overhead was turning from white to grey, and it began to drizzle.

'Sorry, Aoife, that was so rude of me. It's really none of my business. Let's talk about something else.'

And so we did. He asked me whereabouts in Ireland I was from, and told me he'd been born in Edinburgh but that his family had owned land in the Highlands for centuries. We talked for so long that by the time I was turning to leave, we were both flushed with cold and beaded with rain.

'Maybe I'll see you again soon?'

'Maybe,' I said, 'I hope so. I walk this way most days, after lunch.'

'That's good to know.' He smiled again, and I watched for the creases by his eyes. 'Oh, and Aoife? About your accounts. I'm no expert, but I find with things like that, the worst thing you can do is keep going over the same things again and again. It might help for you to try something different.'

'Thanks,' I nodded, 'I'll give that a go.'

And so, on the evening which marked four full days since Elijah had stormed out, I decided to change my approach. My fears about some possible mistake I'd made in the transcription of our accounts had kept me up the night before, and an afternoon of fruitless number crunching had left me feeling restless and fed up. I was just about to call it a day when I remembered the trouble Elijah had had in selling the old computer before we'd left the city. And I couldn't remember us leaving it in the flat with the desk and the other bits and pieces we were unable to sell or move. Which made me think that possibly, for some reason known only to him and God, Elijah had decided to bring it up to Halcyon after all. And *if* he had brought it with us, there was only one place it could possibly be – his office. As I returned all of the ledgers to their shelf, I weighed up my options. I had never been in there before, and there was an unspoken rule which put the space out of bounds for everyone but him. The possibilities turned over in my mind. On the off chance that the computer was in Elijah's office, and that he hadn't wiped the floppy disk which held our accounts, and that I was able to find where the missing money had gone, would he be pleased enough with me that he would neglect to ask how I'd found it? And if I got to his office and the computer wasn't there, he would never have to know that I had been in at all.

The more I thought about it, the happier I was with my idea. I would have to time it properly though. Ruth and Deborah didn't know that the money was missing in the first place, and even if they did, I couldn't trust them not to tell Elijah. Deborah especially would not be above using such an indiscretion to win favour with him – she was on shaky ground herself, after all. I would have to get through the evening like normal, and then find a way into the office once they were in bed.

After the lamplight of my own little office, it took my eyes a moment to adjust to the brightness of the kitchen, where a single electric bulb hung, naked, over the table. Ruth was washing her hands in the sink using a clump of Deborah's hand-made soap, while Deborah stood in front of the oven. Even with her back to me I could tell that she had cheered up slightly since the last time I had seen her; her hair was freshly plaited, and she stood a little taller than she had before.

'Hi, Aoife.' She turned her head and gave me a smile. 'You're just in time. I was just getting ready to plate up.'

Since Elijah had left, Deborah's communication had been monosyllabic at best, so I was almost surprised to hear her speaking normally again. In the interest of appearing normal myself, I forced a response.

'Lovely,' I said, wrinkling my nose while her back was turned, 'what are we having?'

I had used my lightest tone, but Deborah and Ruth exchanged a brief glance before Ruth spoke up.

'Deborah has made a barley and vegetable stew. And we have some boiled eggs, and some fresh bread.'

I rummaged through the cutlery drawer for knives and forks,

trying not to grimace. For as long as I lived, I would never ever get used to Deborah's cooking: rubbery meat; vegetables boiled until they were grey; dense, stodgy loaves. For someone so desperate to play the dream wife, she put on a poor show in the kitchen. I kept my mouth closed, though, this time around.

Ruth and I took our places at the table, and Deborah laid our plates out before us, setting mine down with a little more force than she did Ruth's. I pushed the stew around with my fork, trying to identify any of the ingredients which had gone into it.

'Thank you, Deborah, this looks delicious. Shall we say a word of thanks?'

Deborah blinked.

'Yes, let's,' said Ruth. 'Deborah, would you like to lead us?'

I gripped my knife and fork so hard that my nails dug into my palms. Deborah tossed her plait over her shoulder and gave a benevolent smile.

'For what we are about to receive, may the Lord make us truly thankful.'

'Thanks be to God and our Holy Prophet.'

As we spoke those final words together, I couldn't help but look over at the empty chair where Elijah usually sat. Where, I wondered, was our Holy Prophet now? And most importantly, what was *he* praying about?

Despite it being almost inedible, I managed to finish my meal without retching. Even without Elijah there I couldn't bear to leave a morsel on my plate; we had all learned our lesson about that the hard way. Ruth began to clear the dishes, and Deborah put the kettle on the stove to boil. Outside, I could hear John leading the rest of Halcyon in evening worship, the voices of the congregation carrying across the darkness from the warmth and light of the church. The three of us listened in silence. We should have been there ourselves, really, spending time amongst the congregation instead of sitting in the kitchen. But there we were, sipping our mugs of heather tea, not saying a word. All I had to do was wait for them both to go to bed.

Deborah was the first to break the spell when she rose from the table to fetch the sewing box.

'Does anyone have anything they need mended?' she asked.

'I do,' said Ruth, 'but I won't bother you with it. I can do my own.'

Before Deborah could say anything more, Ruth had already disappeared upstairs. She returned moments later with an armful of clothes piled so high that it almost obscured her face.

'Crikey, Ruth, you'll be on forever getting through that lot!' Deborah's eyes widened.

'I don't mind,' Ruth replied, 'I'm not tired.'

'Well, my stuff can wait. I'll help you,' said Deborah. For once I was glad of her.

'Yes,' I agreed, 'I'll help too, or you'll be mending until two in the morning.' I had no intention of waiting up that long.

Deborah and I reached into Ruth's pile of mending, ignoring her half-hearted protest. There was no clock in the kitchen, or anywhere else in Halcyon, but we must have been there for hours before we had finally worked through the lot, because it was pitch black outside and my eyes were stinging. When I stood up, my exhausted reflection stared back at me through the window. I was relieved when Ruth finally yawned and excused herself to go to bed. Deborah, though, remained seated.

'You look exhausted,' I said, 'why don't you get yourself off to bed too?'

She shrugged, but didn't move. 'I think I'm okay here for a bit. You go, though.'

I drummed my fingernails on the kitchen counter. The noise they made was the only sound in the room.

'It can't be good for the baby for you to be up this late. Go to bed.'

Deborah stared over at me, and for a moment I worried she might say no. Instead, she pushed back her chair and rose, unsteadily, to her feet. The woman really did look wrecked. She turned and left the room without saying a word.

'Goodnight,' I said, but she was already gone.

From down the hallway, I heard her bedroom door close with a bang.

Alone at last, I decided to retire to my own room for long enough to give the others a chance to fall asleep properly. The last thing I wanted was for one of them to hear me clattering about and come to investigate. My bedroom was dark and cold, and my heavy duvet looked too cosy to resist. I slipped off my shoes and slid under the covers, just to keep warm while I was waiting. Time passed, although I couldn't guess how much, and by some miracle I managed to keep myself awake. Even so, it was so difficult to leave the warmth of the bed behind that I was tempted to abandon my mission for another time. Only the threat of Elijah's impending return, which could come at any moment, gave me the motivation to leave my cocoon.

I closed the door behind me as quietly as I could. My room led straight into the deserted kitchen and I followed my instincts through the blackness towards the hall. Elijah's office was upstairs, which meant that not only did I risk waking Deborah, whose bedroom was directly next to the staircase, but also Ruth, who slept just off the landing. My stockinged feet made no noise on the hardwood floor, but I knew that the creak of a single board could give me up. Being caught in the kitchen was one thing, but it wouldn't be so easy to explain being upstairs in the middle of the night.

The farmhouse felt different in the dark. Unfamiliar and eerie. For some reason, the darkness made me feel more exposed than the light – like anyone could be watching me as I tiptoed like a child towards the one room I had never visited.

When we were young, Grainne and I had a book of fairy tales, and we would sit in her bed and read them together. She did voices better than anyone I'd ever met. We joked that she could have been on the stage. The book we shared was full of what Grainne called 'proper' stories.

'None of that Walt Disney rubbish,' she would laugh as we poured over gruesome illustrations of bleeding feet and crow-faced witches.

She liked the gory parts best. The scary parts. She could build the tension to the point that I would be clinging to her arm, white-knuckled, my knees pulled to my chest. Her favourite story, and the one she read most impressively, was 'Bluebeard'. As I walked towards Elijah's office, I could almost hear Grainne's childish voice, filled with the tantalising combination of fear and barely disguised glee, narrating my every step. It wasn't until I reached the door that I remembered the key. In the story, of course, Bluebeard gives his young wife a bundle of keys, the smallest of which opens the door to his secret room. Elijah, when he left, had given me no such gift. I had no key. I had no idea of where to find the key, and for all I knew he'd taken it with him. After all that. If I wasn't being so careful to keep quiet, I would have screamed. I reached out a hand to give the handle a dejected, frustrated rattle, but instead of stopping with the lock, my hand continued moving downward, taking the handle with it. Noiselessly, the door swung open.

I held my breath and stepped inside, half expecting to brush up against the hanging bodies of Bluebeard's murdered wives. What I did not expect to see was Deborah, her startled face illuminated by the blue-tinged light emanating from an unfamiliar computer.

# Chapter Twelve

## Ruth

I made my bed in the dark, tucking the loose sheets under the mattress as neatly and quietly as I could. It would have been faster to leave it, but I was feeling guilty enough and didn't want to add leaving an unmade bed to the ever-growing fog of shame which hung heavily in my head. I looked out of the window to where Mim was waiting, the white of her nightgown reflecting the moonlight like a ghost. I grabbed an extra sweater from my wardrobe for her and headed down the stairs and out the door.

'Hey,' I whispered, 'are you ready?'

'Yeah,' she said, 'all the towels and blankets and stuff are in the barn where the cows are. I wasn't sure where to leave them.'

The cattle barn was probably not the most suitable place; it was too open and exposed though the day.

'That's okay. We can find somewhere quieter together. I don't want to disturb the cows.'

Even with the moonlight it was difficult to make her out properly, but I thought I could see her nod. We walked side by side, as close as we could be without touching, along the worn dirt path between the farmhouse and the barn. It was a quiet night, and with every step something seemed to crunch underfoot. Even our breathing, shallow and nervous, seemed deafeningly loud to my sound-starved ears. It wasn't until that moment, surrounded by darkness halfway between the house and the barn, that I realised what a dumb thing it was that we were doing. Not even just dumb. It was a sin. I thought about how poor Aoife and Deborah had ended up helping with my big pile of mending, the pile I had brought down to give me an excuse to stay up until I could be sure they had gone to bed, and felt like the most awful person in the world. And if that wasn't bad enough, I would have to keep this secret from them, and from Elijah, for goodness knows how long. It wasn't even as though we'd had the good sense to make a proper plan. If I was the type of woman to curse, I would have cursed then. As it was, I gritted my teeth and kept on, slowly, carefully, towards the barn.

The whole mess had started when Elijah left. I had slept badly that night, tossing and turning so much that when I woke my sheets were tangled around me and my hair was damp with sweat. I had been raised in the firm belief that everything would look better in the morning, but when the three of us gathered around the kitchen table for breakfast without him, everything just seemed much worse. At the time we should have been filing down the hall for temple, Aoife and Deborah took off for work as though they didn't even notice there was a huge chunk missing from our morning. I sat in the empty temple room alone and closed my eyes, pretending that we were all there together in silent prayer. Even though I left the farmhouse at the same time I always did, and sat in my usual seat for church, the whole day was off. John delivered the sermon, but I found it hard to concentrate on what he was saying. I spent the service picking at a hangnail on my thumb and casting occasional glances at Deborah. Her hair looked as though it hadn't been brushed, and she had heavy purple bags under her eyes. She was looking up at John, fixing him with a dull, unblinking stare.

Once everyone was dismissed, I headed straight to the cattle barn. The scent, thick and sweet, calmed me from the very second that I stepped inside, and I took my time greeting each cow, patting their soft brown necks and looking into their big wise eyes. We kept three cows, big, beautiful Jerseys, but only two of them were giving milk at the moment. The oldest, who I took the most time with, had stopped producing several months ago and would most likely be slaughtered by Christmas, and when the next lot of calves were born we would not sell them all, like we usually did, but keep one to replace her. The methodical process of milking soothed me further, and by the time I was done I had almost convinced myself that Elijah would be back before the day was out if only I could follow our normal routine and keep on as though nothing was the matter. I reminded myself that Elijah often left Halcyon alone to do missionary work, although then he always said when he would be back. And he never stormed out.

Even though the milking was finished, I was still perched on my wooden stool with my head pressed against the cow's warm stomach when Mim arrived. She announced her entrance with a gentle knock on the lintel of the barn door, and I jumped to my feet, startling the cow in the process. Mim flushed and looked away. It took me a second to realise that she was not going to speak first.

'Can I help you?' My words sounded blunt, but I was too flustered to try and soften them with any sort of follow-up.

'Helen sent me over. We've run out of milk in the schoolhouse. It got spilled. And now there's none, and we were wanting to get prepared for lunch.' She looked down at her feet as she spoke, and her voice was so soft that I had to strain to hear her.

I looked at my pail, which was still full of milk.

'You can take this,' I said, 'will it be enough?'

Mim leaned forward from her place in the doorway, but her feet remained stuck to the floor. Really, I should have taken the bucket to her so she could examine it properly – I could see that she was nervous – but I always took personal offence when people were frightened of the cows and I wanted to show her that there was nothing to be scared of. I beckoned her in with my free hand, and reluctantly she came forward, keeping as far away from the animals as she could. Eventually, she was close enough to peer into the bucket.

'I think so,' she said.

Her eyes darted nervously from cow to cow, and they looked back curiously. I'd never had very much to do with cattle at all until we came to Halcyon, other than seeing them from a distance or maybe on TV. Their gentleness had surprised me. I had thought that they would be dopey, bovine being an insult as far as I was concerned, but it hardly took me any time at all to figure out that they had their own little quirks, and that they were friendly and sweet. Eventually, I came to see them as big, gentle dogs.

'They like you,' I said.

Mim looked unconvinced and wrinkled her freckled nose.

'Look,' I put the heavy milk pail down on the ground and stepped closer to the oldest cow, who was tethered to her post, 'look how interested they are in you.'

They were lined up together, blinking gently at us with

their thick lashes. Mim didn't respond but she did inch towards them, gingerly.

'I always think they look like genteel old British ladies,' I said, looking at the cows instead of Mim, 'as though they should be wearing flowery straw hats.'

By her silence, I could tell that she remained unconvinced. I turned to look at her, and she made a polite face.

'I guess I must have got the idea from a movie or something.'

Once I said it, I realised that Mim would never have seen a movie, and that her frame of reference for them would have come from one of Elijah's sermons. Fortunately, the comment seemed to go right over her head.

'Do they bite?'

'No,' I said, 'no, they're very sweet natured.'

She reached out a tentative hand and laid it on the neck of the youngest cow, the one I had delivered myself.

'It's quite pretty,' she said. 'Are they boys or girls?'

At first, I thought she might have been trying to make a joke, but when I looked at her face I could tell that she was completely serious.

'They're all girls,' I said, 'that's how we get the milk from them.'

She gave a serious nod. 'They look like girls.'

I wasn't sure what else to say, and really I just wanted her to leave so I could get them out to pasture. I was trying to come up with a tactful way to end the conversation when we were interrupted by the clacking of Russell's little feet on the concrete floor. She was a common fixture in the barn because it was her job to keep the rats away from the feed and I was used to her being there, but her arrival startled Mim, who pulled her hand away from the cow with a jerk. I had no idea how someone who lived on a farm could be so jumpy around animals.

'It's just Russell,' I said, bending down to nearer the dog's level. She waddled towards me.

'Russell?' Mim's voice betrayed her surprise. 'It has a *name*?'

My stomach turned over. Russell's name was not general knowledge in Halcyon. I fought the temptation to babble. *Play it cool*, I thought, *what would Aoife do?*

'Yeah,' I said, 'she does.'

That seemed to be enough for Mim, who had now turned her attention fully from the cows to the dog.

'Is there something wrong with her?'

It was a fair question. She was pacing up and down the barn, looking for a place to settle, and letting out a small, low whine. Even when I patted my thigh to call her over, she kept her distance, turning in circles as if she was about to lie down, and then picking herself up again and moving to a different spot. She was a pitiful sight.

'She's carrying a litter,' I explained, 'she might be getting ready to start whelping soon.'

'Whelping?'

'Having her pups,' I said.

'Oh!' Mim suddenly looked properly interested for the first time. 'Can I help?'

'Well, she's not having them right this moment,' I paused and took a closer look at Russell, who had finally curled up on a pile of hay, 'or I don't think she is.'

We were both kneeling down to get a better look at the dog when there came another knock on the wall of the barn. I turned to see Helen standing in the doorway. Mim turned too. As soon as she saw who it was, she shot to her feet.

'Mim! You're still here!' Helen's voice startled Russell, who raised her little head in weary surprise.

Mim stood there, silently staring at her feet.

'I'm sorry, Helen,' the sound of my own voice took me by surprise, 'this is my fault.'

'Oh no, Ruth, please don't apologise. I just wanted to make sure that Jemima wasn't bothering you. Jemima... do you think you might have taken up enough of Sister Ruth's time this morning?'

After that, things went back to normal very quickly. Mim collected the pail and followed Helen back to the schoolhouse. I finished my brief examination of Russell, and when I was satisfied that her pups weren't going to arrive any time in the next couple of hours, I got back to my work. I didn't even think about Mim again until the next morning, when she followed me to the barn after church. Before I could even ask her what she was doing there, she burst out:

'I just wanted to check on the dog.'

'Does Helen know you're here?'

Mim shook her head so vehemently that the two plaits which hung down by her ears lifted into the air.

'Look,' I said, 'I don't want to get you in any trouble.' I also didn't want to get *myself* into any trouble, but I thought it might be best not to say that part out loud.

'You won't, I promise.'

Famous last words. By this time, Russell had taken herself off into a quiet corner of the barn, and after some close inspection I predicted that she would be ready to have her litter later that day.

'Can you come and get me when she does?' Mim asked.

She didn't look at me when she spoke, but this time she wasn't staring at her feet; instead, she was looking right into Russell's face, their noses almost touching. For someone who had jumped at the sight of the dog the day before, she certainly had warmed to her.

'Dogs usually don't have their pups during the day,' I said, 'a bit like ladies. They tend to come along in the middle of the night.'

She looked up at me, crestfallen.

'Well, honey, I won't be here either. She'll just have them on her own.'

Mim's mouth fell open. 'On her own?' There was more emotion in her voice than I had ever heard there before.

'Honey, she's a dog. It's not like a human giving birth. Dogs are made to do this sort of thing without any help.'

I couldn't help it; my mind turned to Aoife ten years before, sitting in the living room of her and Elijah's flat, squatting with her back to the wall as I counted her contractions. It was wintertime, and Elijah had just returned from church. I could feel the cold radiating from him, smell the sharp freshness of outside which clung to his coat.

'How is everything progressing?' he asked, glancing at his labouring wife.

It touched me to see his vulnerability. He usually wore his confidence like a second skin.

'Perfectly,' I said. 'Textbook.'

Aoife looked up at us with a weary smile, 'What can I say? I know what I'm doing.' She closed her eyes for a moment, and I noted the time on my pad. 'So does Ruth.'

'How many babies have you delivered, Sister Ruth?' Elijah asked, 'I'm sure I've asked you this before.'

I could see his confidence was returning, and he looked me straight in the eyes as he spoke. This was a habit of his which I was still getting used to, and it sent a rush of hot blood to my cheeks. I lowered my gaze.

'Oh,' I said, busying myself with the contents of my medical bag, 'too many to count! Plenty.'

'More than one, then?' he smiled.

I nodded.

'Well, Aoife, she trumps you, so make sure you pay attention,' he said. 'I just called back to check in on you both, I have to run back to the church. Before I go, Sister Ruth, can I speak to you for a second?'

Aoife rolled her eyes and smiled at me as I followed Elijah into the corridor. I enjoyed being called Sister Ruth, not in the medical sense, but in the religious sense. I liked the idea that in God's eyes, the church of Heaven on Earth was one big family.

Once we were alone, his jovial attitude disappeared. The mood in the living room had been one of eager anticipation and nervous excitement, but out in the dim light of the hallway things felt more serious. Suddenly, I was very conscious that I had only officially completed my midwifery training the year before, and that this was my first delivery outside of the hospital. He ran a hand through his dark hair and shook his head gently. I allowed myself to make eye contact with him.

'I can't tell you how much I appreciate this, Ruth, your presence here is a real blessing. And I know that Aoife appreciates it too, despite her bravado.'

I felt my cheeks grow hot and my breath come out short. I think I must have been a little in love with him, even then.

'We have every faith in you, and your confidence is very reassuring.' He paused. 'However, I realise you're still new to our church and our life, so I feel I need to be very clear about what we need from you.'

'Sure,' I said. 'I mean, of course.'

'You know our beliefs. We follow God, and we turn away from what is not Godly. There are many things in this world that go against our teachings, including those in charge.'

I nodded, unsure where this impromptu sermon was leading.

'And you know that nobody outside of the church knows that Aoife is pregnant. No midwives, no doctors, not a soul. That can't change, Ruth, no matter what happens here tonight. I need this baby to live free, free from government tracking and Western medicine and the whole nightmare – I need to do that for him, I need to give him that gift. So hospital is not an option.'

He looked at me searchingly, waiting for me to say that I understood, holding my gaze.

'I understand.'

Elijah smiled and left. When I opened the door to the living room of their small flat, I saw Aoife, my patient, pacing in front of the window. Imposed against the darkness of the night outside, she looked even whiter than normal. Her fine black hair was plastered to her forehead with sweat. Her eyes were the very lightest blue I'd ever seen. I was only twenty-two at the time, so she couldn't have been much more than twenty-four or twenty-five, but she was my hero and I wanted to be just like her: Godly and beautiful.

When I entered the room, she looked straight across at me.

'Did he tell you about the hospital?' she asked.

'Yeah.'

I was still overwhelmed, both by my responsibility and how close I was to Aoife. This was the longest time we had ever spent together. I tried not to let it show in my voice.

'Who needs hospitals? We have everything we need right here.'

She smiled. 'That's what I like to hear. Oh, and Ruth?' but before she could speak, Aoife was interrupted by a contraction. My training eclipsed my nerves, and I imagined that I was in an ordinary delivery room, with trained professionals with years and years of experience waiting just outside the door.

Once the surge of pain was over and she had regained the ability to speak, she picked up from where she had been forced to leave off.

'Ruth, I want to apologise about before, if you thought I was being proud. I certainly didn't mean to suggest that I was as experienced as you. I only meant... Well, I only said it, because last time it was just me by myself, and I managed all right. Not that I'm not grateful for you being here, Ruth, you're a blessing...'


Back in the barn, Mim spoke again.

'But she's so little!' There was no petulance in her voice, no hint of a whine, which I appreciated.

I looked down at Russell. She really did look very small, lying there in her nest of hay.

'Okay,' I sighed, 'if she starts through the day I'll come and fetch you.'

'And if it happens at night?'

I deliberated for a second, but only a second. 'And if she's not started by the time I'm finishing up for the day, we can come check on her in the night.'

Mim let out a squeal of delight, and then immediately covered her mouth with her hand. Her reaction took me by surprise. I guess I thought it was a bit childish, although I really shouldn't have been shocked at that. She *was* a child. Gleefully, she planted a kiss on Russell's head and made her exit. For the rest of the day I kept a close eye on the dog. She paced and whined, but when I examined her I saw nothing that indicated the imminent arrival of her litter.

That was how I ended up walking in silence with Mim by my side, too frightened to even turn on my torch while we were still outside, towards the barn in the middle of the night. By the time we arrived, Russell was lying flat on her side, four tiny wriggling pups suckling at her teats in the torchlight.

'We missed it!' Mim's disappointed whisper filled the barn.

I was too busy kneeling at Russell's side to respond, trying to feel her stomach as gently as I could to make sure she was all done. 'What a clever girl you are,' I whispered. She turned her tired eyes up to meet mine. I wished all the labours I was responsible for went this smoothly.

I could feel Mim close behind me, her breathing loud by my ear.

'What do we do now?'

I gritted my teeth. Mim, who had once been so quiet, so reluctant to talk, to make a pest of herself, was suddenly hanging on to me like a little lost puppy. The irony was not lost on me, but I wanted to stand up and shake her off. Instead, I took a deep breath.

'Now we need to take her out for some air, so she can… potty. And then we need to move them all somewhere a bit out of the way, so they can rest up.'

'Oh, they're so *sweet*! I wonder if Elijah would maybe let us give them names too, like Russell?'

She clearly hadn't listened to a word I had said, but that wasn't what made me stand up so suddenly. At the mention of Elijah's name, it was as though an icy finger had touched my spine and turned my entire body cold. Even Elijah's absence could not make me forget a very frustrating and very relevant conversation we had had when I'd first discovered that Russell was carrying a litter. He had been adamant, then, that we did not have reason to keep an entire litter of pups, nor did we have the resources to feed them. He said we could keep just one. All of this had been before his decision to cut us off from the outside world, so I had assumed we would sell the puppies to someone in Abercraig when the time came. Now, though, I had no idea what he would want to do with them. I looked at Mim, who was carefully scooping water from the cows' trough into her small pale hand and carrying it across to Russell, who lapped at it gratefully. *Shit*, I thought, *shit shit shit.*

# Chapter Thirteen

## Deborah

It wasn't as though I hadn't thought of going into Elijah's office before. I don't know of anyone who could live in a house with a locked door and not wonder what was behind it, but for a long time I was the sort of person who could resist a lot for the sake of a simple life. I would walk past that locked door every time I went to clean upstairs, never going in, because the only way I could imagine life in Halcyon being much worse was if I actively went against Elijah's wishes.

Still, even though Elijah was a clever man, at times scarily quick and intelligent, when it came to hiding places he was almost disappointingly unimaginative. I found the ring which held the spare office key while clearing out his underwear drawer, tucked inside a balled-up pair of woollen socks in a chest of drawers on the upstairs landing, outside Ruth's bedroom and just along from his office. That was just a few months after we'd settled in Halcyon. It took me all of two seconds' thought to figure out what the key was for, but I dutifully returned it to its hiding spot. I can see now how idiotic I was being, but things were very different in those days. I was newly married, and even if I didn't necessarily *love* Elijah, I certainly cared enough to respect his privacy. My mother had been completely devoted to him, and I was still looking at him through her eyes. It was for the sake of her memory that I decided to believe that he had nothing to hide, because for her, he could do no wrong.

When I was seventeen years old, my mother took ill in our flat. We had only just moved in, and she had been tired and sick since the landlord – one of the men from the church – handed over her keys.

'Bloody typical,' she had said from the bathroom floor as I unpacked our things. Heaven on Earth had done a big donation drive for us, and I was suddenly in possession of more stuff than I ever had owned in my life before.

'Are you okay in there? You're missing out on all the fun.'

I entered the bathroom, a reinforced shopping bag of towels and loo rolls and toiletries in hand, just in time to see her empty her guts into the avocado toilet bowl.

Three days later, when Elijah called round to put up some shelves, she was lying in bed. I'd never really spoken to Elijah outside of church before. He was in his thirties and strict, and he scared me a little bit, with his heavy dark eyebrows and stern, unsmiling eyes. Still, I was glad to see him.

'I think there's something really wrong with her,' I said. We were standing outside her bedroom door, so I kept my voice low. 'She's been sick so much even her skin looks weird. She's hardly eaten anything since we moved.' Elijah left his toolbox on the floor and knocked gently.

'Cheryl? It's me. Deborah says you're under the weather. May I come in?'

There was a little murmur from inside the room, and I pushed the door open.

My mother had always been a skinny woman, but three days of illness had turned her into a skeleton. Her skin, usually pale, had taken on a yellowish tinge. She hadn't seemed so bad until Elijah had got there – it was only now that I saw her through his eyes that I realised what a state she was in. Sensing his shock, I felt like a kid again, standing next to a social worker and noticing, suddenly, just how bad things were.

Elijah took my arm and guided me gently back into the hall.

'Has your landline been installed yet?'

I nodded.

'Good,' he said, 'because I think you need to phone an ambulance.'

I had sat through enough church services to know that Elijah did not trust hospitals. For him to say we needed an ambulance, meant this must be serious.

Elijah sat by my side at the hospital that day as the doctors ran tests on my mother. When a nurse or doctor questioned if we both needed to be there, he shut them down straight away.

'This girl is a child,' he said, 'she can't be expected to do this on her own.'

The day ran on, and every so often when it seemed like it might be about time to eat, Elijah would excuse himself and return with food – sandwiches, crisps, scalding cups of soup from vending machines.

'Look at all this shit,' he said, pointing at the list of ingredients on the back of the sandwich box, 'no wonder everyone in this place is ill.'

By the time the evening staff came on shift, we had started to talk. He asked me about what it was like living with my mother again after so long, and I actually answered him. At first, I did it because it felt like I owed him something for being so good to us, but then the words kept on coming and soon I had told him everything – what it had been like growing up with her, then being moved around, never feeling quite at home anywhere. He nodded and listened. By the time I had finished my throat was hoarse from talking and exhaustion.

'Why don't you try and get some sleep? I'll wake you if there's any news.'

I shut my eyes against the harsh fluorescent hospital light and leaned my head back against the wall. When I woke up a few hours later, it was resting on his shoulder.

There was nothing the doctors could do about her kidneys, but Elijah had done something irreversible for her soul that night and she saw him as more of a saviour than ever before. His most loyal disciple, she would say over and over: 'This is what a really good man looks like, Debbie. I can't believe it took me forty years to meet one.' She'd say it after services, when he dropped her to the hospital for dialysis, whilst watching him play with his kids in the park next to the church hall. Her final words to me had been about him. How she was sorry she wouldn't get to be at our wedding, and how happy she had been to see us engaged. 'I know he'll keep you safe, pet.'

Now, when things got worse in Halcyon, I would return to the key. I would hold it in my hands, the cold metal acting as a reminder that if things got bad, like *really* bad, I would be able to use it. There were days when I was tempted, once or twice I even got as far as slipping the key into the lock, but I never turned it, never touched the door handle. Things were bad, but never really bad. Never as bad as they'd been before, not even as bad as the stuff I'd grown up watching on telly. Yeah, everything I did was an act, but I was safe in Halcyon. My kids might have been living in a different building and might not understand I was their mam, but I got to see them every day. And maybe some days Elijah scared me, but he never smacked me about or screamed at me. If I went in, I'd have to admit that things had got bad enough that I was ready to go against him, to step away from Halcyon and Heaven on Earth and everything I had there. Which was everything I had at all.

As soon as I left the schoolhouse, I felt the pull of the spare key calling me. All I could think of was putting one foot in front of the other on the hard, frosty earth, and making my way to its hiding place. Halcyon was waking up around me, but I was too focussed on my goal to stop and talk to the people leaving their caravans. I didn't even bother to look in on the kitchen to check if Aoife and Ruth were there before heading up the stairs. If I had ever wavered at the thought of entering the office in past, that fear was gone. Once my mind was made up, my only worry was whether or not Elijah would have thought to take the key with him, wherever he had gone. The original was worn on a loop on his belt, along with the keys to all of Halcyon's other locks, and if his departure had been as unplanned as it had seemed, he surely wouldn't have thought to take the spare one with him. I held my breath as I pulled open the drawer, but at first glance things seemed hopeful – the neatly folded rows of underwear and balled up socks looked undisturbed from the last time I had tidied them, which made me think that Elijah hadn't had a rifle through before leaving. The socks I was looking for were always kept in the same place, pushed up against the far right corner. I didn't even need to look; my hand knew exactly what to feel for. I would be able to recognise the exact shape, the particular bristle of the fibres, if I was blindfolded. And there they were, exactly where I had left them, an innocent looking woolly bundle containing, quite literally, the key to everything.

I moved as if I was in a dream, slowly and purposefully unrolling the socks and slipping the key out and into my hand. I was at the office door, key poised by the lock, when the front door banged open. *That's him,* I thought, *he's back.* My heart hammered so fiercely that it ached, and I worried that I would have a heart attack and collapse on the spot. The protective aura of my pregnancy would not be enough to save me from Elijah's wrath if he found me there. The rules had been changed, after all, the second he had lobbed a plate at my head. The key was back in its rightful place before I knew where I was, panic making the time skip.

'Elijah?' I called down the stairs, clinging on to the banister to stop myself falling, 'Elijah, is that you?'

Did my voice give me away? Would he know as soon as he heard it that I'd been up to no good? I listened out for his response, planning my excuses for being upstairs, rehearsing what I'd say when I saw him.

'No,' came the reply, 'sorry Deborah, honey, it's just me.'

Ruth. Not Elijah. Just Ruth. Just lovely Ruth. I felt the hard floor under me as I sat down heavily on the top step, one hand still clinging to the banister, the other gripping my head.

I don't know what I hoped to find inside the locked office, the inner sanctum, the Holy of Holies. Throughout the day my brain swam with possibilities – piles of Bibles, stacks of girlie mags, files of boring legal documents – but I didn't really care. I wasn't going in there to find anything specific; all I wanted and needed was one less secret in my life. The chance to take away a little bit of Elijah's power, to put my disobedient thoughts into action, so that I didn't lose myself completely. The thought of it thrilled me so much that I spent the whole day on a knife-edge, my brain too jittery to settle on a single thought or task. Every time someone turned to look at something behind me, I thought Elijah must be standing there. After he delivered the church service, John told us that he had an announcement, and when it didn't relate to Elijah at all, just the new bunking arrangements for the caravans, I let out an actual sigh of relief. When Aoife came in late for tea, I worried that she was caught up in talking to him, that they would stroll in together, hand in hand. I became so convinced that Elijah would be coming back that evening that I even prepared enough food for four. Through the scraping of plates and the chewing of food, I listened out for the noise of the gate opening or the car pulling in. By the time we finished eating I couldn't sit still any more. I lifted the kettle onto the hob, boiling water for cups of heather tea that nobody had asked for, worried that the whistling of the steam would cover up any sounds that might warn me of his return.

After hours and hours and the latest night the three of us had had in a long time, Aoife pushed her pile of mending to the side and told me to go to bed, almost like she knew what I was going to do and wanted to stop me. I could have stood my ground and told her no, but I didn't want to raise suspicion. If I started talking back, she would notice and remember, and she would suspect something was going on. Also, I'm not ashamed to say that a big part of me was properly frightened of Aoife. As she towered over me, arms folded, eyes bloodshot with exhaustion, I did not fancy my chances. And so I took myself into my bedroom and changed into my nightdress, not even daring to make my usual journey to the outhouse and using my chamber pot instead. I stopped short of actually getting into bed, though. Instead, I waited until I was sure that everyone was safely turned in for the night, and made my way carefully upstairs.

I gripped the banister tightly, waiting until both feet were firmly planted on the bare wood before taking another step, counting my way up. My biggest risk at this point, other than Elijah suddenly coming home and deciding to go straight upstairs or to my bedroom, was Ruth. Of the three of us she was the only one who slept up there, and I knew that she was a light sleeper. She could step out at any time and she'd find me where I had no right to be. As risks went, this one didn't worry me too much. Although the chances of Ruth finding me were fairly high, she was the sort of person who only cared to see the good in others. I imagined that if she saw me looming over Elijah's sleeping body, brandishing a butcher's knife, she would wait patiently for me to explain myself and then nod and leave me to it. She and Aoife were also barely speaking, which made it unlikely that she would grass me up the next day. There *was* the chance that concern for my wellbeing would lead her to tell Elijah, if he ever came back, but I would cross that bridge if I came to it.

I stopped outside Ruth's door, my ears straining to hear anything other than the sound of my heart slamming into my chest at double time. When I was as satisfied as I could be that she was sleeping I allowed myself to slide the drawer open, lifting it up from its mount to avoid the sound of wood sliding against wood. I kept the key inside the sock until I reached the office door, frightened that my shaking hand would drop it and wake Ruth. The keyring held one key and a flimsy plastic crucifix charm. The darkness and my shaking hand made me miss the keyhole so many times that by the time I finally felt the key slot in I could feel tears of frustration and relief stinging my eyes. The heavy metallic click of the turning lock echoed in the hallway and I froze, ready for Ruth's door to creak open. For a second, the absolute madness of the situation hit me. I didn't let myself get caught up in that madness for too long, though – it was a thread I didn't want to pull, and anyway, I had other things to worry about.

Opening the door was an anti-climax because the room was almost as dark as the hallway had been; the milky half-light cast by the full moon was barely bright enough to penetrate the glass in the window, let alone illuminate anything of interest inside. I closed the door gently behind me and leaned against the sturdy wood while my eyes adjusted. Before too long, some familiar shapes began to emerge from the gloom. A filing cabinet. A chair. A desk. Something else, resting on the desk, a frame? A box? I took a step closer, careful not to lift my feet too far from the ground in case I tripped. It wasn't until I was right on top of it that I could see what it was, and I had to reach out and touch it to be sure. It seemed to be a computer, but nothing like any computer I had seen in real life before. It was slim, and there was no big boxy hard drive. I felt its edges. It didn't even seem to have a mouse attached. It was only then that I realised it wasn't a proper computer, of the sort we had had in the labs when I was at school, but a portable laptop with its lid open. Taking the greatest care not to scrape the legs against the floor, I pulled out the chair and sat down. I felt the baby turning somersaults in my belly. Computers were not my area of expertise, fancy new computers in the dark even less so. Hell, it had been about ten years since I had sat at a desk. I ran my hand lightly across its surface, searching for something that felt like an 'on' button. It must have been much more sensitive than any machine I had used at school, because I barely grazed a little indentation at the top of the keyboard when the whole thing sprang to life. All at once the room was bathed in electric light from the screen, and a tinny tune burst from some concealed speaker. My heart leapt into my throat and stayed there long after the sound had stopped. A blue screen told me that it was 00:17. I couldn't even think when I had last known what the exact time was. It felt strange to remember that we shared a world with people who might need to know that it was precisely seventeen minutes past midnight, and that once upon a time, when I had lived in a world of buses and metro trains and appointments instead of chickens and babies and prayers, I had been that kind of person myself.

The keyboard glowed invitingly, but the lack of a mouse had thrown me and I wasn't sure how I was supposed to actually get the thing to work. I was still deciding what to do next when the door creaked open.

# Chapter Fourteen

## Aoife

I couldn't even begin to guess how long we stayed there in silence, blinking at each other in the near darkness. It was as though what was happening was too strange, too unlikely, for either of us to comprehend it, and so we had to wait for our brains to catch up. When the silence was finally broken, it was because we both spoke at once.

'This is ridiculous. I'm turning on the light.'

'You were supposed to be in bed.'

Even though I knew she couldn't see me, I shook my head and pressed my hand to my temple. I didn't know what to say, so I felt along the wall for a switch, certain that Elijah had thought to have the room wired with electric lights. The darkness heightened my senses, and the cold of the stone travelled from my fingertips and into my core. I was glad the light was still off, so Deborah couldn't see me shiver. My hand found the switch-box, unmistakably smooth and hard and plastic, jutting out of the wall. I knew that as soon as I flicked the switch, the situation would go from an absurd dream, from which I could wake at any time, to something very real. It was as though I was about to skim a pebble into a still and quiet lake, without any way of knowing how far the ripples in the water would spread, or what the pebble might hit on its way down.

'I thought you said you were going to switch the light on.' She was whispering, but I could hear something in her voice that I had never noticed there before. Fear, maybe? Or defiance.

Before she could say anything more, I turned on the light. The switch turned out to be attached to a single bulb which hung bare and dim in the centre of the room, directly above Elijah's desk. And above Deborah, who was perched as daintily as a pregnant woman could perch on the edge of a high-backed leather chair. Her mouth hung open as if she had been about to say something more before deciding against it. She had changed clothes since I'd seen her last, into a long flannel nightgown much like my own, and her hair was loose, its blonde waves crimped into the shape of the plaits she had been wearing all day. I had waited years to see what was in that room, but all I could see was her.

'I can't believe it.'

'Look, Aoife, I'm really sorry…' her voice cracked as she spoke, and she shook her head as though she was in disagreement with the whole situation.

'Shut up,' I snapped. 'Just shut up.'

I knew I had spoken too loudly, but as soon as Deborah widened her eyes and drew her finger to her lips to shush me, a vicious heat rose inside me. I could feel it colouring my cheeks, which prickled like flames. I stepped towards her and slammed my hands onto the desk. She winced.

'How *dare* you? How *dare* you tell me to lower my voice? How dare you tell me what to do *at all*?!' Despite my protest and my rage, I was careful to keep my voice to a whisper. Even so, I must have frightened Deborah, because she curled into herself, drawing her hands around her swollen stomach on instinct. That made me even angrier, and I leaned in further, until I was as close to her as I could get without climbing onto the desk. 'What are you flinching for? You think I'm going to hit you? I'm not going to hit you! Sit up properly and get a grip on yourself!' Tears were starting to burn the back of my eyes, and I banged the desk again. My palms stung.

The sound of my hand hitting the wood must have stirred something in Deborah, because she rose up out of the chair and looked me straight in the eye as she spoke.

'You must be kidding?' she asked, 'Why wouldn't I think that? Bashing around, shouting on. You're definitely bloody acting like someone who wants to hit me.'

'Really?' I said, 'Well, I'm not going to. So, stop acting like a baby, and start explaining yourself.'

I tried to prepare myself for what she was about to say, but I couldn't imagine what Elijah had been thinking when he decided to let her in there instead of me. What little plan could they have been brewing together?

'Please don't tell Elijah.'

I had not prepared myself for that. I stared at her, silently, waiting for her to go on. It didn't take long, and when she started speaking, it was as though she might never stop.

'I found the spare key in the drawer. I found it ages ago. I'm sorry. I just wanted to see what was inside, and it had to be tonight, because I don't know when he'll be home, and I just couldn't go any longer not knowing. And I don't know what's going to happen when he gets back. I'm so sorry, Aoife, I don't know what else to say, I'm so sorry.'

Finally, she fell silent. It was like she had just run out of words. She looked stunned, as if she couldn't quite believe what she had said. I couldn't believe it either.

'He doesn't know you're here?' I asked, hardly daring to hope that I had understood her correctly.

'No,' she said. 'Please don't tell him.'

My face must have given something away, or maybe she just put two and two together based on the surprise in my voice, but it looked like the reality of the situation had begun to dawn on her too.

'He doesn't know you're here either, does he?' she asked.

I shook my head. There was no point in lying. I could tell that, like me, she was trying to think of what this meant for the both of us. I was still toying with the possibility that she was hiding the truth from me when she let out a peal of hysterical laughter.

Then it was my turn to put my finger to my lips. She had looked ashen before, but all of a sudden there was colour in her face. She sat back down in the chair with a heavy *thump* and leaned back so she was looking at the ceiling. I stared in disbelief as her entire body shook with the effort of keeping the laughter in.

I hardly knew what to say. This frenzied, trembling woman in the chair in front of me was not the Deborah I knew. Where was her infuriating calmness? Her serene piety? I put my hands to my hips and tried to keep some authority in my voice.

'I don't know what you think is so funny! You look like you're having a fit!'

She heaved herself forwards, gripping on to the arms of the chair, until she was sitting upright. With a trembling hand, she wiped tears of mirth from her eyes.

'Oh, drop it, Aoife!' She had stopped laughing, but it was as though the laughter had left a trace of itself behind and it lingered in her voice. She went on, 'You can drop the act now. We're both just as bad as each other. You don't have a leg to stand on any more with that attitude.'

She was right, really. We were both sneaking around our house in the middle of the night, going behind our husband's back. Still, I wasn't ready to give up all of my authority. We were there in that room together, yes, but one of us had to be in charge, and by God and His Holy Prophet, that person was going to be me.

I cast my eyes around the room, looking for some inspiration. It was small and dark, even with the glow of the electric blub and the computer screen, and had the dank, cloying smell of damp. The walls had obviously been plastered once, but this had flaked and crumbled to reveal great patches of dark stone. On the wall behind the desk there was a large map of what appeared to be Halcyon, and the other two walls were lined with homemade shelves – the sort you put together when you're a skint student and all you have are a few planks of wood and some bricks. The shelves themselves were bursting with books, their spines turned inwards. Ordinarily, the books would have been my first port of call, but there was something else that drew my attention even more, and that I was desperate to explore. Something that made up for the ordinariness of Elijah's cell. His laptop.

'What have you found so far?' I asked, gesturing towards it.

Deborah shook her head. 'Nothing. Nothing yet. I don't even know how to use it.'

I could feel the smugness in my smile.

'Let me try.'

I made my way around the desk to where Deborah was sitting, and together we looked at the blue screen, on which the time had just changed to 00:30. She turned to look at me expectantly.

'It doesn't have a mouse,' she said. 'And the screen looked different before.'

I leaned forward and touched the tracker pad with a tentative finger. It had been such a long time since I had touched something like that, not since I'd left university fourteen years before, and it felt cool and artificial against my skin. The screen with the clock disappeared and was replaced by a cluttered desktop. Deborah looked impressed, and I tried my best to conceal my pride.

'Easy,' I said, 'look, look at all this stuff.'

'What is it all?' Deborah asked, squinting at the screen.

'Let's find out.' I clicked on a document called 'Timeline FINAL' and held my breath.

A little grey box popped up on the screen.

'Please insert removable drive D,' Deborah sounded the words slowly and deliberately.

'Thanks, Deborah, I can read,' I snapped.

This was not supposed to happen. He was not supposed to have a load of secret files stored on a secret laptop in a locked room. We were supposed to be a team. I was meant to be his *wife*. Halcyon had been *our* dream, *our* project. And now, clearly, it was just his. And where did that leave me? I no longer cared about the missing money, no longer wanted to win back his trust. It was too late. The realisation didn't enrage me the way I thought it might. Instead, it hollowed me out and brought a sinking emptiness which made my chest ache.

Deborah raised her eyebrows, but all she said was, 'What's "removable drive D"?'

I didn't answer. Instead, I tried another file. 'Strategy_optA'. What the hell was that supposed to be?

'It's just saying the same thing again,' said Deborah, pointing at the box which had popped up again on the screen, 'that removable drive D thing. What's that? Do we have one of those?'

I tried another, and another. I tried every file which I could see on the desktop, and for each one, the same message appeared.

'It must be the floppy disk,' I said, weakly, feeling around the sides of the machine for a slot, 'or a CD-ROM. Or something.' But I couldn't feel anything the right size or shape.

'Well,' said Deborah, 'should we have a look in the drawers?'

Elijah's desk had three deep drawers, all of which were locked. Deborah pulled and rattled each one hopelessly and then swore under her breath.

The desk was a cheap, lightweight one, and if we had really wanted to, we could have broken the lock with a few sharp blows, but then there would be no hiding what we had done.

'What do we do now?' she asked.

But I was one step ahead of her. I clicked the familiar blue 'e', the only other button I recognised, and said a silent prayer. If I couldn't read any of his files, the least I could do was try to get on the internet, maybe take a look at his search history. I knew it was a long shot, and to be perfectly honest I had no idea how I thought it was going to work. There was no wire attached to the laptop, and I couldn't see a router box anywhere. If I really thought about it, I would have realised that we had never had anyone come to install any such thing, but I was determined and practically giddy at the prospect of connecting with the outside world. The time might have passed for me to please Elijah, but now I was even more determined to drag him down.

A blank webpage appeared. I had expected it, but that didn't stop the disappointment winding me like a blow to the chest. I was just about ready to close the machine and take a look around the rest of the room when Deborah raised her finger to the screen again, this time pointing at a little icon in the bottom right corner.

'What's that?' she asked. 'That one there, that looks like a signal with a cross through? Is that something?'

I clicked on it.

'Look,' said Deborah, leaning close to read what was on the screen, 'it's got an internet thing, a connection or whatever! That bit that says, "portable Wi-Fi network". Click on it!'

'No,' I said, 'that's just what the laptop has connected to before. See, when I press it, it says it can't connect. "Portable Wi-Fi network not present".'

I could see from Deborah's face that she was puzzling something out.

'That can't be right though, can it?'

'Of course I'm right. What do you mean?' I said.

'No, I don't mean you. I just mean, if it's saying this laptop has been connected to Wi-Fi, that can't be right, can it? I've only just thought. Because we're not allowed to use Wi-Fi.'

Deborah was right. We weren't allowed to use Wi-Fi. Even when we lived in the city, Elijah had been adamant that it was dangerous, that it allowed the government to see everything you were doing, that it gave off radioscopic waves which messed with your mind and gave you tumours and miscarriages. I remembered one sermon in particular, which Elijah delivered after one of the congregants bought a mobile phone. *The rays from things like this,* he had said, holding the phone between his finger and thumb as though it was a dirty nappy, *are the government's most effective method of population control.* Deborah had only just joined us when that happened. It might have even been her phone for all I could remember. Either way, the perils of wireless internet and the mind-bending carcinogenic rays emitted by mobile phones were common subjects in Elijah's preaching.

'Why would he use something that he thinks is so dangerous?'

I shrugged. There were so many possible answers. Maybe he sat there in a tinfoil hat. Maybe he didn't care. Maybe he had changed his mind about the whole thing. Maybe it was simply one rule for him, and one rule for us. Once I would have puzzled it over, desperate to find a possible scenario that painted Elijah in the best light, determined to understand his thinking, but that time had certainly passed. He was no longer a man I could recognise. I closed the laptop's lid and took myself across the room to the thin window. If it had been daytime, I would have been able to see almost all of Halcyon's populated zone from there, but it was night and the moon was obscured by a cloud, so as it was, all I could see were the faint outlines of caravans and outbuildings. Behind me I could hear Deborah rising from her seat, the floorboards creaking gently as she walked over to study something else in the room. I knew that I should be doing the same – taking the opportunity to explore Elijah's secret space – but I no longer wanted to. I suppose I was worried about what else I might find, but I was also suddenly very tired, and the bright digital glare of the laptop screen had incited a throbbing pain behind my left eye. So instead of looking around the room with Deborah, I stayed at the window, gazing out over the sleeping colony below.

'Huh,' I heard her say quietly, 'hey, Aoife, did you know that Elijah still has his passport? It's in his old name, even.'

It must have been the movement that caught my eye. It was only slight, but in the stillness of the night any motion was hard to ignore. At first, I thought it must have been a trick of the darkness, or a side-effect of my headache, but a sliver of moon had found its way out from behind a cloud and I was suddenly certain.

'Turn off the light.' I moved away from the glass as quickly as I could.

'What?' said Deborah. She was busy flipping through the passport.

'Turn off the light! I think there's someone outside!'

Her face grew ashen, and she lumbered across the room to the light switch.

Neither of us spoke again until we were in the kitchen. I sat at the table, resting my head in my hands as Deborah made us cups of tea in the flickering candlelight. I was amazed at how swiftly she had locked the door behind us, how efficiently she had returned the key to its hiding place, how silently she had come down the stairs. I had lit the candle for us, reluctant to risk turning on another electric light in the middle of the night. The sound of boiling water did something to soothe my jangling nerves, and by the time I was holding the mug in my hands, inhaling the rising steam as the warmth seeped into my bones, I felt almost normal. Whatever normal was, then.

'God, I miss real tea.' Deborah's whisper took me by surprise.

'Really?'

'Yeah,' she said, 'sometimes I dream about it.'

I wasn't sure how well she could see me in the half-light of the dancing flame, but I smiled anyway.

'Me too,' I said.

'Sometimes the dreams feel so real, it's like I can actually taste it, you know? Do you ever get those?'

I nodded. 'The other night I dreamed I ate a jacket potato covered with melted cheese and baked beans and butter. It was incredible.'

'Oh,' she said, 'what I wouldn't give for some proper cheese right now. Or some crisps. Or pasta. When I was pregnant with Susannah, there was an entire month when I would have sold my soul for one of those huge cookies you get from kiosks in shopping centres. I would wake up in the middle of the night convinced I could smell them.'

'Do you have any cravings this time around?'

'Oh, I don't know,' she said, 'my freedom, maybe?'

She gave a short, awkward laugh and rolled her eyes. I reached out and took her hand from across the table; it was small and warm. I think it must have been the first time I had ever touched her.

'I just keep feeling so *angry*. Do you ever feel like that? Like, all I want to do is scream and throw things. It can't be good for the baby. Although that seems a bit redundant, really, because what part of this is good for the baby? For any of the babies? I mean, I had as shitty a childhood as the next person, shittier probably, but even when I was in care I was allowed to be a kid, you know? I went to school, I went to the park, I could have fun. You know?'

I nodded. I knew I should say something reassuring, but I couldn't think of anything at all, so I gave her hand another squeeze. If I was honest, I never let myself think too much about the children. Constance must have been about twelve. She was my first baby. She was almost seven when we arrived in Halcyon, and old enough to remember what it was like when we lived in the same house. It was hard for her, at first, only seeing me at church. It had been hard for Faith, too, I remembered, although even when we had lived together much of the caring had fallen to Ruth or the other women in Heaven on Earth. I had been busy supporting Elijah and working for the church, and he had been firm, even then, in his beliefs about how families should function, how dangerous it could be for parents to love their children too much. I saw myself as a nurse or a teacher, whose job it was to see them through from one end of the day to the other, and Elijah's preaching helped me to understand that my lack of affection was not a deficiency. Still, I saw the way that other women – and men – behaved with their children. The way their souls slotted together like pieces of a puzzle.

Halcyon and Humility never knew any different – to them, I was always just one of their father's wives, one of three 'mothers' who meant no more to them than any random woman working in the schoolhouse. And then after Humility the babies had just stopped coming, even though I was definitely still young enough to be having them. Elijah and I had seen it as a curse, but perhaps it was a blessing. I pushed the thoughts away and refocussed on Deborah, who had started speaking again.

'But then, if I left, and somehow managed to bring them with me, what would I do then? I don't even have any GCSEs. I've never had a job. We'd be on the street, and then they'd get taken away, and surely it's better to be in here with them, than out there without them?'

We were quiet for a moment. I sipped my tea.

'I don't know.'

It was all I could say.

# Chapter Fifteen

## Ruth

I didn't have the heart to tell Mim the real reason we needed to move Russell and the pups out of the barn and into one of the outbuildings. Instead, I said it was so the cows weren't disturbed, and so the dogs could have some peace. It wasn't a complete lie, and definitely better than the truth, which would have just upset her. I gathered the pups up into one of the cleaner towels and placed them in Mim's eager arms, and in my own I carried Russell. At first, she squirmed, her small, stocky body twisting in an attempt to get closer to her litter, but I shushed her and stroked her and it didn't take long before she was calm and still. I turned off the torch and tucked it into the pocket of my nightgown.

'I can't see anything!' Mim squeaked.

If she hadn't been holding the puppies, I was sure she would have grabbed hold of me. Instead, she came as close as she could. I could feel her shivering.

'It's okay,' I said, 'walk by me. The outbuilding we need is just outside.'

Together, we inched along the outside wall of the barn towards the nearest lean-to, where we kept the spare tarpaulins. It was the best place I could think of for Russell and her litter to hide out until I decided what to do with them – it would be less draughty than the barn, and there was less chance of someone stumbling across them. The few feet of empty space between the end of the barn and the start of the outhouse seemed to go on for miles, and I was so frightened of tripping over and dropping the dog that instead of lifting my feet, I shuffled forwards so the stony ground scraped the soles of my boots. I let out a sigh of relief when I finally came up against the cold corrugated iron of the outbuilding.

'We made it,' I whispered, more to myself than to Mim, whose breathing had become more irregular and shallow the further we got from the barn.

The night air was freezing cold, and I was reluctant to take one of my hands away from Russell's warm fur in order to reach for the latch. I fumbled, but it didn't take me long to find it. Relieved, I slid the bolt across and tried to pull the door towards me. It didn't budge. I tried again, using as much of my strength as I could without disturbing the dog, and when nothing happened, I tried to push instead. It was stuck fast.

'What's happening?' whispered Mim, her breath hot and clammy against my ear.

'I think it's locked.'

'Locked? Why?'

I could feel myself growing frustrated. I was tempted to ask her to go back to bed and leave me to it, but instead I said: 'I don't know why. We'll have to find someplace else.'

*Someplace else.* Where else? There were other outbuildings, sure, Halcyon was littered with them, but I didn't know how easy it would be to find them in the dark. Not only that; Halcyon's ground was rocky and slick with mud, and it was hard to tell what was the worn path and what wasn't, so I was worried that I would end up straying off into the night. I closed my eyes and tried to picture the settlement as a whole, running through possible hiding places and mapping out our route. The torch in my pocket banged against my leg, a reminder of how much easier it would be if we could have a little light. I resisted the temptation, and somehow we managed to shuffle our way to the next shed. That one was locked too. By the time we reached the third outbuilding my legs were beginning to shake, and my arms were numb with cold and the effort of carrying the dog. I had no idea how long we'd been out, and though the darkness didn't seem likely to break any time soon, the threat of dawn added a greater sense of urgency to the whole escapade. I was also very conscious that if *I* was cold, the puppies must have been even colder, and there was a very real chance that they would freeze to death while I was trying my best to save their lives.

'Make sure you're keeping the pups warm,' I said to Mim, as my frozen hands fumbled with yet another latch.

'I am.'

The relief I felt when the door swung open seemed to come from my very core; it was the same feeling I got after a tricky delivery ended well. As soon as Mim and our charges and I were safely inside and the door closed behind us, I got down onto my knees and said a prayer of thanks. Russell, who had been quiet and still, must have noticed her sudden proximity to solid ground and twisted herself free of my grasp. The click of her claws against the poured concrete floor pulled me back into reality, and I went into efficiency autopilot, firing instructions at Mim and piling up blankets and towels to build a nest for the dogs. I shone the torch around the rest of the shed in case there was anything else in there that we could use, but the space was almost entirely taken up with empty tins of paint and other prospectively useful odds and ends that had been saved for a rainy day. Nothing which would be any good for keeping dogs warm, but at least it was unlikely that anyone would venture in there any time soon.

'Okay,' I said, turning to face Mim, 'now I need to go and get the rest of the stuff and bring it here. You wait with the dogs, and I'll be as quick as I can.'

As I turned to leave, she grabbed my arm. 'Please can I come with you? They were talking about some man that's been spotted around the compound in evening worship today.'

I ran the possible outcomes through in my head. For the effort it would cost me to convince her to stay there alone, I decided it would be faster to agree. As for the potential intruder, I had no time to think about it.

'Fine,' I said, 'you can help me carry everything.'

I interrupted her eager nod by switching off the torch.

We walked back to the barn in silence, but when we got inside it was as though someone had flipped a switch inside Mim's brain, and suddenly all she could do was talk.

'I think this is the most fun I've ever had in my life.'

'Hmm,' I said. And then, 'Here, please hold the torch so I can see what I'm doing.'

She took it from my hand. From the swaying of the beam, I could tell that she was moving from one foot to the other. If I ever did that growing up, my mom would scold me. *Have you got ants in your pants or something? Stay still – you're making me seasick!* I bit my tongue and concentrated on making up the bundle.

'I don't know how I'm ever going to go back to the schoolhouse after this.' She giggled and then went quiet for a second before adding, 'Of course, I won't be there for much longer. Probably.'

I didn't say anything.

'You know,' she said, 'because I'll probably be getting married soon.'

The silence that fell was a heavy one. I had no interest in encouraging this line of conversation, so even though I knew Mim was holding out for a response I was reluctant to give one. I made another noncommittal *mmm* sound. She continued:

'It'll definitely be good to get out of the schoolhouse. Helen said she's going to be sad to see me go, but I can't wait. It's going to be so nice not to worry about getting woken up in the middle of the night. And I think it must be quite fun being married.'

I'm a quiet person. I like to watch, and I listen pretty well, which means that I've always been good at letting other people speak. Because of this, I seem to be the sort of girl that people enjoy spilling their secrets to. I can imagine there are lots of people in this world who would enjoy having that effect on others, but it's a skill that is wasted on me. I had no idea what to say to Mim. I had no idea what she wanted from me. Did she want me to tell her I was excited for her, happy for her? It was none of my business if she and Elijah married. Silently, I passed her the dish of water and took the torch from her hand.

I was relieved when she didn't say anything more as we walked back to the dogs. It was still pitch dark when we got back outside, but muscle memory guided me back to the outbuilding and I didn't have the worry of dropping Russell this time, so we made much faster progress than before. When we arrived, the dog was lying contentedly on her side with all four pups suckling greedily. Mim seemed antsy, and despite what she had said earlier, seemed keen to return to bed, so I arranged the fresh towels and dish of water quickly. As happy as I was to see Russell so content, I was eager to get back too, so we said a quick goodnight at the door before going our separate ways.

It was good to be back in the farmhouse, and I took great pleasure in closing the door against that strange, long night. My body was achy with tension and frozen from the biting cold, but my hands felt dirty and I knew that I needed to wash up before bed. I don't know what made me go to turn on the electric light in the kitchen – I knew the room well enough to navigate it in the dark – but fate or God guided my hand to the switch. Something in the room seemed out of place. *What's wrong with this picture?* Still in the doorway I cast my eyes around, blinking in the harsh light, trying to figure out what it was. It didn't take me long to notice. On the kitchen counter, by the sink, were two mugs laid out to drain. On the table was a candle, its flame extinguished, burned halfway down.

# Chapter Sixteen

## Deborah

The morning after our long night, Aoife and I followed our usual routines. Ruth was with us at breakfast so we didn't get the chance to talk about what had happened, although I had been desperate to – 'You hate him too now, right?' I wanted to say over our bowls of porridge and glasses of water. 'How long have you hated him? Do you hate him more than you hate me?'

'Please pass the honey,' I said instead.

I hadn't been addressing either of them in particular, but I was still a bit disappointed when it was Ruth who slid the heavy ceramic pot across the table and into my hand. I'd hoped that Aoife would take it as an opportunity to give me some kind of meaningful sign, and then I felt stupid for hoping.

It would be too much of a risk to go back up to the office during the day, and even if I did go, I knew there was nothing I could really do without being able to look at the laptop files or go onto the internet. The books might have held some clues to Elijah's state of mind, but there were so many and it would take me forever to even read one. It just wasn't worth it. Instead, I wished my sister wives a good morning and went to my work.

The children all seemed bleary-eyed and exhausted that morning as we walked from the schoolhouse to the bunker to work on some preparations for the End. I was carrying my little Susannah, breathing in the scent of her as she rested her head against my shoulder, her skinny legs wrapped around my bump. I wouldn't be able to carry her for much longer. She smelled of fresh air and laundered clothes and milk, her eyelids pink and fluttering, lashes long and dark. She was my reason, along with

Jonah and Noah, for sticking around. I tried to remind myself of that, that it hadn't been for nothing. Still, I'd have to do better for them. I took another deep breath in and Susannah raised a hand to my cheek, resting it on my face just as Helen turned around.

The bunker was a short walk out of the central cluster of Halcyon's barns and outbuildings, so it didn't take our group long to get there. It wasn't much to look at from above ground – heavy corrugated metal covered in turf like a giant Anderson shelter for eighty – but it still made my stomach dip whenever I approached it. Once every couple of weeks we would take the children from the schoolhouse for a day under the ground, getting them used to the space that we were planning to spend the time, either days, weeks, or months, from the onset of total societal breakdown until God was ready to take us. We'd have them rotate the food in the stores, scrub the floors, clean out the vents. It had taken about two years and almost all of our savings from donations and tithes to build, and now, thanks to the children, it waited, gleaming and immaculate for the End.

Helen turned the heavy handle and pulled open the vault door, and we followed her into the cold and clammy darkness. The air in the bunker tasted of damp earth and sat in my lungs like a freezing thing, and it was so thick that I felt as though I should be able to bite down and leave tooth marks in it. The door swung shut and we vanished into the dark. We always spent the first couple of minutes with the electric light off, but it never got easier. I squeezed the sleepy Susannah closer to me, working hard to manage my breathing and keep my heart rate steady. However many times I went in, it never stopped feeling like a tomb.

Helen clicked her wind-up torch on and shone the dim beam to the floor, making the phosphorescent arrows appear. I tried to focus on them, and Susannah and the twins who I knew were nearby. Usually by this point I would be feeling better, not quite so claustrophobic, but the sense of being trapped just got heavier and heavier the further into the bunker that we walked. To either side of me, faintly illuminated by the torchlight, bunk beds and travel cots for eighty lined the walls. When we reached the end of the main space and the door to the storage room, Helen flipped on the electricity and the long florescent light pinged into flickering life overhead.

The main section of the bunker was the largest. As well as beds, it contained a long bench across one wall which doubled as both a seating area and a storage space. The seat of the bench lifted up in various places to reveal carefully packed sleeping bags, boxes of foil blankets, all the stuff you might need for a camping trip or an apocalypse. The bench, like everything else in the bunker, was made to last. The hinges were strong and oiled, so the lids raised without a single creak. The wood was solid pine. Elijah had insisted on the very best of everything. He had even insisted on selecting the colour of the walls himself – a cool, pale blue, which he had chosen after about a month of research into something he called the 'psychology of colour'. Elijah was the father to twelve children, but the bunker was more his baby than any of them. Even the food store in the next room along was organised to the hilt, with labelled shelves of canned goods running in alphabetical order from anchovies to water. He hadn't lowered himself to do the organising, but he had overseen it closely and would sometimes come down when the children were in to supervise their upkeep of his most sacred space. Elijah's attention to the bunker went all the way down the concrete steps to the lower floor, where more strips of fluorescent lighting illuminated our bathroom (three toilets ordered specially from the United States, lots of loo roll, thousands of baby wipes – all exotic luxuries compared to what we had in Halcyon itself), and the panic room. The panic room was closed off behind another heavy metal door, just like the one which opened into the main body of the bunker, with a round handle like the wheel of a ship. If worst came to worst, and the rest of the bunker was infiltrated or compromised, the panic room was built to keep us safe for up to a week, after which point the food down there would run out.

Elijah had spent hours with his Bible, doing complicated-looking sums using numbers which he seemed to choose at random from passages in the Book of Revelation, and when he had finished he announced that God wouldn't make us wait for more than two weeks from the start of the End until he brought us to join Him in Heaven. In that time, though, we could be subject to anything. Crazed sinners descending on our community, determined to steal our food and medical supplies; extreme weather, covering Halcyon in snowdrifts as tall as buildings or intense heat burning anyone outside to a crisp; nuclear war, some pathetic little man with his finger on the button blowing the world into oblivion. Elijah made no promises, other than: 'the End is coming' and 'we will be ready'. We had enough supplies for over two months.

'Well done, everyone,' said Helen, clasping her hands together in delight. 'I know we don't like that very much, do we? But we were all so brave today! And we'll all be so ready if those nasty outsiders break our wind turbines or our generator at the End.'

Jonah and Noah were standing apart, at opposite sides of the group, their dark curls hidden under woolly hats. Jonah was staring up at Helen, listening with the intensity of a three-year-old Elijah. Noah was busily fiddling with the belt loops on his corduroy trousers. Neither of them was looking at me. The sudden brightness stirred Susannah and she lifted her head from my shoulder, squirming to be put down. I held her tighter – it was rare that Helen allowed me to hold her at all.

'We won't be scared, will we?' Helen asked.

'No!'

The sound of all of the children shouting their answer rang in my ears. Even with the lights on, I was still so aware of being under the ground, of how easy it would be to become trapped beneath corrugated metal and tonnes of earth.

'That's right, everyone! We're God's bravest soldiers, because we have our Holy Prophet leading us.' Helen pointed to the mural of Elijah on the storeroom door. It was a good likeness, and showed Elijah in his argyle jumper and ancient jeans leading the population of Halcyon up a golden ladder, away from a flaming city and the grasping hands of sinners and up into a set of heavenly white clouds. There was no depiction of Heaven itself, because that would be sacrilegious, so it looked like the crowd were about to disappear into nothing. All of the church members had haloes, to set them apart from the sinners, but Elijah's was the largest and brightest. It was picked out in gold leaf, which Elijah said he had found lying around somewhere when he had been on a mission trip.

I knew the mural very well, because I'd painted it, but the light was too bright and I couldn't make it out properly. Something about the brightness and my dizziness and how hard

I was suddenly finding it to catch my breath meant that the Elijah in the painting seemed to be looking right at me, smiling. Helen was still talking, but her voice seemed very far away. A grey mist crept across my vision and I felt myself falling slowly backwards as someone grabbed the writhing Susannah from my arms.

# Chapter Seventeen

## Aoife

I kept going out of my way to walk around the perimeter fence to look for Malcolm, and he kept on being there, waiting for me. Our talks had kept me going in the days Elijah had been away, but my sad little epiphany in the office had made me reluctant to see him again. I imagined myself through his eyes – a deluded, pathetic, lonely woman – and felt even more ashamed than I had been already. He was only there because he was interested in our land, and I was some pitiful sideshow to be laughed at when he got home. I had spent the whole of my silent breakfast running through the situation in my head: how long had I been deluding myself about my position? When had my power started slipping away? And why, after everything we'd been through and everything I'd done, did he not love me any more?

*Idiot. Who's to say I ever loved you?*

Still, I didn't turn to my accounts that morning at all, or to the community barn or to Deborah (what to say to her, now?). Instead, I wrapped myself up and made my way around the perimeter fence to the spot where Malcolm usually waited for me. Everyone else was already hard at work, but again, nobody seemed to care about where I was going, or at least no one was brave enough to stop me. I had that authority still, which was a mercy. I wasn't like the others, who had to worry about neighbourly eyes catching secret stumbles and turning them over to John.

Halcyon had also been covered by low-lying cloud, which meant it was impossible to see more than a few feet ahead; the mountains which usually guarded our horizon were completely obscured, shrouded by the soupy whiteness. I was far enough away from the centre that nobody would be able to see me, even if they were looking. I could feel little beads of moisture settling on me – my skin, my hair, the fibres of my clothes. The air smelled peaty and damp. I passed the sheep, grazing peacefully by the stream, their fleeces thick and ready for winter, and kept walking until I saw Malcolm's figure emerge from the fog. He must have already spotted me by the time I saw him, as he was waving cheerfully. His smile seemed so pleased, so genuine, that it lifted me and quickened my pace. That wasn't the smile of a man who was just there to talk about buying land. I felt a flutter of pride. I might have been a fool, but *Malcolm* wanted to see me. He was *excited* to see me. He *liked* me, and he didn't need to know about anything that might make him feel differently. *Look at you*, came the voice, familiar and scathing, *how shallow can you get? Your whole life is a lie, and everything is suddenly all right because this* man, *this* stranger, *seems to be showing an interest? He'll see right through you.*

I was shaking my head to clear the voice away when I noticed, with a little jolt of panic, that Malcolm's left hand was tucked behind his back. It was obvious from the way he was holding himself that he was hiding something there, a tactic favoured by Elijah when he wanted to catch me out for some apparent wrongdoing in the early days of our marriage. He would come in, all smiles, and then out from behind his back would appear something of mine which he'd found and decided to be a tool of the devil: a tinted lip-balm, a can of diet cola, a box of tampons. Swiftly followed by a lecture, a punishment, or days of silence, depending on his mood.

Elijah would draw it out, waiting for me to notice he was hiding something, letting me sweat, but Malcolm clearly wasn't the sort of man for such games. As soon as he was sure I'd noticed, he revealed a shiny tartan-patterned tin with a delighted flourish.

'Morning, Aoife! Look what my housekeeper made.'

I'd barely arrived at the fence when he opened the tin to reveal rows of shortbread biscuits, neatly nestled side by side.

'I thought you might like one.'

He passed a slender golden slice of shortbread through one of the gaps in the chain link with a leather gloved hand. I took it without thinking; it was still warm.

'How lovely. Thank you, Malcolm, you shouldn't have.'

I hadn't tasted anything so delicious in years.

'These are incredible,' I said, mouth full of crumbs, 'you need to give your housekeeper a pay rise.'

I flinched as soon as the words were out of my mouth. Any such comment made to Elijah, however light-hearted, would be met with rage. *How dare you tell a man what to do?* But Malcolm just smiled again and nodded.

'I'll take that as a solid piece of advice, coming from a church accountant with half a business degree.'

He was being sarcastic, but sweetly so; his gentle laughter was with me, not at me. This kindness, combined with how little I had left to lose, made me bold.

'I suppose that's the reason you're here today, and the other days? To talk accounts, and business?' I raised an eyebrow in what I hoped was a subtly flirtatious way, but my voice turned unintentionally hard as I asked my final question. 'Are you still interested in our land?'

Malcolm's smile vanished, but he didn't seem angry. He closed the lid of the biscuit tin and studied my face, his seriousness unfamiliar and thrilling.

'You're clearly an intelligent woman, Aoife. I have a feeling you know that's not why I've been coming here every day.'

I felt my cheeks redden, and I twisted my wedding ring around my finger. The thin, gold band was as cold as my hand, and loose enough that it spun easily.

'Then, why have you been coming here every day?'

*You sound so needy. He knows you're married.*

He seemed to be considering his answer, weighing up responses in his head.

'I think,' he said, 'that you're an interesting person. I enjoy talking to you. You're someone I like spending time with.'

I met his gaze for a moment before looking down at my feet. I could still sense the colour in my cheeks, and was ashamed of myself.

He broke the silence that followed with a rough clearing of his throat.

'I actually have a question for you this morning, too. I've been wondering for a little while.'

I must have looked sceptical because he smiled his warm smile again.

'It's okay,' he said, 'you don't have to answer if you don't want to. And I promise it's nothing personal. I just wanted to ask how long you've been here.'

'Do you mean me, or the church?'

'Well, both, I suppose. Did you come to the church, or with the church?'

To the church or with the church? I *was* the church! Was. Everything seemed to be in the past tense.

'With the church,' I said. 'I came with the church. We've been here for five years.'

'Five *years*?' He sounded stunned. '*Here*? But why?'

I sighed, my breath curling in the cold air.

'The city wasn't the right place for us to live the way we wanted to live. There was too much pressure, too much outside influence. It's hard to be a Christian in the truest possible way when you live in a society like that.'

'What do you mean?'

'When you live in the city, working a job, buying food from supermarkets, paying taxes and utility bills, you end up giving your time and your money to places that use it badly. Do you know how much modern slavery is behind so much of the stuff you buy every day? Fruit picked by children in Morocco, and all the little ones trafficked into the cocoa industry?' I could see he was about to interrupt, so I went on, quicker, 'And even if you don't buy the strawberries or the chocolates, even if you just go in to buy a pint of milk, you're still giving money to that supermarket. And when you pay your taxes, the government that takes that money is the same government that sells weapons which wind up blowing up schools and hospitals in Syria. That's just the tip of the iceberg. And it's our children too, the church's children. They were seeing stuff in the streets, hearing things that children shouldn't be seeing or hearing. We did our best but it's impossible to properly protect them out there. The way things are going, we just didn't feel safe. And that's not how God wanted us to live.'

I stopped myself before mentioning the End, the breakdown of society which had felt so inevitable, the arrival of God on Earth to save the righteous and condemn the sinners. I'd spoken to enough people about Heaven on Earth and our work to know how to pace my evangelism. It had been a long time since I'd delivered a speech like that. Remembering why we'd come made me sadder about where we were now. I still believed those things. I still wanted to be the sort of Christian who lived them.

Malcolm nodded again.

'I get it,' he said, 'I can see the appeal of that. And now you're here, and you're all self-sufficient, do you feel closer to God? Excuse me if that's too personal, I'm not really a… man of faith. I don't want you to think I'm being patronising or anything. I suppose I'm just curious.'

I thought about Elijah and his punishments and his secrets. His rages and his games. Did listening to the sound of choking and retching as a room of my friends and neighbours drank what they thought was poison make me feel closer to God? Did watching my husband slide his arm around the shoulders of a teenager make me feel closer to God? I looked up at Malcolm's face, so open and kind and interested. He liked me. He was a good person, and to like me, he must have thought that I was a good person too. I couldn't bear to tell him that I wasn't.

'It's more complicated than that,' I said.

I made my excuses to leave, and had already turned to walk away, when Malcolm spoke again.

'Maybe things don't have to be complicated. Maybe they could be easy. I'm not judging, and I might have got the wrong end of the stick here, but I just want to say it. If you ever want to leave, Aoife, you just have to say the word. I'll be here.'

# Chapter Eighteen

## Ruth

Some nights, when my soul was heavy, I would lie in bed and think of my early days in Heaven on Earth in the hopes that the happy memories would send me to sleep.

I'd been attending the church for a few months when my relationship with Elijah shifted, and I wondered if the little tug I felt in my heart every time he looked my way might have been reciprocated. Grey city snow was piled in slushy drifts on the sidewalk, and I had been shivering at my bus stop for half an hour after service, my return ticket clutched in my frozen, gloved hand. I was beginning to wonder if I should make my way on foot when Elijah appeared from around the corner, deerstalker hat pulled down over his ears and scarf up to his chin.

He raised his hand to greet me.

'Ruth!' he called, his voice as loud and confident in the street as it was in church.

I waved back, suddenly warm despite the flakes of snow which were melting down the collar of my coat. I had lent my scarf to one of the trainee midwives at work.

'I'm glad I caught you,' he said once he was close enough that he didn't have to shout. 'Let me walk you home.'

'Oh, that's okay, you don't—'

But we were already on our way.

We were about halfway back to my place when Elijah slowed down. On the edge of the sidewalk was a patch of virgin snow, untouched by footprints or grit or mud. He stepped to the side and stamped down purposefully, leaving an imprint of his boot behind.

'I can never resist.' He shrugged, and I laughed.

The action had been so joyful and childish, so out of character, that I hadn't been able to help myself.

He looked at me, a smile playing on his lips. I was reminded of one of my favourite British words – cheeky. His smile looked almost *cheeky*.

'What's so funny?' he asked.

'I guess I just would never have expected you to do that. It seems like such a—' I tried to think of a word other than 'childish', because I didn't want him to think I was being insulting, 'light-hearted thing to do. It made me happy to see it, I guess because I could tell it made you happy to do it.'

'You don't think I'm a light-hearted sort of person?'

'No, not really,' I said.

Something about being side by side made it easier to speak openly to him. We were still walking, but I could feel the sleeve of his winter coat brushing mine. If I had been a different kind of woman, I might have pretended to slip so he would catch me and take me by the arm.

'Care to elaborate?'

'Well, you're just very serious. I didn't think people who were so smart and holy did things like that.'

Then it was Elijah's turn to laugh.

'We're all of us more than we seem, Ruth. Like you. On the outside you're a shy, devout woman. You're charitable and kind, a bit of a rule-follower. But then, you came here from America all by yourself. You do a job that's incredibly physically challenging and emotionally draining. You're tough, and brave, deep down, in a way that lots of people who seem more confident than you just aren't.'

Aoife's name hung in the air between us, unsaid.

'You're being very generous,' I said, 'but I'm not so sure how brave I am. Before I found the church, I was so lonely that I started to feel like I wasn't even a real person.'

'Are you homesick?'

I shook my head.

'Good, I'm glad. I'd hate for you to feel homesick, especially now I hope you've found a family here with us.'

I smiled as demurely as I could, but inside my chest, beneath the layers of my coat and sweater and blouse, my heart thumped hard against my ribs. Emboldened by his words, I allowed myself to look up at Elijah's face. His nose had turned a little red with the cold, and his cheeks were pink. I wanted to rest my hands against them, to warm him.

'I should have done this ages ago,' he said. For a second I was terrified that he might try to kiss me, but instead he unwound the scarf from around his neck and draped it gently over my shoulders.

'There, that's better.'

When we reached the door to my apartment, he waited until I had fished the key from inside my purse. It took me an embarrassingly long time, because I was wearing my gloves, but he didn't sigh or shiver. When I finally got the door open, I went to take off his scarf.

'No,' he said, 'you keep that.'

I brought the scarf with me to Halcyon, when we moved.


'Ruthie?'

I must have drifted off, because the sound of my name being whispered woke me.

'Ruthie?'

I heard my name again and sat up in bed. The voice was coming from outside my bedroom door, and I knew it better than I knew my own. It was Elijah. My heart convulsed with a mixture of relief and fear. He was back, alive and well. But also he was back, alive and well.

The door opened, and he stepped inside.

'Put the lamp on, Ruthie Angel, I want to see your face. I've missed you.'

We had been preparing for our wedding when Elijah learned that my middle name was Angel, and he'd been pleased. 'Suits you', he'd said. He called me his Ruthie Angel sometimes, when he was feeling affectionate, and it embarrassed me although I never told him so. I guess I never said anything because it was nice that he cared enough to give me a pet name, but also because I could never really put my finger on why I disliked it so much.

I leaned across to the electric lamp by the side of my bed and switched it on. The bulb was dim but it still dazzled me, so I could smell Elijah before I saw him. The scent of hard liquor and cigarette smoke, and something else I half recognised but couldn't name, came off him like a vapour. He looked like he hadn't slept in the whole time he'd been away from Halcyon, his eyes red raw and circled with purple. He was still wearing the clothes he'd had on when he'd left, and I noticed that one of the buttons had come off his sheepskin coat. Had he been trying to preach in a bar? That was the only explanation I could find for the smells, so out of place in Halcyon, and the way he looked – as if he'd been in a brawl. Had the Godless outsiders attacked him?

'Elijah.' My voice was hoarse and deep with sleep, and I tried to make it a little higher before continuing. 'Welcome home. We've missed you too.'

He smiled then, the way he did sometimes that didn't make it up to his eyes, and shrugged off his coat. It landed with a heavy thump on the bare floorboards.

'That's what I like to hear,' he said, his words slurring. 'You know, Ruthie, why I came to you tonight?'

I was relieved when he didn't give me the chance to answer.

'You don't ask questions. I can trust you to just shut up and not ask stupid questions. Aoife would be asking me where I'd been, just outright, no respect. She doesn't respect me, is her problem. She thinks she's something. And Deborah, she'd try and be clever, she thinks she's clever. She wouldn't ask but she'd ask, you know? She'd ask, but without asking. Thinking she's clever. You *know* you're not something. You *know* you're not clever. That's what I like about you, Ruthie, that's why you're the Angel. You're the best of them, you are. You're my favourite.'

The whole time he'd been speaking, his words slow and low, sliding into each other, he had been walking towards the bed where I was lying, shedding his sweater and then his plaid shirt, and finally his long thermal vest. Then he was kicking off his boots and working the clasp of his belt with his left hand, steadying himself against the bed with his right.

'You're my favourite,' he said again, this time into my neck. He was lying beside me, and I could feel his mouth, wet and hot against my ear. He was so close now that I could tell the stink of liquor was coming from his skin, from inside his mouth and through his pores. He had been drinking. He was *drunk*. 'Did you hear when I said that? What do you say?'

'Thank you,' I whispered.

My arms and legs had turned heavy. Sometimes that happened, when he was in one of his moods and he still wanted to make love. My body would freeze and I'd have to breathe, in for four and out for eight, like the breathing I did when I birthed my babies, to stop myself getting too tense and making him mad. But this time was different, because I'd never seen him drunk before, never been kissed by a drunk man before, or by a man whose whole mouth tasted of cigarettes. I'd only ever kissed Elijah, and Elijah never drank, never smoked. We didn't even use communion wine any more.

The warmth I'd trapped under my blankets was replaced with cold as Elijah tried to join me under the covers, his jeans still half on. He moved jerkily, getting caught up in my quilt and his pants, and I could sense his frustration growing. It was almost a relief when he finally made it, if only because I knew he wouldn't get madder, but even so that was short-lived. His belt and fly were unbuckled, leaving his hands free to push up my nightdress. It was like being touched by ice.

'You're so warm,' he said, his mouth on mine.

I closed my eyes. *This is normal*, I told myself, *this is all right. He's had a few drinks, because he's stressed, but the rest of it is normal.* He guided my hand to his crotch and held it there. *The only difference is the alcohol. He's still your husband. This is what it means to have a husband.*

With my eyes closed, it was easier to distract myself. The feeling of him moving between my legs, his grunts, the creak of the bed, could almost be drowned out. I could almost imagine it wasn't happening. I thought about my day, and about poor Deborah, who had fainted in the bunker in front of all of the children. Her blood pressure had been low, which was normal for a woman at the start of her third trimester, but still something to keep an eye on. I would have to make sure she was drinking enough water, maybe check our first-aid supplies to see if we had a pair of support stockings that might fit her. She would be recuperating in her bed downstairs, in the room below mine. I hoped that the creak of the bed wasn't disturbing her. I would be so embarrassed if it woke her up. *In for four, out for eight.* Elijah's mouth was no longer covering mine, which made my calming breaths easier. It also meant I could no longer taste him, and that made it easier to pretend that the whole situation was normal. Normal, and soon to be over.

Elijah rolled off me with a shudder, and I turned off the lamp.

He had his back to me, and I thought he was about to fall asleep until he spoke.

'I've been wandering the desert, but now I'm back and I'm here to stay. Now I know what it really feels like to be God.'

I took another deep breath in, counting to four, trying not to let the air catch in my throat. He was quiet for a long time after that. When I was sure he was asleep, I let myself cry.

# Chapter Nineteen

## Deborah

I was back on my feet less than twenty-four hours after my fainting spell in the bunker, ladling out porridge into bowls when Ruth, who had been sitting at the table for a good while, gave a little cough. Aoife and I looked at her.

'I don't know if you two heard,' she said, speaking into her half-empty mug, 'but Elijah got back last night.'

I dropped my ladle into the saucepan where it sank down into the sticky, bubbling oats. Aoife turned white, and I watched her eyes flicker as she tried to decide what to say. She opened her mouth but seemed to think better of it and closed it again. In the nine years I had known Aoife, I had only seen her lost for words twice: the first time was in Elijah's office, and the second was just then.

'He said he's back for good now,' Ruth went on, still staring into her drink, 'but he won't be coming to breakfast this morning.'

This seemed to knock Aoife back into herself.

'Not coming to breakfast? Really? Is he joking? He goes away to who knows where for days, and then doesn't even have the decency to come to breakfast when he gets back?'

'Did he say why?' I asked, hoping to give Aoife a chance to calm down before she said something she might regret in front of Ruth. I used my best 'Prophet's Wife' voice, light and breezy, with all the rough edges sanded down.

Ruth shook her head, and Aoife snorted. I kicked her under the table, a swift smack to her shin with the side of my boot which she managed to ignore.

'Did you ask him where he'd been?' Aoife was leaning towards

Ruth now, determinedly trying to catch her eye. She looked as though she was ready to take Ruth's face in her hands and turn it towards herself.

'No,' Ruth said, 'he didn't seem like he was in the mood for conversation.'

I wondered if that was supposed to be a euphemism. Clearly Aoife did too, because she let out a sharp, cruel laugh and rolled her eyes. I wanted to shoot her a warning glance, but she was too busy staring at Ruth to notice me, and I wasn't brave enough to kick her again.

'Did he say anything at all, other than the thing about breakfast?' I asked Ruth, as softly as I could.

I had barely got the words out of my mouth when she stood up and whipped around to face me.

'No,' she said, 'I already told you that he didn't want to talk.' She was as close to shouting as I'd ever heard her. 'I don't know what you expect me to do.' Her last words caught in her throat, and she practically choked them out.

Aoife and I turned to look at each other at the exact same moment, and she looked as shocked as I felt.

'Hey, hey, calm down,' she said, raising her hands in mock surrender, 'we were only asking.'

Ruth pushed back her chair. 'And I was just answering you! I don't appreciate you both giving me the third degree.'

She stormed towards the door, shoulders high and tense.

'Wait!' I said, 'You've not even had your breakfast!'

But she was already gone.

Never in a million years would I have imagined seeing Ruth like that. She was always so calm, so nice. She didn't argue with anyone, she gave everyone the benefit of the doubt. She was everything I had been pretending to be, but for real. I was so stunned that I'd half forgotten what the argument had been about in the first place. Aoife broke our silence.

'Well,' she said, folding her arms across her chest, 'I'm getting a bit sick of people storming out of this room in a huff.'

'You shouldn't joke, Aoife,' I said, 'I'm a bit worried. That's not like her at all.'

Aoife arched one wry eyebrow in response. 'Yes it is. She's not said a word to me these past few days.'

I thought back. I couldn't vouch for anything that had

happened during my blackout, but since then I supposed that she hadn't spoken to me either. It wasn't as though she was ordinarily very chatty, but she would usually at least ask how I was feeling, if I'd been sleeping well, that kind of thing. She'd looked after me the day before, after my wobble, helped me back to my bed from the bunker and brought me water to drink, but she hadn't really said anything even then. I felt a little bit bad that I hadn't noticed the change in her mood sooner, but I'd been stressed and distracted, and Helen had been needing my help a lot more in the schoolhouse. This was the first time I'd even had the chance to speak with Aoife since our midnight meeting in Elijah's office.

Aoife must have been able to tell that I was worried, because she came and put her hand on my shoulder. I flinched, still not used to her friendliness and definitely not ready to take it for granted.

'Hey,' she said, 'don't get yourself worked up about it. She's just in a bad mood, okay? Maybe she's on her period or something.'

I shrugged.

'You know I'm right. Now,' she sat herself back down at the table, 'let's eat.'

I looked down into the saucepan full of porridge, which had bubbled over and splattered onto the stove top. I sighed and picked the drowned ladle out with two fingers, trying not to scald myself. Maybe Aoife was right about Ruth just being hormonal. It was nicer to believe that than to imagine something being really wrong. I sat down next to her, and we warmed our hands on our bowls of porridge.

'So,' she said, 'he's back.'

I nodded. It was a relief to have him back, just because it meant that I could finally stop dreading it. *He's here now*, I told myself, *and whatever happens, happens. You'll be okay, Deborah. You always are.*

'I wonder when he plans on showing his face.' Aoife's words were bold, but I noticed that she kept her voice low. We both looked to the door, half expecting him to burst in, ears burning, itching for a fight. When he didn't, she went on: 'The most important thing is just to go on as normal. Don't let him think that we're any different to what we were when he left.'

'That's what I had planned to do anyway,' I said. And then, 'but what about Ruth, though?'

'What about her?'

'Well,' I said, glancing back up at the door, 'what should we tell her?' Even as I asked the question, I wondered what on earth I thought there even was to tell.

Aoife looked up from her breakfast. 'What makes you think that we should tell her anything?'

'Look,' I said, setting down my spoon and turning to face her fully, 'if something comes of this, and if we decide to leave—'

'When we leave,' Aoife interrupted.

'If, when, whatever. We can't go without her. It's not like we can just pack up with our kids and bugger off, and say to her and Eli and Abe and Leah and Moses and Abigail, "oh, sorry, you all just have to stay here, enjoy the rest of your lives".'

She was quiet for a second, and I could tell that she was trying to think of something clever to say.

'Leah and Moses and Abigail were born here, they don't know any better. And it's not like we'd be stopping to say goodbye.'

I shook my head in disbelief.

'That's not the point and you know it,' I said. 'All of my kids were born here, that doesn't mean they're safe here. We can't leave them.'

'We can't take them either.' She lowered her voice even further. 'You saw Ruth just there. She won't want to go anywhere with us, and you know she'd tell Elijah. Plus, she might not see an awful lot of the kids, but I can bet that she would come after us with a machete if we took them away from Halcyon, whether we told her beforehand or not.'

Something in my face must have shown that I agreed with her, because she continued with renewed confidence.

'And anyway, where do we draw the line? Do we take all the kids? What about everyone else?'

I thought of Mim, and wondered what would happen to her if we took off.

'We should take whoever wants to go,' I said.

'And the people who want to stay?'

I sighed.

'Those people should stay, obviously.'

'So, we're agreed.' She looked smug. 'We can't take Ruth.'

We were so deep in conversation that we must have missed the sound of footsteps in the corridor, because we both jumped in our seats when the knock came at the kitchen door.

'May I come in?' I recognised Helen's sweetie-pie voice straight away.

I fixed Aoife with what I hoped was a stern stare and hissed: 'We don't know *what* Ruth wants.'

She didn't respond. Instead, she called out to Helen.

'Of course, come on in, make yourself at home.'

She needn't have bothered; the door was already swinging open.

Helen was always put together. I had never seen her with a hair out of place, even after a long day in the schoolhouse, and although I knew there was no iron in the whole of Halcyon, her clothes always seemed to have been freshly pressed. When I first joined Heaven on Earth I had respected Aoife, but I was scared of her too. Helen was different; gentle and motherly in a way Aoife absolutely wasn't, and in a way my own mother hadn't been. When I was seventeen and new to the church, I'd been stunned that people like Helen existed. She'd been like an advert for Elijah's brand of Christianity, giving off a glow of holiness that I had found weird, then pathetic, then inspiring. Now she just made me tired.

'Oh girls,' she squealed, 'John has just told me the good news!'

Her voice was breathless, as if she'd been running.

'Yes,' said Aoife, 'it's really grand to have him back.'

I managed a smile.

'Thanks be to God and our Holy Prophet!' Helen clasped her hands together. 'This is such an exciting time for us all. A really momentous time.'

Momentous seemed like a strange way to put it. Had she missed Elijah that much?

'Why don't you sit yourself down, Helen, and join us for some tea?' Aoife suggested.

'That's very kind of you, Aoife, but no,' she said, 'I actually came to collect Deborah. It's all hands on deck now, getting the children ready. And we're having a bit of a morning.' She shrugged her shoulders gently but didn't say anything more.

'I'd love to join you, but now that Elijah is back I'll need to go to temple before I can come out and help.'

This time it was Helen's turn to be confused.

'But Elijah isn't going to temple this morning. I just left him, he's with John and a couple of the other men by the bunker. He says he has too much to do.'

I glanced at Aoife, waiting for her response.

'Yes, sorry Deborah, I forgot to mention. He did tell me to let you know.'

Although it was clearly a lie, her tone was so casual and her face so bland that I almost believed her.

'Oh,' I said, 'well, I'll just finish up my breakfast and be straight along?'

I hoped that Helen would take the hint and leave me and Aoife alone again, but she shook her head.

'Actually, Deborah, we really do need you now. Like I said, we've had a bit of a trying morning and we could use your help.'

With as polite a smile as I could manage, I left my porridge half eaten and followed Helen to the door. Before crossing into the hall I turned to glance at Aoife, hoping for some sign of solidarity; instead, she was sipping her tea and looking peacefully out of the window as though nothing out of the ordinary had ever happened to her in her entire life.

I didn't have very long to worry about Aoife's lie or our conversation before we reached the schoolhouse. As soon as the door was opened, I could tell that something was wrong. The younger children were sitting silently in a huddle in the classroom, watched by some of the older ones. They looked cowed and red-eyed. It was with relief that I spotted Jonah, Noah, and Susannah amongst them. Helen took my arm and guided me towards the sleeping quarters, but before we entered she stopped to face me. She looked as though I'd just caught her with her hand in the biscuit tin, her eyes darting from side to side in search of an excuse. Eventually, she placed her hand on my arm and spoke:

'Now, it's not as bad as it looks.'

I shook free of her grasp and ducked through the gap in the tarpaulin. Once I was in, it took me what felt like a long time to make sense of the scene in front of me. It reminded me of a painting I had seen on a school trip to an art gallery years before; bodies in motion, illuminated by firelight, surrounding something I couldn't quite make out. I took another step forward. I recognised Danielle, Annie, and Mim as the figures, but what were they doing, and who were they doing it to? They were speaking, but I couldn't tell what they were saying. My heart was pounding fit to burst through my chest, and I could hear the blood pumping through my body, rising like a red tide into my head. But the noise I was hearing wasn't my own blood – it was water sloshing in a metal tub. I took another step closer, but Danielle and Annie's backs were still blocking my view; as far as I could tell they hadn't even noticed I was there. Eventually Mim glanced up and saw me. She looked distraught, like she'd been crying, and her cheeks were as red as a slap. Water or sweat had plastered her hair to her head. I was searching her face for signs of what was happening, when slowly, she looked down.

I followed Mim's eyes as they landed on the boy in the bath. Oliver. He wasn't one of my children, or Aoife's or Ruth's, but I knew him well from my time in the schoolhouse. I knew them all so well. He was a wispy boy, around seven years old, with a skinny body and a large head of shaggy mouse-coloured hair. Lying there, though, he seemed even smaller than usual, and his hair was slick and wet. I felt my body slacken with relief, and for a brief moment I wondered what all the fuss was about, why I'd been called in to help give someone a bath. It was only then that I realised Oliver was shaking, and the front of Mim's dress was drenched with water from trying to hold him still. He looked like a wild rabbit caught in a trap.

Slowly, I became aware of a wet hand tugging on my skirt. At first I thought it was Oliver's, but his arms were drawn tightly across his chest. The tug came again. It was Danielle.

'Deborah!' she was saying, 'are you listening to me?'

Danielle was the same age as me, and we had been close friends when I had first joined Heaven on Earth. I had taught her how to French plait hair, and later I had helped her dress for her wedding. It was strange to see her kneeling like that, looking up at me as though I would know what to do.

'I said we need to warm him up!' she said, rubbing Oliver's arms.

I lowered myself slowly so I was kneeling by the bath, and reached in with my hand. The water was hot, made hotter by the roaring fire, but Oliver's skin felt like ice.

'What's wrong with him?' I tried to keep the fear out of my voice, because I could see Oliver's eyes growing wider with panic as every second passed.

'I just told you,' said Danielle, 'he's too cold. It's like he's got hypothermia or something.'

'We've made the water as hot as we think he can take,' said

Annie, tucking a sodden strand of hair behind her ear, 'and we put mustard powder in it, from the kitchen.'

'Mustard powder?' I asked.

'Yeah,' she said, 'you know, like a mustard bath?'

I shook my head. I didn't know what she meant, but I wasn't about to waste time by asking for a more detailed explanation. Instead, I turned my attention to Oliver.

'How long have you been this cold, Ollie?' I asked, stroking his head. He was shivering so hard that his body was vibrating, and every nerve in my body was telling me to run away from something which I should not be seeing, which I should have no knowledge of.

He opened his mouth, but no words came out. Danielle answered for him.

'We only just got him in the bath before you came in, but he's been shivering for about an hour.'

'An *hour*?' I turned to look at Helen, who was standing against the gap in the tarp with her arms crossed. 'He's been like this for an *hour*?'

The word *hour* came out in a screech, and Helen winced.

'Keep your voice down,' she said, standing in place. 'We had it under control.'

'Clearly not!' Her calmness made me angrier, and it was all I could do not to get up and shake her.

'Well,' she said, 'you're here now, so help.'

I looked back down at Oliver. I could still feel him shivering, and his breathing was becoming laboured and shallow. I racked my brains for anything I had ever seen in a film or a TV programme that might come in handy, but there was nothing. Years of hospital dramas had vanished from my mind, wiped out by panic or just faded by time. There was only one thing I could possibly think to do:

'We need to get Ruth.'

Annie and Danielle shared a look of concern, but neither spoke against me. It wouldn't have mattered either way, though, because at the sound of Ruth's name Mim nodded, shot to her feet, and sprinted out of the barn.

'I had hoped we could keep this a little bit quieter if I'm perfectly honest, Deborah,' said Helen as we watched Mim disappear through the tarp. 'There are much more important things happening in Halcyon at the moment. We don't want to distract people.'

With Ruth safely en route, and Annie and Danielle continuing to soothe and calm the shaking Oliver, I allowed myself to rise to my feet and face Helen. I stood as close to her as I dared. She had been in Heaven on Earth longer than me, and was older than me, but I was Elijah's wife and ready to pull rank if necessary.

'I know exactly what you mean,' I hissed, 'all of the excitement that you were so thrilled about when you came to collect me from the farmhouse.'

She flushed with embarrassment.

'I can't believe it, Helen,' I went on, 'coming in all chatty and *giddy* and poor Ollie lying here frozen half to death. You didn't even think to mention it.'

*He's your son*, I wanted to add, suddenly remembering. But I thought better of it. 'You're making a big fuss out of nothing,' she said, gesturing at Oliver, 'he's absolutely fine. We have more pressing things to worry about, and you of all people should know that.'

At any other time I would have stopped to wonder exactly what pressing things Helen was talking about, and who knows, maybe I should have done then, but all I could think about was Ruth, and when she would arrive.

It didn't take long for them to turn up, and they were both panting; Mim must have told Ruth to run.

'What's the emergency?' she said, zeroing in on Oliver and rolling up her sleeves before any of us had the chance to respond.

Annie and I stepped out of her way, but Danielle stayed by Oliver's side. Ruth took one look at his shivering body and snapped into action. Within minutes we had lifted Oliver out of the hot water and dried him off as gently as we could. It was difficult to reconcile this confident, authoritative version of Ruth with the quiet woman I usually knew, but she seemed to shed her shyness like a snake skin, emerging glistening and assertive – a brighter, more powerful version of her normal self. Under her command, we gathered as many blankets as we could from the other beds. With a firm but gentle hand, she took them from us and swaddled Oliver like an enormous baby.

If time had jarred and jolted before, Ruth's arrival set

everything on a smoother course. Before too long Oliver stopped shaking and had warmed up enough that Annie and Helen were able to go next door and tend to the other children. Ruth was perched on the side of Oliver's bed, taking his pulse. All I could do was stand there at the foot of the bed, watching the scene and allowing the adrenaline to drain from my body.

It was during the newly settled calm that it dawned on me. I turned to Danielle, who was mopping up a puddle of spilled water by the tub.

'Are the others okay?' I asked.

She looked up from what she was doing.

'What others?' she asked, wiping sweat from her head with a damp forearm.

'What do you mean "what others"? The other children! If they were all sleeping in here together, and Oliver managed to catch this cold, should we not get Ruth to check that they're all all right?'

The room was dim, but the glow from the fire was enough that I was able to see Danielle's cheeks colour. She touched her hand to the side of her head, as though looking for a strand of hair to play with. When she couldn't find one, she brought her hand back down to her thigh. It must have been wet, because when she moved it again, I saw that it had left a dark print on her skirt.

Eventually she spoke.

'No,' she said, 'no. They're fine.'

'Well, should we just check? Or have Ruth check? Like I said, if it's happened to Oliver...'

I trailed off in disbelief. Danielle had gone back to mopping up the water with the towel.

'Are you listening to me?' I asked, trying to keep my voice from going too loud.

Danielle sighed. 'I already told you, Deb, the others are fine. It was just Ollie. It just happened to Ollie.'

Whether it was the fact that she couldn't meet my gaze, or the shame in her voice, I couldn't be sure. I was winded by the thought that what had happened to Oliver might have been something more than a horrible fluke. My anger was boiling over again and I wanted to shout, or to take her by the shoulders and shake her and make her tell me what had happened. Maybe I would have, if Ruth hadn't called me over when she did.

'Deborah?' she said, her voice no more than a whisper, 'can you come over here for a minute?'

I looked at Danielle, but she was wringing out the towel into the tub and her head was down. Ruth was waiting for me, still perched on the edge of Oliver's bed. She patted a space next to her, and I sat down gently.

'Everything is all right now,' said Ruth, her voice so low that I could barely hear her, 'and Ollie is stable. But I want you to know you called me just in time.'

I nodded, and she went on:

'I don't know whose idea it was to put him in the bath, but that was the dumbest, most dangerous thing that they could have done. He could have died.'

Ruth wasn't looking at me while she was speaking. Instead, she was staring down at Oliver. He was pale, and the delicate skin under his eyes was tinged with a blueish purple. He looked peaceful though, and still.

'I don't know what happened here,' I said, 'because I got here just before you did. But we need to find out.'

It was only then that she looked at me.

'You need to speak to him as soon as he wakes up.'

# Chapter Twenty

## Aoife

Malcolm's words were echoing around my head as I sat alone in the kitchen after breakfast. Ruth and Deborah were long gone, and I could hear the people of Halcyon at work outside, but I couldn't bring myself to move. I was thinking about how easy he had made everything sound, how confident he had been that I could just leave, that he could help me. I had toyed with the idea of sharing his offer with Deborah, but I wanted to speak to him again first. Now that Elijah was back things would be trickier, and I needed to know Malcolm was serious. Also, I needed to think about what I would say to him, how I would explain myself and Halcyon without driving him away. The last thing I wanted was to find myself speechless again.

I was still in the kitchen, turning the Malcolm situation over in my mind, when the bell rang. The bell at Halcyon was a bit like a fire alarm anywhere else; if you heard it, you were to drop whatever you were doing and head straight to the church. A spirit drill, we called it. I left the dishes I was washing in the sink – not my job, but as a gesture of goodwill to Deborah I'd decided to do them anyway – dried my hands on my dress, and headed for the door. Our front porch was home to an array of boots and coats and I chose some at random, ending up with a pair of poorly repaired wellies that were probably on their way out two winters ago, and a thick navy fleece of Elijah's which smelled of clean sweat and wood-smoke. It was a beautiful sight, stepping outside and seeing the whole of Halcyon converging on the church together. There must have been similar scenes in Biblical times, with people teeming from all directions to hear the word of Christ. It was easy to forget, as I watched the congregation flock into the church, how determined I was to leave.

I managed to make my way through the crowd easily enough and was one of the first to enter the church. Elijah was there already, standing like a statue behind the pulpit. I hurried down the aisle and to my place at the front, secretly glad to notice that neither Ruth nor Deborah were there yet. I looked up at Elijah, hoping that he would have noticed too, but he continued to stare ahead, watching as each person walked through the doors. It was only then that I noticed John was standing at the corner of the raised platform, holding his clipboard. He was also watching the congregation, his eyes darting from person to person. Everyone had been chatting as they walked, but as soon as they entered the church something in the atmosphere turned them quiet. Even as the room filled up, the eerie silence was maintained – the only noise was the sound of footsteps on the concrete, and the scraping and squeaking of chairs as people sat themselves down. Ruth and Deborah were the last to enter, and I couldn't help but feel a pang of jealousy when I saw them walking in together. Deborah looked at me questioningly as they took their seats, but I kept my gaze forward. Now was not the time to appear in cahoots.

Up on stage, Elijah was whispering something to John, who checked his clipboard before beckoning Helen up to the front. She looked around her as she walked self-consciously to where the two men stood. I didn't hear what John asked her, but I saw her cheeks turn red as she replied. I caught the words *not coming* and *ill in bed*. Whatever she'd said had clearly displeased Elijah, who spoke loudly enough that his voice echoed and carried through the silent church.

'I. Don't. Care,' I heard him say to Helen. 'Go and fetch him.'

Helen's face fell, and she looked imploringly to John. Elijah turned to John too.

'I don't have time for this, John, control your wife.'

My throat tightened as I watched John grab Helen's forearm and yank her towards him so hard that her head jerked backwards. He hissed something in her ear before turning to Elijah, who nodded with absent approval when Helen turned and hurried out through the still open doors. Nobody seemed alarmed by what they had just seen, and I felt surprise even though I knew I shouldn't. After all, how many punishments had this barn witnessed? Instead, the congregation waited, soundlessly and for what felt like an age, until she returned.

When she did, even I allowed myself to turn and look. Holding Helen's hand was Oliver, wrapped in a cocoon of blankets which trailed out a little way behind him like a cape. His eyes looked tired, and he was hunched over and shuffling. I remembered when he was born, the April after Ruth and Elijah married and the year before our move. We shared a birthday.

Children were always seated at the back of the church as a rule, so the younger ones could be taken out by the older ones if they became fussy, but Helen walked him all the way down to her place directly behind us. I felt Ruth go to rise, and saw Deborah reach out a hand to keep her in her seat. They were the only ones to move, however – the rest of the congregation remained still and silent, too focused on Elijah to pay attention to the little scene. These weren't heartless people; in usual circumstances, it wouldn't be in anybody's nature to ignore a child who was clearly unwell. They were just captivated. Elijah had been away for days, without having told anyone where he was going, and then there he was, larger than life, back in their midst. Even I was spellbound in spite of myself. Looking up at him sent my heart fluttering in the way it used to when we first met – he buzzed with a familiar pent-up tension which spoke to some deep desire inside me. But it was more than just that. I don't know if I could think of anyone else who could command a room without saying a word. It was an effort to remember that I was no longer supposed to be enthralled by him, that he had made a fool of me, that I wanted to leave him. If he'd looked at me then, if he'd called me to him, I would have been up on my feet without a second thought – a magnet pulling towards its mate.

Eventually, the sermon began. He spoke quietly at first, his voice so low and deep that everyone leaned forward in their seats.

'There are dark times ahead.'

Dark times. Since coming to Halcyon, I'd heard more sermons about 'dark times' than I'd had hot dinners, and the phrase brought me back to my senses somewhat. I forced myself to listen to what he was saying; despite the familiarity of his words, Elijah seemed more tense than usual and I didn't want to miss anything. He paused before speaking again and in the heavy silence I studied his face, searching for a sign of what was to come. I suppose that, with one thing or another, I had not really looked at him properly for a while. Suddenly he seemed old; there were lines on his face that hadn't been there before, and specks of white were showing through the black of his beard. Even his eyes were different – bloodshot and dull, as though he hadn't slept for days. When he started talking again, his words came slowly. At first, I thought he was doing it on purpose, some sort of public-speaking technique to draw us in and hold our interest, but after a while it became very clear – to me at least – that he was trying to keep from slurring his words. Was he really that tired? As he went on, he started to speed up. Words fell from his mouth and tripped over each other, sentences seeping and merging. I wondered, as I sat and listened to him, whether anyone else had noticed the grinding way his lower jaw was moving – surely they must have done?

From what I managed to make out, he was speaking about his recent trip to the outside world. He spoke, in this new, chaotic way, of the downfall of society. 'We must be ready,' he said, over and over again, 'we must be ready.' Every so often he would punctuate his rambling descriptions of rabid locals looking for a safe haven and government officials coming in search of survivors with a strike of the pulpit. I was frightened, but not at the thought of some hypothetical invasion. What scared me was how unhinged Elijah appeared, how detached from reality and his usual self he was. I remembered the night before he disappeared, when he had seemed like that, and I had held him and he had calmed and slept. If we were alone together, I could have taken his face in my hands and looked into his tired eyes and brought him back, but there, with everyone watching, I couldn't have even if I had wanted to. And really, the more he talked, the less I did want to. With every word I felt myself drifting further and further away from him until I no longer cared what he said or what he thought. That glimmer of feeling I'd experienced when I'd seen him again had vanished. The rest of the congregation listened, rapt, apparently unfazed.

It was as though someone had cast a spell over him. Eventually, my husband looked to the side of the stage where John was standing; John's glance must have reminded Elijah where he was, and after a short pause he seemed to pull himself together.

'John,' he said, 'will be supervising bunker checks.' His speech was slow again, but his voice seemed steadier. 'Any stores not in the bunker will need to be moved down there, and we'll need to redouble our work to fill the stockrooms. We're preparing for the worst here everybody, but we've been preparing for a long time.' This time when he paused, I could tell straight away that it was for effect. When he spoke again, he was more coherent. 'When God told me that the time was drawing near, I could never have hoped it would be this near.'

The people of Halcyon, who had been so silent throughout Elijah's sermon, found their voices all at once and the room filled with the rising sounds of fear-tinged excitement. Everyone except for Deborah and Ruth, who sat unmoved and unmoving, staring straight up at Elijah. He, in turn, was surveying the entire room. When he had started his sermon, he had been vacant and hardly there, but the congregation's reaction must have bolstered him, because all of a sudden he seemed more like himself again. He raised a steady hand.

'Quiet.' His voice echoed around the room, and he waited until the final reverberation had faded before continuing. 'We have been preparing for this moment for a long time – some of us for thirteen years. We have nothing to fear. The people who would harm us, now *they* are the ones who should be frightened. *Satan* is the one who should be frightened! We are God's army, and we are ready to fight!'

As soon as the words had left his mouth, I was deafened by a loud roar. For a second, I thought Elijah must have been right, and that something of Biblical proportions was about to happen – a heavenly host descending from the clouds, or a thunderstorm indicating the start of a second flood. None of those possibilities frightened me as much as the reality, though, which was that the entire room had heard Elijah's battle cry and erupted into a wild cheer. It worried me that they could sit through such an incoherent speech and still place their faith so unwaveringly in the person who had given it. But if I was so confused and infuriated by their reaction, why did I feel so sad not to be cheering with them? I felt left out, as though I had missed the punchline of a joke that everyone else had understood, but it was as if that feeling were multiplied by a thousand. I put my hands together and tried to drown out my grief with applause. One of the babies at the back started to cry, but the noise did not stop. Instead it grew louder, and eventually the baby's wail became indistinguishable from the congregation's wild cheer. Someone started to stamp their feet, and soon the whooping and applause was joined by the smack of hard-soled boots against concrete. Someone else gave a loud, high whistle. The barn rattled and shook, and the air was thick with sound.

Elijah watched from above as the congregation whipped itself into a frenzy, and when sufficient time passed, he raised his hand once again. This time he did not even have to speak. The crowd muted instantly at his sign; even the crying baby had given up its tears. He surveyed the panting crowd with pleasure.

'In order to strengthen our army,' he said, his voice clear and strong and familiar, 'I will be taking our sister Jemima as my new wife. God has spoken.'

I felt the room rise around me as the noise erupted again. This time, I couldn't bring myself to join in the cheer. Instead I remained in my seat, numb and dazed, until the congregation fell into an exhausted silence. John took to the stage to give out new orders for the day, but even though I had known this was coming I was too distracted to hear a word. My heart was crashing against my chest, not even beating any more, but clenching like a great raging fist. I could feel it reverberating through my body until even my brain started to throb. When John finally finished and the congregation began to file out, I rose, shaking and sick, to follow behind them. My body was so numb to everything except its own movement that I could barely even feel my feet on the ground. I became vaguely aware of a hand tapping on my shoulder, the sensation permeating my numbness like a figure emerging through the mist. Turning, I was surprised to see John, his arm still outstretched, his mouth half open.

'Can I have a quick word?' he asked.

I scanned the room. Ruth and Deborah were already at the door, and Elijah could have been anywhere. I nodded, confused, and together we walked back to my usual seat. He gestured for me to sit down. When the final person had left the church and the door was pulled closed, he gave an awkward cough. I studied his face. Pale stubble was growing on his chin, and I wondered when he had last shaved. Usually he was so clean-cut, the only similarity I had ever been able to observe between him and Helen, other than their shared devotion to the church. Or in John's case, I supposed, devotion to Elijah. He had helped Elijah start up Heaven on Earth back in the city, when Elijah decided that the preacher at their old Methodist church wasn't a 'true Christian'. When Elijah and I had met, they were still working to convert some members of the old congregation. I had always thought of John as something of a third wheel, an irritating and intense figure hovering on the periphery of mine and Elijah's relationship. And John made no secret of the fact that he felt the same way about me.

'Elijah has asked me to speak to you today about something a little...' he paused, 'sensitive.'

At any other time those words would have drawn out some reaction from me, but as it was I couldn't think of anything that he could say to me that was more shocking, or indeed more sensitive, than Elijah's announcement had been. John was not one to be deterred by a silent conversation partner, though, and he went on.

'I don't intend to be insensitive here, Aoife, but I think that it would be best, given the circumstances, to be as forthright as possible.'

I sighed. I was desperate to get back to my office, where I could sit alone and quietly untangle my thoughts.

'Can you just get on with it, please? I have work to do.'

My voice sounded unfamiliar – flat and quiet. I looked down at my lap, embarrassed to sound so weak in front of John.

'Elijah is worried that you have been putting too much strain on yourself lately.'

'Strain?' I asked.

'That you've been spending too much time doing work that isn't necessarily appropriate for a woman of your station in the community, or, to be quite frank, Aoife, a woman at all. He believes that the pressure on your brain has had an influence on, well... on other things.'

'Excuse me?'

'I'm not sure how to put this delicately, so I'll just say it. Elijah is concerned that your work in the office has led to your current inability to conceive. He wanted me to remind you that he's encouraged you to give up your work in the office before, but he says he wants to do everything he can to get things right. He hopes that it won't be too late.'

I could see John's mouth moving, and hear the words which

were coming out, but my head was filled with a swirling fog and I couldn't decipher his meaning. The confusion must have shown in my face, because he coughed again before clarifying.

'Elijah has decided that it would be best for you if you were to give up your role in the office.'

For the second time that morning, I felt the floor disappear from beneath my feet. I forced myself to look John right in the eye. I had hoped that he would at least have the decency to pretend to feel ashamed or awkward, but there was a barely disguised glee hiding behind his façade of formality.

'Don't worry,' he said, 'you won't be idle. It will be all hands on deck getting things ready for the bunker. I was speaking to Jess earlier, and she's offered to teach you how to use the loom. The deepest circle of hell is ice cold after all; we'll want to be wrapped up warm when it ascends to Earth.'

He smiled.

My head was swimming, but I knew that I had to say something. I pulled myself out of the depths and took a deep breath.

'I appreciate your concern...'

'Elijah's concern.'

'I appreciate Elijah's concern,' I said, 'but my work in the office is very important. I can't just *stop*.'

'Well, Aoife, I'm afraid you have no choice. And I'm sorry to burst your bubble, but the important work at the moment is the work that helps us prepare for the End times. *Not* files and accounts. I'm sure you agree.'

I no longer cared about the accounts or the files. The missing thousands, once an obsession, a charm which I had believed had the ability to bring Elijah back to me if I could recover it, meant nothing. But the removal of my very last ounce of power hit me hard. The final nail had been hammered into the coffin of my life as I'd known it. The room was starting to get chilly in its near emptiness, and I didn't trust myself not to shiver. I hoped that the more amenable I was, the sooner he would let me go. It wasn't usually in my nature to go down without a fight, but I wasn't stupid and knew how to pick my battles when I needed to. Also, I was remembering the way Helen's head had snapped backwards when he had pulled her towards him earlier. I couldn't seem to shake the thought.

'Very good.' He looked surprised, but relieved. 'Very good.

Jess is with the rest of the ladies in the community centre. You can head over there now. *Straight* there mind, Aoife, no detours.'

John clapped his hands together as he rose to stand and looked at me meaningfully. I stood up too, but felt myself wobble as I understood his last words. Had he been watching me take my walks? Did he know I'd been talking to Malcolm? Did *Elijah* know? Oh God. The thought made me feel sick. He gestured for me to walk out ahead, and I made my way outside on shaking legs.

I could see Elijah standing with a small group of men outside one of the outbuildings. John must have seen them too, because as soon as the door was locked he hurried across to them without even a backward glance. I watched until they disappeared into the outbuilding and then I took my chance. If John was on to me, I might not have another opportunity to speak to Malcolm. Elijah's speech had inspired a flurry of activity in the colonists, and they were so preoccupied with their work that nobody seemed to notice as I snuck away from the centre of Halcyon. Still, I quickened my pace as I followed the familiar route around the fence.

To my relief, I saw Malcolm almost straight away. I'd left so unceremoniously the day before that part of me had been worried he might not come back. He gave a languid wave, and I forced myself to smile back. As I got closer, I saw his expression change from one of happiness to one of concern. He gave a big, exaggerated shrug and mouthed *what's wrong?* I shrugged back and hoped that he was still too far away to see the corners of my mouth tremble.

When I reached the fence he asked me again, but this time there was no exaggeration, no hint of humour in his face.

'Aoife! What's the matter? What's happened?'

I couldn't hold it in any longer. He had barely got the words out before I burst into tears; the sort of huge, gulping sobs that you might expect from a toddler who had just finished throwing a tantrum.

*Go on then, cry.*

'Hey, hey,' he said, pressing his gloved hands against the chain link of the fence, 'take a breath. It's okay. Take a second.'

The way he spoke made me wonder whether he had children. For all of our conversations, I had never even thought to ask him. I couldn't even remember if I had told him about my own children, and the thought made me cry even harder.

'I'm so sorry,' I sobbed, wiping my eyes and nose on the sleeve of my coat, 'I'm so embarrassed. Just ignore me, I'm being ridiculous.'

'You've nothing to be embarrassed about,' he said, 'please don't be sorry. Do you want to talk about it?'

And then I did. I talked and I talked, and I told him everything. I told him about Ruth and Deborah and Elijah, and about Halcyon. I told him about Mim, and losing my job in the office, and the secret computer, and about Jess and her loom, and then about Mim again, and all the time he stood there and listened, his face completely expressionless. *He'll hate you*, came the voice as my words tumbled out, *he'll judge you. He won't understand. Nobody from out there could ever understand you.*

When he was sure that I was finished, he exhaled deeply through his mouth.

'Well then.'

# Chapter Twenty-One

## Ruth

I had tried not to look at Elijah while he preached, and it was like trying not to look at the sun during an eclipse. I'd managed to keep my eyes off of him, but I could still hear him, his voice slurring and halting like it had been the night before. Instead, I concentrated on my hands, clasped in my lap with my thumbs crossed over each other like I was praying. We'd been taught to sit like that as kids, my sisters and me. I had enjoyed looking down at my neat little hands when I was younger, liking how tidy they looked, folded up like a sweater. When I held my hands like that it made my elbows tuck into my sides, so that all of me felt compact and dainty. And good. Sitting in Halcyon, I was thirty years and thousands of miles away from the little girl I'd been when I was first taught to sit that way, but there I was, still doing it. Still being good. I thought of what Elijah had said the night before, about how I was his favourite. Wasn't that all I'd ever wanted to hear? Not because I was competitive, or because I wanted to be better than my sister wives; I just wanted to know I was pleasing him. So why had it made me feel so awful? As my mind ticked over, Elijah's words dripped into my brain in a slow, steady stream: on, and on, and on. I kept my hands clasped through his announcement, through the cheering, until we were dismissed.

Time had lost all meaning during the spirit drill, as it always did, and when it was time to leave I felt drained and disorientated. The sky above was white, and there was no sun to tell me the time of day. From the grumbling in my stomach I guessed that it might be around lunch-time, although I hadn't eaten breakfast so I couldn't be sure. Either way, I had no interest in returning to the farmhouse where I imagined Aoife and Deborah were now gathered, digesting Elijah's news together over steaming mugs of tea. I decided that the best thing to do would be to return to the cowshed where I could be out of the way, surrounded by creatures who were simple and sweet, and who looked forward to my arrival every day. Russell was there too, and it would give me the chance to check on her. I had decided to remove the pups and Russell from the outbuilding where Mim and I had hidden them. It was too risky for me to sneak in and out of there, and the prospect of getting caught had made me tense and jumpy. The cows seemed to enjoy their company, I reasoned, and it wasn't like anyone other than me spent much time in that barn anyway.

As soon as I was safely inside, I fell to my knees. Prayer had been my comfort and my joy for so many years. My lowest lows and my highest highs had been punctuated by conversations with God, but at that moment there was nothing for me to say. It was God who had told Elijah that he had to marry Mim. And if it wasn't? I opened my eyes. Prayer was pointless either way. I remembered Elijah's words, how lucid they had been after his drunken whispers: 'now I know what it really feels like to be God.' They had shaken me the night before, but kneeling there on the floor of the barn they crushed me like a hand under a steel-capped boot. I had no prayers but was too hopeless to move, so I just stayed there, hunched over on the freezing, hay-strewn floor, hoping against hope that no one would come in.

It was Russell who brought me back to reality. She had left her pups and tapped her way along to where I was kneeling. When she reached me, she stuck her inquisitive face into mine, her nose cold and wet against my cheek. I don't know how long I had spent down there, but when I rose my joints were stiff and achy. It felt self-indulgent to stretch, though, so I didn't. Instead, I shuffled over to check on the pups, who were sleeping peacefully in a nest of towels. A lump formed in my throat at the sight of them. I could only hope that Elijah would be too distracted to remember Russell and his plans for her litter. There was so much else for him to focus on – his wedding, the End. I winced. He had sounded so sure about the End during the spirit drill, and everyone had been so excited about it. I would have been too, if the announcement had come a month or a week, or even a few days before. I had been waiting for the End for years; I had literally dreamed of it on the rare occasions I slept long enough to dream. And now it was apparently just around the corner, and I felt nothing.

A figure appeared silhouetted in the doorway. It stood there a second before it spoke.

'Hi.'

I recognised the voice immediately, although I wished I hadn't. Russell must have recognised it too, because she waddled across to where the figure was standing, her stubby tail wagging in greeting.

'What is it, Mim?'

Even I could hear the dullness in my voice, but it didn't seem to faze her.

'Please may I come in for a minute?'

Mim's voice was so soft that I could hardly hear her from where I was standing. The fact of it annoyed me, and I wanted her to leave. Instead, I nodded.

'Fine,' I said, 'come on in.'

She walked slowly, running her hand along the hard metal edge of the cows' trough, and stopped a little way away from me. In the half-light of the barn she looked paler than normal, drawn and tired.

'Can I talk to you?'

With a sigh, I gestured to my milking stool. Mim perched herself down, but I remained on my feet, arms folded.

'What's the problem?' I asked. 'I'm a bit busy here.'

'Of course. I won't keep you,' she said. After a long pause, during which Mim stared at her hands, she spoke again, 'I suppose I just wanted to speak to someone. I just feel a bit…' she mimed freezing up.

'Oh?' I said.

'Yeah.'

We sat in awkward silence again. I could tell that Mim was waiting for me to say something encouraging but everything about her was frustrating to me, from her simpering voice to the way she was picking at her cuticles, and I didn't feel like making things easier for her. I was done making things easy for people.

'It's just,' she went on, 'you're the only person I feel like I can really talk to.'

This surprised me.

'Really?'

'Yes,' she said, 'well, it's pretty hard to talk in the schoolhouse.

And the other women are always so busy.' She looked worried for a moment before continuing, 'Not that I mean to say that I don't think you're busy or anything, but you always seem to have time to talk to me. And you're always nice.'

I flinched.

'What was it you wanted to talk about?' I asked, even though I was certain that I already knew the answer.

'Well,' she said, 'you were there today, at the spirit drill. You heard what he said.'

I gave a slow nod, guarding myself against what she might say next.

'I've known it was going to happen for a while, I mean, I knew we were getting married soon, but this just seems so sudden. And I just feel like I don't really know anything. About being married.' Mim's face turned pink as she spoke; even the tips of her ears had coloured.

I could feel my body tensing up, and my jaw hurt from clenching. I sensed her staring up at me expectantly, but instead of looking her in the eye I turned around and busied myself with the cows. When I spoke, I spoke to them, not her.

'Look,' I said, 'I get it. But now is just... not a good time. I have a lot to do. I have to take the cows out to pasture.'

I heard her rise to her feet.

'That's all right,' said Mim, 'I can walk with you, I don't mind.'

'Well, I mind,' I said, turning to face her. I was surprised by the anger in my voice. 'I mind. Now is not a good time, Jemima.'

She seemed to crumple right before my eyes, and for a second I thought that she might cry. Instead, she gave a single nod and scurried out the way she had come. When I was sure she had gone, I sat myself down on the newly vacated milking stool. It was still warm, which made me uncomfortable, and I leaned forward and rested my head in my hands. Mim in general made me feel uncomfortable. I couldn't work her out. She seemed to fluctuate between deferential and conspiratorial, which made it difficult to figure out what it was she wanted from me. Flightiness – that's what it was. I wondered what Elijah saw in her. I wasn't so naïve as to believe any of Elijah's marriages, myself included, had been solely love matches. Or else, if they were, it was our usefulness to the cause that had formed part of his attraction to Aoife, Deborah, and me. We each had our strengths. Something we could offer.

I was nothing special as a person, but I had my nurses' training and I was good at pacifying him. Mim, well, there was nothing to her. She was just a teenager. That was it. *Of course* that was it. I don't know why it took me so long to work it out. She was young and pretty and biddable. He wanted someone who he could boss around, and someone to... I winced. I thought of Mim, with her two long plaits and her big doe eyes. She had come to me thinking that I was her friend, and all I'd done was send her away.

I pulled myself up from where I was sitting. The cold was still lingering in my bones and joints, and I ached with every movement. I would have taken the physical discomfort any day, though, over the shame. I caught a glimpse of my reflection in the metallic cladding of the big milk silo which sat in the corner of the barn; it was warped and flat. *Seems about right*, I thought, closing my eyes and screwing up my face in pure distaste at myself. In my head, I ran through every curse word that I knew before putting on my coat and leaving the barn in search of Mim.

# Chapter Twenty-Two

## Deborah

After the spirit drill, I felt like I had been hit by a bus. My brain was too fried from trying to follow Elijah's manic, rambling sermon to even begin to digest what he'd just said, and all I could think of was how much I needed my bed. The farmhouse, which in reality was just across the yard, felt cruelly distant, and when I finally reached my room I barely managed to pull my boots off before burrowing myself under the covers. The sheets were so stiff with cold that I was frightened to move once I got in, just in case a glimmer of bare skin became exposed to the chill. I could feel my nose running, but I was too frozen and exhausted to raise my hand and stop the flow. Instead, I felt the warm trickle down my cheek and closed my eyes.

I don't know how long I slept for, but it couldn't have been too long because when I woke up I could still see daylight coming through the net curtains in my window and hear the bustle of people outside. It took me a minute to remember exactly where I was, and why, and for a delicious moment I stretched my sore muscles, relishing the warmth now trapped inside my blankets in a state of blissful ignorance. The sound of Helen's voice passing outside my window was what brought me back to my senses again and I swung myself out of bed, my stockinged feet landing softly on the rag rug which covered the hard, chilly floorboards. The room spun, but my mind and purpose were as focused as the point of a knife and I was out of the house faster than it would have usually taken me to get my shoes on.

For the second time that day, I left the farmhouse for the schoolhouse. The cold bit and pinched at my flesh, burrowing through the loose knit of my jumper and slipping shamelessly up my skirt. I regretted not taking my coat the second I was out of the door, but I was only heading across the yard and I didn't plan to be outside for long. With everything that had happened with Ollie that morning, and Elijah's crazed sermon at the spirit drill, I knew that was where I needed to be. Even if all I could do was see my kids.

Annie was standing at the door of the barn, looking nervously around and clutching a heavy shawl about herself. She didn't see me until I was almost on top of her, and when she did she jumped and blushed.

'Oh, hi Deborah,' she said, 'what are you doing here?'

I couldn't tell if she was kidding. Annie had never been much of a joker, but I couldn't think of another explanation. Where else would I be?

'Erm, I'm just here for work,' I said, struggling to keep my tone light, 'you know, like I am every day?'

I heard my voice lift at the end of the sentence, so it sounded like I was asking her a question. Elijah hated it when I did that – he said it made me sound simple.

She shook her head, unable to meet my eye.

'I'm sorry, Deborah,' she said, 'I was sure someone would have told you. John made it sound as though he'd already spoken to you.'

'About what?' I asked, my heart beginning to flutter in my chest.

'They told me not to let you in here any more.'

Annie's voice shook a little, but her face was serious. I knew that I'd have to choose my next move carefully. Talking to people in Halcyon was like playing chess, or at least what I imagined playing chess would be like. Thinking four steps ahead of yourself: *if I say this, they'll think that, so they'll say... but then they'll actually... and I'll end up...* The trick was to always be very sweet to everyone at all times, so they would give you the benefit of the doubt if you ever found yourself in a situation where it would be useful for someone to give you the benefit of the doubt. It was an exhausting way to live, but it usually worked.

'Look, Annie,' I said in my nicest voice, 'I don't know what's going on here, but I think there must have been some kind of misunderstanding. I'm just here to do my job, just like you, just like I always do.'

'I…' she started to speak again, but I reached out my hand and touched her arm – a gentle reminder that I outranked her.

'I know that you're just doing as you're told, which is great, it's what I'm doing too.' I paused for a second, plotting my next move. 'No one has told me not to turn up to work duty. If I wasn't meant to be here today, don't you think Elijah would have said something to me himself?'

Annie's face started to soften, and I could tell she was thinking about what I had said. I clutched my belly and shivered in an attempt to hurry her along. Just as I thought she was about to step to one side and let me in, though, she raised her hand and waved at someone behind me. I turned to see John coming towards us.

'Sorry about this, Sister,' he said to Annie, who looked as relieved as I had ever seen anybody look. 'I'll take it from here.'

Annie nodded her thanks and disappeared into the schoolhouse, leaving me standing in the cold with John. As soon as she was safely inside, John stepped across and blocked the door with his body. He wasn't a tall man, but he was taller than me, and suddenly I was a kid again, standing in front of a teacher and getting ready to be told off. My shoulders squared automatically. It was the wrong move for John, who liked his women timid and submissive, but it was too late to change my tactic. I had committed, so I would just have to hope for the best.

'Can you please tell me what's going on here?' I asked, my voice as calm as I could make it, 'I just want to go to work?'

Another questioning lift at the end, but never mind. John already thought I was an idiot.

He raised his eyebrows; instead of being fazed, he looked mildly entertained. Was he humouring me? He reached out to take my arm, and I jerked away in shock. Men in Halcyon did not touch women who were not their wives. John knew that.

'Deborah!' he said, in exaggerated surprise, 'I'm not going to hurt you. I just think it would be a good idea to talk about this inside. You look half frozen.'

He was right; I was shivering, and the tips of my fingers were turning blue.

'Fine,' I said, 'let's go inside, and you can explain to me why I'm suddenly not allowed to see the children. Or do my job.'

He smiled in the big, wide way Elijah sometimes did when he was preaching. I wondered if he had been taking lessons. This time when he reached for my arm, I let him take it, surprised by just how strange it felt to be held by someone different. His grip was less confident than Elijah's; he seemed to be putting more effort into clinging with his fingers, while Elijah would use his whole hand. His hand was smaller too, and he was shorter. I kept my own arm limp and did my best to avoid touching any more of John than I had to, like a loyal wife, and together we walked back towards the farmhouse. When I had said 'inside', I'd meant the schoolhouse, but I should have known better. I forced myself to take a breath and begin again. I knew that if I was to get anywhere with John, I would have to restart the submissive act. The walk was slower than I would have liked, but it gave me the chance to look around at the people of Halcyon. Hardly anyone was in the courtyard – lots of people seemed to be at the bunker already, their voices carrying on the wind, and the people who were around paid us no attention at all. I watched Alfie hauling a box of crockery from the community barn out in the direction of the bunker, with Lois following closely behind holding a laundry bag. I wanted to wave at them both with my free hand – 'hey, Alfie, Lois, look what this crazy guy is doing! Call Elijah!' They probably wouldn't have looked up even if I had shouted. The people of Halcyon were all very good at ignoring things they weren't meant to be seeing. Myself included.

When we reached the farmhouse, John pushed the door and it swung open with a creak. He waited until I had wiped my boots on the doormat and was safely blocked into the porch before walking in himself and closing the door firmly behind him. I was surprised when we passed the door to the kitchen, and instead continued straight down the hall. We stopped outside Aoife's office. She was protective of the space and I had only ever been in there a couple of times before. John motioned for me to enter. *Aoife's not going to be happy when she hears about this*, I thought. Still, I didn't say anything.

The light in the room was dim, so I didn't notice anything unusual at first. There was electricity set up in there, but either John didn't know about it or he had decided to save on power. I watched as he struck a match. For a moment, his face was illuminated by the raw, yellow glow of the flame. Somehow that made the room seem even darker, and for the first time that day I worried that I might be in danger. My hands slipped down to my belly, and I wondered whether I would be able to get to the door before John if it came down to it. I was busy plotting possible escape routes when the room was suddenly bathed in light. John had used the match to light a paraffin lamp and was looking at me expectantly. I glanced around the room; it didn't take me long to guess what he was waiting for me to notice.

'Where's all Aoife's stuff gone?' I asked.

All evidence that the room had once been an office had vanished. The desk had been replaced by a roughly crafted double bed, and the lamp itself was resting on a bedside cabinet. The Bible scenes which Aoife was so pleased with had been taken down, and the whitewashed walls stood bare and cold, even in the paraffin glow.

'Things are going to start changing around here,' said John as he sat down on the bed. 'For starters, this isn't Aoife's office any more. It's going to be her bedroom from now on, and we're giving Mim Aoife's old one. Seems a shame for that barren witch to get the best room in the house.'

I should have felt enraged on Aoife's behalf, but I was too focussed now on the potential danger of the situation I had let myself into to spare a thought for her potentially hurt feelings. John was breaking one rule after another; he had taken my arm, brought me into a room alone and unchaperoned, and there he was insulting one of the Prophet's wives. What else was he capable of? There was a large space next to him on the bed, and he patted the quilt invitingly. I stepped backwards, so I was as far away from him as I could be while staying in the room. Every fibre of my body was screaming for me to turn and leave, but I fought the urge. *Stay calm. Let's hear what else he has to say.* I think I really believed that if I went along with whatever power-play John was running, we would be able to walk out of the farmhouse and back to the schoolhouse, where everything would miraculously return to normal.

He shrugged, as if to say *fair enough*, and continued.

'Elijah thinks, and I agree, that you wives have been kept on too long a leash. It's time to rein you in.'

'I don't understand.'

John shook his head.

'Don't play dumb please, Deborah. It's embarrassing for us both. You couldn't have thought you would be able to keep your position in the schoolhouse indefinitely. Helen has told me that you favour your own children. All of the other women who work there can maintain the appropriate boundaries but apparently you can't.'

*Bloody Helen.*

'Where's Elijah?' I asked. 'Why isn't he telling me all of this himself?'

'*Where's Elijah? I want to speak to Elijah,*' he mimicked, his voice a high and whiny copy of my own. 'When will you girls realise that Elijah has more important things to do than worry about you? You're not the centre of his world, Deborah. You're not even a *third*, not even a *quarter* of his world. He's our most Holy Prophet. The end is nigh!' He stood up then, apparently too angry to stay seated. I wondered if he was going to hit me. Instead he sighed a heavy, frustrated sigh and shook his head again. 'You really are irredeemably fucking stupid, aren't you?'

My mouth dropped open in shock. I'd known John since I was a seventeen-year-old convert to the church, and had never heard anything remotely close to a swear word pass his tight little lips. But it had come out so easily, as natural as could be. He was right - I was stupid. Stupid to have ever believed that there wasn't one rule for us and one for the pair of them.

John must have realised that he had crossed a line because he stepped towards me and gave me a gentle pat on the shoulder. I winced, but he didn't laugh.

'Look,' he said, his voice stern but not unkind, 'we are at the very end of times. Not even just the final days. We're in the final hours.'

I nodded, gulping back my urge to scream in his face.

'And you,' he said, placing his hand on my belly, 'are carrying a very precious cargo. We can't have you wearing yourself out with preparations like everyone else. You need to rest. The children are being well taken care of.'

I thought of Ollie, shivering, too cold and frightened to even cry. I still didn't know what exactly had happened to him, but I was familiar enough with the punishments inflicted on rule-breaking adults that I feared I could guess. It was strange to think that I'd been by his side in the schoolhouse just a couple of hours before – it felt like a lifetime ago. I nodded again.

'Good,' he said, 'good. I think it would be best for you to stay in the farmhouse for now, and we can find something nice and stress-free for you to do. Knitting, or something. It'll help you take your mind off things, and I know how keen you are to be of use to everyone.'

I walked with John to the front door and watched from the porch as he locked it behind him. Once he was safely out of sight, I moved as quickly as I could to the other door at the other side of the house – the one that led to the back garden and the outhouse. Aoife would be out there somewhere, and I wanted to find her and talk to her. But even as I was walking, I realised that the whole thing was pointless. I knew that the door would be locked tight, but I tried the handle anyway. Sure enough, it didn't even budge.

When I pushed open the kitchen door, three heads turned to greet me. Aoife, Ruth, and – I did a double take – Mim. A conference of wives. Was that right? Was there even a collective noun for a group of wives, or had no one ever thought to come up with one? Not that Mim was a wife yet, I reminded myself, although it wouldn't be long.

It wasn't until Aoife stood up that I finally snapped back to reality.

'Ah, Deborah! Looks like we've got the full complement.'

I closed the door and took my seat amongst my sisters.

# Chapter Twenty-Three

## Aoife

I had returned from my walk to find Jemima sitting alone at the kitchen table. She must have been hoping for Deborah, or even Ruth, because when she looked up and saw me standing in the doorway she burst into tears. I didn't know Jemima – Mim – particularly well. For a long time she had just been another one of Halcyon's multitude of young people. But still, part of me was hurt to see her react that way to my presence. Who could blame her, though? She had obviously come looking for sympathy and she had been met by the person she considered to be Elijah's right-hand woman. How strange of me, how out of character, to be so offended by Mim's fear when I had spent years carefully cultivating a persona which inspired just that. And yet I was relieved to feel it. I was embarrassed and resentful and hurt, and I took that to be a good thing – a sign that I might be a nice girl after all.

*Since when have you cared about being nice?* chimed the voice in my head. It was Elijah's voice, I realised. It always had been. I blocked it out and pulled up a chair next to Mim, whose sobs were slowly becoming less hysterical. I placed a tentative hand on her back, and she turned to face me. She existed in my head as a small, faceless teenager with limp hair and no distinguishing features, so when I pictured her with Elijah, that's what I saw. In reality, she was quite pretty in a bird-like sort of way, like a sharper, more petite version of Deborah. Or maybe even, and my heart skipped a beat when I saw it, a fairer, younger *me*. I wondered if I should be flattered. Her hair was mousy – I'd been right about that – and had been twisted into two long plaits which hung on either side of her face down to her waist. There was a sprinkling of red spots across her chin, something which endeared me to her even more. At her age, I had suffered with the most appalling acne and as an adult was left with pits and scars on my forehead and cheeks. The only blemishes on Mim's cheeks were the heavy red blotches which had come from crying, and a fine dusting of freckles, which I didn't really count as flaws. Grainne had had freckles.

I had thought that Mim would pull away from my attempt to comfort her, but she leaned into me, resting her sodden face in the crevice between my neck and shoulder. With my free hand I touched my own face. The cold Highland air must have dried any tears my sleeve had missed, but I worried that my eyes or cheeks would somehow give me away. I longed more than ever for a mirror. I was ready to be nice, but I wasn't ready to be weak, and the thought of anyone catching me red-eyed like Mim sent my heart into a spasm. On some kind of instinct, I clutched her closer, and the tears picked up again.

'I'm so sorry, Aoife,' she gasped between sobs, 'please don't tell on me.'

I raised my eyebrows in surprise, although Mim's face was still burrowed against my neck and there was no one else around to see. It seemed like such a childish thing to say, although she could have been no older than fifteen or sixteen. I flinched and hoped to God that she was at least sixteen, before shooing the thought into the back of my mind to be dealt with later.

'Shh,' I said, 'it's all right. No one is going to tell on you.'

I tried to mimic the tone that Malcolm had used with me less than half an hour before and hoped that I sounded tender and comforting. We stayed like that long enough for my arm to start aching, but I didn't want to pull away. Instead, I tried to focus my attention on Mim. Looking at the top of her head made me wonder what was going on inside her mind in that moment, a thought experiment which was surprisingly difficult after such a long time devoted to trying not to think too deeply about such things. I had always acted on the assumption that life would be much more difficult if I allowed myself to consider the feelings of others, but it began to dawn on me that life had been pretty difficult anyway.

When I had opened up to Malcolm, I was surprised to find myself embarrassed to tell him certain things. I had known that some parts of my confession would be difficult, but I felt more shame than I'd expected about aspects of our lives that I had considered normal. Actions that had felt appropriate and ordinary became strange and cruel when relayed to someone who was not a part of Heaven on Earth. It was as though I had spent the last twelve years of my life in a parallel world and speaking to Malcolm had broken the spell which had kept me there. Suddenly my universe had shifted, and I was able to look into myself from the outside. I held Mim closer and rested my cheek against her hair.

'It's okay if you don't want to get married.'

I don't know why I said it. I suppose everything was so up in the air, and I still felt slightly lightheaded and vulnerable after my own crying jag. The kitchen had transformed into a sort of liminal space where everything mattered, so nothing mattered, and I could say anything at all. Mim twisted herself out from my embrace and fixed me with a doubtful look. Her eyes were even redder than before, and her pale lashes were wet with tears. With a straight face I met her gaze.

'I have to.'

'But do you *want* to?'

'It doesn't matter what I want. It's what God wants, and I need to do what God wants me to do.'

She was looking down at the tabletop by then, and I moved my head in an attempt to meet her eyes again.

'I didn't ask what you think God wants,' I said, 'I asked what you want.'

When she didn't respond, I worried that my voice had sounded too stern and had frightened her. It wasn't until I heard the uncertainty in her eventual reply that I realised she had merely been thinking, and that she had been quiet for so long because nobody had thought to ask her what she wanted before. I wondered if even Elijah had, or if she had just been informed one day that she would be getting married in the same way that you might tell a child that it was time for bed.

'I suppose I never really thought about it.'

'Well,' I said, 'you can't be all that thrilled about the whole thing if you've come in here crying.'

She gave a damp-sounding snort of laughter before bursting into tears again.

'Oh, hush now,' I rubbed her back gently, 'please don't cry

again. There's been enough crying for one day. I already told you that it's all right if you don't want to get married right now. How old are you, anyway?'

'Sixteen,' she replied, 'so I'm old enough.'

It was my turn to snort then. If you'd asked me earlier that day, I would have agreed that Mim was certainly old enough for marriage, just not to my husband, but after talking to Malcolm the mere thought of it was absurd.

'You know,' I said, lowering my voice, 'when I was your age I was still at school. I had a job at the local shop, stocking shelves.'

She gave a sniff and wiped her red nose on the sleeve of her cardigan. It left a slick line of wetness on the dirty white wool. Usually that sort of thing would have turned my stomach, but instead it just made me feel unbearably sad.

'Really?' she asked.

'Yes,' I said, 'I wasn't ready for marriage then, and I don't think that you're ready for it now.'

She nodded in agreement for the briefest moment before shaking her head again.

'But what am I supposed to do? I don't want to make Elijah or God angry.'

I hated myself then. I had tried to be the kind voice of reason, but all I had done was raise her hopes. What was she supposed to do? She could hardly say no. God was the ultimate authority in Halcyon, and Elijah was His man on the ground, His Holy Prophet. Elijah's word was law, and I couldn't see a refusal of marriage ending well for anyone involved. But at the same time, I couldn't bring myself to look at Mim's sad little face and do nothing, knowing what I did. Only one solution came to mind.

'Deborah and I have been thinking.' I paused then, considering my words. Mim was upset in that moment, but that didn't mean that she wouldn't turn around and grass us up to Elijah before the day was done. Before I could decide whether or not it would be a good idea to continue, Mim spoke.

'I think I know what about,' she said, 'or at least, I can only think of one way out of it. But it's a sin, and anyway I'm too scared.'

I decided to hedge my bets.

'What were you thinking of doing, Mim?'

'Well,' she took a deep breath in, 'there are lots of sharp things in the sheds. And ropes.'

'Good grief, Mim! You were going to kill him?'

Mim's eyes widened in shock, and her face turned pink.

'No! No! I was thinking I could maybe kill me. Like Judas. But I know it's a sin.' She looked at me expectantly. 'Isn't that what you and Deborah were thinking about?'

I gripped her hands tightly in mine while waiting for my words to be returned to me. My throat was tight, a pair of invisible hands around my neck.

'Oh Mim,' I said, 'no, that's not it at all. We were going to leave.'

'Leave?' She seemed genuinely shocked. 'Leave for where? Where would you even go?'

'Well,' I said, 'we hadn't quite decided yet. There are places out there where people can go when they need help. Shelters, things like that. And there are nice, kind people who would want to help us if we left.' *People like Malcolm*, I thought, *and I have a sister, somewhere*. But I couldn't bear to tell her about *him*, nor did I want to lay a jinx on the possibility of Grainne's support. It had been such a long time, and things had ended so horribly between us that the idea of her forgiveness was almost impossible.

'But what about the End?' she asked, frustration bubbling through the sadness in her voice. 'Even if places like that did exist once, they'll be gone now. It's a mess out there, Elijah said.'

I thought of Malcolm again. When I had got to the point in my story about Elijah's sermon at the sprit drill, he had placed his hands against the fence. *I need you to know*, he had said, *that none of that is true. But I think you know it already.* He had sounded almost angry when he said that. Angry and kind.

'No,' I said, 'no, it's not. Don't ask me how I know but I do, I promise. The End isn't coming.'

'But... but why would he say it was?'

She looked dazed, and I squeezed her hand again as kindly as I could.

'I don't know.'

It was then that the front door banged open. Both Mim and I jumped and let go of each other's hands. My heart was still racing when Ruth appeared in the doorway. She stood, motionless, as though she was working out the scene before her. I often forget that people can perceive me in a way that is different from how I perceive myself, so while I believed it was obvious that I must have been comforting the tearful Mim, Ruth clearly saw me as the cause of her distress. She fixed me with a cold glare before turning her attention to Mim.

'I'm really sorry,' she said, 'I was so rude to you earlier. I don't know why I acted the way I did. Well… I guess I do, but it was mean and I'm so embarrassed. I looked for you all over.' Then she turned back to me. 'On my way over here, John stopped me and said not to worry about the animals from now on. That Alfie and Adam would be taking care of them until we have to slaughter them. Do you know anything about that?'

She didn't sound accusatory, which I appreciated, but I was too concerned by the fact that John had also got to her to focus too much on her tone.

'I can't believe it,' I said, 'you too?'

'What do you mean, me too? What's happened?'

I sighed. 'I was also sacked today. It's a theme, apparently.'

Ruth sat down heavily on her usual chair. She covered her eyes with her hands and massaged her temples. I thought I heard her swear under her breath, but I assumed I must have imagined it.

'This is crazy,' she said, 'this doesn't feel real. What are we going to do?'

There was no question any more of whether we should share our intentions to escape with Ruth, but before I could fill her in on the subject the door banged open once again.

'Do you think it's Deborah?' Mim asked.

In perfect synchronisation, Ruth and I raised our fingers to our lips. Out in the hall came the sound of two sets of footsteps, and then two voices. One was unmistakably Deborah's, and the other belonged to a man. John. Ruth opened her eyes wide, and Mim furrowed her brow in confusion. I tried to maintain a calm exterior, but inside my mind was whirring through all the possible reasons for Deborah and John to come into the farmhouse together. None were particularly promising. I heard the familiar creak of my office door as it opened and then closed again. What were they doing in there? The three of us sat in tense silence, waiting for something to happen.

# Chapter Twenty-Four

## Ruth

Part of me was relieved when it was Deborah who finally appeared in the doorway, but another part was worried. I had the sense that we'd all been backed into a tight corner, and there was no way out. Aoife and Deborah were talking about how things had gone too far and how the only option now was to leave Halcyon, saying stuff like 'it's now or never' and 'we can make a clean break'. But even if we managed to leave Halcyon, which I doubted we could, we'd never escape it. It was in us. There could be no such thing as a clean break.

'What's the use?' I asked, not bothering to wait for a break in the conversation.

Aoife and Deborah fell silent as they turned to face me. They looked shocked, as if they had forgotten that I was there.

'I mean it,' I said, directing my words to the tabletop, 'what is the point? We can't even get out of this building. How do you expect us to leave Halcyon?'

*And what the heck are we meant to do with ourselves once we're out?* I didn't add.

'Well, we have to try,' said Deborah in the voice I imagined she used to convince the children of Halcyon to wash their hands after visiting the outhouse, 'even if it's just for Mim's sake.'

I sighed.

'This isn't a movie, Deborah. This is real life. We can try as hard as we like but you've already told us that this door is locked and we know the front gates are locked, and also there's a seven-foot-tall fence around the place. Anyway, if Elijah really meant what he said in the sermon, pretty soon we'll all be stuck in the bunker, which has quite literally been built to be impenetrable. So.'

Mim's face crumpled, and for a second I felt a little twinge of guilt even though I knew I was right. It was over. We were all stuck there, at the mercy of whoever had been given the key to the door. By that point the sky outside was pitch black, and the window had become a dark mirror. The thin light coming from the electric bulb was enough to illuminate the scene at the table, and I caught myself unable to tear my eyes away from our reflections. By some strange trick, we all looked more hunched and haggard in the window than we did in real life, and I wondered which was the truer picture. I had no idea how *I* looked in real life, but I certainly felt as beat as my reflection suggested. My daze was interrupted by the sound of someone's stomach growling.

'Sorry,' said Mim, blushing deeply. 'I haven't managed to eat anything today.'

Aoife stood and squeezed Mim's shoulder. It surprised me to see her acting with such tenderness. In all the years I had known her, she had never been one for casual affection. She almost seemed motherly.

'No need to be sorry,' she said, lifting half a loaf out of the bread bin. 'If God wanted us to starve, He wouldn't have let us get locked up in a kitchen. Although...' She paused, her face peering into the cupboard we used as a pantry. 'It appears that we've been looted.'

'What do you mean?' asked Deborah, craning her neck to see where Aoife was standing.

'Well,' she said, 'it looks like someone's been through and taken all of our non-perishables.'

Deborah shook her head and raised her hands in frustration.

'Shit,' she said, 'they must be filling up the bunker already.'

'Never mind,' said Aoife, 'at least they didn't take the bread.'

She turned towards us again, holding the plated-up sliced bread. With two plates in each hand, she reminded me for a second of a waitress in a diner. I half expected her to say *order up!* but of course she didn't. Instead she laid the plates out before us with a hollow smile.

'Eat up,' she said, 'there's no more where that came from.'

I hadn't expected to have any appetite, but as soon as the food was set down my mouth began to water. My hand was already halfway to my plate when Mim piped up again and in her small, nervous voice asked:

'Aren't we going to say a prayer of thanks?'

Aoife, Deborah and I looked at one another in the heavy silence which followed Mim's question. Everyone's face seemed to ask the same thing – *should we?* Both options seemed equally impossible. How could we have even considered eating without blessing our food, but also, who could we pray to now? Thankfully, just as Mim looked ready to either apologise or cry again, Deborah spoke.

'Yes,' she said, 'I think that might do us good. Aoife? Will you lead us?'

Aoife cleared her throat and adjusted herself in her chair.

'Thank you, Deborah,' she said, her eyes closed tight, and her hands clasped in prayer, 'for the bread which you have made. May we be strengthened by it.'

Instead of saying 'amen', the three of us followed Aoife's lead and nodded solemnly. I was ready to reach out once again for my bread when Deborah smacked her hands against the table excitedly:

'Wait!'

We watched in confusion as she rose and disappeared out of the kitchen. She was back again within seconds, holding a half-empty bottle of red wine in one hand and grinning mischievously.

'*Where* did you get *that*?!' I asked, my mouth open wide in astonishment.

'When Elijah decided that we should stop using wine for communion, he told me to pour it away.'

She gave a shrug, as if to say *but then I didn't*, and turned to fetch four mugs from the cupboard. Aoife took hold of the bottle and poured it eagerly so great splashes ended up landing on the table, where they left dark stains on the untreated wood. The pungent smell of alcohol made me wince, and I remembered Elijah the night before, with his hot, reeking breath in my face.

'How many years ago did Elijah ban communion wine?' Aoife asked, swirling the dark, heady liquid around her mug.

'About three,' I said.

Deborah readied herself for a sip, but before the wine touched her lips she stopped and looked at me.

'Will this be okay?' she asked, one hand on her protruding stomach.

I thought back to my training, and the holy trinity of *no*'s for our expectant mothers: no cigarettes, no drugs, no alcohol. Eventually I spoke:

'I think that a couple of units of wine floating around its bloodstream is the last thing that baby needs to worry about.'

Deborah let out a little laugh, and Aoife said, 'I'll drink to that.'

Maybe on some level we all had an idea of what would happen next, and that was why the evening took the turn it did. Even though the wine was terrible and I could hardly bring myself to take more than a mouthful, it gave off the illicit glow of harmless contraband and that alone was enough to make us giddy. For a while we laughed and ate and drank as though the End wasn't right around the corner. And it was around the corner, I was sure, just not in the way we'd prayed for all those years. Even Mim seemed to relax a little, although her own mug of wine lay untouched on the table. The spectre of Elijah's sermon still hung over me, but I had managed to forget that we were locked in the farmhouse until the spirit drill bell rang. The harsh clang reverberated around the room, and the mood changed as suddenly as if a spell had been broken. We had never had two drills in a single day before.

Mim shot to her feet.

'What are we supposed to do?'

As she spoke I heard footsteps in the hall. Aoife must have heard them too, because she grabbed the bottle of wine and thrust it under the table just in time for the door to swing open and John to appear.

'Follow me,' he said.

If he could smell the rancid wine in the air, he gave no sign of it. His face was tired and flushed, and he seemed to be annoyed at the sight of us. I got the feeling that if it was up to him, we'd all just be left in the kitchen forever. He looked at Deborah, and I wondered what had happened between them in Aoife's old office – had she of all people given him trouble? I found it hard to imagine, but then there were a lot of things that I knew for a fact about Deborah that I found difficult to reconcile with the version of her that I saw every day in Halcyon, so it wouldn't have been outside the realms of possibility. We had all heard the stories of her wild youth; she had managed to fit a lot in, if Elijah was to be believed, before she'd joined us at seventeen.

When we got out into the hall, we were met by Niall. He was

standing with his back to the porch door, and in his hand he held one of the big torches we had bought to go in the bunker. The light which came from it was whiter and brighter than any I had seen in years, and I squinted against it.

'Follow me please, ladies,' he said.

One by one we filed out of the farmhouse and into the bitter night, with Niall and his torch leading the way and John bringing up the rear. Everyone must have already been in the church by the time we set off, and Halcyon felt strangely deserted. The path to the church was illuminated by the alien light, and I wondered if maybe I was dreaming. The whole day had been so strange that it didn't feel unlikely, and who knows, maybe I would have passed the whole thing off as some kind of lucid nightmare if it wasn't for the constant reminders of my physical waking body – the freezing cold, the sudden, splitting headache, the rising lump in my throat.

Niall pushed open the door of the church to reveal the entire population of Halcyon, wrapped up in their warmest clothes and staring expectantly up at the stage upon which Elijah was pacing. The air hummed with tension. I'd been to thousands of evening services with the church, but none of them had felt like this. It was familiar and unfamiliar at the same time, like watching a movie with the sound just a little out from the actors' moving mouths, or the slightly distorted reality of a dream. Wrong enough to notice. Evening services had once been my very favourites, back in the old days when we had been city folk, and I tried not to let the strangeness of the situation tarnish the safety and joy wrapped up in those memories.

It was after a session of evening worship, way back when we were still living in England, that Aoife had pulled me aside to talk to me about marrying Elijah. While everyone else was pouring their herbal teas and nibbling homemade biscuits, she took me to the other side of the hall and sat me down on one of the hard plastic chairs which had been lined back up against the wall. She leaned towards me.

'How would you feel about joining our family?'

I looked for some hint in her piercing blue eyes which might indicate the kind of answer she wanted to receive. Did she seem reluctant? Hopeful? Sad? I couldn't tell. Her entire expression was inscrutable, and I wanted to choose my answer carefully.

'I'm not sure I understand, Sister. Am I not already part of the church's family?'

Aoife pulled back slightly, and it almost looked as though she was trying to avoid rolling her eyes.

'I think you might know what I mean, Ruth. Obviously, you're already part of our family in Heaven on Earth, a major part of it. And really, Ruth, that's a big part of the reason that we wanted to ask you this question. Elijah and I would like to invite you to join *our* family. We want you, if you would like, to marry Elijah. That is, to be his wife, his second wife, along with me. To marry him and come and live with us.'

I nodded.

'Right.'

'Are you surprised by my question?' she asked.

I shook my head. Maybe I should have pretended that the thought of marrying Elijah had never crossed my mind, but I couldn't lie to Aoife. For the past few months, Elijah had been keen to spend more time with me than normal: picking me up from work in the church van, helping me close up the soup kitchen when it wasn't his shift. As a church, we had never been against polygamy. Plural marriage was a Biblical phenomenon, and Elijah often preached about Moses and David and Solomon, who had been blessed with more than one wife, so when his interest became so obvious that even I couldn't ignore it, I was only shocked that he seemed to have chosen me.

'You can think about it, you don't have to say anything now.'

'No,' I said. Aoife straightened, and I hurried on. 'No, I mean, no I don't need to think about it. My answer is yes.'

Aoife let out a short sharp exhale and leaned back in her chair, then, after a moment of thought, leaned forward and pulled me into a hug. I could feel the tension in her body, even though she held me at a distance from herself, by the way she gripped the tops of my arms. I placed my own arms around her back, careful not to let my face touch hers, aware of the congregation eating their cookies and drinking their tea at the other end of the hall. They were as much a reason for my 'yes' as Elijah was. I loved them like family – more than my own family, who I had barely spoken to since I had moved to Newcastle – and I wanted to wedge myself in amongst them.

It was strange to think that it was this same group of people I was looking at now, almost exactly, who I had loved so deeply that I'd been willing to give up any semblance of a normal life to be with them. They were so intent on watching Elijah that not a single soul turned to look as we shuffled in, and no eyes followed us as we made our way down the centre aisle to our usual seats. There was Danielle, whose baby I had delivered two years ago, a little boy – breach. Adam, who had put a nail through his hand while making repairs to the community barn after a storm. I'd been so terrified that he'd get an infection that I'd kept changing his dressing every day for a week after I'd needed to. Lois was fiddling with the tassels on her scarf; people were speaking to her again, and the relief glowed off her. I realised I didn't like the gawping, starry-eyed crowd that my friends and neighbours had become, and fought the temptation to go up to each person individually and give them a shake. Had I ever looked at Elijah like that? I shook my head gently. Of course I had. And as I took my seat, and Elijah took his place behind the rostrum, I tried with all my might not to do it again.

# Chapter Twenty-Five

## Deborah

I couldn't have guessed how long the spirit drill had lasted, but by the time we were finally dismissed the sky had begun to lighten. I had managed to stay awake for the duration of Elijah's sermon, but just barely, and all I could think about once it was over was going to the outhouse and then curling up in my bed. My throat was raw from cheering along with the rest of the congregation, my ears were ringing, and my eyes stung with exhaustion. Ahead of me, I could see the dim outline of Mim leaning sleepily against Ruth's shoulder as they walked. Aoife and I also walked as a pair, which I appreciated; it would be good to have someone to grab onto if my legs finally gave way. The bodies of the other congregants moved around us, slow and silent, heading for the comfort of their caravans to catch a couple of hours' sleep before having to wake up for the day.

In the half-light, I could make out the shapes of the older children carrying the younger ones, although it was still too dark for me to recognise any particular faces. I thought of Jonah and Noah and Susannah, and my heart ached. Being away from them never got easier, but I had got more used to it. I had had forty days with the boys, where they had stayed with me in the farmhouse in my room. There had been some debate about that, apparently – should I get twice as long because I had birthed two? Elijah and John had decided eventually that no, I shouldn't. Ruth and some of the others had looked after me, while I looked after the babies. I could still feel their small, wriggling bodies, the latch of their hungry mouths on my nipples. When the forty days were up and they were moved to the schoolhouse, I had felt a literal tearing in my chest.

'I'm so sorry, honey,' Ruth had said.

I lay back against my pillows, still in my nightdress. I knew that if I didn't force myself to stay lying down, I would have chased after them, those two tiny bundles in Helen's arms. I bit back tears and closed my eyes.

'I need them with me,' I croaked.

It was a risky thing to say, even to Ruth. She could so easily have told Elijah. Instead, she lay down next to me on the bed and put her arm around my shoulders. With her other hand she pushed the hair away from my face.

'I know,' she said, 'I know.'

I remember how grateful I had been that she hadn't given me a speech about how it was our burden as mothers, or how it was for the best, or that I would still get to see them in the schoolhouse every day, and 'really, Deborah, they're just across the courtyard, don't you think you're being a bit dramatic?' which Aoife had said to me the following day at breakfast, once Elijah had left.

When it was time for Ruth to go, I was still lying like a corpse on my bed. My hair was unbrushed and unplaited, fanned out around me, and my eyes were dry and stinging. Milk had soaked through my nightdress, leaving a sodden patch over each breast.

'Don't let him see you like this,' she said.

She was right. Elijah would be there soon, and if he saw me in such a state he would never allow me to keep up my work in the schoolhouse. In a hormone-addled haze, I rose and washed my face, combed my hair, dressed myself. I used the ghostly reflection in my window to practice a smile.

When I'd had Susannah, Elijah had been irritated by the birth of another daughter, but I had been relieved – the Biblical period of purification was longer. With her, I'd been allowed eighty blissful days before the third chamber of my heart was torn out, and it was time to welcome my husband back into my bed.

I must have slowed my pace a little, because Aoife took my arm and propelled me forwards. We walked the rest of the way to the farmhouse door like that – her firm hand gripping me so hard that I could feel it through my layers of coats and jumpers. It wasn't until we came to a stop that I realised Mim was still with us, clinging tightly onto Ruth.

'Please don't make me go back there,' she sobbed. 'I want to stay with you.'

Whether they were tears of fear or exhaustion was anyone's guess, but either way I felt bad for her. I was almost ready to relent when Aoife spoke:

'I know,' she said, 'but they're expecting you at the schoolhouse. If you don't turn up, they're just going to come looking for you.'

She was right, but Mim remained unconvinced.

'But I don't think I want to go back!'

Her voice was choked with emotion and seemed to carry into the hills. By that point I was feeling less sorry for Mim, and more worried that someone would hear her. Somewhere behind us, I was sure John must be watching and listening. To my surprise, before I could say anything, Ruth chimed in.

'Aoife's right,' she said, turning to face Mim, 'but look, it's almost dawn. You'll only be there for a few hours, and then we'll all be up again. Nothing bad is going to happen in a few hours.'

I thought of Ollie, frozen and shivering, and I knew Ruth was thinking of him too. For a second nobody spoke, and I waited for Mim to argue back, to say that both Ruth and I had seen with our own eyes exactly the sort of harm that could be done in a few hours. But she didn't. Maybe she was just too tired to argue, or maybe her upbringing prevented her from talking back any further. Either way, I'm ashamed to say that I was relieved. My brain and body were running on fumes, and there was no energy left in me to think too hard about what might happen if we forced a recently betrothed teenager to return, unsupervised, to a place that clearly terrified her.

Once Mim had disappeared safely into the half-light, Aoife opened the farmhouse door. None of us even bothered to take off our coats and boots before going our separate ways. I guessed that I would get in about three hours of sleep before it would be time to wake up, but ironically I was too exhausted to worry about it. When I reached my room, I just about managed to kick off my boots before curling up under the quilts. My eyes closed before my head even hit the pillow, and I fell into a heavy, dreamless sleep.

When I woke up the following morning, it was to the sound of more bells. I hadn't moved an inch from the spot in which I'd fallen asleep, which made me feel as though I hadn't slept at all. That, combined with the noise, made me feel disorientated, and for a second I couldn't even bring myself to get out of bed. Still dressed from the night before, I pushed back my quilt and felt the trapped heat evaporate into the chilly room. Condensation had built up on the windowpane, and I gave it a half-hearted wipe with the sleeve of my jumper. Little grey fibres stuck to the wet glass and I tried to pick them off with my nail while listening to the bells ring on. My bedroom was at the back of the house, which meant that all I could see were looming, craggy hills, and in the near distance, the heavy metal gate which separated Halcyon from the outside world. Two men, too blurred by the streaks of water for me to be able to make out their faces, stood guard. Strangely, they didn't seem to be moving towards the church at the sound of the bells, which continued to ring. Elijah's paranoia must have reached new heights if he would allow two of his congregation to miss a sermon for guard duty. I stood and watched them for a bit longer, waiting to see if they would move, before I turned with a sigh and walked towards the door. My hand hovered over the handle – usually I aimed to be one of the first to respond to the bells which called us to the church, but such attempts to win Elijah's favour seemed more than redundant at that point, and I had no other reason to want to be there.

Pretty soon, it became clear that I wasn't the only one who didn't want me to join the congregation in church. The handle, when I eventually tried to turn it, moved an inch and then stuck fast. I gave it another try, and then another. I attempted to move it the other way, as though that would do something different. No matter what I did, though, nothing changed. The door was locked, and I was stuck.

# Chapter Twenty-Six

## Aoife

Bleary-eyed and stifling my yawns, I found myself sitting in my usual seat in church just a few hours after I had last left it. To my left was Ruth, who looked as though she had managed even less sleep than me. She was staring up at the rostrum where Elijah stood, once again, taking in the crowd which had gathered before him. The atmosphere was quiet, as though the congregation had used up all of their fervour the night before and was now struggling against an emotional hangover. For once, I allowed myself to turn and survey the room. It was almost full, but amongst the flock of familiar faces there was no sign of Deborah, Mim, or Helen. That they were all three absent seemed like too much of a coincidence, and I was about to turn and ask Ruth if she knew where they were when John appeared in front of us.

'Excuse me,' he said, gesturing at the slim gap between me and Ruth, 'may I?'

I gave a silent nod and fixed him with a glare as Ruth shuffled along to the neighbouring chair where Deborah usually sat. John was smaller than I was, but his presence between us made it impossible for me to catch Ruth's eye. I wished that I had waited in the farmhouse for Deborah, but my body seemed to have a Pavlovian reaction to the sound of the church bells – the first burst of their familiar clang had me out the door before I even knew what was happening. My clothes were still rumpled from sleep, and I could feel the hair escaping awkwardly from my bun. Not that Elijah would care. He hadn't even looked over since I walked in. If anything, he seemed to be actively avoiding catching my eye. At first, I had thought that he was surveying the entire congregation, but I soon realised that he was actually staring fixedly at the door. I was desperate to speak to Ruth, but every time I moved to look at her John seemed to find a way to block my view.

By that time the atmosphere was tense and heavy. We were all waiting for something to happen when the doors swung open. I turned, expecting to spot Deborah, but she was still nowhere to be seen. Instead, silhouetted in the doorway against the white sky stood two other figures clinging tightly to one another.

# Chapter Twenty-Seven

## Ruth

I figured it out the second that John came and sat between me and Aoife, but it didn't matter; there was nothing that I could do anyway. It was too late. And by the time the doors opened and Aoife and the rest of them realised what was about to happen too, it was even later, and all we could do was sit there and watch as Mim and Helen walked arm in arm down the centre aisle. The sight of the young bride and her mother seemed to perk up the congregation, and I found myself wishing that Mim would play the part of blushing bride in a way that matched the enthusiasm of everyone else in the room; it would have made it less painful to watch. Instead, she shuffled forwards, her eyes glassy and dazed, her feet catching the hem of her too-large dress on every other step. Someone had taken her hair out of its plaits, and it hung long and crimped down her back. There were no flowers.

It said a lot about the way things worked in Halcyon and Heaven on Earth that I had managed to forget, up until then, that Helen and John were Mim's biological parents. I'd never noticed them paying her any particular attention, and she never talked about them even though they had all lived together before the move to Halcyon in Mim's early childhood. It surprised me that Elijah had allowed Helen to walk her daughter down the aisle. The tradition of a parent giving away their child into marriage suggested that the child had previously belonged to the parent, instead of to God. That was how it was explained to me when Elijah and I became engaged and I had suggested flying my parents and siblings out to attend the wedding. I had barely spoken to them in years – the odd call at Christmas or a birthday, never being sure what to say and so never saying much. They knew I was working, and going to church, and they were happy enough with that. My godmother had cut me off completely long before my engagement, telling me to call her when I was ready to be normal again. In the end I decided not to tell them that I was getting married, so our only guests were the other members of Heaven on Earth. I had worn Aoife's wedding dress, the same dress that Deborah later wore on her wedding day and the dress that Mim wore now. It really was far too big for her, and the white satin bodice hung loose around her skinny waist. The puffs at the top of the sleeves, which I had remembered as being so elegant, looked comically large on Mim. Helen was holding onto her arm with a grip so tight that the fabric of the sleeve was bunched and creased. I winced at the thought of what that grip might be doing to the skin underneath.

The pair reached the front of the church, and Elijah greeted them with a smile. He had lost weight from his face, so when he smiled his skin and lips stretched too thin over his teeth and he looked like a skeleton. Mim turned nervously to look at the crowd; it was the first sign she gave that she had half an idea of what was going on. I wondered if she was searching for me, but she was looking in the opposite direction to where Aoife and I were sitting. That was one small mercy; how could I have looked back at her if she had spotted us? What expression would I have been able to arrange on my face that would have done her any good? Whatever she did see didn't seem to have done her any good either, because she let out a high-pitched squeak. John shifted in his seat when she did that, and Helen tugged her arm hard. Slowly, Mim turned her head back round, but she didn't look up at Elijah. Instead, she kept her eyes fixed firmly on the floor. John relaxed. When it became clear that Mim wasn't about to fall over or run away, Elijah gave a nod and Helen let go of her daughter's arm. As Helen returned to her seat, I managed to glimpse her face. She looked as drawn and tired as everyone else in the room. Her hair was pulled back tightly, but it had escaped in fine wisps which curled out from her scalp like a greying halo. Her jaw, I could see, was tense, and her mouth was set in a tight, thin line.

When Helen had taken her seat, Elijah cleared his throat and reached out a hand to Mim. Hesitantly, she took it and made the small step up to join him on the low stage. As soon as she was by his side, her gaze returned once again to the floor. Elijah didn't seem to notice. His attention was focussed outwards.

'Good morning, everyone.' I could tell that he was trying to sound normal, but his voice had a manic edge to it and his right hand was shaking. 'I am so very happy to see you all gathered here today, to witness this most joyful occasion.'

# Chapter Twenty-Eight

## Deborah

By the time the bells had stopped, I was lying on my side on top of the covers of my bed, watching a small beetle make its way from one end of the bedside table to the other. My stomach rumbled, and I had already had to use the chamber pot under my bed. Inside me, the baby squirmed and kicked. I placed my hand on the spot where I had felt what I imagined was its foot, and took a deep breath in. If it wasn't for the baby, I might have been worried; after all, finding yourself unexpectedly locked in a room is rarely a good thing. But the baby growing inside me made everything different. When I was pregnant, I was safe by default. I thought back to Elijah's game with the glasses of water, how confident I had been that mine was clean, how quickly I'd gulped it down to keep up my good wife act and impress him. I remembered the sight of the plate flying through the air in the kitchen the night before Elijah left. I had ducked on instinct, but even then I had been certain that he was aiming for the space above my head.

I loved how protected I was when I was pregnant, but I loved my babies too. I had always loved babies. I always thought that if they hadn't been married to Elijah, Aoife and Ruth would never have had so many children, but I'm sure I would have. Even as a child I was desperate to be a parent. I was the kid who insisted on tucking the baby dolls in every night, and if the foster family I was placed with had little children I would be thrilled. Way back when I lived with my mother the first time around, I always hoped that she would have another baby. In hindsight, I'm glad that she didn't, but at the time all I wanted was some small person to fuss over and care about. As I grew older, parenthood became an idealised state. When I was a parent, I thought, everything would be all right. There would always be someone there to love, and always someone to love me back. What a thrilling prospect that was to my affection-starved little self.

The reality of parenthood was different. By the time I gave birth to the twins, we had been in Halcyon for just over a year. The schoolhouse was well established, and Elijah's beliefs about the dangers of the family unit had taken root in the hard Highland ground. In the months that followed Jonah and Noah's removal to the schoolhouse, I spent tearful hours alone in my bedroom, an old-fashioned manual breast pump clamped to my raw, ravaged nipples, trying to drain sufficient milk from myself to fill enough bottles to satisfy the two of them. It was then, with empty arms and empty womb, that I had started to hate him. Until that point, I had convinced myself to believe in the work we were doing and had trusted in Elijah's plan. Everything would be so different for those babies, I had thought, so different to how it had been for me. They would be raised within a community. They would have so many people to love them, and they would be safe, and they would grow up surrounded by God and His wonder. And then I'd gone and lost them, like my mother had lost me, only worse. When I was seventeen, I'd found my mother again, and I got to know her and I got to love her not just because I was half her, but because of who she was. I'd seen her clean and happy. I'd watched her face light up when Elijah preached. I'd heard her voice raised in song. We'd been reunited. I got the feeling that my own children would never get to know me like that.

Not long after giving birth to the twins, I found out that I was expecting again. The first time around there had been hope, and I had stared in wonder at my growing, changing body. My pregnancy with Susannah was very different. Every bout of morning sickness, every stretch mark, every flutter and kick in my belly filled me with dread. Still, at least I knew that for as long as I was pregnant my body was off limits. I was a holy vessel. I no longer had to keep one eye open for minute shifts in Elijah's mood, or fear his strange punishments. After the twins, but before I became pregnant with Susannah, I had taken the Lord's name in vain. A minor sin by most standards, but in Halcyon there was no such thing – a broken rule was a broken rule, and the sinner had to be absolved before they brought the wrath of God down on everyone. I had spent hours pumping, but when Annie came to pick up the bottles, she'd dropped one. Elijah thought that plastic was poison, so the bottles were made of glass, and of course it smashed as soon as it landed on the hard wood floor. I remember being hit with an almighty wave of anger and sorrow, and I had screamed so loudly that Elijah had heard.

'Jesus Christ!'

Pretty tame stuff, especially for me, but as far as Elijah was concerned it couldn't have been much worse. As soon as Annie had left with the surviving bottle, apologising all the way out of the door and almost in tears herself, he crouched down and rummaged around the cupboard under the sink. It was where we kept our cleaning things, and some of the less easily replaceable cooking ingredients. I watched his back as he rose and fetched a mug, into which he poured a mystery liquid. For a second I wondered whether I would allow myself to drink bleach if it turned out that that was what he had served me. As soon as the mug was in my hand, though, one sniff told me exactly what was inside. Cider vinegar. He must have emptied the entire bottle in there; it was full to the brim. He watched coolly, his arms crossed over his broad chest, as I drank the entire thing. By the time I'd finished my mouth and throat were burning, and my stomach was cramping so much that I could barely stand. It was all I could do not to vomit, but something told me that would have been a bad idea, and I forced myself not to. 'It's for your own good,' he had said, as I retched dryly over my wash basin, saliva running from my mouth. He brought me a glass of water, afterwards, and rubbed my back. 'You're forgiven. I love you.'


Lying on my bed, I could still just about see the two guards by the gate. One was facing inwards, towards Halcyon and the house, and the other was looking out into the world beyond. I closed my eyes.

# Chapter Twenty-Nine

## Aoife

Satellite delay. That's the only way I can think to describe it. I watched the doors open and saw Mim walking down the aisle towards Elijah. I saw that she was wearing my wedding dress. I even heard Elijah begin preaching as he held her limp, white hand. All that, and my brain didn't seem able to comprehend what was going on until the service was well underway. Once I had caught up with my senses, I was met with the urge to stand up, to object, to somehow stop the whole thing. The instinct surprised me, but as soon as I moved to act on it, John's hand touched my thigh.

'I wouldn't,' his whisper was so low I could hardly hear it, 'if I were you.'

His breath was hot, and it made me squirm. I kept my eyes fixed ahead as he continued.

'Jemima has told us everything. She's named Deborah as a traitor. Something about an escape?'

I must have tensed, because he let out a satisfied exhale.

'The three of you can do whatever you like for all I care, but you won't drag my daughter to Hell with you.'

Fear hardened into a lump in my throat. Traitor seemed like such a big, serious word.

'Where's Deborah?' I breathed.

In the periphery of my vision I saw John shake his head and raise a finger to his lips. *Shh.*

For as long as I could remember, being told to be quiet had filled me with a hot rage, but I had other things to worry about. There was Deborah, of course, but in light of her condition I wasn't too worried about her safety – at least her physical safety.

More pressing was Mim, who seemed to be swaying gently, her eyes red from tears, or lack of sleep, or both. She was a sorry sight, up there in an ill-fitting wedding dress which had seen all three of her soon-to-be sister-wives as well as her mother up and down the aisle. I almost felt sorry for that dress. I had been so happy to wear it. It had been the most beautiful thing I had ever worn. It made me feel like a woman. The only sadness I had felt on my wedding day was the knowledge that my sister would never see me in it. Grainne had refused to come to the wedding. She and I had had some disagreements. I told her I disapproved of her lifestyle, and she told me that she disapproved of mine. Now, looking at Mim, I didn't see a bride; I saw a victim. I wondered if that's what Grainne would have seen in me if she had been at my wedding. If she had heard it in my voice when I had called her to tell her that I was getting married to Elijah.

'You're just a silly little girl, Aoife,' she'd said, her voice cold and distant through the phone. 'You'll regret it one day, giving your life to this nutter.'

'His *name*,' I had said, 'is Elijah. And he's not a nutter. He's the best man I've ever known. The best person I've ever known. Better than you, certainly.'

Next to me on John and Helen's sofa, Elijah had squeezed my hand. John and Helen were standing in the kitchen, I remembered the way they were shadowed in the door's frosted glass panel. Mim would have been there too, I supposed, in the kitchen with her parents. Strange to think of it then, as I watched her on the stage. She would have been four years of age when Elijah and I married. I took a deep breath.

'Mammy and Daddy will be turning in their graves, I hope you know that. At what an eejit you're being, cutting yourself off from everyone, leaving your job. To do what? Wait hand and foot on your man who thinks he's some kind of Messiah?'

I remember the feeling of the receiver in my hand – hot, and sticky with sweat. I leaned in to Elijah, as closely as I could. His body felt strong and safe.

'Ha,' I'd said, 'that's rich, coming from you. Are you still shacked up with that woman? It's shameful.' I was almost spitting down the phone. 'I'm ashamed to even know you, I wish you weren't my sister. Elijah was right, I should never have called you. I don't want you at my wedding anyway.'

'Is that right? Then why *did* you call me, Aoife?'

I hung up, then. She didn't call back. It was the last I'd ever heard from her. Elijah drew me into a tight hug as soon as the phone was back on the hook, and stroked my hair as I wept.

'We'll pray for her,' he'd said.

But that was all in the past. In the present, John's clammy hand remained firmly on my leg; my initial burst of adrenaline had faded, and common sense had taken its place. I had no choice but to watch the service. Elijah delivered the exact same words he had spoken when we had married, down to the intonation of his voice. The only difference was that John had officiated our wedding, and this time Elijah was leading it himself. I wondered what that meant. Mim continued to sway, and I doubted she could even hear him. Her part was coming up, the part where she would have to agree to the pledge. The closer it got the tighter John's grip became. I could feel his palm sweating through my skirt. Not so long ago, he would not have dared to touch me.

The unfamiliar sound of the siren surprised us all. Unlike the church bells, the siren was to be used only as a warning for the End. For all of Elijah's warnings about an imminent invasion and the impending End of Days, he seemed more shocked than anyone. For several seconds his mouth continued to move, but no words came out. As panic rose around the room, spreading through the rows from person to person like a virus, the realisation of what was happening dawned on him. His face morphed into a mask of pure elation – the look of a man vindicated – and he raised both of his arms heavenward. No one in the room spoke as Elijah's voice rose up against the sound of the alarm.

'My dear, dear friends! My brothers and sisters! The time we have so eagerly awaited has finally arrived. God is raining down the End of Days upon us. Soon we will all be judged, and we will take our seats beside Him!'

Chairs and benches scraped against the concrete floor as the crowd rose around us. They whooped and cheered with a volume so unholy that it set my flesh and bones reverberating. Elijah, apparently forgetting his almost-bride, stepped forward until he was at the very edge of the stage. He clenched both fists and shot them hard into the air.

'Yes!' he cried, his voice so deep and loud that it fought against the chaos and came out clear and strong over it. 'Yes! Yes! Yes!'

With each call, he pumped his fists into the air again. Briefly, he looked my way. His eyes were wide, but his pupils were so small that it seemed they were all whites and irises. He pulled his lips into a great, manic smile which stopped my heart and made my stomach flip, before turning away and clapping his hands. At that, the crowd fell quiet again. His voice almost shook as he spoke.

'Everyone to the bunker, now! The time has come – it is the last hour! We are vindicated!'

He leapt off the rostrum and into the aisle. John rose next, scurrying to catch up with Elijah before he reached the door. The congregation swarmed out behind them. In the commotion, I reached out to Ruth and pulled her up by her sleeve. She seemed to be frozen in shock, but moved with me easily enough. When she was on her feet, I dragged her into the aisle before turning to Mim, who hadn't moved an inch since she first took to the platform. The wail of the siren combined with the noise from the receding congregation meant that I could shout for her without drawing too much unwanted attention to myself, and that's what I did.

'Mim!' I called, waving in the hopes of catching her eye, 'Mim! Come on!'

Mim slipped back into consciousness, and within seconds had jumped from the rostrum with as much eagerness as Elijah had done just minutes before. She moved as a white blur, and before I knew it she had taken hold of my free hand. Together, the three of us followed the final dregs of colonists out of the church. Once we were outside, we pulled away from the crowd, who were moving en masse towards the newly stocked bunker. Instead, we turned and headed in the opposite direction, towards the farmhouse, and Deborah.

# Chapter Thirty

## Ruth

My first thought, when that horrible screaming siren first sounded, was that we'd all been wrong. Or, I guess, that we'd all been right at first, right to listen to Elijah and join Heaven on Earth and marry him and move to Halcyon. And then we'd been wrong, oh so horribly wrong, to fall away from him. It was hard to get my head straight, with the noise and the panic, but I suppose that somewhere in my muddled and anxious brain I began to worry that it was disobedience – mine in particular – that had brought about the End of Days. It all started with the puppies, and my duplicity. And then it had been Mim, and then Deborah and Aoife, and all of their talk and all of their sin. Surely the Devil himself must have been sitting with us in the farmhouse that night – last night, or the night before? Time meant nothing to me then. All I could think was *Elijah was right*, and all I could worry about was the fate of our four souls.

When Aoife pulled me up and out of my daze, I assumed that she had had a similar revelation and that we were going to follow everybody into the bunker, but of course I was wrong. My instinct, when I realised where we were actually going, was to let go of Aoife's hand and run away to be with Elijah and the rest of the colony. I'm not ashamed to admit it. The only thing that stopped me was Mim. Keeping pace alongside us, she looked like a kid playing dress-up in her mother's wedding gown. That would have been bad enough, but what shocked me back to my senses wasn't the fact of the wedding itself so much as the sheer relief with which she seemed to feel at running away from it. I'd seen that look before, in the various hospitals I'd trained in, on the faces of patients who had come close to dying but had been saved. I'd seen it on the faces of the mothers who gave birth to silent babies when those babies finally gave their inaugural cry. Relief made even more precious by how close they had come to something unthinkably, unbearably awful.

And so I kept running, away from the promised safety of the bunker and the company of the people I had grown to love so deeply over my years in the church. Away from my children, as they were herded off by women who they knew better and trusted more than me. I was running from Elijah too, I knew. We had been married for eight years, and that thought was like a lasso around my middle, wrenching me backwards, making each step in the other direction a battle against almost a decade of memories. Happy ones, not just from our marriage, but from the two years before when I had been just another member of the Church of Heaven on Earth. The little glances we'd shared across the church hall, the drive to the food bank when we'd just gotten engaged and he placed his hand in mine for the very first time, how filled with joy I'd been then. *You're special, Ruthie*, he would say, if I ever got sad, *God brought you here for a reason. You're not like any of the others, not even Aoife. You've got a goodness in you.* Or, *I'm blessed to have you in my life.* As we lay in bed, he would lean in to me and whisper, *I thank God every day that I get to spend eternity with you.* But I thought again of Mim, and I pushed the memories to one side. It was different now, and it had been for a long time.

And so I gripped Aoife's hand all the harder in the knowledge that God was present in Halcyon that day – just not in the way everyone thought. He wasn't there to usher in the End of Days, but to deliver Mim from evil.

# Chapter Thirty-One

## Deborah

At the sound of the siren, the two figures who had been watching the gate deserted their post and legged it into the centre of Halcyon. Because of where my bedroom was, I couldn't see exactly what was going on, but I could see my chance, so I took it. As soon as the guards had disappeared around the side of the farmhouse and I could be certain that they weren't keeping an eye on me through the window, I began to shake my pillow out of its case. We had no bags or luggage in our rooms – why would we need those, when we were here until the end? But we did have pillowcases.

The last time I had packed my things into a pillowcase, it was under the watchful eye of the social worker who had come to remove me from the squat I was living in with my mother and her friends. He had been amazed that we had nothing else in the house that could do the job. *Not even bin liners?* he'd asked, and I remember wondering if he was new. I probably had even fewer things to pack in my room at Halcyon than I'd had back then, and that was saying something. I was wearing most of my clothes because of the cold, so I only had a couple of changes of underwear and a vest to pack, and there was little else. I'd only managed to keep hold of a few things from the time before Halcyon – a pristine bar of soap which I had discovered after we moved, a receipt from the first 'date' Elijah had taken me on when we began courting, our wedding photo. The two of us in the centre, me in a white dress with puffy sleeves and a garland of pink flowers in my hair and Elijah in his one grey suit. I was beaming, fresh-faced at twenty-one years old, with

Elijah looking smug and handsome, his arm around my waist. Next to me in the picture was Ruth, smiling, her hands clasped together and resting across her stomach. Aoife was standing next to Elijah, with a face like a smacked arse. Both she and Ruth were pregnant in the photo. Two days after our wedding, we'd all moved to Halcyon. The only other thing I took with me was a picture which had been taken of me and my mother just a couple of months before she died. We were sitting together in the church hall we had used for Heaven on Earth gatherings, and we had our arms around each other. She was frail and thin, her hair wispy and grey even though she was barely into her forties, but she looked happy and so did I. Elijah had been the one to bring her off the street. He'd driven her to and from her AA meetings, given her work in the church's soup kitchen, brought her back to life. He'd even helped her find me again. Because of Elijah, we'd had three happy years together in Heaven on Earth before she died of liver failure. I slipped the photo into my makeshift bag, carefully flattening it against the side to keep it from creasing, and wondered how the Elijah of before could possibly be the same man I had grown to hate. Halcyon had changed him, somehow, for the worse. Just like it had changed the rest of us.

The sound of the siren drowned out the knocking at the door, but when I finally heard it my heart jumped into my throat and stayed there. The pillowcase bag was still in my hands, and I stashed it under the quilt. Then, with shaking legs, I walked around the bed and up to the door.

'Who is it?'

'It's us! Can you open the door?' Aoife's familiar voice sounded through the wood, overwhelming the siren to become the most powerful sound in the room.

I pressed myself as close to the door as I could, and positioned my mouth against the crack between the door and the frame.

'Who's us?' I asked.

'It's Aoife and Mim and me,' said Ruth. Her voice was quieter than Aoife's, but I could just about hear her. 'Are you stuck in there?'

'Yes!' I was surprised to hear the desperation in my voice. 'Yes, I'm stuck. I think someone's locked me in. What's going on out there? Why is the siren going off?'

'We'll explain in a minute,' said Aoife, 'but for now we need to get you out of that room.'

The siren cut off mid wail, and despite the ringing it left behind in my ears I could hear their muffled discussion taking place through the door. When the discussion was over, Aoife's voice once again travelled low and clear into my room.

'We've decided,' she said, 'to keep it simple. We think that the best way to get you out is just to knock the door down. Ruth and Mim are going to grab something heavy for us to use as a sort of... battering ram, I suppose. And then we're going to start bashing. Okay?'

'Okay,' I said.

What I really admired about Aoife was her ability, in spite of the strangeness of our situation, to sound truly excited about the prospect of knocking down a door with a makeshift battering ram. She really was wasted in Halcyon. She should have been a general. I wanted to tell her, but it didn't seem like the right moment for any kind of light-hearted comment. Something big was clearly going on out there, plus I didn't want her to think I was taking the piss. And so we stood in silence, on either side of my bedroom door, until the sound of footsteps echoed along the corridor.

'We're back,' panted Mim.

I'd almost forgotten that she was there.

'Great,' said Aoife, her voice less clear than it had been – she must have been facing away from the door. 'This will be perfect.'

I was just about to ask what they had brought when Ruth spoke directly through the gap between the door and the lintel:

'It's the bench from the hall,' she said, 'it's the only big thing we could carry.'

There was another minute of deliberation out in the corridor before Aoife called out:

'Right, we're in position. Deb, you get as far back as you can – shout when you're ready for us to get going and we'll swing on the count of three.'

I moved back around to the other side of my bed and lowered myself slowly onto my hands and knees.

'I'm ready!'

They wasted no time. The words were barely out of my mouth

before Aoife gave the count, and the first bang rang out. My heart slammed against my chest, and the baby kicked and squirmed. I wanted to place a hand against my stomach to calm it, but I was still kneeling behind the bed and needed both arms to support myself. My wrists and forearms began to shake.

'Okay,' Aoife shouted, 'we're going again.'

There was another crash of wood against wood, followed by an almighty splintering crack. I raised my head up above the side of the bed, but everything was still intact. Before I could duck back down, the door burst open with one final explosion of sound and smacked hard against my bedroom wall. Together, Aoife, Ruth and Mim stumbled into the room amidst a shower of plaster dust, propelled by the momentum of the bench.

All I could do was stare in stunned silence as I took in the scene. My bedroom door was battered and splintered, hanging limply from one hinge, and the wall had a deep crater where the door's heavy brass handle had hit it. The bench where I usually sat to put on my shoes was cracked straight down its middle and lying sadly on its side on the floor. All things considered, I supposed that the damage wasn't really all that bad. What really shocked me, far more than the mess of plaster and wood, was Mim.

'Why is she wearing my wedding dress?' I asked, leaning heavily on the bed for support as I pulled myself up to stand properly.

Her mouth opened and closed silently until Ruth stepped in and took her by the hand.

'The first bell,' said Ruth, using the gentle voice she usually reserved for labouring mothers, 'was to call us to the church. It looks like Elijah wanted to get the wedding done sooner than we'd thought. If it wasn't for the emergency siren, Mim would have been married by now.'

I stepped backwards and leant gratefully against the solid security of the wall as Mim gave a weak nod.

'Yes,' said Aoife, 'it's been a rough morning for everyone. After the siren went off everyone got a bit excited and headed off to the bunker, and we came here to find you.'

A hundred questions fought in my mind, desperate to be raised.

'Do we know why it went off?' I asked. 'I mean, what was the emergency?'

Ruth shrugged her shoulders sadly as Aoife spoke:

'We don't know. Elijah ran off almost as soon as it started.'

Her sharp jaw clenched. 'But that means it could be anything, and I think we should make a move while we can – everyone's so distracted they've probably not even noticed that we're not in the bunker yet.'

I swallowed hard. There were too many things I wanted to say, and the prospect of actually leaving – not thinking about leaving or planning to leave, but actually, really getting away – was so dizzying that I couldn't even begin to comprehend it. I must have paled or wobbled, because Ruth raised a concerned brow.

'Are you all right?'

'Yeah, no, I'm fine. I suppose we'd better get going then. Where are the kids?'

# Chapter Thirty-Two

## Aoife

My arms were still aching from the effort of breaking into Deborah's room as the four of us made our way down the corridor and towards the front door. The plan had seemed simple enough when we had agreed on it just minutes before, but the closer I came to re-entering Halcyon proper, the faster my heart started to beat. There were too many what-ifs. What if Malcolm didn't show up to see me, even though he promised that he would? What if someone came looking for us? What if Ruth or Deborah or Mim got cold feet? It wasn't unlikely. Mim was only a teenager after all, and Deborah wasn't happy about leaving the children behind, even though we'd assured her it was the only way, and that we would come back for them before the day was over. Various worst-case scenarios played out in my head, but I forced myself to block them out. There was no point in dwelling on the things that could go wrong. I took a long, slow breath in, trying to fill myself up with confidence as well as air before reaching out for the handle. Before I could push it down, I felt Ruth's gentle hand on my arm.

'This person who can help us,' she said, 'it's your sister, right?'

My breath caught in my throat. Part of my argument for leaving now had been to do with Malcolm, although I'd not referred to him by name. All I'd said was that there was someone nearby who had a car big enough to pull down a section of the perimeter fence, and that they'd take us to the police station. I'd assumed that years of learning how not to ask too many questions had been the reason behind their lack of interest in who this person was, but apparently I was wrong.

'No,' I said eventually, my hand still hovering over the door handle. 'No, it's not my sister.'

Deborah stopped in her tracks.

'Wait,' she said, 'if it's not your sister, then who the Hell is it?'

The three of them stared at me expectantly as I fumbled for the answer that would raise the least number of follow-up questions. Eventually, I settled on the truth. After everything, it seemed like the only safe way to go.

'A little while ago...' I spoke slowly, trying to give myself some thinking time between each word. I knew I needed to be honest, but I also had to handle this tactfully. 'I met a person, a man, while I was walking around the perimeter fence. We started talking, and as the time has passed we've spoken more and more. He knows everything. He told me that he'd be back every day, and that if I ever wanted to leave all I had to do was say the word.'

As I spoke, I watched their faces change. Ruth and Mim's eyes widened in sheer surprise – Mim in particular looked as though her entire worldview had been toppled for the second time in twenty-four hours. Deborah's expression betrayed something else. She shook her head slowly, a wry little smile playing on the corners of her lips. I could feel a blush rising from my chest and up to my cheeks, and I placed a cool hand on my neck in what I hoped was a very subtle way.

'Well,' I said, 'there you go. I assume nobody has a problem?'

None of them spoke.

'Grand. Let's get going.'

As I opened the door a gust of wind pushed me back, taking my breath away and almost throwing me off my balance. The farmhouse was far from warm, but it was sheltered, and the sudden icy blast was a shock to my system. I was already wearing as many layers as I had access to, but I pulled them close around me while I waited for Deborah to close the door behind us.

'Okay,' I said, raising my voice above the rising wind. 'Everyone should be in the bunker by now, so all we need to worry about is someone coming out and looking for us. Mim, you stay in the middle. We don't want anyone to spot you. Deborah, keep an eye to the right. Ruth, keep turning back in case someone starts to follow. I'll keep a look out for Malcolm.'

Mim and Deborah nodded quickly and made to start walking, but Ruth brought a slender finger to her lips.

'Listen,' she said, 'do you hear that?'

I strained my ears, trying to hear anything above the whistle and roar of the wind. I shook my head and was about to lead on when Deborah furrowed her brows in concentration.

'Yes,' she said, 'I do hear something. It sounds like voices? I think it's coming from over by the bunker.'

Before I knew it, the three of us were following Deborah around the edge of the farmhouse, inching our way towards the possible source of a sound I still wasn't certain I could hear. Eventually, we broke away from the safety of the farmhouse wall and headed towards the church. From the other side of the barn we should be able to see the small portion of the bunker that existed above ground. Deborah was still leading the way, and she turned the corner around the church barn first. She was barely there for a second when she stepped backwards, raising her arms out to her sides to form a barrier between us and whatever it was she had seen.

'What is it?' I asked, resisting the urge to push myself past and see for myself.

She turned silently and beckoned us forwards. 'Slowly,' she mouthed, 'don't make a sound.'

I had expected Halcyon to appear entirely abandoned – after all, I had watched the entire population head underground as we had left the church. Instead, every member of the Church of Heaven on Earth except for the four of us was standing together, filling the sizable clearing outside the bunker with shivering bodies. Piled up to one side of the cluster of people was a heap of what looked like heavy sacks. I squinted to get a better look, but then wished I hadn't. In reality, the heavy sacks were the lifeless bodies of our three cows, piled up against each other, brown fur soaked with crimson blood. Next to me, Ruth gasped and covered her mouth with her hands. None of the crowd were looking at the cows, though. Instead, they were all staring in the same direction, through the chain-link fence, and out into the wide world beyond Halcyon. I followed their gaze until my eyes landed on the most surprising sight of all. Three police cars, their lights off and their sirens silent, were parked in the near distance. As I watched, they slowly moved closer to the colony, three white vultures with their eyes on the prize.

As one, Ruth, Deborah, Mim and I turned back the way we had come, heading towards the farmhouse as quickly and as noiselessly as we could.

# Chapter Thirty-Three

## Ruth

Before I moved to England, I didn't have much of an idea of what it would be like. My world was confined to the areas of our town that my father would let me visit, whatever was preached at church, and a short family vacation to Galveston, Texas when I was about eight years old. I'd receive a birthday card once a year in the mail from my godmother in London, but it was too expensive to call her. The rare occasions when she came to visit us, she would spend most of her stay talking with my mother, who she'd gone to high school with, and I would be too nervous to speak to her. That's how we were all raised, my siblings and I: to be seen and not heard around grown-ups who were not our direct blood relations. But also, she scared me a little. She had a loud voice and a big laugh and wore colourful drapey clothes with bright patterns which I thought of as vaguely African. She was nothing like anyone I had seen in my town, but I didn't think of her as English either. Her accent was like ours, although she did mispronounce certain words – water as *woh-ta* – in a way that made my siblings and I giggle behind our napkins at dinner.

So even when I moved to England, my concept of the English was a little hazy. I half imagined England to be full of tall white men in those black suits with long tails and big stovepipe hats, sipping cups of tea with their pinkies sticking up in the air. My funny little fantasy faded about as quickly as I'd expected it to when I arrived, but one thing that did strike me was just how much tea everyone seemed to drink. I remember my first day on the ward at the training hospital, and the ward sister telling me that my tea break would be at four and thinking that she was teasing me.

When our ladies were delivered of their babies, the first thing we would give them was a cup of tea. It was a quirk that never became normal for me in all the years I lived there, so when we returned to the farmhouse and Deborah's first move was to boil the kettle and spoon leaves into the teapot, I could hardly believe my eyes. I felt for sure that Aoife would scold her for not taking the situation seriously enough, but when she passed the mugs around Aoife took hers with more gratitude than I had ever seen her express. I curled my hands around my own mug, allowing the warmth to seep through to my hands and the rising heathery steam to lap at my face. As crazy as it seemed to sit drinking tea while Halcyon was surrounded by police, I had to admit that there was something about it that soothed me. Maybe I'd been there too long.

'So,' said Aoife, 'how are we going to get around the fence without anyone seeing us?'

Deborah, who had been taking a long sip of her drink, returned her mug to the table.

'Well, it's obvious, isn't it? We're not.'

Aoife raised a sceptical eyebrow, and I shrank back into my seat on instinct.

'And why is that?'

'Well, because it's not physically possible. There are too many of us for a start, and *way* too many of them. And we don't know why the police are here. What if they think we're all planning something crazy, like a mass suicide or a – I don't know, what was that thing those religious people did on the metro in Japan? Some kind of bomb thing?'

'Ah, yes,' said Aoife, 'makes sense with all the mass public-transport systems we've got around here, to go with all of our weaponry and bomb-making equipment.'

Deborah let out a frustrated sigh. She was a very pretty woman with very delicate features, but her entire face had hardened.

'A mass suicide then,' she said, 'whatever. It doesn't even matter. What I mean is, if they think we're going to do something dangerous, they'll be willing to use force. I'm not going to leave my kids here alone surrounded by armed police even if I could get out, which as we've already established, is now impossible because of said police.'

'I didn't think police in Scotland were armed.' My fight-or-flight response activated at the thought of it.

All three women turned, looking as surprised as I was that I had spoken.

'Sorry,' I said, noticing the red blotches appearing on Deborah's cheeks, 'it was just a thought.'

Aoife pointed at me in a way that said *see, Ruth knows what she's talking about*, and Deborah ran her hands through her hair.

'You just don't get it,' she said. 'It doesn't matter to me if they have AK-47s or bloody pepper spray or even just a really strong hose. I'm not going to leave my kids here. And I know *we* know we're not going to do anything daft, but they don't know that! What if some pissed-off local from Abercraig has told them we've got a munitions factory in the community barn or something?'

As Deborah spoke, her voice rose higher and higher, her frustration growing with every word. She seemed just about ready to pop, so I was relieved when, after a pause, Aoife nodded her head.

'You're right,' she said, looking Deborah in the eye, 'I'm sorry.'

Deborah bristled, and shuffled uncomfortably in her seat. Clearly, she had been gearing herself up for a lengthier debate.

'Okay, well, good.'

'Good,' said Aoife, 'let's come up with a new plan.'

The wind howled outside like a wild wolf threatening to blow the house down as the four of us huddled together around the table. With every moment that passed I felt my chest tighten a little more.

'Let's try and think about this logically,' said Aoife, clasping her hands together, 'the most important thing is—'

'To get the kids out,' interrupted Deborah.

Aoife faltered. 'Well, yes, obviously long-term the most important thing is getting us and the children out, but before we do that we need to speak to the police. They need to know that we're not dangerous, and that the four of us want to leave.' She paused for a moment. 'And that there are a lot of children here who need to leave too. We need to tell them not to use force.'

Deborah nodded, satisfied. 'And how do we do that?'

'I suppose there's only one way. We can't wait for them to come in, or it'll be too late. One of us will have to go and speak to them. Tell them what we want to do, and get them to pull down the gate or cut a hole in the fence or something.'

My palms grew clammy with sweat at the thought of going

out there, and I prayed silently that I wouldn't be chosen to go. Aoife had just begun to say 'maybe Ruth—' when my prayer was answered in a way that made me wish it hadn't been.

The low chuckle from the doorway made us all jump. I turned to see John standing there, his arms folded across his chest. The whistling wind must have drowned out his approach, and I couldn't bear to think how long he might have been listening to us. He shook his head indulgently before he spoke.

'I don't think that would be a very good idea.'

Deborah rolled her eyes. 'Fuck off, John.'

A sharp laugh bubbled up through my throat and burst from my mouth. I had never heard anyone speak to John that way before. I smacked my palm over my lips but I was too late. John glared in my direction before returning his focus to Deborah.

'Don't get me wrong, Deborah, I was just trying to help. Ruth is apparently half the reason the police are here.'

I felt as if the blood was evaporating in my veins. I wanted to ask what he meant, but the words came out as a dry croak. Nobody else spoke.

'Yes, well apparently,' John continued, 'when someone comes into a country on a student visa, and then they stay on a work visa, the government gets a little… cross, when that person stops working. And when that person starts using the skills they learned while working here to deliver countless unregistered babies, they get even crosser.'

He shrugged his shoulders.

'You're lying.' Aoife's voice was barely a whisper. 'How could they possibly know she was here?'

'That's where it gets even better,' he said. 'You see, it seems like you have a mole in your little coven here. Someone, and I couldn't possibly say who, has been chatting with a very friendly undercover officer who's been visiting all the way from Edinburgh for the past – how long would you say it's been, Aoife?'

I was too busy reeling from the knowledge that the police were here for me to fully comprehend the meaning behind John's final revelation, but Deborah did. She turned with the full force of her body to face Aoife straight on.

'You fucking *idiot*! What were you *thinking* of, talking to some random bloke about all of us? And telling him our names? What else did you tell the police, Aoife? I have a birthmark on my hip and a scar on my foot, did you mention that to your little friend? You seem to have blabbed bloody everything bloody else!'

The louder Deborah grew the broader John's smile became. I wanted to tell her to stop, that he was saying these things because he wanted us to fight, but I couldn't get the words to come. Instead, all I could do was sit and listen and watch as John grew smugger and Deborah grew angrier and Aoife shrunk deeper and deeper into herself.

'And if one traitor wasn't bad enough…'

This time John turned to Mim, who until then had been sitting in stunned silence, and flashed her a smile. Even Deborah stopped yelling at Aoife and refocussed her attention on John.

'We know all about your little plots,' he continued, 'and your secret wine parties, and the treacherous things you gossip about when the decent people of Halcyon are busy working themselves to the *bone* for this community.' A vein had begun to throb in his temple, but he managed to keep his voice level. 'I will say, I was very proud when Mim trotted in and told Elijah and I all about it last night after the spirit drill. But it seems that the glamour of sin is still too much for her little mind to resist, and she's found her way back to your witches' den.'

# Chapter Thirty-Four

## Deborah

Aoife had turned as white as a sheet, and with all the colour drained from her face she suddenly seemed to be much older than she was. Thin lines ran across the horizon of her forehead and in between her brows, and it was only now that I noticed how deep the purple bags were under her eyes. I don't know whether those features stood out then because of some sudden change in her, or because I had never allowed myself to notice anything so human about Aoife before. It made it worse. I hated seeing her so sad and small and sorry, not because I didn't want her to be all of those things, but because it didn't seem fair that she could do something so awful and then turn herself into a victim. It would have been better if she had shouted back at me, or even if she had apologised to Ruth. But instead she just sat there, shrinking, making me angrier and angrier. My attention was so focussed on Aoife that the rest of the room blurred into nothing and all I could see was her. Somewhere in my periphery I could sense John standing smugly, watching the scene he had caused with pleasure, but I was past caring about giving him the satisfaction. *Let him enjoy it*, I thought, *why the hell not?*

My focus was broken by a stifled cry from across the table. Mim was gripping the sides of her face with her skinny bird hands. She looked almost as awful as Aoife, with huge red splotches spreading over her cheeks.

'I'm so sorry, Deborah,' she choked, 'I'm so ashamed.'

I had been so fixed on Aoife's betrayal that it took me a moment to connect her tears with John's exposure of her own short-lived deflection from our little group. Ordinarily, I would have been hurt, maybe even angry, but the more immediate threat of the police circling Halcyon had done wonders for my perspective. Mim's apology only made me more upset with Aoife than I had been before, and my frustration at her turning the situation towards herself coloured my response.

'Don't worry about it,' I said, itching to turn back to Aoife, 'there are bigger things to focus on right now.'

She shook her head desperately.

'No,' she said, 'it's not just that. I told them it was all you because I trusted you the least, and I was so upset about Ollie and I thought you knew all about it because you spent so much time in the schoolhouse but I was wrong, I can tell now that you didn't know anything about any of it.'

When Mim paused to catch her breath, I took my chance to interrupt. A creeping sickness was spreading over my body, and I needed to know that she didn't mean what I thought she meant.

'What are you talking about? What about Ollie in the schoolhouse? What actually happened to him?'

Mim gave a great sniff and wiped her running eyes and nose on the sleeve of our wedding dress.

'He was being bad so they took him out back with the bucket. They do it all the time.' She worked to hold in a sob. 'I thought you knew! I thought you were in charge!'

Words and images flashed through my mind, but they were too many and passed too quickly for me to stop and focus on one. The room spun around me, and I clung to the tabletop to keep my balance. Ruth's voice, slow and considered, pulled me a little closer back to earth.

'What do they do all the time?' she asked.

'Everything!' Mim practically wailed. 'The buckets, the water, the night drills, the beatings, making you stand outside even if it's cold and dark. I thought she knew!' She turned to me again, her eyes full of shame and sadness, 'I thought you told them to!'

Before I could speak, before I could even look around to see Ruth and Aoife's reactions, John clapped his hands together as if he was distracting a group of unruly children.

'Right,' he said, 'I think I've had just about enough of this ridiculous whinging and crying. If you would all follow me.'

It took me a second to realise that we were all waiting for Aoife to respond. She had become our unofficial spokeswoman, and her silence left us momentarily without a voice.

'We're quite happy here,' I said, shifting my hand over my bulging stomach, 'thank you.'

And that was when he brought out the gun.

I didn't know what it was at first. The idea of there being a gun in our kitchen, or in Halcyon at all, was so alien that even with it right there in front of me, my brain couldn't believe my eyes. There had never been firearms in Halcyon. Elijah had been insistent, even when it was pointed out that lots of people who lived off the land had guns because they needed them to slaughter livestock or shoot pests. He was completely stubborn about it. Jesus Christ had never held a gun, after all, and in Biblical times people had slaughtered their animals with their own hands. Elijah explained to us that this was the most respectful practice, because you had to really appreciate the fact you were taking the life of one of God's creatures – albeit a creature God created for humans to eat – something that could not be achieved with the pull of a trigger.

John had removed the gun from the waistband of his trousers, where it had been concealed under his jumper, in a way that suggested he had been practicing. The situation was obviously dangerous, and far more volatile than any of us could have imagined, but the rehearsed-ness of the move allowed me to relax just slightly. It made everything seem a little less threatening and reassured me that we were all still living in the real world; a world where nobody instinctively knew how to handle a deadly weapon, even if they had somehow managed to gain access to one.

Ruth rose to her feet and raised her hands above her head as soon as the gun was drawn, and the scraping of chair legs against the wooden floor made me jump.

'Where on earth did you get that thing?' I asked, pulled back to my senses by the sound.

John smirked, the tilt of his head suggesting that there were a lot more things we didn't know about. Instead of answering me, he jerked the shaft of the gun towards the door.

'Up you get. Elijah has enough to contend with today without the lot of you making his life even more difficult.'

Mim was the next to stand. She shuffled over to Ruth, then clung to her side like a limpet. Aoife followed, dead-eyed and zombified. I wondered if she had even noticed John was apparently armed, or if she had just moved because that's what everyone else seemed to be doing. The three of them stood, clustered, along the kitchen wall, Mim and Aoife copying Ruth's raised-hands pose. John was still blocking the doorway, clearly not wanting to give up his tactical advantage any sooner than he had to. Once he was satisfied the other wives were not going anywhere, he turned his attention and his gun back to me. Despite the whirlpool of emotions ripping through my body, I was determined to stand my ground and remain in my chair, straight-backed and as defiant as a pregnant Joan of Arc. He seemed less than impressed.

'I won't ask you again,' he said. 'Get up, Deborah.'

I let out an unimpressed *pfft* sound, which came out louder and more sarcastic than I had planned.

'I bet that thing isn't even real,' I said.

Although my heart hammered in my chest, I couldn't help but feel proud of the confidence in my voice. I had always been a versatile actress, and this time I had taken to my new part so well that I almost had myself convinced. Almost, but not quite. John's finger moved slightly towards the trigger and I forced myself not to flinch.

'If you hurt this baby,' I said, 'Elijah will kill you. You know he will, John.'

Up until that moment, John had been pointing the gun towards me, clutching it stiffly and unnaturally in a white-knuckled hand. Once I had finished speaking, though, he lowered his arm and shook his head. There was nothing forced or false about the look of pity and disgust in his featureless face. He stepped towards me and crouched down so we were eye to eye.

'Deborah,' he said, 'this is the End. It's here. We've been waiting for this moment for *years*. Elijah has been tearing himself apart getting ready for this. It's all he cares about now.'

He was so close that I could practically taste his breath, stale and rank. He lowered his voice.

'He's already decided that you're a liability. You're not coming into the bunker, so either way it's a death sentence. You and the baby. Elijah's orders.'

He stood back up, and when he spoke again it was loud enough for the whole room to hear.

'Sorry to break it to you, Deborah. The choice is yours.'

Except, there was no choice. I rose unsteadily to my feet.

# Chapter Thirty-Five

## Aoife

I expected John to lead us out of the kitchen and shepherd us straight out of the farmhouse door. Instead, he closed the kitchen door then took us to my room. My bed was still unmade from the morning, the tangled quilt and sheets showing everyone what a poor night's sleep I had had. The curtains were closed too, and I was conscious of how strongly the room still smelled of my sleeping body. A pile of dirty clothes sat shamelessly on the floor by my wardrobe. Fortunately, my numbed brain could not bring itself to care about how vulnerable or human my bedroom made me appear. They had already seen the very worst of me, and I already loathed myself more than they ever could. Somewhere in the back of my mind came a whisper of a thought about Malcolm and what he would think, before I remembered that he was the reason for all of this in the first place.

Without a word John left us, the click of the key in the lock his parting remark. I wanted to perch myself on the edge of the bed – according to the little voice straining to be heard through the fog in my brain, this would make the best impression – but as soon as I touched the mattress my body took over and I found myself lying down flat, like a cadaver on an embalming table. And so I waited, tense and ready, for the inevitable onslaught of anger.

Nothing was said at first, but it didn't take long for Deborah to oblige. It was as though she had spent years and years with her lips sewn together, and all of a sudden the threads had been cut and she was free to voice all of the vitriol that had been bubbling in her mind all that time. And in her defence, that was very much what had happened. We were past the point of reality and were all sharing the same lucid dream, where anything could be said or done without fear of consequence. It was fine, though. I could barely hear Deborah at all. I could tell her words were harsh, but they washed over me like water over a rock, smoothing me out, wearing me away. Even if I'd wanted to defend myself, I had no fight left. She might have gone on forever if Ruth hadn't interrupted her.

'Stop it, Deborah, please! I can't take it any more!'

I opened my eyes but didn't dare lift my head, and Deborah's rant stopped.

'I'm absolutely not going to defend Aoife, but don't you think we have more important things to worry about? Elijah wants us to sit here and fight and tear each other apart because it saves him the job. Deborah, I know you're mad at Aoife right now but aren't you even madder at Elijah? We need to remember who the real bad guys are, and I personally don't think that there are any in this room.'

'Are you kidding me?' said Deborah. 'I appreciate what you're trying to do here, Ruth, but don't you get it? They don't care about us any more, they think this is real and they're leaving us here to die! And it's her fault.'

Out of the corner of my eye, I saw Deborah point an accusatory finger in my direction.

'Deborah, please—'

'Oh come off it, Ruth, why are you defending her? She *hates* us.'

I waited for Ruth to speak up again, but instead of coming to my defence, she stayed silent. Did Ruth think I hated her?

'I can trace every single issue in my marriage back to her.'

I pushed myself up so I was resting on my elbows and turned to face Deborah.

'Really, Deb? Every issue?'

'Yes, *Aoife*, every issue. I worked and I worked to make something of this,' she gestured around her, 'and to keep him happy, and there you were, every time, whispering away in his ear – *Deborah's fake, Deborah doesn't really believe in this life, Deborah doesn't deserve you.*'

'I never said that,' I spat. 'You were always the one going on to him about me. He told me all of your nasty little opinions, that I'm past it, and stuck-up, and—'

'I never said that,' Deborah practically screeched.

'I know you—'

'Oh for goodness sake, listen to yourselves!'

I had never once heard Ruth raise her voice, and Deborah, Mim and I all turned at once to look at her, too stunned to do anything but listen. She was sitting cross-legged on the floor with her back to the door, and even in the fading light I could read the exasperation on her face.

'How do you not see what's been happening here? How are you missing this? How did *I* miss it?'

'What are you talking about?' I snapped.

I was itching with annoyance at being interrupted, even by Ruth.

'He was lying, Aoife,' she said, her voice calm and patient, 'he was making it all up.'

Embarrassment hit me as suddenly and overwhelmingly as a wave of nausea. He had been lying. Of course he had. But why did this particular constellation of lies, this messy, petty web, stand out amongst all the others as such a cruel betrayal?

Deborah, too, seemed felled by the realisation. The mattress sank as she sat down heavily at the foot of the bed. It was strange to look at her there, knowing what I did. Even as we had started to get along better in the days since we met in Elijah's office, I had been storing an undercurrent of resentment towards the woman who I had thought had laughed at my vanished fertility, pitied my age, loathed my personality. Now that was gone, or going, at the very least – years of dislike do not fade so easily – she seemed more real. The careful way she cradled her stomach with her arms, even with her head in her hands, no longer seemed like an affectation or a subtle brag. It was just the action of an ordinary woman.

'How could I be so stupid?' Deborah's voice was muffled.

'He said the same to me,' said Ruth, 'but that you'd both thought I was lazy. I guess it makes sense. Divide and conquer. We're easier to manage if we can be kept apart.'

'So,' I said, taking my chance, 'you were right, Ruth. We're not the bad guys.'

Deborah raised her head.

'Oh, you would say that. This doesn't change the fact that you dobbed Ruth in to that policeman.'

I bristled, a familiar flash of anger striking through my chest.

Maybe my thoughts of peace and forgiveness had come too soon. We all looked at Ruth again, waiting for her to speak.

'I think,' she said, eventually, 'that if we're going to get out of here, we need to stop fighting with each other.'

'Thank you,' I replied.

'As for you,' she raised her eyebrows and pulled herself up from the floor, 'you're lucky I'm a very forgiving woman. I'm trying to think of a single other person on God's green earth who would have the grace to react the way I am to you right now.'

Deborah snorted.

'I know, I'm so sorry, Ruth.'

'Apologise to me later, when we're all safely out of here. For now, why don't you worry about helping us decide what we're going to do next?'

I had never known Ruth speak with such confidence outside of a delivery room or some other medical emergency. Something about the authority in her voice caused my body to react to her command, and before my brain even knew what was what I was sitting up and surveying the room. We had no guarantee of how long we could expect to be left alone, which was my first concern. There was no point in spending hours coming up with a foolproof plan only for John to return with his gun before we had a chance to actually do anything, and I said as much. The others nodded. Even Mim, who was doing her very best to disappear into the corner, let out a vague murmur of agreement.

'You're right,' said Ruth, 'and with that in mind, I think our best bet is to get out of this room as quickly as possible. Once we're out, Aoife will have to find a way to speak to her police officer – I guess he's one of the ones out there right now.' She looked down at me, her dark eyes focused and bright. 'Aoife, you'll have to tell him exactly what's going on, and that we all need out, us and all of the kids. Make sure he knows who I am and what I look like and that I'm not going to put up a fight about the deportation or arrest or whatever it might be. Deborah, Mim, you need to give Aoife an exact number of children so the police know how many to look out for.'

All we could do was agree.

'Great,' she said, 'now, how are we going to get out? I mean, the obvious answer is through the window, but I don't think that's going to work for everyone.'

Four sets of eyes turned to my tiny bedroom window. Although my room was on the ground floor, the window was built high enough into the wall that you could only see out of it if you were standing up. Deborah raised her hand.

'There's a key to Elijah's office in the chest of drawers at the top of the stairs,' she said, 'and I'm pretty sure Elijah will have a spare set of keys to all of our rooms in there somewhere. That way only one of us would have to go out of the window. Whoever does that can come back in through the front door, go upstairs and fetch the keys, come back down and let the rest of us out.'

'That sounds good to me,' Ruth said, before casting her eyes around the room again. 'So, who's going to be able to fit through the window?'

'Wait, wait, wait,' I said, 'I know we agreed that we have to move quickly, but don't you think there are a lot of variables here that we haven't considered? Like, what if John locked the farmhouse door, or if Elijah has moved his spare key from the drawers?'

I looked hopefully from face to face, waiting for someone to agree, but nobody did. Ruth shrugged.

'If that happens, then we're back to square one. But at least we've tried something.'

I bit the inside of my cheek.

'Fine. In that case, I suppose I should be the one to go out of the window.'

Again, nobody spoke. I clambered over the bed so I was on the right side, opened the curtains, and peered through the glass and out into Halcyon. From here I couldn't see any of the police cars, or the gathering of colonists – only a cluster of beehives and some outbuildings. Even the hives seemed deserted in the dim light of the late autumn afternoon. I don't suppose I had ever really paid much attention to the window itself before that day. I had not ever felt inclined to open it – even in the summertime, I was never so warm as to need that – and I hadn't thought enough of the view to look out very often. So it wasn't until then that I noticed the frame of the window itself had no handle or hinges by which it could be opened. There were just six small panes of glass, welded together with heavy leaden piping. I pulled my bedside table underneath the window to act as a stepping stool and gave a weak push. Unsurprisingly, it didn't budge.

'Oh, get off there,' said Deborah, raising an arm to help me down from the table.

I took it gratefully, but let go the instant my feet touched the ground. Her feelings about me were clearly still cool, and I didn't want her to think mine had changed too much either.

She bent down as best she could and picked up the bedside table. 'Stand back!'

Ruth, Mim and I moved as far away as the space allowed in the seconds between Deborah's warning and the forceful smash of wood against glass. She dropped the table for a moment and panted, her hands resting on her thighs, before picking it up again and clearing the rest of the frame. Once the window was completely gone, Deborah sat down heavily on the bed.

'Well, I hope no one heard that.'

I doubted it. As empty as Halcyon looked, the sound of police sirens and nervous chatter was enough to block out any noise from the farmhouse.

Before I even got the chance to return to my spot by the window, Ruth shook her head.

'Sorry, Aoife,' she said, inspecting the gap, 'but there's no way you're going to be able to fit through there. I'll have to try.'

We watched in silent awe as Ruth found her balance on the bedside table – still sturdy despite its dealings with the window – and pulled herself up so her forearms were resting against the window ledge.

'Careful,' said Deborah, her hands pressed against her mouth, 'there might still be some shards.'

Ruth nodded and returned to the ground.

'There are going to be shards there whatever we do,' she said, 'I think we'll need to get the whole frame out somehow.'

I nodded, and Deborah stepped forward.

'The plaster around the wood is all crumbly – we should be able to dislodge it if we both push as hard as we can.'

I watched as together they pushed the window frame free from the wall. It seemed to come away easily enough, a testament to the age and decrepit nature of the house, leaving more plaster dust in its wake. By this point we were filthy with it, each of us covered head to toe in a thin grey film.

Once the frame was safely removed, Ruth pulled herself up again, this time thrusting her torso forward and out, until her front half was clear of the room. It soon became apparent, though, that her hips were going to be too wide to make it the full way through. Defeated, she slowly eased herself back down.

'Well, that idea's a bust. Does anyone else have another plan? Maybe we can try and knock this door down too?'

With the window gone the sounds of outside seemed louder than ever, and the cacophony made it almost impossible to think. I was wracking my brain for any other possible escape routes when Mim's reedy voice piped up from the corner.

'It's not a bust. I mean, it might not be yet. I think I could be small enough to squeeze through.'

The idea of Mim, as petite as she was, having the physicality needed to launch herself through a window – wearing a wedding gown of all things – seemed almost funny, but by that point she was our only chance. I could tell from Ruth and Deborah's silence that they, too, were reluctant to give her the job but whatever their reasons were, they were clearly not pressing enough, because within moments Mim was halfway into Halcyon.

# Chapter Thirty-Six

## Mim

By the time I realised what I was doing I was already perched, knees to my chest, in the empty window frame, looking down at the pile of broken glass below. Getting up there had been a lot easier than I had expected, but I suppose I hadn't really considered the fact that I would also need to get down. The thought of it made me freeze up, all except for my stomach, which churned and growled and made me worry that I might be sick. I tried to remember that I was safe because I was being upheld in God's righteous right hand, but that made me even sicker, because I wasn't sure if God *was* upholding me any more.

I could pinpoint the exact moment that things had started going really wrong. Right in the middle of the second spirit drill, just as Elijah was warning us about the oncoming tide of sin, my bleeding started. I could feel the warm wetness between my legs, and whenever I moved the nasty smell of blood wafted up into my nostrils and made me queasy. It had been Deborah who had first explained things to me the day the first streak of rust appeared in my knickers. She called it my 'monthly cycle', which I found confusing. The name made it sound like it would arrive once a month, which it rarely did, and last a short amount of time, which it never did. Once it lasted straight through from one full moon to another. I became so sick and worried that I confided in Helen, who told me that I must have been doing something very wicked for it to have lasted that long, and that God was clearly very angry with me. Since then I began to see the blood as a punishment or a bad omen. And I must have been right, because look at all of the things that had happened since the blood spilled in church. They were too many and too awful to even think about.

I took a deep breath in, filling my lungs as much as I could in my crouched position. My body must have needed the air, because straight away I began to feel a little bit better. I was still scared of the drop and nervous about my heavy menstrual rag slipping and bleeding into the wedding dress, but at least I could think a little more clearly.

'Please can somebody pass me something that I can throw down to land on,' I called in to Aoife's bedroom, 'so I don't cut myself on the glass?'

I tried not to look down too much, but I could hear the commotion in the room behind me as they looked for something suitable. Aoife's arm reached up and handed me the rag rug. It was the first thing my eyes had landed on when I entered her room because I had made it myself, way back when we had first arrived in Halcyon. The gesture seemed like it might be symbolic, but I couldn't quite figure out how.

There was just enough of a gap between my scrunched-up body and the window frame for me to throw the mat out. I shook it as best I could with my left hand, while my right held tightly onto the inside wall, hoping that it would land flat enough to cover plenty of the glass. Jaw clenched, I watched it fall quickly and heavily to the ground; it managed to fold itself almost clean in half, but at least the biggest patch of shards was covered. I muttered a quick prayer of thanks.

'Are you okay up there? Do you want to change out of the dress before you jump?'

It was Ruth. The concern in her voice warmed my heart, but at the same time I didn't want her to think that I was less capable or brave than the rest of them. I also didn't want to have to climb back down the way I had come to change into something else in case I couldn't bring myself to go back up again. I knew that my voice would shake and give me away if I tried to answer, so I just repositioned myself to let my legs dangle down against the outside wall. I had an idea in my mind that I would be able to use my arms as levers and lower myself slowly enough to avoid a real drop. My muscles – what little of them there were – had other ideas, and I had no sooner attempted to support my own weight when they gave up entirely, leaving me to fall gracelessly in the vague direction of the mat.

The second I landed I forced myself to stand up, knowing that if I waited on the ground for any length of time, I would find it impossible to move. I looked down and surveyed the damage, my body still shaking from the impact. Most of me had managed to find the rug, but my left hand had gone straight down on a thick shard of glass which was now sticking out of the centre of my palm. The back of the wedding dress was another victim of the fall; it had torn badly from scraping against the rough stonework of the outside wall and was hanging in sad, tattered strips. Thanks be to God, the satin had provided enough of a barrier to prevent the backs of my legs from facing the same fate.

'Mim!'

I turned to see Ruth's worried face sticking out of the window.

'Are you hurt?' she asked.

'Not really,' I said. 'Just—'

I raised my left palm up to her, and she winced.

'Before you do anything else,' she said in her nurse's voice, 'I need you to pull that out.'

A lump rose in my throat, and I turned my back to the window. Breathing heavily, I took the glass between the thumb and forefinger of my right hand. The touch alone was enough to make me shudder, but I knew she was right. The longer I left it the worse it would be. If I had learned one thing from my years in the schoolhouse, it was that painful things were best to get over quickly. I had also learned that I could handle more than I thought I could. The first time I was sent outside, soaked from wetting the bed, I had thought I would die from the cold – but I didn't. Every beating I took had felt like the most I could take, but then they would go on and I would realise I could take more. This was just like that. I thought of Christ, and the nails they had driven into his palms, as I tightened my grip and pulled. My skin released the glass with a gentle spurt of blood, and I turned back to Ruth, who was still waiting anxiously in the window. Once she was satisfied that the glass was gone, she allowed herself a small smile of relief.

'Now tear off some of the wedding dress and wrap your hand with it, tight as you can. Then take another strip and wrap it round your wrist, like a tourniquet – do you know what a tourniquet is? To stop the flow of blood.'

I did as I was told. Even with the sound of sirens in the background, the rip of the fabric made me shudder. I hoped Aoife and Deborah would forgive me.

'Good job,' she said. 'Now round you go. We'll be waiting.'

Before she could say anything more, I hurried around the corner of the farmhouse. My lungs struggled to take in the cold air, even though my body was desperate for it. My heart still hadn't slowed at all. I leaned against the wall, not trusting my shaking legs to support me on their own. That was when I heard the voices travelling on the wind. I inched along and peeked around the corner so I could get a better look at the front of the house, where the voices seemed to be coming from. John and Elijah were standing by the door. I ducked straight back around. Could I run back to them, maybe? Fall to my knees at Elijah's feet and beg his forgiveness? But before I could make my mind up, John spoke.

'All I'm saying is, I don't know what we're waiting for,' he said. 'We should grab Mim and get the marriage done. She'll be no bother, once she's away from those—'

'I said no.' Elijah sounded angry. 'Forget about Mim.' The sound of my name made my heart race. 'The police have enough on me already. If they catch me with her, I'm a dead man.' He almost sounded scared when he said that.

'Nobody is going to catch you! We've been preparing for this, that's what the bunker is for. They'll never get in, and by the time we're out of provisions, the Lord will have called us to Him.'

'What a mess,' said Elijah in a low voice that I could only just hear. 'I can't believe I'm risking jail for this lot.'

My head was spinning as I leaned against the wall, listening to the sounds of papers changing hands. If Elijah was frightened, surely we all should be?

'No one is going to jail, mate. The police can't touch you.'

Why was he so worried about the police, I wondered? Didn't he trust the bunker to keep everyone safe? I was still trying to figure out what was going on when I heard their footsteps crossing the courtyard. As they came into view, I pressed myself as close to the wall as I could. They were walking in the direction of the bunker, and Elijah had his hands in his pockets.

'Let's just go back to the bunker for now. You'll feel better when everyone is safely inside. I can always come back up for

Mim later if you change your mind. And I thought I told you to lay off that stuff today? I know you say it helps you focus, but it's got you all on edge.'

Elijah spun round to face John and swung a fist in his direction. My hands rose up to my face as John was knocked to the ground. Elijah looked down at him and said something too quiet for me to hear before walking off, leaving John to pull himself to his feet. I watched him running to catch up, and stayed where I was until they were both out of sight.

Aoife, Ruth, and Deborah would be wondering where I was. I had no idea how long I had been standing there, listening to the men talking. What if they managed to find another way out, and they came looking for me? I knew I was going to have to move, because if they found me there and asked what I'd been doing, I would have to tell the truth. And I wasn't sure that I wanted to tell them. They would have so many questions, and I wouldn't know the answers, and anyway, maybe it hadn't been as bad as it had looked? How could I know for certain what I had seen and heard? It was probably better to pretend it hadn't happened at all.

I inched back around the wall. In the gaps between the farm buildings I could see two figures patrolling the fence. I squinted. It was Niall – I recognised him by his lolloping gait, even though he was obviously trying his best to march – and Mark, his red hair standing bright against the darkening sky. I craned my neck so I could see more, and the first thing I spotted was the cluster of police cars, surrounded by officers dressed in black. I hadn't seen anything or anyone like them since we left the city when I was ten. They looked like crows pecking around, just waiting for Halcyon to die so they could swoop in and pick it to pieces. The thought of it made me feel uneasy. I didn't want to get married to Elijah, or go back to the schoolhouse, but at the same time I didn't want Halcyon to be over, not fully over, its corpse being pulled to bits by hungry police officers who didn't understand us and didn't want to. I remembered Elijah's warnings about the police, and their cruelty, and how even in Biblical times the upholders of the law of man had persecuted Christ and His followers. If he was scared, there was no wonder.

I knew that I needed to keep going, to get to the door and go up to Elijah's office to find a spare key to let everyone out before someone spotted me, but my legs had turned wobbly and weak. I closed my eyes so I could focus on the rough stone against my back and the way the cold was coming out of the wall and into my body. I felt the sting of my scraped skin, and the dull throb of the cut in my palm. My heartbeat slowed, and my legs seemed a little sturdier. I tried to keep concentrating on the little things as I opened my eyes and kept moving towards the front door, blocking out the wail of the sirens and listening instead to the crunch of gravel under my feet.

Just before I reached the door, I allowed myself to turn around. I could see that everyone was still congregated in front of the bunker, the only difference being that now the children were leaning against each other, clearly exhausted. The pile of cow carcasses was still there, and I hoped they weren't frightened of them. Ordinarily, I would have been there with them, holding their hands and keeping them calm. Instead, I was looking over from afar, preparing to bring their whole world crashing down. The thumping of my heart forced me to pull myself together and turn away before I froze up again. The door was locked, but Ruth had mentioned that there was always a spare key under the boot scraper next to the front step. The schoolhouse did not lock, and so I had never actually had to use a key before; I tried it one way, and then another, and then with a heavy click the door opened.

Despite the setting sun outside, the darkness of the farmhouse hallway overwhelmed my eyes. With every door closed and no other source of light, I had to fumble my way to the staircase and climb with my bad hand on the handrail and the other flat against the wall. I had never been upstairs in there before, and I wasn't used to stairs in general – this was the only building in Halcyon with a second storey – so I wanted to be careful. I was very aware that God might no longer be watching over me. The first door I tried swung open with ease, but my relief didn't last long. It wasn't Elijah's office, but Ruth's bedroom. I allowed myself to linger for a moment in the doorway before moving on to the only other door up there. I filled my lungs with the stale indoor air and pressed down on the handle. It was already unlocked.

The curtains were open in the office, and I could just about see all I needed to see with the fading afternoon light from outside. At a glance, everything looked orderly; books lined shelves like rows and rows of Christian soldiers, pens and pencils stood to attention in their pot on Elijah's desk. All as it should be. Gently, I closed the door behind me and stepped further into the room. *If I were a key, where would I be?* As tidy as the room was, there were a host of places things could be hidden. Inside the pages of a book, under a floorboard, inside the desk. I cast my eyes around and decided to start with the obvious. If Elijah never expected anyone to come into his office, I reasoned, why would he go to the lengths of hiding something as innocent as a set of keys? The first drawer I tried was locked, as was the second. *So much for my theory*, I thought. But still – if you were at your desk and needed something from a drawer, you wouldn't want to go far to find the key to unlock it. The only thing on Elijah's desk was an old mug filled with pens and pencils. Not wanting to waste a second, I tipped them out onto the desk. They bounced off the wooden surface and onto the floor, but the small flat key stayed where it landed – right under my nose.

I didn't have any expectations of what I might find inside the drawer, but I was still surprised. Brightly coloured packages caught what little light there was in the room and glistened temptingly. I knelt down so I could see them better, all pain suddenly taking a back seat to my curiosity. The sight of the packets and bags unlocked a pre-Halcyon memory from deep in the recesses of my mind, and a laugh bubbled up from nowhere.

# Chapter Thirty-Seven

## Ruth

The threat of deportation meant very little to me by then, if it had ever meant much in the first place. All I could think about as I paced back and forth in Aoife's room was getting us all out. The children, of course, but the adults too; good, honest people who just wanted to live better and do better and love one another, who had been taken in and turned into something else entirely. Or, mostly good. Mostly honest. The world outside may not have been perfect, but it was better than what we had here. The little capacity for caring that I had left over was spent on worrying about the animals – the poor cows had already been slaughtered, but Russell and the pups' fate was a mystery to me. Someone would have had to go into the cow shed where the dogs were, and I could only hope that whoever it was had been too focussed on their task to care about a small terrier and her litter.

Nobody spoke; there was nothing to say. The darkness set in around us as we waited. We all jumped when the front door opened, and I prayed that it was her. There was no way to know for sure, though the soft footsteps up the stairs were reassuring, but if it was, it had taken her a long time to get back into the farmhouse. I had become so immune to the sound of the sirens that I couldn't say when they stopped exactly – I only noticed the silence from outside when I realised that I could suddenly hear the small sounds from within the house. Upstairs, Mim – or the person I hoped was Mim – opened and closed two doors in quick succession. *Come on, come on.* Time stretched and warped. It was a race that my life depended on, but I could see none of the runners, and I had no idea how long the track was or how many obstacles would come between them and the finishing line.

Aoife had returned to the bed. She lay flat on her back, and when I passed her on my short loop of the room, I could see her lips moving in silent prayer. Deborah was still standing by the window, staring blankly out of the pane-less frame. They both must have been listening too, straining to hear any sound that might give away Mim's position and tell us how much longer we'd have to wait, because the creak of the top step pulled them out of their freeze frame. Together, we stood and watched the door.

# Chapter Thirty-Eight

## Deborah

My heart was halfway into my throat as I listened to Mim struggle with the keys on the other side of the door. It took all of my strength not to scream at her to hurry as key after key was pushed into the lock and key after key got jammed and we had to listen as she wriggled it out. When the door did finally swing open, I had to blink to make sure the dark wasn't playing tricks on me. She closed the door with one hand, because with the other she was holding an armful of crisp packets and chocolate bars.

'You'll never believe what I found in Elijah's desk,' she said, dropping her loot on the bed.

'I'm pretty sure I could take a guess,' I said, looking down at the snacks with hungry eyes. Somehow, the sight of the once familiar food calmed me a little. 'Is that what took you so long?'

Mim shook her head as we crowded round the bed.

'The keyring was right at the bottom of the drawer, and the drawer was full of all of this stuff. I thought I might as well pick some up, in case anyone was hungry.'

I was starved, but Ruth and Aoife both shook their heads, so I shook mine too.

'Did you see what was happening outside? Are the police still there? Is it safe for us to make a run for it?' Ruth asked.

Even before Mim spoke, it was obvious that she was not going to give us an answer we wanted to hear. She described the scene outside in stilted detail without looking up from her feet.

'I don't understand why they're making all of the children stand out in the middle of everything? They don't need to be seeing all of this, and they look so tired.'

She sounded sad, as if out of everything, this was what disappointed her the most about Halcyon.

'Surely they just want them where they can see them?' I said.

Aoife stirred from her seat on the bed and shook her head.

'No, I don't think so. They'll want them where the police can see them. They don't want them charging in with hoses or tear gas or whatever riot police do to break up crowds.'

My stomach sank.

'Tear gas?'

Aoife shrugged and lay back down. But the thought of tear gas or anything like it coming anywhere near my children made every cell in my body scream, and I clutched my stomach – at least I had one baby with me.

'Well, what are we going to do now?'

I could feel myself panicking, but I didn't even try to keep the rise from my voice. I was past the point of caring what Mim and Ruth and even Aoife thought of me. Ruth leaned across and took my hand in hers. My skin had been so starved of touch that Ruth's cold fingers sent an electric shock through my nerves and made my heart beat even faster.

'It's okay.' She looked me in the eyes as she spoke. 'I think we need to stick to our original plan; it's the only chance we have of getting out of here by the end of the day. I just think that instead of all of us leaving together, it might be more sensible if only one of us went. That way, we have less chance of getting caught.'

Immediately, Mim raised her hand.

'I'll go,' she said, 'I've done it once already, so I know where everyone is. I think it would be, you know – the sensible choice.'

I shook my head, pulling my hand out of Ruth's.

'Nope, not a chance. You've done enough, Mim. It's Aoife's turn now. She knows which police officer to speak to, anyway. I'm sure she'll be glad to see him.'

The last few words to leave my mouth were coated with an undeniable film of venom, which made Ruth flinch.

'I don't know—' she began, before she was interrupted by Aoife.

'No,' she said, her voice croaky and tired. 'Deborah is right. It wouldn't make sense for anyone else to go.'

Before any of us could say anything more, Aoife rose one last time from her bed and glided as purposefully as a ghost towards the door. Mim put her unbandaged hand up to her mouth, and Ruth began to gnaw on her nails. My heart tugged after her, which I didn't expect or enjoy. I swallowed the lump in my throat and turned my attention to the pile of snack foods on the bed. I unwrapped a bar of Dairy Milk, the purple sheen of its wrapper winking at me as I wolfed down the whole bar in nine swift bites. Once I had finished, I folded the wrapper into a small triangle, laid it on Aoife's pillowcase, and selected two packets of crisps: one cheese and onion and the other prawn cocktail. Even the puff of air which escaped the bags as I popped them open contained more flavour than I had experienced in six years. I could sense Ruth and Mim looking down at me and felt their silent concern, but I was overcome by what I could only describe as a vicious animal hunger. I shovelled the crisps into my mouth in great handfuls, licking the greasy crumbs off my fingers whenever they became too coated for me to easily pick up any more. As the night air whispered through the hole in the wall where the windowpane had once been, and the room became colder and darker, I continued to eat.

# Chapter Thirty-Nine

## Aoife

Mim's description of the scene outside had been enough to worry me, but it was still not enough to prepare me for what I saw when I left the farmhouse. The police cars had turned their headlights on, and four sets of bright white lights were casting strange shadows from the once-familiar figures and structures of the colony. I secreted myself behind the wall of the church, and from there I could see straight into the cluster of people in the centre of the settlement. Barely twenty feet away, I could hear the muffled whines of exhausted children and the hushed prayers of terrified adults. The whole thing was obscene. Elijah and I had planned for Halcyon to be a utopia, but there it was right before my eyes, transformed into a Jonestown or a Waco; the kind of place you would see on the news and shake your head and wonder at just how people got themselves into such a mess. Thankfully, I didn't have the time or the mental reserves to connect the dots and realise that *I* was now the sort of person people might wonder those things about. Instead, I turned towards the source of the blinding headlights in an attempt to make out the figures of the police officers. One was holding a large white loudspeaker. When she turned it on, the nails-down-a-chalkboard squeal cast a studded silence over the people of Heaven on Earth.

'My name is Courtney Ballantine. I am a Detective Sergeant in the Highlands and Islands police force.'

She spoke with a confidence which I found reassuring, although I worried it wouldn't do her any favours. A confident woman was not something to be appreciated in Halcyon, especially by the man in charge.

'We have spoken to one of you individually, but now we feel that it is time to address you all. I think it's only fair that you all understand what is happening here tonight. None of the officers here want to do you any harm. We have been made aware that there are children here – I can see them all now, and they look cold and scared – and we have a duty to check on their wellbeing.'

I watched as Annie broke away from the huddle of children crowding around her. Illuminated by the headlight beams, she stepped towards Courtney Ballantine and pointed an accusatory finger in her direction. She looked emaciated, her hair coming loose from its braided bun, eyes wild and gleaming. Had she always been so thin?

'Go away! Our children are fine! Go home and worry about your own children, and leave us alone!'

Ironically, Annie's screech set two of the smaller children off crying, but the rest of Halcyon didn't seem to care. Their cheers masked the cries of the babies, and the Detective Sergeant waited for them to stop.

'I understand that this is a very intense situation.' If she was angry, she wasn't showing it. 'We want to make it as stress-free as we can, for all of you, but especially for the little ones. I can see that you love them very much. We need to come in so we can check on them, and we need to speak to your—', she stopped for half a second, '—leader, in person. We ask that you open your front gates and let myself and my colleagues inside. If you do not comply, we will use force to enter your compound and we will arrest anyone who attempts to stop us from doing our job. I don't want that to happen, and I'm sure none of you want that to happen either. It's up to you to decide on the course of action you would like to take.'

The loudspeaker clicked off, and I moved to the other end of the building where I hoped to get a proper look at the detective. She was speaking quietly to another person who I now realised was Malcolm. I held my breath. He didn't seem to be paying very much attention to what she was saying, or at least he wasn't looking at her. He was busy scanning the crowd. I imagined his green eyes straining through the darkness and wondered if he was looking for me. I wasn't sure if I wanted him to see me or not, or what I would say to him if we spoke. I had thought of him as a friend, a person I could trust – someone kind who found me interesting and possibly even attractive. But in the end, he was just another man who had taken me in, the gullible fool that I was. *Prick*. The voice in my head was suddenly my own. I drew my eyes away and snuck back round so I could regain my view on the crowd of colonists. Elijah was nowhere to be seen, but John was there giving instructions to Mark S., a young man who had grown up in the church. Mark nodded and scurried off into one of the surrounding outhouses, returning with his own loudspeaker clutched to his chest. The bright white plastic looked out of place on the Halcyon side of the fence, and I struggled to remember if I had ever seen the loudspeaker before. It didn't seem familiar, but then nothing seemed familiar that night – not even the people.

John signalled for the hum of whispered conversation to stop before he raised the loudspeaker to his lips. There was no ear-splitting screech this time, and even from a distance I could sense his disappointment at the lack of dramatic effect.

'Halcyon is a peaceful community,' he began, 'and we have lived here for almost six years without causing any trouble to anyone. All we want to do is follow the Word of the Lord and of our Holy Prophet without disturbance from the outside world.'

A brief pause was followed by a cheer from the crowd.

'But now the outside world has come to us, you have left us with no choice. In order to move into the next life, we must be here, where we can follow our way of living. We would rather die in Halcyon and meet our Lord in Heaven, than live and burn in hell. And we would rather take our children with us than let them go with you and follow your sure path to damnation.

We will do what it takes to protect ourselves from your heathen ways. We have a stockpile of explosives here which we are ready and willing to use if you leave us no other choice. Either you leave this land now and never return, or we will burn this place to the ground and take ourselves with it!'

At first, I thought the screams and cries were ones of terror, but the more I listened the clearer it became – they were sounds of rejoicing. Choking back the bile which had risen to my mouth, I took the moment of distraction to run out from behind the safety of the church and towards the nearest outbuilding to the perimeter fence. The noise of the crowd and the blood pumping past my ears combined into one deafening roar as I ran, so I felt more like I was running through a nightmare than in real life. The outbuilding – a small tin shack where we stored surplus wool from our sheep – welcomed me like a beacon.

I had not planned to actually go inside; I'd hoped instead to use the cover it provided as a stopping place on my way to the perimeter, a point where I could hopefully attract the attention of someone on the other side of the fence. Once I was there, though, I couldn't resist. The prospect of having somewhere dark and quiet to gather my thoughts and catch my breath was too inviting, and I had barely stopped running before I pulled the heavy door open. Almost instantly, a hand shot through the darkness and grabbed hold of my skirt, pulling me in and knocking me off balance.

'Oh God! I'm so sorry! Please forgive me!'

As panicked and tearful as the voice was, I recognised it immediately.

'Helen? Is that you?'

'Aoife! Thank God! Have you seen Mim?'

Her hands, as frozen and ridged as ice, searched for mine and I almost felt sorry for her, but her desperation made me want to pull away and I shook her off in disgust.

'Well, she's certainly not in here, is she?' I whispered. 'What are you doing, Helen, hiding like a kid?'

'What am I supposed to do? What can any of us do? It's gone absolutely mental out there, Aoife, you must have seen it. There are police outside, and then John—' she broke off in tears before continuing, gasping and gulping, '—saying what he just said – did you hear him? I never thought I'd live to see it, Aoife, it's like a nightmare.'

Even in the darkness I could see her vague shape, curled up and quaking on the floor by my feet. It was unsettling to hear the fear in her voice. Usually Helen seemed incapable of presenting any negative emotions at all, but now her sweet baby-talk voice was gone. Even her words sounded so unfamiliar that I wondered for a moment if she was possessed.

I said the only thing I could think to say:

'Pull yourself together. There's plenty you can do if you actually want to help, instead of hiding out and feeling sorry for yourself.'

With a sniff, she fumbled for my hand once again. I allowed it, but gripped her a little tighter than I needed to as I pulled her from the floor.

'We're going to get everyone who wants to get out, out,' I said, 'but I can't do it alone.'

'We? Who's we?'

I sighed. 'Me, Ruth, Deborah, and Mim.'

'Mim! Mim's helping you? She's all right?'

'Yes, yes, she's fine. Or she's fine for now anyway, as fine as the rest of us. I need to get to the fence to speak to the police, but I can't get there if everyone is looking that way. Can you distract them?'

She sniffed again, wiped her nose with the back of her hand.

'Distract them how?'

# Chapter Forty

## Ruth

My nails, which had gone unbitten for ten years, had been torn to shreds in the minutes between Aoife leaving the room and the police officer's speech through the loudspeaker. I had been working away at them so distractedly that it was only Deborah's crumb-covered hand gently touching my own that even brought my attention to it. It was getting too dark to see clearly and none of us wanted to turn on the light, so I just sat there, running my fingertips over the ragged ends of my nails, waiting for anything to happen.

When the officer began her address, Deborah, Mim and I moved towards the empty window so we could hear better. We could have left, but although the door was unlocked, an unspoken agreement kept us where we were. We didn't even dare to lean up against it. Since Aoife had disappeared through it, I couldn't escape the feeling that she had been swallowed up, that there was no longer a hallway on the other side but some kind of swirling portal like you might see in a cheesy science-fiction movie – the sort I'd watched with my godmother in the early London days. The unfamiliar voice, tinged with a mechanical echo, did not do much to relieve my mind of that particular fantasy. It occurred to me that I hadn't eaten anything all day and I worried that I might be delirious. That made me feel faint, and I was concentrating so hard on not falling over that I missed almost all of what the officer said.

'Well,' said Deborah, once the speech had been delivered, 'they won't like that one bloody bit.'

I nodded, unsure whether or not she could actually see my head moving, and resumed my nail-biting, frantically searching for an unchewed end with my teeth. I watched as Deborah's shadowy outline shuffled away from the door and back to the bed, where she sat down with a heavy groan.

'Are you okay, Deborah?' I asked, removing my finger from my mouth for as long as it took me to speak, before replacing it.

'Yeah,' she said, 'yeah, I'm just tired. And I feel a bit sick. I think I ate too much crap. How about you, Mim, are you okay?'

Even though we were all stuck in Aoife's pokey bedroom, I kept forgetting about Mim. I mean, I knew she was there – I could hear her breathing and the anxious rumbling of her stomach. It was more that I was starting to forget that she was real in the same way that I knew Deborah and I were. As much as I'd taken to her over the past week, the stress of the last eight hours had eclipsed her personhood in my mind. It was as though my soul couldn't bear to care about another person and had followed a strict 'last one in first one out' policy, expelling Mim to sit alone in Aoife's darkening bedroom, shivering against the cold from the broken window.

She responded to Deborah with a sad squeak and knelt down as if she was planning to pray. I reached out for her shoulder and gave it what I hoped was a reassuring pat, and she lent her head against my hand. I could feel the tendons in her popsicle-stick neck pulling as she moved. That appealed to the nurse in me, and I left my hand there to slowly turn numb under her heavy head. I managed to relax slightly, just in time for John's voice to blare out through his own loudspeaker and send all my nerves on edge again.

This time we stayed where we were. If anything, I wanted to take myself further away from the sound – throw a pillow over my head or cover my ears with my hands and hum or something – but I just stood at Mim's side and listened. Once it was over, it was my turn to speak first.

'I think he's faking,' I said, my quaking voice not doing much to back up my words, 'I don't believe they could even if they wanted to. That gun is one thing, but I think one of us would have noticed if they had started hiding explosives around the place. It's a front, or a test, like Elijah's game with the water at the Feast of the Prophet. For all we know the gun was a fake too. He never fired it.'

Deborah let out a noncommittal *hmm*, but before she could say anything more Mim's shoulders began to shake.

'I believe it,' she said.

She was straining to keep herself from crying, I could tell. I'd worked with enough labouring women to know that.

'But Mim, where would they even keep stuff like that? We're a small community. We keep livestock, we grow vegetables, we pray. We don't blow things up. Someone would have seen something and said something long before now if it was true.'

I was trying to reassure myself more than anything, and I think they could tell.

'I'm not so sure, Ruth,' said Deborah. 'First of all, would you recognise an explosive if you saw one? Would any of us? And if you're looking for a place to hide something, you could do a lot worse than Halcyon.'

My mind turned to the night with Mim and the puppies, and those locked doors.

'Should we get out of here?' I asked.

'And go where? Aoife's already out there, and I think we'd have heard if they'd seen her. For all we know she could be speaking to the police officer right now. We just have to trust her. I trust her.'

It was reassuring to hear Deborah sound so calm, and I believed what she said when she talked about trusting Aoife, but I could not help but worry that after years in Heaven on Earth Deborah just needed desperately to have faith in someone. Even if that person was Aoife.

# Chapter Forty-One

## Deborah

My back ached and my stomach ached and my head ached. My earthly body felt heavy and worn out. Even the new life which I was supposedly nurturing in my womb felt like a stone. I wished that I had the energy to pray, like Mim was. I could hear her muttering under her breath, words like *saviour* and *peace* and *forgiveness* floating past my ears as they made their way to God's. Or maybe just to the ceiling. It was hard to see God in Halcyon that night.

When I was growing up with my mother, in and out of friends' flats and B&Bs and squats, my knowledge of God came solely from what I'd seen and heard on TV. He was as fictional to me as Dot Cotton or the Fresh Prince of Bel-Air, and a thousand times less interesting. It wasn't until I was taken into care and started going to school that the magnitude of this all-powerful, all-knowing, all-loving being was revealed to me and inevitably I got really into it. I remember coming home from school one day and telling my foster carers about my new discovery.

'Did you know about God?' I asked them, wide-eyed.

They had nodded, tactfully, waiting to hear what I had to say.

'Do you know that God loves *everyone*? And that God made the whole *world*?'

If they had wanted to laugh, they managed to keep it inside. Neither of them was religious; they never took me to church or made me say a prayer before bed, but when my childish fanaticism began they didn't do anything to discourage me. When I asked to bless the food we were about to receive they dutifully said their *amens* without even the flicker of a smirk, and when I begged to rent *Jesus Christ Superstar* from the video shop they sat and watched it with me. In hindsight, I suppose they were just happy that the skinny little girl who had come to their house covered in fleas and bruises was finding something that made her feel happy and loved. They were nice people, after all, and I like to think that's what I would have felt if I were them. God died when I left that placement and entered my teens, and then He was resurrected when my mother and I reunited and I saw how happy and healthy she had become since joining Heaven on Earth. That evening in Aoife's bedroom it was as though God was comatose, and He would either pull through or disappear from my world forever depending on what happened next.

When the singing began, I wondered if Elijah had been right all along. Had a host of angels descended from heaven to carry the good people of Halcyon to eternal peace at the feet of their Lord? No. Barely two lines into 'Morning Has Broken' it was clear that the singers were too familiar to be celestial. Still, there was something heavenly about the sound of all those little voices, exhausted as they were, joining together in song. 'Morning Has Broken' was one of the songs I had taught the children. It was the first religious song I'd ever heard, the song which had brought God into my life, a fact that allowed me to convince Elijah that it would be suitable to be sung in Halcyon. He had otherwise believed it to be too secular – our other songs were written by him. I tried to remember if I had told Aoife that story.

'Do you think that's something to do with her?' asked Mim, hopefully.

For the first time that day my heart beat with joy instead of terror. My aches and pains were practically forgotten – background noise to the thrill of hope coursing through my veins and playing on the ends of every nerve in my body.

'Yes.' I said, 'Yes, I think so, Mim.'

I felt myself coming back to life.

# Chapter Forty-Two

## Aoife

Just as I had hoped, the children's song proved to be enough of a distraction that I was able to sprint from behind the shed to the perimeter fence. Courtney Ballantine was the first to see me, and she pointed to a dark patch of fence which the lights from the police cars hadn't reached. By this time my eyes had adjusted to the lack of light, and I was able to get a better idea of her appearance. She looked older than she did when she had been illuminated by the headlights, and shorter too, although she exuded the confidence of a person for whom nothing was new. It must have been an act, considering the location of her constabulary, but I admired her for it nonetheless.

'I need to speak to whoever is in charge,' I said, keeping my voice as low as possible, 'I'm Aoife.'

I imagined that she widened her eyes in recognition, but it was too dark to tell for sure.

'Aoife,' she said, 'DI Andrews, Malcolm, has told me all about you. I'm glad to see that you're all right. Where are—'

'Aoife!'

It was Malcolm; I had been so focussed on Courtney that I hadn't seen him approach the fence. His smooth whisky voice was hushed but relieved. I ignored him.

'Where are…?' I said to Courtney, urging her to continue.

She looked at Malcolm, and then back at me. She seemed ready to speak again, but Malcolm beat her to it.

'Aoife, please. I know they must have told you about me, and who I am. I'm sorry if you feel as though I've misled you. I know you must be angry with me, I understand…'

I was watching Courtney Ballantine as Malcolm spoke, willing her to step in and shut him up. I couldn't bring myself to look at him. With every word that left his mouth, I grew more and more enraged. This man had lied to me. He had seen how vulnerable – as much as it pained me to admit it – I was and he had taken advantage. He had been nice to me and he had *flirted* with me and drawn me in. He had made me like him. He had done everything Elijah had done.

'No,' I said.

'Pardon?'

'No. Stop it, just stop it. You're sorry if I *feel* misled? Bullshit, Malcolm. Bullshit, DI Whoever You Are. What does that even mean? I don't *feel* misled, or if I do, it's because I was. By you.'

'I—'

'Shut up. I am sick,' my voice cracked, 'I am sick of listening to men say the word "I". How dare you make this about you? You have put us all in so much danger here tonight. I came out here to tell you and your colleagues that there are two women and a teenage girl in our farmhouse. One of the women is pregnant. We need you to get us out, and we need you to get our children out. How do you plan on doing that, Mister Policeman? Because that's all I care about right now. Not some half-arsed apology.'

For a brief moment before he regained his composure, his usually open face looked wounded. Had I hurt his feelings? Did I care? I wasn't sure, and I had no time to dwell. He cleared his throat.

'We're doing our best, Aoife,' he said. 'DS Ballantine and her team have found a tunnel which leads into your compound.'

'One of the boys has just come back from investigating,' said Courtney Ballantine, 'but there's a trapdoor at the other end which is locked or jammed from the other side.'

'I don't know about any tunnels,' I said, folding my arms across my chest. 'If I did, I'd be out by now.'

'I understand,' she said, 'I wasn't implying—'

'Where did you say this tunnel leads?'

Malcolm was the one to answer. He pointed in the direction of the schoolhouse, away from the bunker and the crowd.

'It's in that direction, and judging by the distance it opens up in one of your outbuildings.'

Courtney shook her head softly, apparently frustrated by his answer to my question.

'That doesn't matter now,' she said, 'it's a dead end for us because we can't get in. What we'd like to ask you, while you're here, is what you know about these explosives. DI Andrews told us that you'd never mentioned them before. Do you know anything about them?'

'No,' I said, 'that was the first I heard of them too.'

'Thank you. I realise this may be a difficult question for you to answer, Aoife, but can I ask if you believe his threat? We're treating it as real either way, but I would appreciate your insight.'

'I'm sorry,' I said, 'I just have no idea any more.'

No idea at all. About anything. I felt as though I was lost out at sea, no land in sight. The only thing I could see to cling to, the single piece of flotsam, was the tunnel. I had said that I didn't know of any tunnels, and at the time that had been true, but suddenly I remembered the short-lived project of a few years ago. Hadn't some of the men started work digging out a fully underground shelter, one that would eventually connect to the bunker? They had used one of the outbuildings to conceal the trapdoor entrance, although I couldn't remember which one, but they'd had to give it up – something to do with the ground being too hard. Had that been a cover? Had Elijah had them build a tunnel instead, some secret way in and out of Halcyon?

'Here's what's going to happen,' I said, sounding more confident than I felt. 'I am going to find the entrance to the tunnel, and unlock it. Then, I'm going to send my sister-wives and Mim through to you. Once they're safe, you can come in and do what you need to do. Get the kids out first, then whatever you need to do with the rest of them.'

'Aoife, don't be ridiculous,' said Malcolm, coming as close to the fence as he could. 'That's far too dangerous. Anything could happen to you. We'll find another way to get you out, I promise. We have specialists coming in now, professional negotiators, they're twenty minutes away. Please just wait here with us.'

I shook my head. It felt good to say no.

'This will be quicker.'


We had erected some of the sheds and outbuildings ourselves when we first moved to Halcyon, although there had been an abundance of them even before then, remnants of the farm which had been here before us. If some of the members of Heaven on Earth were annoyed that they had to sleep in rusty caravans when our stores got to enjoy the comfort of a real element-proof building they never said, but I imagined a few might have had some private thoughts of complaint to be confessed and repented later. For a relatively small community who had renounced all worldly possessions, we did seem to require a large amount of storage space. Once they were built, I never made it my business to go inside. That was too operational for someone of my status, and anyway, what would I possibly need? Even Ruth, whose job it had been to tend to the animals, didn't have to rummage round for chicken or cow feed herself. Someone was assigned to do that for her and leave whatever she might need in a convenient place. Much like Elijah's office, the outbuildings of Halcyon were a series of closed doors which I had never really cared to look behind. Unlike Elijah's office, though, the thought of exploring the outhouses had never once crossed my mind. I wondered what awful things that might say about me. Did it make me a snob, or just brainwashed? And which was worse?

The first shed I tried was held closed by a great rusted padlock. I had neither the time nor the inclination to go searching for a key, so I scrabbled around on the ground, turning over pebbles and bits of moss until I found a suitably heavy rock. It felt reassuringly solid in my hand. Breath held, I bashed the padlock with all of my strength, but as rusted as it was, it didn't budge. I raised the rock once again, ready to give it a second try, when I was struck with an idea. Feeling carefully around the padlock I located the flimsy hook it was attached to and swung at that instead. It snapped off easily, the closed padlock still swinging, and I pulled open the door. It was far too dark for me to make out any of the shapes, so I pocketed my rock and got to my knees so I could feel around for any trap doors. The floor of the shed was gritty with dust and dirt, and I could feel the undersides of my fingernails growing thick with grime. I found a couple of towels – cold and damp – and other bits of clutter, but no handle or join which might indicate a passage. I gave up and moved on to the next outhouse, a larger one where I knew we stored some of the inherited farming equipment which no one had got around to fixing yet. It seemed a likely enough spot for a trap door, but the floor was poured concrete throughout.

As I searched, I could hear the sounds of rising tension coming from the crowd inside Halcyon. They were obviously anxious for some action to be taken. I thought of my sister-wives waiting in my bedroom and moved on quickly to the next outbuilding. I was running out of options as well as time – there was only one more spot to check after this, and if it wasn't there then I had either missed it, or it had been entirely blocked up. There was a padlock on this door too, but it was already unlocked. I worried that might mean there was somebody inside, but when I pushed the door open I found the building empty except for towering piles of plastic bags filled with raw wool. Wool and grain had spilled out onto the floor and embedded themselves into the palms of my hands as I felt for a hatch or a door. I was getting ready to give in and try the final outbuilding when my finger caught on the sharp edge of a metal hinge. Desperate, I pushed a pile of bags to one side to reveal a thick sheet of plywood with a rope handle. I gripped the rope tightly and pulled but my position on the floor made it difficult to raise the board, which was jammed tightly. I was about to push myself up to stand when I heard the door swing open.

# Part Three

# Chapter Forty-Three

## Mim

'Mim?' said Mel, 'is that right?'

Mel was to be my new carer, and her Scottish accent was so strong I had to strain to understand a single word she said.

I nodded.

'Well, that's not one I've heard before, and I've heard a lot of funny names in my line of work. Is it from your,' she paused, 'church?'

When she said the word 'church' she lifted her hands so they were level with her shoulders, and waggled her fingers. I didn't understand the gesture – it turned out there were a lot of things I didn't understand – and that made me bristle. But my social worker Caro, the lady who had taken me from the hospital to the group home, and then to Mel's house, had told me to be on my best behaviour, and so I smiled nicely.

'It's a Christian name, from the Bible,' I said. 'It's short for Jemima, who was one of the daughters of Job.' I paused before adding, 'From the Book of Job.'

I stopped talking when Mel's eyes began to glaze over, but I didn't mind too much. Everyone who went on mission trips to Abercraig and beyond said people were rarely receptive at first, and that you had to keep trying. I decided then to treat my sojourn from Halcyon as a mission trip. It would be difficult, I knew that, but it would give some purpose to this new season of my life. And it would give me an extra reason to be as nice and pleasant as possible; I was representing Heaven on Earth, after all.

'Well,' said Mel, 'that's very nice, I'm sure. You've a very posh voice you know, Mim. When they said you were all living up by Abercraig, I thought you'd have a nice Highland accent.'

Before I could tell her that we'd moved to Halcyon when I was ten, and that before then we'd lived in England, and that actually I had never been to Abercraig, Mel started speaking again.

'And what's that you've got in your wee bag?'

She pointed at the reinforced shopping bag I was clutching, her finger as pink as the sausages we'd eaten the evening before at the group home.

'Just my toothbrush and toothpaste,' I said, 'and some pyjamas they gave me when I left the hospital.'

Mel sighed and shook her head.

'And is that all? Just those bits and the clothes on your back?'

I nodded.

'You poor lamb. Not to worry, my daughter is about your size, and I've set you aside all of the clothes she doesnae wear any more.'

'Won't your daughter mind?'

'*Won't your daughter mind?*' Mel mimicked, laughing, 'Naw, she's off at the uni now, down Dundee, got a student loan to buy herself all the new clothes she fancies. Now you get yersel up them stairs and have a try of some of those clothes, and you can give me a fashion show. That's what Jodie used to do, when she was wee.'

All this time we had been standing in the centre of Mel's living room. It reminded me a little of the living room John and Helen used to have before we moved to Halcyon, except the sofas at Mel's were made of a shiny white material, and there was a television in the corner. There were some framed photographs on the wall, of Mel and a girl who I presumed was Jodie smiling against a woodland background with their shoes off. I must have been staring a little too long because Mel took me by the shoulders and turned me around until I was facing the door to the hallway, and then gave me a gentle push towards the stairs.

'Off you go then,' she said, 'your room is the first door to the right.'

I took the stairs one at a time, fear of falling keeping me from going any faster. My stomach started to flip when I was barely halfway up, and my heart began to race. I kept going though, up and up, one wool-stockinged foot and then another, until I reached the top. My body, that is my stomach and my heart, had been entirely out of control since the night we all left Halcyon. At first it frightened me, especially because it was accompanied by an overwhelming sense of impending doom, but then I realised what was going on, that it was God giving me a warning, telling me to look out, and that made it less frightening. It's always good to be ready for things, and knowing that God is still looking out for me despite the fact I'm living away from the rest of His True Church is a relief too.

I wondered, as I turned the handle on the door of my new bedroom, what danger lay ahead. The room itself was pretty bare, which was nice; white walls with bobbly paper, thin blue carpet, a wooden bed made up with flowery sheets, a lamp, and a wardrobe. Nothing to worry about yet, but my heart and stomach wouldn't stop fluttering. I wanted desperately to curl up on the bed and lie there until I felt normal again, but if I knew one thing it's that when God gives you a challenge, you have to face it. And so I opened up the wardrobe to see what kind of clothes Jodie had left behind.

It became very clear as soon as I pulled out the first item of clothing what God's warning had been about this time; the denim skirt in my hand looked as though it would barely cover my behind. The fear rising, I lay the skirt on the bed and looked for something longer, but to my horror the only things in there that would reach to my calves were two pairs of trousers. My breath came in jagged gasps as I pulled out immodest garment after immodest garment: tops with straps as thin as pieces of string, or necklines low enough to show my chest. I wanted to cry out, 'there's a problem here', but I had hardly got the first word out when I imagined Mel's mocking voice in my head and stopped myself. The words which were stuck in my throat turned into a hard lump, and before I knew it I was weeping and so loudly and forcefully that I could hardly breathe. I had never cried like that in my life. By the time Mel had made her way upstairs I was practically screaming.

'Jesus Christ, Mim, what's going on up here? Why are all of your lovely new clothes all over the floor?'

I did not answer. I felt Mel standing over me and I knew that I should be ashamed, but the more I cried the harder it became to breathe, and the more terror I felt. When she pulled me up by the arm I allowed myself to rise, but I still could not stop weeping. My neck snapped back as she took me by the shoulders and shook me, the shock of it stopping me mid-wail. I had been shaken like that before, and the familiar jolt and grip returned me to my senses.

'Pull yourself together, woman,' said Mel, her voice quivering, 'and tell me right now what all of this crying is about.'

I swallowed and pointed to the pile of clothes which lay in a creased and tangled mess across the floor and bed.

'The clothes? What's wrong with them?'

'They're not modest,' I said, fighting to keep any more tears away, 'and there are trousers, which aren't appropriate for me, because the Bible says that "a woman shall not wear a man's garment, nor shall a man put on a woman's cloak, for whoever does these things is an abomination to the Lord your God."'

Mel rolled her eyes.

'And what does the Bible say about crying on like a mad woman?'

I didn't answer. Instead, I closed my eyes and silently recounted the verse from the Book of Revelation which Elijah had read to us all so many times, and which had given us all so much comfort. *He will wipe away every tear from their eyes, and death shall be no more, neither shall there be mourning, nor crying, nor pain any more, for the former things have passed away.* I let the words fill my heart.

'Just what I thought. Now go and wash your face and brush your teeth. Then I think it's time for you to go to bed.'

I nodded and took my toothbrush and toothpaste into the bathroom. I hadn't eaten anything since lunch at the group home, and it couldn't have been later than six o'clock, but I was happy to follow Mel's instructions.

When the bathroom door was safely closed, I stood and looked at my reflection in the mirror above the sink. I was pale, and my eyes were red and puffy with tears. I ran the tap and splashed my face with cold water before dabbing it dry with a rough pink towel. When I returned to the mirror my face looked pinker, but I didn't study myself for too long; the last thing I wanted was to end up becoming vain. Instead, I ran the tap again and wet the bristles of my new toothbrush. I left the toothpaste on the side of the sink; we had no toothpaste in Halcyon because of the fluoride turning your brain to mush, and when the nurse at the hospital had insisted I use it my mouth had felt as though it was full of ice. Just to be safe, I squeezed what I thought looked a reasonable amount of paste out of the tube and into the sink, so if Mel were to check it would look like I'd used it. I knew that was both wasteful and deceitful, but my week in the hospital and my day in the group home had taught me how strongly some people felt about the strangest things, including horrible minty toothpaste. And anyway, it's not really wasteful if the thing you're not using is something dangerous like toothpaste, and you can't be deceitful to a sinner.

I didn't sleep at all that first night, but it's been a few weeks since I've been with Mel and sleeping comes a little easier now. I'm still getting used to having a room to myself, but I've started having dreams about Halcyon, so at least I have something to look forward to. I've not told anyone about my dreams; not Mel and especially not Doctor Beck, the therapist they're making me see. I don't tell Doctor Beck anything at all, because of therapists being agents of the Devil, but I do try to be pleasant to her, because I want her to see how well Godly people behave. She talks to me lots about Helen and John, who she calls my mum and dad, and asks if I miss them. I say no, not really, and then she writes something in her little book. Doctor Beck was the one who explained that Helen wasn't allowed to look after me and Ollie at the moment because of everything that went on in the schoolhouse. She says that Helen seems very sorry, and has been helpful to the police, so maybe we'll get to live with her again one day. I know that John is in jail, but I don't know why. Doctor Beck talks to me as though I'm a child, even though I was almost married. Doctor Beck is not married.

In my dreams I return to Halcyon, and everything is how it was before things got bad. People smile and greet me as I walk to the church; they treat me like I've been away on a mission trip. Aoife and Ruth don't speak to me in the dreams, and when Deborah speaks it's to talk about teaching the younger children. Sometimes the dreams feel more real than real life does, and I wish I could think about them during the day. But thinking about Halcyon through the day makes me feel sad, because I know it's not really there any more, and guilty, because I know it's my fault Halcyon is gone. I'm too scared to ask anyone about Deborah or

Ruth or Aoife – I don't really know how to feel about them now – so I don't know if they feel the same way.

When I'm not thinking about Halcyon, I'm thinking about school. Mel wanted me to start straight away, but the social worker said that it's too close to the Christmas break and there's no point, and I should start in January. Mel's house is near to the school, and in the mornings and afternoons I watch the flocks of teenagers as they swarm around the building and its surrounding streets. They jostle and shout and swear, and it makes my heart race, but I can't look away. Mel takes me to the library to look at textbooks and makes me watch documentaries on television, but they make my head spin. She also makes me watch other television programmes with her, because she says I need to learn about the real world if I don't want to get eaten alive by the other kids. I don't like those programmes, and spend a lot of my time covering my eyes and ears to avoid being exposed to sinful things. When I told her I'd never been to school before, even before I came to Halcyon, she said that explained a lot.

I hear her talking about me to Jodie and her other friends on the phone. She has a lot of friends, so sometimes I hear her telling the same story over and over again. *You'll never guess what Mim said today*, she'll say, or *that girl, honestly, it's like she's been dropped from space*, and then she'll relay something I've said or done, usually something I hadn't even thought twice about, and laugh. I try not to let it upset me, because of course I deserve it. I've been praying a lot, and I think God is telling me that this is my punishment for destroying Halcyon and scattering the members of Heaven on Earth to the winds. I lie in bed and imagine going back in time, running up to Elijah and John talking outside the farmhouse and telling them that they need to leave now, and begging them to take me too. I pray that when my punishment is over, I can be the one to bring us back together again.

# Chapter Forty-Four

## Deborah

Once the police pulled down the fence, things moved quickly, and my memories of the night are jumpy and disjointed. I seem to remember sitting in hospital *before* sitting in the police car, but I don't recall actually being driven anywhere or speaking to anyone until the next morning. The smell of smoke mixes with the smell of bleach. Over the days that followed, countless people – doctors, nurses, detectives – greeted me in a way that suggested we had met before or mentioned previous conversations which I could have sworn had never happened. I've had to piece things together from what I've been told, and what I've read in the papers or seen on television.

Elijah had apparently instructed John to hold the fort before leaving on foot shortly before the police broke in. I remember John, loyal to the end, looking around for Elijah as he was bundled into a police car, the way his voice changed from desperate to angry when he realised he'd been had like the rest of us. It's a fond memory, the only fond memory I have from that night. Of course, Elijah never came back to Halcyon. Instead, he stole a car parked somewhere just outside of Abercraig and was arrested the following day at Glasgow airport after trying to board a flight to Turkey. It turned out that Elijah had been raiding Heaven on Earth's coffers regularly for over a year and using the donated money to buy whatever kind of amphetamine he could get his hands on. Before that, he'd been siphoning money off for a running-away fund – a few hundred here, a couple of thousand there, and it had all added up. The picture they showed of him on the news was a mugshot taken after his arrest, so I suppose I shouldn't have been so shocked by how much he looked like a criminal. He had the start of a black eye, and a puffy gash on his cheek. His dark beard, which had once lent him such an air of respectability and authority, made his face look sunken and cruel. I felt embarrassed that that was the version of him the public was going to see, not for Elijah, but for myself. People would look at him, I thought, and wonder how we could have believed a word he said. How so many people could have trusted a man like that. And, now that I was back in the real world, I wasn't even sure I could have given them an answer. All my reasons for joining the church, then staying there, for marrying him and having his babies and getting up and getting on day after day trapped under his thumb, seemed deficient all of a sudden. Thinking about them was like interrogating a dream, and coming to realise that nothing made any sense.

I wondered if something about Halcyon had stopped us from seeing anything as it really was. When I first looked at myself in the mirror in the hospital, I couldn't believe my eyes. I looked gaunt and pale, and so frail that I could not believe that my body was able to support itself, let alone the baby I was carrying. Back in Halcyon I had thought of myself as plump, glowing, the picture of maternal health. Even my hair, which was easily long enough for me to see without a mirror, was suddenly as dry as straw. I had even pictured its colour wrong. In my head I had hair like spun gold, but in reality it had turned a sort of mousy beige, streaked with fine strands of grey. I looked so much like an old woman that the police officer was visibly stunned when I told him I was twenty-six.

They made me stay in the hospital for almost a week. I lay there quietly on my drip, trying to feel my strength returning. Whenever a kindly nurse suggested I take a little walk up and down the corridor I would shake my head. I only rose on my own to use the toilet, which I allowed myself to do twice a day and where I would stare at my reflection in the full-length mirror on the back of the door as I relieved myself. Sometimes I'd be wheeled off to the maternity unit for scans and blood tests. I'd never had an ultrasound before, or heard one of my babies' heartbeats. I stared at the small stranger on the screen, fascinated by its tiny movements. The midwives were all very nice to me, but I could tell they thought that I was a negligent mother and I was always relieved to be back in my bed.

One of them started talking about folic acid, and when I looked blankly at her she shook her head. Eventually they said I was well enough to leave. I was given two white paper bags bulging with boxes of pills and forced to change into some clothes which I had never seen before. For the first time since I was seventeen years old, I pulled a pair of tracksuit bottoms over my legs and slipped my feet into some canvas plimsolls. There was a T-shirt too, grey and soft and V-necked, which clung too tightly to the sharp edges of my body. I took a deep breath in as I lifted it over my head. It had the anonymous smell of something that had just been washed in an unfamiliar detergent. As exposed as I felt in my new clothes – too pregnant, too many limbs, too much skin – I liked their anonymity. My social worker, Jade, pushed me in a wheelchair to the front doors of the hospital, and then I had to get out and walk. She took me by the arm, and we moved slowly together towards her car.

I watched in awe as the world outside the window whizzed past us. Beige pebbledash homes, children on scooters, big green parks; I couldn't tear my eyes away. Even the River Ness in November, which was as grey and miserable as any stretch of water could be, swelled my heart. I could have sat there quite happily for hours, watching the world go by, but we had barely been driving for ten minutes when Jade flicked on her indicators and pulled into the car park of a modern-looking apartment building.

'Well,' she said, unbuckling her seatbelt, 'this is us.'

I liked Jade. Her hair was dyed an unrealistic looking red, and she wore it short and spiked upwards. She didn't look like a Jade, and I liked that too; I never thought I looked like a Deborah. I wondered how old she was – maybe in her late twenties, so just a little older than me? Or Ruth's age, or Aoife's? My frame of reference was limited. Unlike the social workers I remembered from childhood, she seemed competent, and I trusted her. She opened her door and came around the side of the car to open mine.

It was a women's refuge, the sort of place I might have stayed as a young child with my own mother, with hard-wearing and serviceable furniture and hard-wearing and serviceable staff. Curious faces peered through doorways as I followed Jade and the corridor to my bedroom. The room was set up with a narrow single bed, two camp beds, a cot, and a chest of drawers. Jade must have noticed me staring at them.

'Don't worry, Deb, we'll get you and the kids some bits and bobs to fill those up with. You're not the first lass to come here empty-handed and you won't be the last.'

I nodded.

'When will they get here?'

Jade glanced at her watch, which looked like it was made of red rubber. I fought an almost primal urge to reach out and touch it.

'Not long, an hour or so. The foster carer says they've been asking to see you.'

I smiled. It didn't seem likely that the boys would have been asking for me – Elijah, maybe – but it made me happy to hear it nonetheless. Mainly I was happy that I would get to see them again, and hold them, and play with them, and sleep in the same room as them. All through my time in the hospital I had felt their absence like a physical ache. In all their lives I had never been more than a hundred feet away from them, and then, all of a sudden, I didn't even know where they were. They were playing in rooms I had never seen, being cared for by people I had never met. The thought of it made me feel as though I was being ripped apart from the inside, my heart and gut tearing at the seams, pulled away from me in the unknown direction of my children.

Allegations had been made against the other women who worked in the schoolhouse about the punishments they had apparently been dishing out when I was away. Children telling police about being drenched in cold water and left to stand in the freezing Highland night, beatings with belts and sticks and anything else they could lay their hands on. The police interviewed me at length about that, thinking like Mim had that I must have known, even if I wasn't doing any of the punishing myself. I found myself thinking about it a lot when the lights were off and I was lying on my side in the hospital bed; had I known? I knew Elijah's feelings about sparing the rod and training up. I knew how deeply the women believed in him, how important they felt their task was, how desperate they were to please. I had never seen anything, but how hard had I been looking? Like so many things in Halcyon, maybe it had just been easier not to see it.

I complied with the police in their investigations, telling them that my suspicions had only been raised when I'd been brought in to help look after Ollie just a couple of days before. Once the police were convinced that I was as much of a victim in the whole thing as it was possible to be, I was told that the separation from the children would only be temporary. That knowledge did not make it hurt any less. I had no concept of time. Only of grief, and pain, and shock.

All of Halcyon's children were taken into care, initially anyway. Even Mim, who was of course only sixteen and therefore still a child in the eyes of social services. There was no way of knowing, Jade told me, if or when they would be reunited with their parents. Apparently some people, although no names were named, were still swearing their allegiance to Elijah and Heaven on Earth. The only person I pestered Jade about was Ruth. The last time I had seen her she was being led into a separate police car, wrapped in a foil blanket. Jade said she was looking into it.


I had been in the women's refuge for three days when Shriya, one of the members of staff, called me into the office and handed me the phone. I held the cool plastic against my ear and breathed into the receiver.

'Hello?'

Jade's familiar voice greeted me through the line.

'Hi Deb, how are you? How are the kids?'

Jonah and Noah had barely looked at me since they arrived. They spent their days bouncing off the walls, kicking and biting me and each other and sometimes even the other kids in the shelter the second something didn't go exactly their way. My arms were covered in red welts from their sharp piranha teeth. Serious little Jonah screamed at me so loudly when I asked him to put his new pyjamas on that his face turned purple and the tendons in his neck bulged. Quiet, introverted Noah cried at the drop of a hat, but smacked me away if I came to comfort him. Susannah was the opposite. She clung to me like a limpet, wailing if I put her down, sitting on my knee even when I was on the toilet. I dreaded to think what would happen when my growing bump became too large and I couldn't carry her any more – already I'd developed a chronic back ache and my knees felt ready to explode whenever I stood up.

'We're okay, thanks,' I said, adjusting Susannah on my hip,

'just getting used to everything, you know? Are you still coming down tomorrow?'

'Ah good stuff, Deb, I'm glad to hear it. Yeah, I'll still be down tomorrow but I wanted to call you today because I've just spoken with the police, and they've been able to give me some information about Ruth. I thought you'd want to know as soon as possible.'

I swallowed. Shriya was working at the computer with her back to me and there were no other staff in the office, but I pressed the handset as close as I could to my ear and lowered my voice before speaking again.

'What is it? Where is she? Is she okay?'

'She's all right. She's in police custody. She's going to be extradited to the US – deported. For outstaying her visa. According to the officer I spoke to she has a lot of family over there who have been looking for her, and they're arranging everything with them so she can be released into their care.'

I took a second to digest what Jade had just said.

'And the kids? What happens to them?'

I imagined, briefly, taking them in myself, but I knew they would never allow it.

'They'll be going with her.'

'All five of them?'

'All five of them.'

A sigh of relief left me and I loosened my grip on the phone.

'It really is the best she could have hoped for, Deb, in the circumstances. If you like I can try and arrange for you to talk to her on the phone from the detention centre?'

I didn't know what to say. Earlier that day I would have done anything to speak to Ruth again, but the thought of her being trapped in some dingy detention centre made me want to cry. We'd been apart for less than a week, but already our lives had diverged so rapidly that I couldn't imagine what I would possibly say to her.

Jade must have sensed the uncertainty in my silence, because she spoke again.

'Don't worry, I know how strange this all is for you. Have a think and you can let me know tomorrow when I come to see you, all right? Oh, and before I leave you to your day, there's something else. Aoife's kids are out of care.'

My attention had already drifted away from the call, but the sound of Aoife's name brought it back. Aoife. I couldn't think about her without feeling angry and sad.

'And? Who are they with?'

I knew they couldn't be with her. For a wild moment I wondered if Elijah had somehow managed to get custody, before remembering that he was currently behind bars himself.

'As soon as the story broke about Heaven on Earth and Halcyon, Aoife's sister apparently came forward. She and her wife have taken them all in. She seemed pretty keen to speak to you – Grainne I mean, the sister. But like I said about Ruth, don't worry too much about it right now. There's no pressure there.'

The phone call didn't last long after that. Once it was over, I returned to my bedroom, ignoring Shriya's concerned look and passing the open door of the lounge where Jonah and Noah were playing with some of the other women in a rare moment of peace. It was a good news call, I knew, but my heart felt heavy somehow. We were all scattered. As overjoyed as I was to have Jonah and Noah and Susannah there with me, there was still a gaping hole in my heart where the rest of Heaven on Earth had once lived.

The weeks that followed now seem blurred and lazy. I was supposed to be preparing to apply for work but my CV was almost ten years out of date and, to the disbelief of everyone around me, I have no paperwork whatsoever. Before we moved to Halcyon, we had all burned our passports and birth certificates and cut our national insurance cards in two – except for Elijah, apparently. While others work hard to make me a real person in the eyes of the government, I spend my days in and around the refuge. I have become a minor celebrity amongst the women here, a status which bestows several privileges, namely: everyone is generous with their snacks, and no one makes me share the remote control. Because of this, I am able to spend many hours munching my way through bags of crisps, inhaling their heady saltiness, cleansing my palate every so often with a knock-off brand biscuit bar or a packet of sweets, and staring at the TV. Susannah curled up at my side, I watch as our story is hashed out on daytime television, and then the news, and then on late-night talk shows. Panels of women start sentences with: 'I just feel like, as a mother...'; reporters talk over footage of Halcyon with cold, emotionless voices, focussing on the botched police response; groups of well-spoken men analyse Elijah and the concept of 'new religious movements', or sometimes in relation to male mental health. I don't know which is worse, but still I consume it all, growing frustrated every time the topic changes. I have been asked to appear on one of the programmes, a big one that I remember from before I joined Heaven on Earth, and have decided to say yes.

# Chapter Forty-Five

## Ruth

During the six years I spent in Halcyon, I was just a woman, and my trials and troubles were the same as my sisters'. As soon as the police broke down Halcyon's fence, I became Black again – with a capital B. Bundled into a police car and taken straight to the station, it wasn't until I spoke to Deborah's social worker much later that I learned Deborah and Mim had been driven directly to the hospital. And after that it was the little things. The young female officer looking uncertain as she handed me a toiletry bag before my first shower, and then snatching it back from my hands and removing the small bottle of shampoo before returning it to me. The new officer who drove me to the airport asking where I was being sent back to, and the surprised look on his face when I said the US. 'Oh, is that right?' he had said. 'I thought it might be somewhere a bit more… exotic.' And suddenly, I had to worry about my children too. Eli and Abraham had been so tiny when we had moved to Halcyon that I had never had to let them out of my sight, and then before I knew it, they were gone. The others had never left Halcyon at all before this. Who were they with? How were they being treated? I hadn't ever needed to speak to them about those kinds of things, and now they were suddenly going to be mixed race in a place where that meant something, without me or even the other Halcyon children who looked like them by their side.

Things have been better since I arrived back home. I try not to think too much about the lost time between leaving Halcyon and landing back in the States. The only good thing to happen in that period, the only part worth remembering, was the look of confusion on the officers' faces when it became clear that I thought the raid on Halcyon was because of me and my outstayed visa. My visa, it turned out, was low down on the long list of infractions – both minor and major – of which Halcyon was guilty. Most of them related to Elijah. He had never insured the car, he paid no taxes on the land, and had recently got himself into a whole lot of trouble with some drug dealers in Aberdeen. My mom and my siblings and their husbands and wives and children met me at the airport. The kids were holding a banner, dotted with love hearts and hand-prints, which read 'Welcome Home Auntie Ruth'. I collapsed at the sight of them, my legs weakening and giving way; I was knocked out by the tidal wave of their love. The only person missing was my father, who had died after a series of heart attacks three years before, and my own kids, who were arriving later. That night we stayed at my little brother's apartment in Des Plaines, because it was close to the airport. My mother and I shared a futon, and lying there in the darkness of my brother's living room, I tried to explain myself.

'Mom,' I said, turning to face her, 'I just wanted to say—'

She untangled her fingers from mine, and pressed them against my lips.

'I don't want to hear it.'

'But Mom, please, I need to explain—'

I felt her shake her head.

'That's all over now, Ruth. We need to forget that it happened.'

Her fingers were still resting on my lips when I woke up the next morning.

The arrival of the kids was tougher than I had expected. They landed a few weeks after me, once the lawyers my family found to take my case managed to convince Elijah that things would go better for him in the courts if he showed some decency by waiving his parental rights. I was surprised that he agreed, but also not so much – any lingering power it might have given him was not as attractive as potential time off his sentence, and I knew that self-preservation was his main priority. For the first few nights none of them slept, and Eli, the oldest at seven, started to wet the bed. It bothered my sisters and my mom that the children didn't call me mommy or momma or even mum, and that in fact, they didn't seem to know what to call me. Mom and I had stayed those weeks with my brother; I wanted to stay as close to the airport as possible, and they indulged me. The day they arrived we made the long journey to my childhood home together. All the siblings had moved out, so it was just me and Mom and the five kids. Nothing much had changed there, except for the way it felt. When my mother pushed open the front door, I'd expected to experience the same suffocating feeling which used to grip me as a teen whenever I stepped into the house, a feeling I'd been remembering and dreading since I got on the plane. I waited for the familiar rush of anxiety to strike, ready to bat it away, but it never came. The sense of something or someone watching over my shoulder, waiting for me to slip up, which had haunted the house when I last lived there, was gone.

The TV has played a big part in the kids' transition to their new lives. The first words three-year-old Moses spoke to his granny were: 'Excuse me, do you have Peppa Pig in this country?' Which drew a big laugh from everyone but me.

'What on earth is a pepper pig?' I asked him.

He blinked up at me with his big, serious brown eyes.

'She lives in the TV with her family.'

'And how do you know that?' I asked, incredulous. There had been no television sets in Halcyon.

'From Alan and Gemma's house.'

'Oh,' I said. My sister squeezed my hand as the room swayed.

Abigail, who is barely one, hardly seems to notice that anything new is going on. She babbles happily on whoever's knee she is placed, and grasps for her bright new toys with sweet starfish hands. Moses stares, fascinated, as the world continues to reveal itself to him. He clings to his older cousins, who must remind him of the other children at Halcyon. My sister Anthea has promised to take him to the amusement park at Bloomington before Christmas, if the snow holds off.

It's been twelve days now since the kids arrived in Illinois. Eli's bedwetting is less frequent, and all five children have started calling me Momma, a transition which came much quicker than I'd expected. Abraham and Leah still won't sleep in their own beds, but I don't mind that one bit.

Abigail is napping and I'm sitting on the vinyl couch watching Leah and the boys play marble run with their big cousins. The clatter of plastic and the sound of children's laughter is slowly becoming the soundtrack to my new life, and Halcyon is already starting to feel like it happened a very long time ago, to someone very different. There has been no word from anyone back in the UK, which helps Halcyon fade into memory. Mom must have gotten to everybody already, because none of my family mention it at all. They looked for me, they found me, and in their eyes it's all over. My oldest sister, Candice, whispered something about finding a therapist, but the thought of talking about that part of my life to someone who wasn't there feels sacrilegious. How could I explain to someone what it feels like to wake in the night in your childhood bed, only to cry when you realise you're not in a crumbling farmhouse in Scotland? How Halcyon haunts my nightmares, but also colours my dreams?

My mother sends the kids to play in the kitchen, places a cushion on the floor, and turns on the TV. She sits on the couch, comb and scissors in hand, and I settle myself between her knees, adjusting my position on the cushion until I'm comfortable. There are no soap operas on the TV this afternoon, so we watch a home makeover show as she combs out my damp, freshly conditioned hair. By the time it's combed through, we've watched three episodes. In Halcyon I would comb my hair with my fingers, before winding it into a bun.

'I'll just snip those dry ends off, baby,' she says, 'then we can braid it,'

But it's clear to both of us that my hair is too dry, too damaged from years of washing only in water and homemade soap, to be rescued now. She snips and snips, dark coils falling heavily to the floor until I'm sitting in a nest of curls. I hear my mother sigh.

'There's just so much of it. What do you say we just cut it short?'

I nod.

More hair falls, and I can feel the air as it caresses my scalp.

'I'm just going to get Daddy's old razor, to tidy you up.'

I shift in my spot as Mom squeezes past, and then again as she returns with a battery-operated razor in her hand. The buzz of the razor feels strangely pleasant against my scalp, and when she's done my mother passes me her enamel hand mirror so I can look at my reflection. Behind me in the glass I can see her face. She looks anxious, which is unusual.

Elijah hated short hair on women. It occurs to me that the half centimetre of growth on my head is likely the product of the past month, which means that there's not a hair on my head that Elijah has touched. The thought makes me feel weightless, as though I could float away. A silent stream of tears falls down my cheeks.

'Oh baby, it'll grow back,' Mom says, taking the mirror from me. 'I can call Candice and ask her to bring some wigs over when she comes for Mimi and Tyler.'

I nod and wipe away the tears with the backs of my hands. Together we sweep my shorn hair, a relic of another time, into a garbage bag.

The reverence of the moment – even my mother seems to feel it, and is quiet – is interrupted by a squeal of delight from the kitchen.

'Mailman!' shrieks Moses.

His accent is still so British that it's weird to hear him use the American words which have entered his vocabulary since our arrival. Garbage, refrigerator ('fridator'), and of course, mailman. Moses has become entranced by the mailman, and his greatest pleasure is reaching up and unlatching the front of the mailbox in Mom's yard to retrieve the letters. I hear someone open the door for him so he can run out and fetch whatever mail has been delivered.

'Here, Granny,' he says, passing her a handful of flyers before turning his attention to me.

He's only been outside for a minute, but his hands are cold as he rubs them over my buzz cut.

'I want my hair like this!'

'Oh don't you worry, baby,' says Mom as she flicks through the pile of letters, 'I'll keep my clippers out and you'll be—'

I think she is going to say 'next', but instead she trails off into silence. I look away from Moses and up to her. Amongst the colourful fliers and take-out menus there is a fat, white envelope. She's holding it between her thumb and forefinger, as though it's dirty.

'This one is for you, Ruth. It's got an airmail sticker.'

I disentangle myself from Moses and stand to take the letter from her. It feels heavy and thick.

'I'll open it for you,' she says, reaching to take the letter back, but I pull it to my chest.

At that moment, Abigail wakes from her nap and starts to cry. There's a short stand-off before Mom takes Moses by the hand and goes to soothe the baby, and then I am left alone with the letter.

The handwriting on the envelope is messy and unfamiliar. I tear it open to reveal sheets of lined paper, folded and thick with the same large, untidy writing. The edges are ragged where the pages have been torn from a ring-bound notebook.

*Dear Ruth*, I read, *I hope you don't mind me writing to you.*

I leaf through the rest of the letter, my eyes skimming over words and phrases: *miss you... been tough... prison... not what I expected* until I reach the final page, desperate to see the name, to know for sure who it's from.

*I have put my address on the back of the onvilope, in case you want to write back. Or if you like you can call me at the womens shelter, the office number is online. I really hope I get to hear from you again.*

*Lots and lots of love from Deborah (and Jonah and Noah and Susannah)*

*XOXOXOXOXOXOXXO*

With shaking hands I retrieve the discarded envelope from the floor and turn it round to see the name of the shelter where Deborah is staying. I type the name slowly into the browser of my new cell phone, which is actually my niece Mimi's old one. It all seems too easy, once the webpage loads, to hit the blue call button under the shelter's name.

# Chapter Forty-Six

## Aoife

'Good to see you on your knees, Aoife.'

I stopped pulling at the rope handle and turned to face my husband. He was holding a lantern in his left hand, and it illuminated the small shed with an eerie yellow light. Looking up at him from my position on the floor, he seemed taller, more imposing than ever.

'I hope you're praying for forgiveness?'

His voice was hard with anger.

'Forgiveness?' I asked.

'Don't play dumb, please,' he said, hanging the lantern on a hook on the wall. 'You're many things, Aoife, but you're not stupid. You know what you've done. We all know what you've done.'

I waited for him to continue. I knew him well enough to be sure that he would.

'John told me that you were sneaking around the whole time I was away, talking to that outsider man. That's a commandment broken, Aoife.'

My cheeks burned with indignation. Had John told Elijah that I'd been having an affair? Why else would he think I was an adulteress, as he was clearly insinuating? Unless he'd come to the conclusion himself.

'Elijah, I—'

'It's commandment number one! How *dare* you?!'

Number one? I knew my commandments off by heart, and the commandment to not commit adultery was number seven. Number one was—

'THOU SHALT HAVE NO OTHER GODS BEFORE ME!'

My ears rang and I fell backwards onto the cold, hard floor. Elijah raised his fist, but instead of landing on me it met with the wooden wall, shaking the outbuilding so much that I feared it would tumble like a house of cards.

'Am I a joke to you?'

His voice was a hoarse whisper, but it still dripped with loathing.

I shook my head. The bravado that had allowed me to stand up to Malcolm had melted to nothing in the face of Elijah's white-hot rage.

'You think you can disrespect me like that and get away with it? You think you can bring the Devil to our door and get away with it? I built this place from nothing and you have single-handedly *destroyed* it. I told you they were going to come for me, and now they're here, because of *you*.'

He stepped towards me and bent down so his face was almost touching mine. His eyes glinted in the light cast by the lantern's dancing flame.

'You have ruined *everything*,' he spat.

I held his gaze and lifted myself up onto my elbows. He was so close that I could almost taste him.

'*We* built this place,' I said, my lips moving within millimetres of his, 'together. And we've ruined it separately.'

He lingered for a moment, and rested his hands on my shoulders. He tilted his head slightly, as if he wanted to get a better look at me – for half a second, I even wondered if he was going to try to kiss me.

'You can believe that if you want to,' he said, 'it doesn't matter any more. Halcyon is dead. Heaven on Earth is dead. If I end up in jail, it will be all your fault.'

Did he remember that our daughter, as well as our home, was called Halcyon? I was about to ask him when he tightened his grip on my shoulders and threw me down to the straw-strewn ground. I heard my head crack against the concrete before I felt it. Through the haze of purple spots which clouded my vision, I watched as he moved towards the door.

'Where are you going?' I asked, instead.

Without looking back at me, Elijah lifted the lantern from its hook, the swinging light casting strange shadows on his face so I could barely recognise him. Purposefully, he lifted the glass shield from the lantern and the naked flame flared. He dropped the lantern into one of the bags of wool and retreated out of the door without a backwards glace.

Stupidly, I felt hurt that he left without saying goodbye.

By the time I have realised what is happening, I have also realised it's too late. The door is closed and bolted, and the fire has spread so that it seems to be coming in from all sides, growing faster than I would have thought possible. Time slows as I try to claw at the trapdoor with desperate, blistering hands, and it still won't budge.

*Is this it, then?* I wonder, heat rising, smoke rising, fear rising. *Am I about to meet my maker?*

I am surprised to find my mind spinning back, all the way back to the day I met Elijah in the café. He wasn't even called Elijah then; he was still going by his birth name, Ed. My thoughts continue to spool out filling the smoke around me with visions of the past, but in no particular order; memories of my childhood with Grainne lap up against the building of Halcyon, my work promoting Heaven on Earth curls gently around the birth of my children. Constance, Faith, Halcyon, Humility. I wonder if this is what people mean when they talk about your life flashing before your eyes. It's like it's all there, dancing amongst the smoke and the flames.

Is this what martyrdom is? Am I a saint who will arrive in heaven, flesh mortified, ready to take my place at the side of the Father? Or is this just the start of my eternal punishment?

I am coughing now, and breathing is too difficult for me to waste any more energy on the trapdoor. I lie back and close my eyes to pray for salvation but all I can see is him, imprinted on the inside of my eyelids as clear as if he was standing right in front of me. *Was it worth it?* I can't tell if the voice is his or mine, but I see his hand reach out to me. I know he's not there any more, not really, but I still try and raise my arms towards him. They don't seem to move. The other memories have faded away like smoke, and he is all I have left.

# Epilogue

## Genesis

'That bloke you fancy is in again,' said Sarah, 'if you hurry up you can catch him. His weird mate is already putting his jacket on.'

I looked away so Sarah didn't see me blush, and fumbled with my apron strings while facing the wall. She was younger than me, still at school, and I resented the way she talked as if we were equals.

'I don't know who you're talking about,' I said, tucking a notepad and pencil into my front pocket, 'I don't fancy anyone.'

I turned back around just in time to see Sarah roll her eyes. They were ringed heavily with liner, and her mascara had clumped together so her lashes looked like spider legs.

'Spare me,' she said, 'I don't know why I bother.'

As soon as she left the cramped little stockroom, I flipped open my compact and dabbed some powder on my nose. Then, I took my clip out and shook my hair so it fell about my shoulders in thick black waves. My lips were another matter entirely. I had no lipstick with me, so instead I bit down hard, first on my lower lip and then on the upper one, until they turned red. Then I ran my tongue over them, adding what I hoped looked like a delicate sheen of gloss. It was a Sunday, and he never usually came in on a Sunday.

When I left the stockroom, I was relieved to see that he was still there, sitting at one of the Formica tables with a Rizla in one hand and a packet of tobacco laid out in front of him. His friend hadn't left yet – he was standing there with his jacket on, even though it was July and nowhere near cool enough for a jacket. The friend had a reputation in the café for clicking his fingers to get our attention, and Sarah refused to serve him after his hand lingered on her backside one evening when they were both in alone.

'Anyway, good service today, Ed,' he said, sticking his hands in his jacket pockets. 'I think everything is really starting to come together. Couple of familiar faces from Trinity Methodist, word is obviously spreading.'

Ed moved his head to nod, catching my eye as he did so. He winked.

'Yeah, see you, John,' he said, his eyes still on mine, 'give Helen my best.'

As soon as John was safely out of the door, I collected myself and walked around the counter to his table.

'You know you can't smoke that in here any more,' I pointed to the cigarette he was rolling between his fingers, 'they're really enforcing the new ban, we could get in trouble from the owner.'

My voice shook a little, but Ed smiled.

'I'd hate to get you in trouble,' he said. His own voice was steady and deep. He had no accent – he could have been raised in any upper-middle-class household from Berwick to Brighton.

He ran the tip of his tongue along the paper to seal it, before putting the finished cigarette in his shirt pocket.

'Anyway,' I said, 'can I get you anything?'

The sight of his tongue had felt too intimate, and my pencil shook as I held it poised above my notepad.

'No,' he said, 'I was actually just about to leave.'

'Oh.'

'But I was wondering, what time do you finish today?'

'Me?' I squeaked.

Ed laughed gently, his eyes sparkling.

'Yes, you,' he said, 'what time do you finish? Six?'

I nodded.

Ed dropped a handful of coins into his saucer and headed to the door.

'Great,' he said, 'I'll see you at six.'

I didn't even bother trying to keep the smile from my face as I walked back to the counter. Sarah shook her head.

'Shame you don't fancy him,' she said.


'You smoke?' he asked.

He had been waiting outside the café at six on the dot, the sleeves of his checked shirt rolled up to reveal his forearms. I wanted desperately to say yes, just so I could take the cigarette from his hand and put it between my lips. I imagined him leaning forward to light it for me, cupping his hand around the flame, but I had never smoked in my life and the thought of coughing and spluttering in front of him was unbearable. I shook my head.

'Good,' he said, 'women shouldn't smoke.'

I started to object when Ed laughed, furrowing his brow in what I took to be an impression of myself.

'You're very pretty when you're cross.'

No man had ever called me pretty before, and I laughed along with him. I wanted him to think I was pretty when I laughed, too.

'I'm actually giving it up,' he said, 'too much tax. This'll be my last one.'

'Good for you.' I was unsure how he wanted me to respond. He was fixing me with a thoughtful stare, as though he expected me to do or say something remarkable.

'Do you ever get bored, Aoife?'

My name seemed at home in his mouth, even though I had never introduced myself to him directly. He must have heard it from the girls in the café.

'I work in a café, of course I get bored. Sometimes I feel like I'm bored every day of my life.'

He looked down at me, that same thoughtful look on his face. I hoped that he wouldn't be disappointed by my admission. Didn't only boring people get bored?

'I think,' he said, suddenly very serious, 'that you're made for bigger things. I think that's why you're bored.' He pointed to the thin gold crucifix which hung around my neck. 'You should come to my church some time.'

I nodded, and we began to walk. Ed moved purposefully and I followed, taking two quick steps for each one of his long strides in order to keep up.

'Where are we going?' I asked.

# Acknowledgements

Thanks to Lisa Highton, my incredible agent, for her direction and insight. Thank you for championing me and my work, as well as for your wise words and good humour. I think we make a great team.

I am also so grateful to Cari Rosen, my wonderful editor, for sharing her knowledge and for her unwavering support and belief in this book. The editing process shaped *The Wives of Halcyon* into the best version of itself and has made me a better writer.

I firmly believe that I could not have reached this point without the immense support which I have received from New Writing North and the team there, particularly Will Mackie. Winning a Northern Writers Award put me on the trajectory to publication and the team's ongoing support has been life changing. I can't thank you enough for the time and energy you put into developing and championing writers from backgrounds whose voices are so seldom heard in the literary world. You made me believe that there was room for me in this space. Thanks also to The Literary Consultancy for offering the 'Free Reads' prize, and for the generous and constructive feedback which I received from my assigned reader Sally OJ.

To my very earliest readers, Sarah Rowe, Eleanor Bradford, Ellen Mackenzie and Emily Caulton, for your encouragement, feedback, and kind words. Thanks also to my copy editor Lusana Taylor-Khan, whose eagle eyed reading helped to make this a better book.

To Lucy and Olivia and all the fabulous team at Legend Press who have worked so hard to bring this book to the world – thank you for answering my questions and for your ongoing support, expertise, and friendliness.

Thank you to Rose Cooper for creating the most beautiful cover design; I could not have imagined anything more perfect.

To the wonderful North East Novelists community; how lucky am I to get to spend time with such a talented, supportive group of people? Thank you to Grace and Heather for bringing this group together, and for allowing me to be a part of it.

To my lovely colleagues, past and present, at Newcastle University for your endless encouragement and support. Thanks in particular to my managers Hilary and Lucy, and to Charlotte.

I am lucky to be surrounded by wonderful family and friends, too many to name individually, who have been with me throughout the process of writing and publishing this book – I could not have done this without your support and love. Special thanks to my Mam, for being by my side every step of the way, and for raising me to believe I could do anything I put my mind to.

To my husband Aidan, for being this book's biggest cheerleader. Your confidence in me and my abilities has been unwavering and I am grateful beyond words.

To Nell, the sunshine of my life – you are the reason I do everything, and I'm sorry that this book has no pictures.

Follow Legend Press on X
@legend_times_

Follow Legend Press on Instagram
@legend_times